Mary and The Goddess of Ephesus

The Continued Life of the Mother of Jesus

M E L A N I E   B A C O N

In memory of
Veronica Nuñez, who taught me reverence for Mary, and
Ron Mangravite, who taught me how to understand why she is important
And in gratitude to
Bob and Nancy Bacon, for the honor of being your child, and
Mickey and Tory Kahleck, for the joy of being your mommy

Acknowledgements

Thanks to Jan Thatcher Adams, Caroline Ahl, Roger Ahl, Bob Bacon, Maureen Fetterolf, Mimi Frenier, Mickey Kahleck, Torran Kahleck, and Billie Risa-Draves, who were kind enough to read various drafts of this book. Your comments and suggestions contributed much to the final manuscript, and I am very grateful to you all.

I also want to thank the many people who have encouraged me in my writing over the years. Some of you are: Donna Anderson, Kim Augsburger, Nancy Bacon, Lily Belle, Glory Blair, Risa Christensen, Anji Cornette, Emily Cornette, Sheldon Cornette, Susan Dawkins, Richard Risa-Draves, Sunny Fitzgerald, Gloria Karpinski, Elaine Krom, Helena Moore, Vanessa Stephenson, Linda Van Jahnke and Neva Ventre. I'm also grateful to Ian Leask for an afternoon of helpful tips; my spiritual families Foundation and Dakshina; the faculty and alumni of the University of Minnesota, Morris and United Theological Seminary of the Twin Cities; and my much missed PDW writing group pals Jan, Mary, Rebecca, Sarah, Chuck, Steve, Joel, Dima and Tom. Thanks too to my friends at SPX, Island County, and Lago de Goss; the choir and congregation at Old Waxhaw Presbyterian Church; the confused yet patient fans of hollywoodtarot.com; the folks at Amazon and CreateSpace, the editors at *Writers Digest*, Mike Neff's Algonkian Conference, and the organizers, presenters, and attendees of the Pike's Peak Writers' Conference and the Whidbey Island Writers' Conference.

And thanks to those long-ago editors at *National Lampoon* and the *Morris Sun/Tribune*. Without your willingness to regularly print my early stuff, I probably would not have come back to writing all these years later.

Tory — thank you for taking me to Ephesus, where we discovered together the House of Mary.

Prologue

Ephesus
The Temple of Artemis
Month of Artemision

"Order the gods, goddesses, and emperors into their places," High Priestess Artelia told the priest walking alongside taking notes. Every night of festival began with this annoying pre-sunset chaos. Those highest in rank were the worst offenders.

A slave silently took the wax palimpsest and stylus, and Okeanos cupped his hands to his mouth. "Procession inspection has started!" the priest yelled. "Ready yourselves for the high priestess of the Heavenly Goddess!"

Dignitaries scurried into line. Artelia and her entourage began their inspection walk, quickly reviewing the snaking line of statues, carts, and impatient people that curved around the periphery of the temple precinct. The parade along the Sacred Way, celebrating Artemis as protector and savior of Ephesus, should start at sunset. Tonight's event included a special repeating dance of the Great Goddess exorcising a frenzied female demon rising from the ocean to threaten her beloved city. A new girl played the demon. Artelia doubted she would be fierce enough.

At the head of the procession the dying sun shimmered on the first statue of the goddess Artemis Ephesia, ritually dressed today in gold splendor by the wardrobe and jewelry priestesses, her towering crown and the galaxy of eggs jutting from her torso heavily bejeweled. She rode in an elaborate chariot throne, lit round by torches. Artelia didn't waste time checking on the experienced charioteer who drove her, a long-time festival veteran.

Instead she inspected the statue lineup of gods and emperors, most of which were carried aloft by priests or priestesses of their temples although some figures rode in small wagons pulled by devotees or sacred animals.

Artelia had ensured that the spiritual and imperial dignitaries felt fully honored but not to an extent that infringed on the glory of Artemis. She glanced to see that dung collector slaves were stationed behind each donkey, horse, and oxen cart in order to protect the prestige of these retainers of the gods—or at least their shoes. As she scrutinized the statues she also reviewed the musicians' spacing throughout the processional lineup and spoke with several of them to confirm they understood the music schedule.

"Show some dignity tonight!" she scolded a priest of Dionysus, caught exposing his privates to one of the novices of Isis, whose statue preceded his own god. She also glared at the novice, who didn't seem nearly as shocked as she should, and frowned at the priestess who was supposed to keep her girls in line.

Almost four hundred people participated in tonight's event, and it seemed that half of them were drunk already and bored with the wait. If the procession didn't start soon, fights would break out. She hurried the pace of the inspection.

Midway through the procession was a crowd favorite, Artemis-Diana, the goddess of the hunt, placed in line behind a group of priests carrying a model of the Temple of Artemis on a platform on their shoulders. Several priestesses dressed as the Greek and Roman goddess would pretend to use their bows and arrows to toss wood and metal trinkets and tiny baskets of fruit and nuts into the crowds that lined the Sacred Way. Artelia checked the mule-drawn wagon, decorated with wreaths and ribbons. She saw with relief that there were enough treats to last the entire procession. People would be disappointed and angry if they ran out too soon.

She snapped her fingers under the nose of a curete dozing in the shade of Zeus. Like the musicians, the curetes, Artemis' young male initiates, were spread throughout the procession. Their more prominent activities happened later this spring in the Thargelion festival, which celebrated the birth of the Greek Artemis and her twin brother, Apollo. In that festival, held in the Ortygian grove, the noisy dancing of the curetes kept the jealous Hera away from Leto and her newborns. But in the Artemisia procession tonight, the curetes protected the peace. They ensured that no one got too rowdy and that petty squabbles between the priests and devotees of the different gods didn't erupt into drunken brawls.

Young men and women from all over the region would join tonight's procession en route, hoping to spend a few stolen moments with their prospective brides and grooms before the wedding. The curetes were supposed to make

sure no one used the procession chaos to get to know their future spouse—
or someone else's future spouse—too well. But Artelia privately thought it
unlikely that the handsome curetes, chosen by Artemis for their strength and
beauty, provided much control over youthful lust.

"Remind them to keep an eye on the Dionysians," she told her aide
Okeanos, and he hurried over to speak with a few of the boys.

The mellieras, the female virgin novices, flitted around, all beautifully
attired in golden embroidered chitons. Some depicted the Greek Artemis,
while others held or wore symbols designating them as animals important to
the Goddess such as deer, bees, and quail. Processions gave the mellieras good
opportunity for public practice of the many mythic Temple dances they had
to learn as initiates. Tonight they would dance up and down the procession
line throwing petals, garland, and ribbons into the crowd. Like the curetes, the
mellieras were chosen for their beauty and charm. Artelia had been keeping
an eye on several, and now she scowled at one in particular. She knew from
experience how to recognize a novice likely to be expelled from the Temple at
the end of festival for failure to keep her vows.

The great golden statue of the Queen of Heaven, bedecked with silk and
jewels, stood erect and beautiful in her gilded marble glory at the end of the
procession. This Artemis Ephesia, like the one at the head of the procession,
rode in a chariot pulled by matching horses chosen both for beauty and for
strength enough to pull the large and heavy gold statue.

The sunset colors passed. The full moon lit up the black, star-filled
sky. Artelia gave the signal to light the Temple torches. The high priest, the
Megabysos, stood at the steps of the Temple and called upon Artemis to
bless tonight's festivities. When his ritual was complete, Artelia nodded at
the chief torch bearer. He lit the first torch from the holy fire, and while the
sacred flame lit torch to torch from the back of the line to the front, he gave
an elaborate fiery signal to the music master to begin the first song.

Artelia settled into her litter at the end of the procession, behind the
golden statue of Artemis. A cadre of specially selected curetes lifted the litter
poles onto their shoulders. She rose into the air, praying a few grateful words
to her Goddess as the drummers set the beat for the commencement hymn,
quickly joined by horns and pipes. Joyous music filled the sky and excitement
filled the hearts of the people as the sacred procession from the Temple of
Artemis into the city of Ephesus began, the beat of the heavy drums an echo
of the Goddess's beating heart.

"My sorrow consumes me. I wear my anguish like a shroud."

Mount Kouressos, Ephesus
That same night, twelve months after the crucifixion of Jesus

A far-off unfamiliar melody drifted into the room. Mary breathed out the prayer of her pulse and her guilt before she was even conscious that she was awake: "Adonai, You are the only God. Your name is sacred. Your will be done." She sat up and opened her eyes, then looked over at the open window of the proseuche and frowned. It wasn't morning. The bright stars, seen through the window, filled the black sky without even a hint of dawn. She didn't need to wake up yet.

In the awful early days, the eviscerating knife of her sorrow hadn't allowed her the peace of sleep. But over the last year the sharp, piercing agony had solidified into chains around her heart, dragging her down into a black and bottomless grief. The weight of the sadness was so heavy she shuffled, bent from the burden of it, and all she wanted to do—all she could do—was sleep, heavily and endlessly. She had once been full of energy and excited by every waking moment. Now she couldn't keep her teary eyes open more than four or five hours of the day.

Then she heard it, very faintly. Joyful music trickled through the window of the proseuche, shutters open in the early spring. The sound was so soft she thought she could probably ignore it, probably close her eyes and drift back with the heavy cricket sound into that warm emptiness that served as her only solace...

But another part of her rebelled, a part she'd thought long dead inside her—her curiosity. She wondered about the music that drifted in the air like an angelic choir. If this was the Parousia—her son's return—she must be ready.

She slowly shifted, set her feet on the cold stone floor of her room, and stood. She took her gown and shawl from the peg on the wall and moved her body and arms just enough to clothe herself. She felt around with her feet until they found her cloth slippers and then she shuffled out of her room and through the moonlit proseuche room, opened the door of the small house, and stepped out.

Outside she noticed the fresh, rich spring smell, full of the promise of hope and new life. Reflex tears came to her eyes as her mind filled with re-membrance of last spring's hopes turned horror. Tonight was Passover. She'd turned down the invitation from John's family to join them in the feast of unleavened bread, because just the thought of this season made her feel like vomiting.

He died a full year ago. Yesterday, the actual anniversary of his death, was worse. Whenever she hurt today, she would remind herself: Yesterday was worse. She shook her head and pushed the thoughts away, and dragged herself down the path from her new house, ears bent to the music seeping through the night cricket chorus.

The huge full moon granted her enough light to see the path down the hill, but she walked carefully. She was out of the practice of walking and found it difficult to place her feet steady on the ground, one after the other.

She reached the overlook that John had pointed out to her a few days ago when he brought her up here to live. Although her new home was outside the walls of the city, at the edge of a grove belonging to the goddess of this place, she could see the whole sublime view of the town from this spot. She caught her breath, awestruck.

Down the hill to the west shone the city of Ephesus, its grand marble buildings reflecting the flickering light of a thousand burning lamps, its ancient fortifications twisting down the opposite hill and up this one. The blackness at the far western edge of the city must be the harbor where she and John docked last week when they finally arrived at the end of their long and miserable journey from Caesarea.

But she did not focus on the glowing city. Her attention was captured by the snake of light undulating around the east side of the hill below her, outside of the city walls. That was the source of the music. The snake was a serpentine procession of people waving torches, singing, chanting, and playing instruments. The joy and excitement in the sound was so palpable it almost hurt.

She collapsed to the ground and stared, following the procession with her eyes as it moved closer. It was very long—probably hundreds of people. All of them singing, their happiness alive, almost glowing in the air. "Make a joyful noise unto the Lord," she whispered, reciting a blessing although she knew that whatever this parade celebrated, it was not the Lord God of the Hebrews. She sighed a half-moment of regret as she acknowledged this was not her son's Parousia.

She watched the undulating procession as it rounded the bottom of the hill and headed through the gates of Ephesus, the sound louder and louder as the parade circled the hill until she could actually pick out instruments and harmonies—drums, pipes, horns, cymbals; men's and women's voices together. One woman's voice led the rest, loud and pure, and the others chanted and sang in response. Mary didn't notice her feet and head bobbing to the beat of the music. She didn't notice the unfamiliar faint smile that rested from time to time on her face.

She sat for two hours, watching as the full moon shrank and drifted across the sky, staring at the sinuous line of blazing music until the last flickering torch entered the city gate and was temporarily swallowed up by the reflecting marble buildings of Ephesus. The music rose as inhabitants of the town joined in the singing, and then it faded slowly away as the parade danced through the streets toward the dark edge of the sea. For a while she thought she could pick out the bright string of musical lights as it curved around a corner past the agora near the harbor. It disappeared finally, but she continued to sit under the beautiful canopy of night, smelling the night air and the new spring flowers, hearing again the crickets, thinking about the lights, the singing, and the joy.

She fell asleep on the grass. When the birdsong woke her and she opened her eyes to see the lightening sky, the morning prayer rushed from her lips and she felt as though she was truly awake for the first time in months. She felt that today her secret prayer to find a moment of peace in her heart might finally come true. She shivered in the brisk air, her body damp from dew.

And then she awoke fully at her second miracle of the day: Ten or twelve angels floated down from the purple dawn sky, their large white wings dancing in the air, long horns held to their mouths as they blew silent hymns that only the heavenly beings could hear, although she could hear them shouting to each other in a strange sort of clacking speech. They settled in the tops of the trees, standing tall on their dark legs. Fuzzy details sharpened with the rising dawn. Those legs looked…red.

Red? She strained her eyes to stare at the angels, and as the first rays of the sun finally hit she realized they weren't angels at all, but storks. Huge white storks with long red bills and long red legs settled into the topmost limbs of the old grove. She had never seen white storks before, only black ones as they flew overhead each winter back home, their big black bodies darkening the sky. These white storks had just a bit of black on them, on their tails and the tips of their wings. She could see now that they were settling into old nests, probably the same nests they'd been using for years. The other birds chirped their protests, angry to have their trees usurped by these large intruders. But the storks had no song at all to respond with, just that odd clacking talk.

They were so strange and so beautiful. The blessing of it overwhelmed her, and she remembered that the Hebrew word for stork meant "kind mother," because they gave such loving care to their young. She looked out over the city, awestruck to see the sunlight shining on the wings and backs of dozens of white stork bodies flapping over and around the town and settling on the tops of all the tallest buildings, while others flew over the hill toward the great temple that lay beyond.

"Kind mother." She could almost hear his voice whisper the words to her. For the first time she felt forgiven, and through her tears, for the first time in months, she truly smiled.

She felt as though she had been anointed and felt ready, finally, to be purified. She walked back up the hill to the house to find clean clothes. Too bad there wasn't any hyssop available yet. She'd make do with a cedar branch and sprinkle herself, be her own priest. She didn't care that it was improper to bathe on a Sabbath. Her son forgave her, and she needed to be ready for the Parousia, which all of his disciples believed would happen very soon.

She was ready to use the mikvah herself.

A few women had been up here yesterday, purifying before the feast of unleavened bread. She had met them all, but didn't remember anyone except Deborah, John's sister. Mary didn't even have tea to offer them after their prayers in the proseuche, nor was there anyplace but the cold stone floor for them to sit and visit with each other. The proseuche had a hearth, but no wood or charcoal. She could pray the Shema in Hebrew, which seemed to impress them very much, but she couldn't contribute anything more to the immersion ritual. She held their clothes and toweling, helped them with their hair, and made sure they fully immersed in the icy water at least three times. It was her first time as a mikvah servant, and she felt like a failure because she had nothing to offer the women for their comfort, physical or spiritual, as they shivered with cold. She couldn't even speak with them because she didn't understand Greek. Deborah smiled and said something to her that was no doubt meant to ease her distress, but she could only shrug in response.

She would learn Greek right away. And she would ask John to take her down to the market to buy the supplies she needed to make this a hospitable place, a place of simple comfort. A place of prayer and of purity.

The archisynagogoi had been so kind to offer her this work, and she was determined to do a good job. This generous offer had been made only a few days ago, at the house of John's father, Alexander, where she had been staying since they arrived in Ephesus.

She had been hiding in a warm kitchen corner of the huge house, waiting for a quiet time to slip back to her cot to sleep again, when John found her. "The astrologer says it's a good day to discuss the mikvah with Lavi, the archisynagogos of the other synagogue," he said.

"Oh?" She tried to sound interested.

"Yes." John smiled. "Because he's angry and won't come now, so he sent his son David. David's much easier to talk to." He led her to the exhedra where his father and David waited to interview her.

Like the kitchen, the exhedra opened into the peristyle, the house garden. John told her the large room was used for synagogue meetings. Mary had never attended synagogue in a house, another Ephesian oddity.

Nor had she ever been in such a large and rich house. She'd had to ask John the names and purpose of all the rooms, like the exhedra, which was a large dining and meeting room; the peristyle; the atrium—another room open to the air, with a pool in the middle that collected rainwater; and many other rooms whose Roman names she couldn't remember. This house even had its own bath and, incredibly, an indoor latrine.

It was hard to imagine that John had grown up in this luxurious house, in such a grand and important family.

She felt grateful the interview was not being held in the atrium, where she would have had to look at the shrine honoring Julius Caesar, Caesar Augustus, and, most astonishing of all, Artemis Ephesia. She recognized the two emperors from their statues in Caesarea, but she had never seen anything like Artemis and could not enter that room without staring. Mary could not comprehend an Israelite house with an altar for any graven image, let alone an idol of a pagan goddess. All over the house were decorations of animals and people, paintings, frescoes, statues, mosaics, and decorated cloth, but as barbarous as all of those seemed, nothing came close to shocking her like the image of many-breasted Artemis up on the family altar.

The exhedra held no images at all in its decoration, so she felt almost comfortable when she entered the room and Archisynagogos Alexander introduced her to Archon David and then asked her to sit.

After they prayed, David asked her a question in Greek. She told him that she didn't understand. He then spoke to her in Hebrew, and she was ashamed to tell him that she didn't really understand Hebrew either, except for names of things—animals and plants, for example—and also the Shema and other prayers.

"You can pray the Shema in Hebrew?" he asked in her language, Aramaic.

"Yes." She spoke the words. He nodded, impressed. She would later learn that most of the Israelites in Ephesus could only pray in Greek.

"I believe John has told you that we have a new mikvah and are seeking a mikvah servant who will be acceptable to all who use it, someone who will live at the prayer house, the little proseuche?" Alexander said.

"Yes."

"You don't have to leave my house if you don't want to. You have so many sons that you're not obligated to be under my legal guardianship, but you are welcome to live here with us as part of our family always, because of your loving care for my son John and your kindness in accompanying him back home to Ephesus."

"No." She had no desire to live in this house. "Thank you."

"How many children do you have?" David asked politely.

"I have seven children. Five of them are sons. One is dead."

Then David surprised her by quoting the prophet Jeremiah: "'I make her widows more numerous than the sand of the seas. I bring a destroyer at midday against the mothers of young men. The mother of seven is bereft and faints away. Her sun sets while it is still day and she is filled with shame and distress.'"

Mary had never heard her situation described so clearly. Her eyes welled.

David smiled at her apologetically. "I'm sorry. My desire to show off my scholarship does not excuse causing you pain."

She shook her head. "No, please forgive my silly tears. As you said, I am filled with shame and distress. You are right about me."

"Happily, only one of her children has met the destroyer," Alexander commented, then addressed Mary. "John says that your son Jesus was executed by Pontius Pilate."

"Yes," she said.

"He tells me that Jesus taught in the Temple and had many followers. A great healer, he said."

"Yes."

"Well-respected? A descendant of King David?"

A whisper: "Yes."

"And Pilate saw him as a threat to Rome." This was not a question. Jerusalem was volatile, filled with rebels. Anyone with followers, especially someone claiming descent from King David, would be suspected of treason against Rome.

Silent tears began running down her cheeks, and she lifted the edge of her head scarf to wipe her face.

"Your tears do you no shame, woman. Even here in Ephesus, where we live in harmony with Rome, we hear about the brutality of Pontius Pilate. Your son died as a man, as an Israelite. We will honor you as the mother of a hero."

Her tears overwhelmed her, and she could barely see Alexander's nod to John to lead her away. David said nothing, but from the expression on his blurry face she thought he agreed with Alexander's kind words.

As she reached the door, David spoke. "Alexander, this woman appears to be a respectable widow of sober demeanor. Her Judean manner and customs will be a good example to the women of our community. She is acceptable to the synagogue that meets at the home of my father."

She turned at those words. "Thank you, sir," she said, still mopping her wet face.

He nodded then said, "Do you have any questions of us before John takes you to your new home?"

"Yes," she said. "Who performs the priestly acts for the mikvah? The healing tests and purification sprinkling?"

"No one," said David. "If a priest migrates to gentile lands, he's deprived of his leadership position and forbidden to partake in holy things. We have a butcher who also serves as mohel, but no one goes to him for purification."

Alexander burst out laughing at the thought.

David smiled and continued in his formal way, "The other priestly duties, the legal and civic ones, are done by upstanding men of the community. But we don't have anyone who sprinkles hyssop or performs other purification rites, especially not for women, so you will need to do those things as well. You'll find that only women will be using the mikvah regularly anyway, so it won't be improper. Men use the sea for purification."

"All right," she said. "Does anyone here grow hyssop?"

David and Alexander both smiled broadly, relieved to learn that their new mikvah attendant was actually familiar with purification halakhah.

"You should be able to find some cut hyssop and also some seeds at the Judean market so that you can grow your own," Alexander said.

She nodded and let John lead her away, and he took her and her few belongings up to the house that afternoon.

That had been three days ago.

After she prayed and bathed, she sat on the ground drying her hair in the sun, watching the storks clean and repair their nests. She felt hopeful today. He'd been dead a full year and then today had sent her two signs—the parade of lights and joyful music and the angel storks that told her of his love for her, his kind mother. Today would be her son's Parousia. She was sitting on the ground smiling, thinking about how good it would feel to hold him again, when John arrived carrying a stone bowl. He sat down on the blanket beside her and lifted the lid.

"You look happy today," he said.

"He's coming today," she said. "I can feel it."

John had said those same words to her many times, especially in the early months. He no longer spent each day in idleness waiting for her son's imminent return. "I hope so. But in the meantime, let's have breakfast."

He took a piece of meat from the bowl and noticed her frown. "Don't worry, Mother. We can eat feast leftovers—this lamb was never part of a sacrifice to God. Out here in Asia we observe Passover as best as we can, but there's no Temple here and we don't sacrifice."

This didn't sound proper, but she wasn't a scholar. It didn't seem proper for her to purify people either, yet here she was. Plus she was hungry. She recited a blessing then said, "But no leavening, right?"

"You were there in the kitchen when they removed all chametz from the house," he reminded her.

It embarrassed her to think she was so lost in her own sorrow and desire for sleep she hadn't even noticed something like that going on around her. She had promised her dear worried daughter Anna she would try to pay attention to things, and here was a perfect example of her failure to keep her promise.

They heard a high-pitched shriek coming from the grove. Mary flinched. She'd heard this wild and distressing sound many times in the days since she'd arrived here at the proseuche.

John too was troubled by the sound, but said it must be some kind of animal that lived in the woods. "I'm sure it's nothing dangerous, Mother. Someone would have said if there was anything dangerous up here. But we can ask about it at the next synagogue meeting at my father's house."

It seemed so odd to hold synagogue in a private house. "Why doesn't the community have a real synagogue, John?" she asked. "Aren't there enough Hebrews here?"

He looked at her in concern. "Mother, I told you before."

She patted his hand, tears welling in her eyes at his reproof. She shook them away, annoyed. She was determined to spend at least one day without crying. If Jesus didn't return today, then tonight she could cry.

"Please tell me again."

He leaned over and kissed her, and she felt the faint, sparse beginnings of hair on his smooth young face. The Beloved Disciple was growing up.

"We used to have a synagogue," he said. "Down by the sea. It was destroyed in the big earthquake a few years ago."

"Oh, that's right, I remember now. You went to school there."

"Yes. It was a big synagogue, with a house of prayer, a house of study, and a house of assembly. On Sabbath we all met there and sat in the rows of benches that lined the prayer house—us children over with the women, the leaders at their special bench near the water basin so that they could wash their hands before handling the sacred scrolls. On feast days, there'd sometimes be hundreds of people in the assembly house. It's sad to think there's no place big enough to hold us all anymore."

"Very sad."

"My mother died in that earthquake. She was up at the assembly house early, preparing food before school. She used to be sad when I couldn't sit still and be quiet for Sabbath tefilah. I should have been good, should have prayed with her."

Mary put her arm around him and pulled him close. He allowed her to rock him for a few moments before he pulled away to speak again.

"The synagogue was completely smashed. Part of the mountain collapsed, burying buildings under the rocks." He lay down beside her and hid his thin face in her lap. She felt great sorrow for his pain. His mother had gone there to prepare his food and had died a horrible death. She had been a good mother, and he thought he'd been a bad son. He was too young to bear such guilt. She patted his shoulders, speaking soothing words, and soon he spoke again.

"About a month before the earthquake, thieves broke in and stole all the valuables they could get their hands on—even our menorah. They took the box with the Temple tax. And they took the chest the sacred scrolls were in. I guess they thought there were gold or jewels in there."

"How awful! Were the thieves caught?"

"Yes. They tried to sell some candlesticks at the agora, and someone noticed the Hebrew inscription. Then they tried to take sanctuary at the temple of Artemis, but Artelia, the high priestess, told the Roman proconsul that she didn't want the temple of Artemis to be used as a sanctuary for blasphemers. See, the temple here offers sanctuary to just about everyone in need— criminals, debtors, slaves. But Artelia said that Artemis would not offer sanctuary to people who steal from the gods, and the governor agreed. The men were arrested, beaten, and exiled from Ephesus. And then the governor decreed that theft from our meeting houses is sacrilege, and if anyone steals from us his property will be confiscated and transferred to Rome."

Mary flinched at hearing the Lord God of the Hebrews grouped in with idols as just one of "the gods," but suspected this wouldn't be the last time she'd hear such a thing. In a place with many gods—and the most important of them all a goddess—the laws would be very different than they were back home.

Back home, someone who stole the sacred scrolls out of a synagogue would be stoned for blasphemy.

"What happened to the sacred scrolls?"

"We found the empty chest sitting in the sand at the edge of the sea, not far from the synagogue. The thieves said they just threw the scrolls into the sea and they washed away. We got the menorah, some of the candlesticks, and other stuff back—and then lost them again in the earthquake. Most of the Temple tax was gone—the thieves spent it before they were caught. Now we bank our Temple tax up at the temple of Artemis, because it's the safest place in Asia."

Mary didn't want to think about God's money being banked at the temple of the idol.

"My father says that if the Torah hadn't washed away in the sea, it would have been buried under dirt and rocks a month later. The sea kept it from being polluted. He calls that a miracle. But the other group here—their leader is Archsynagogos Lavi, you met his son Archon David—they view the theft and the earthquake as a double punishment instead. They think someone committed some horrible abomination that profaned the building and the people, so God took our scrolls and our synagogue away from us. I think they blame my father, because he's an elder of the city governing council and tries to get along with the Greeks and with Rome. Well, I'm sure you noticed the altar in the atrium at our house?"

"I did." Artemis with her many breasts, on display in an Israelite home. She'd noticed.

"My father often has important visitors, once even the proconsul. My father says Ephesians fear Israelites because we isolate ourselves, and he wants everyone to know we are honest and trustworthy. He keeps us safe, because the Greeks know him and know he wants the same things for Ephesus that they do."

"And what is that?"

"Prosperity," John said. "Safety. A clean town, with honest people who have decent houses and good food and clean water. A place where people are happy to live."

John finished breakfast as Mary watched a stork welcome its mate to the family nest. She wondered which was the male and which the female. Were storks kind fathers too?

They prayed, and then John asked: "Will you join us for the First Fruits festival?"

"Is First Fruits a significant day, out here in Asia?"

"We offer money to God instead of crops and send it to Jerusalem with the Temple tax. There'll be prayer and speeches, music and dancing. We rent a hall down in the city that's big enough to hold everyone. But since it's the month-long festival of Artemis Ephesia right now, the town is full of revelers who don't understand that our feast isn't open to the public. Festivals were a lot easier back when we had our synagogue."

"There was a procession last night," Mary said. "I could see it from up here. Was that because of this Artemis Ephesia festival?"

"Yes. There'll be another one tonight. It goes right by the hall where we have our feast. So...will you come?"

Mary thought about it. She wanted to just sit here in the shade for the rest of the day, waiting for her son to return. First Fruits, which started to-night, was the day of her son's resurrection. She should spend the day in prayer, in expectation of his return. But she also knew that if he didn't return today, her sadness would be unbearable. She was tired of being sad and alone. Better to be with a crowd. "Yes. I'll come to the festival."

"That's great!" John said. "My sister Deborah and the other women are down at the hall getting everything prepared now. I thought we could go over to my house for a while then go down to the festival with my father."

Mary looked up at the sky. It was only around third hour now. Two more hours until midday. It might be nice to get in a little walk before having a big meal later in the day. Although the Passover feast was last night, it was still High Sabbath...

The women were in town getting things prepared?

"Do you work on the Sabbath here in Asia?" she asked.

"We don't work on the seventh day. But we can't always be so observant about High Sabbaths at festival time, because the rest of the city is usually cel-ebrating their own festivals at the same time and we need to find ways to keep ourselves separate from them without offending them. That's easiest to do if we celebrate during the day because they do most of their celebrating at night. Almost every day in Ephesus is a festival for some god or another—Artemis has this month plus her birthday festival, and there are also major festivals to Isis and Serapis, Dionysus, Aesclepius and Hygeia, Demeter, Ares, Minerva, Cybele and Attis, and Hestia Boulaia. Those festivals all last for many days, sometimes weeks. And that doesn't count the minor festivals, for all the other gods."

"So many gods," she whispered.

"Yes. And for most of those festivals, anyone who wants to join in to celebrate and worship the god is welcome. Naturally the Ephesians don't understand why we don't welcome them to our festivals. We'll celebrate First Fruits this afternoon because the rest of the town will be celebrating the Artemisia tonight."

John looked up at two busy storks cleaning their nest. "I'm glad you have all these storks around you. It's a good sign."

Mary nodded. She went into the house to get a head covering and to put on her shoes for the long walk downhill into the city.

She thought: "My son, why do I keep breathing when nothing matters without you?"

CHAPTER 12

"Hope alone pumps air into my lungs. I endure the wait and ghost-walk through my days."

They walked the path downhill from the mikvah, entering the city through a break in the wall. Once out of the grove she could see the whole of the city below her, because there were almost no trees in Ephesus. John said this was because all wood had been used up long ago in building ships and making sacrifices to the gods. All Ephesians today used charcoal in their braziers and hearths, which they had to buy from charcoal merchants.

Though the path was clear, she kept losing her balance. "I can't think what's wrong with me," she said after John grabbed her arm for the third time to keep her from falling.

"You haven't had any real exercise in a long while, Mother," he said politely, not commenting that Mary had more or less slept the last twelve months away. She hadn't walked from Galilee to Caesarea as he had—she rode all the way, and every time he checked on her, her head was nodding with sleep. Even while they were on board ship she spent all her time sleeping.

"It's also not so easy going down this steep hill," she said.

"You'll get used to it," he promised. "Once you've been here for a while, going up and down this hill will be as normal as carrying water or gathering wood."

"Speaking of that, can I glean wood from the grove around the proseuche?"

"All wood in that grove belongs to Artemis Ephesia," John said. "Any big trees or groups of trees you see around here, you can be sure that they belong to Artemis. You mustn't use any of the wood without permission."

"Whom do I ask for permission?" It seemed foolish to expect Alexander or the synagogues to spend money on charcoal for her when wood lay rotting on the ground all around her house.

"You should ask Artelia, the high priestess. She's very reasonable. We negotiated with her for the mikvah."

They walked in silence for a while and then she spoke.

"I still don't understand why you have graven images in your house."

"The graven images are not idols, they're symbols," John said, and she knew he repeated his father's words. "Julius Caesar and Caesar Augustus are reminders that we are privileged residents in Ephesus. They established our rights to live in accordance with the Torah out here in Asia. Our Temple tax can't be confiscated for any reason, even for taxes for Rome or Ephesus. We don't have to participate in legal suits or other civic duties on the Sabbath or the day before. And even though I'll be a Roman citizen, I'll be exempt from military conscription because it's too hard to keep the Sabbath or comply with the dietary laws when you're out with the army."

"The Romans allow all that?"

"Those are our rights, and they protect them."

"Amazing," she said and meant it. To her, Romans were people who stripped away the rights of Israelites, not protectors of them.

"In Ephesus, we remember Julius Caesar and Caesar Augustus as friends of the Israelites. Of course, they've both been dead a long time, and sometimes there are people on the city council who try to take away some of our rights. So every few years, every time there's a new proconsul of Rome, my father shows the documents to him and to the city council, reminding them that we're privileged residents, and they give him a new decree reaffirming that. Whenever any of them come into our house, they see the busts of Julius Caesar and Caesar Augustus and they remember all that."

"And what about the other?" She didn't know how to refer to the hideous idol with all the breasts sticking out of her chest and waist like eggs popping out of a basket.

"Artemis Ephesia? That's about 'eusebeia'—our devotion to our city. Ephesus is proud to serve Artemis. Half the people who live here have "Art" at the beginning of their name in honor of her. Even my Latin name is Arturius. Ephesians believe that our prosperity and holiness as a city is due to the protection, blessing, and presence of the goddess Artemis Ephesia. See, just like the Israelites think of Jerusalem as the Holy City, that's how the Greeks in Asia think about Ephesus. That little statue in the atrium was a gift to my father from the city council, in gratitude for all the good work he's done for our city. It's a symbol like the busts of the Caesars. It symbolizes the devotion we feel toward Ephesus—and the respect Ephesus has for us."

John sounded like an idol worshipper as he spoke about the city. No doubt Alexander was worse. Mary understood why Archisynagogos Lavi felt that Alexander wasn't true to his faith.

John saw the slight frown on her face. "My father talks sometimes about the Maccabees, who went to war on the Sabbath in order to defeat the enemy. They violated the Torah to protect the Torah. He says that's what he does."

Mary nodded and then concentrated on her walking as the road downhill became steeper.

The area closest to the gate, where they'd first walked through, had large villas with high walls and gardens, fountains, and a few privately owned trees. Alexander's house over on Mount Pion was typical of the style of the villas on both hills. Rich people liked living high up on the hills, away from the thick, dirty air of the city, which fed the demons of disease. Mary and John walked along a rock-lined footpath that wound between many of these beautiful stone and brick houses, down to the main road of Mount Kouressos that they would take the rest of the way down the hill. From this road she could see every detail of Ephesus, including the other, smaller hill across from Mount Kouressos, Mount Pion, where even more elaborate villas lined the top of the hill near the city wall.

The stables for the villas were built for easy access along the higher side of the Mount Kouressos road. Tenement housing was on the lower side of the road. The smell rising up from the poor neighborhoods was as strong as the smell from the stables. The poor people of Ephesus lived in close-built rickety wooden apartments of three and four stories, separated from each other by narrow dirt walkways filled with debris and human and animal filth. Dark, smelly smoke poured out of open windows. The buildings were so close to each other that she could see people high up in one building passing things through a window to people in the next building, and many of the buildings seemed so decrepit that it was only their leaning against one another that kept them from collapsing. Dotted here and there in the neighborhoods she could see open pits where people were supposed to dump their chamber pots; and she did see some people using the pits for that purpose although she saw just as many people simply use the walkways and roads.

And the masses of people living in the tenement neighborhoods—so many people crowded each other in the walkways that it was hard for her to imagine the apartments having room enough to hold them all. The lovely bird and cricket sounds of the grove were no more, supplanted by a buzzing human city cacophony.

Walking inside the city high up on the Mount Kouressos road, she could see details that she had missed from her look-out spot near the proseuche, which was outside the city walls. She realized now that wooden tenement neighborhoods made up most of the city.

Large public buildings, temples, and fountains separated the tenement neighborhoods from one another. Their beauty was quite astonishing when juxtaposed against the filth and poverty of the neighborhoods they served. People crowded the public buildings even more than they did the tenement walkways, because who would want to spend time in their filthy, dangerous houses when they could enjoy the clean beauty of these elaborate fountains and great marble temples and shrines instead?

Street vendors sold food and shopkeepers operated their businesses from the first floors of the tenements where they lived. Mary noticed a bakery, a wine merchant, and a laundry.

She watched as a priest standing at an altar in front of a temple made a burnt offering to his god, a sight she'd never seen at the Temple in Jerusalem since women weren't allowed in the inner court where sacrifices were made. Then she tripped in the road when she saw one of the food vendors receive the offering from the priest and take it away to sell on the street.

John grabbed her to keep her from falling. She patted his hand in thanks and pointed to the temple. "John, I think they're selling that burnt offering," she said.

"Yes," he said. "Most of the meat you buy in this city has been offered to the gods. So if you buy anything cooked, be sure to buy it from one of the Israelite vendors or from our butcher."

The temple was close enough to the road that she could actually smell the burnt offering. "That smells so good," she said. "What is it?"

"Pork," John said, and she felt doubly polluted—for smelling the pork and for enjoying the smell.

John put his arm around her. He was as tall as she was now. When he first started following after her son, he'd been thirteen years old and small for his age. Jesus took a special liking to the solemn and clever young boy, sent by his family to live with neglectful cousins in Jerusalem while he studied at the Temple. Jesus made John feel welcome in his circle, even giving the boy lessons himself when he had time.

When Jesus died, he placed John in her care. Her son hung on the cross in great agony, his blood dripping on the ground, and he looked down at John and her as they stood weeping at his feet and he said, "Woman, here is your son." Those were the last words he ever spoke to her.

"I love you, John," she said.

"I love you too, Mother. And don't feel bad about smelling the pork."

"I won't," she said, but she hoped there would be a chance for her to wash in pure water very soon.

They passed a small meat market, and she grimaced to see hare carcasses on display for purchase as well as chickens tied up above, their broken necks dangling. She could imagine the blood pooling for hours in each animal's head, neck, and torso as they hung by their feet from the rafters of the shop.

John noticed her distaste at the dead chickens and hares. "You would be amazed at the things gentiles will eat. Usually meat that's been sacrificed to the gods. There aren't many meat markets like this in Ephesus, because the priests control most of the meat trade. Vegetables too—you'll want to avoid buying vegetables on the street, because they were probably part of a sacrifice. After the holidays, we'll go to the Judean market and you can meet our butcher."

She was exhausted when they finally reached the bottom of Mount Pion and crossed a wide, busy street into the heart of the city. John, ever thoughtful, asked her if she would like to rest for a bit before they started up Mount Pion to his father's house.

"Yes, for just a moment," she said thankfully. He helped her to a bench near a fountain and she collapsed onto the seat.

She sat with her eyes closed for a while, saying a brief prayer. She opened them when John came over with a clay cup that he had filled with water at the fountain. "Here, Mother," he said gently.

She sipped the water gratefully. It wasn't the pure, sweet water of the mikvah spring, but its brackishness went unnoticed in her thirst. She held the empty cup out to John with a smile. "More, please."

He went to refill the cup, and she looked around. The loose-pebble street, which stretched from the city gate to the harbor agora and beyond, was flanked on each side with innumerable columns and statues. The marble and stone buildings that fronted the street were ornate, lavish, highly sculpted, and brightly painted. Inscriptions had been carved on every surface, all incomprehensible to her. She noticed an ivory plaque of a winged woman erected on a column, with inscriptions above and below, and wondered what it said.

From her bench she could see five fountains of various sizes, not including the one immediately ahead of her where John refilled her cup, the gushing water of the fountains an impressive testimony to the strength of the city's aqueducts. John held his cup to water flowing out of a horn at the mouth of some heathen god, while more water poured from the antlers of the deer that danced around the god's feet.

Before she sat down, John had identified this as the state agora area and this road as the "sacred way." There were several particularly impressive public buildings here, and as she waited for John her eyes examined one long marble building that featured elaborate friezes along the roof and tall statues of important-looking men and women lined across it. In the hand of one statue, a small figure of Artemis Ephesia stood in all her many-breasted glory.

Mary thought this "sacred way" must be the road that the procession had taken last night after it entered the city.

A dirty little boy walked over and stood in front of her, staring and asking her a question in some foreign tongue. She did not think she had ever seen such a filthy child. John returned and handed her the cup of water. She swallowed it gratefully and said, "What does that child want, John?"

John spoke to the boy. The boy answered rapidly and then more slowly when John interrupted him.

"Sorry, Mother, he speaks the old Ephesian peasant language, which I don't understand very well. But I think he wants to know if you're a fortune teller."

"What? Why would he think that?"

John spoke again to the boy then laughed at the response. "He says because you're dressed all in black, like the Judean sibyls at the market. Judean fortune tellers are highly regarded here, you see. It's because they know the secret language."

"What is that?"

"Hebrew. The secret language. And our God has a secret name, which they think gives us very great magic."

Mary nodded. "I see. Well, please tell the child that before any respectable Judean fortune teller will agree to read the auguries for him, he will have to take a bath."

John laughed and repeated her words to the boy. The boy shook his head vigorously and ran off.

"That was a good answer, Mother," John said. "Now, if you're feeling better, I think we should get going before he returns all dripping wet, ready for you to read his signs."

"I agree." She stood to take his arm and start the walk up the next hill.

Many magistrates and government dignitaries lived near Alexander's house on Mount Pion. Even the Roman proconsul lived nearby. Mary was glad to leave the filth and crowds of the tenements behind her and enter the beautiful neighborhoods, even though walking up the small hill of Mount Pion seemed more arduous than the walk down Mount Kouressos.

She washed gratefully at the stone basin near the entrance of Alexander's house before John opened the door. As soon as they entered the vestibulum, they heard angry voices yelling in Greek.

"What's happening?" Mary asked.

John grabbed her hand and hurried toward the sound. Before they reached the room from which the loud voices came, he pulled her into the atrium to listen.

"It's Archisynagogos Lavi," he whispered. "And my father."

"What's wrong?"

He listened for a while, and sorrow seeped into his face.

"You know Rebekkah? My brother Enoch's wife?"

"Yes."

"They've been married for ten years. And Rebekkah has never become pregnant."

"How sad."

"Yes, well, now Aspasia, one of the house slaves, is pregnant. And she and Enoch both say the baby is his."

Mary stared at John. He couldn't look at her as he spoke. "My brother is divorcing Rebekkah and marrying Aspasia. It's against the law here to have more than one legal wife. And Enoch wants Aspasia's child to have his patris."

"Oh, no." Mary liked Rebekkah, a quiet but kind woman, although of course she hadn't been able to talk with her. And she even remembered Aspasia, a sweet girl who had come to get her for meals several times during the few days she had stayed at Alexander's house.

"Rebekkah is Archisynagogos Lavi's daughter," John added.

They heard some people walking near and peeked out the door of the room to see Rebekkah, sobbing quietly, leave the house escorted by several women. Slaves followed behind, carrying trunks, rugs, bolts of cloth, and other items.

One of the women with Rebekkah was John's sister Deborah, who stopped her at the door to give her a heart-wrenching embrace before she left.

There was a last angry shout from the other room. An imposing gentleman stomped past them to follow Rebekkah out of the house, followed by several younger men. Mary recognized Archon David in the group.

Deborah slowly closed the door behind them and turned to see John and Mary now hurrying to meet her.

She greeted Mary quietly, and then spoke with her brother as the three returned to the atrium.

"She was on her way to the hall to get things ready for the festival when Archisynagogos Lavi arrived," John told Mary.

Alexander walked out of the room where the shouting had occurred, followed by a shamefaced Enoch. John's father looked displeased to see Mary, and she was embarrassed to be witness to this private affair.

Enoch and Deborah spoke together for a while. John translated for Mary.

"My father freed Aspasia today so that she can marry Enoch. He removed her collar and gave her papers of manumission."

"I want Aspasia to be baptized at the mikvah tomorrow," Enoch told Mary. He had never spoken to her before, and she hadn't considered that of course he too would speak Aramaic, having been educated in Jerusalem like John.

"Baptized? You mean like John the baptizer used to do?" John had been famous in Judea for his focus on purity and asceticism, his teachings about the end-times, and his legions of followers.

"Exactly like that. I am a disciple of John's. Have you ever seen a baptism?"

She knew baptism was a purification ritual, a reflection and a renewal of one's devotion to God. But she had never seen one. "No. No, I haven't."

"Well, Deborah will be there to help." Enoch nodded good-bye and then he, Deborah, and their father walked away, deep in conversation.

"My father is saying that no one from Lavi's family will be at the feast. He says it will be a long while before we see any of them at any assembly or event. He hopes that they will still use the mikvah and proseuche despite this."

"Oh, I hope so too." She felt very sad for Rebekkah, being shamed in this way for her barrenness. If Rebekkah came to the mikvah, she would be particularly kind to her. Her inability to speak Rebekkah's language might even make the poor woman more comfortable, since she would know that Mary wouldn't be asking intrusive questions or gossiping about her.

"I think we should probably leave the house," John said. "Let's go to the harbor agora. Maybe we can pick up some things for the baptism and then later we can go to the festival."

But as they left the house, John was stopped by a young man at the door, anxious and panting from running. John spoke with him then said, "Mother, this slave is looking for Deborah. His mistress, Adrianna, is a member of our synagogue and she's dying. She has no sisters or daughters living, and her son wants a Hebrew woman to sit with her. Normally Deborah would do this, but now—"

"No," Mary said decisively. "Don't bother your sister. She has enough to deal with now. I'll sit with the poor woman."

"There'll be corpse pollution," John warned. "You won't be able to attend the festival."

Mary thought it more appropriate to spend the anniversary of her son's death sitting with a dying woman instead of attending a festival anyway. "I don't mind. But what about you?"

He seemed disappointed, but shrugged. "There'll be other festivals," he said in his good-natured way. "And you'll need someone to translate with the family."

John verified the location of the family's house with the slave then sent the young man off to tell them that Mary would come instead of his sister Deborah.

"We'll need to take some living water with us," Mary said. "And some oil." They left soon after, John carrying the items Mary needed to purify the dying woman.

"At least now I won't have to baptize Aspasia," Mary said as they walked. She and John would suffer corpse pollution for seven days and must avoid everyone. "I was worried, since I have no idea how to conduct a baptism." She wrinkled her nose. They were nearing another tenement area, and the stench of the streets was getting stronger.

"Aspasia's probably been baptized once already anyway," John said. "When Enoch returned after studying at the Temple, he baptized everyone in the house except Father. But they want to make sure her conversion is legally documented, so that her children will have full Ephesian and Roman citizenship like their father and also be Hebrews with full Judean privilege."

"But will Aspasia's children really be Hebrews?" As Mary said this, she realized the foolishness of the question—was anyone born outside of the land of Israel, away from the Temple of God, really a "Hebrew"?

"Things are different here in Asia than they are in Judea. For example, here Samaritans are considered Hebrews. Samaritans will be using the mikvah too."

This shocked her. Back home, Samaritans were enemies, considered lower than dogs.

"You see, to the Romans we're all the same, since we pray to the same God, follow the same Torah, and have the same rituals and laws. The Romans don't care about the exile to Babylon or the Holy Temple or Mount Gerazim or any of the old history about the two kingdoms. So since there are so few of us here in Ephesus—and there's even fewer of them—we work together when it makes sense. Politics, you know. They wanted a mikvah as much as we did, so we share this one. We don't hold synagogue together, of course, or festivals. There would be too many fights."

They continued the rest of the way downhill, trying to avoid the piles of manure that littered the ground, trying to avoid jostling the people or being run down by the horses, donkeys, carts, and wagons that now filled the roadway. The closer they got to the heart of the city, the busier the road became, crowded with men—and with women. Half the people they saw were women.

Mary couldn't believe the number of women who lived and worked in Ephesus. So different from Jerusalem. Everyone who lived in Jerusalem was associated with the Temple of God, the only industry, and worked mostly in businesses that catered to the pilgrims. People sold sacrificial animals. Tanners used the remains of the sacrificed animals to sell clean leather products to the visitors. Money-changers exchanged the travelers' Greek, Roman, and

Egyptian currencies into the shekels that were the only currency accepted by the priests. People fed, bathed, clothed, and housed the pilgrims who travelled long distances to make their atonement sacrifices, attend festivals, or study with Temple teachers.

But there weren't very many women, other than family members of the men on pilgrimage. Women weren't supposed to live in Jerusalem, although of course many did. But they stayed hidden and quiet. Nothing like here.

Here in Ephesus, she saw women everywhere, running shops, chasing and nursing children, doing laundry, arguing with men. They were present, they were loud, and they were busy. They belonged here.

She realized what a difference it must make to a woman's life to live in a city that was ruled by a goddess. Then she said a quick, guilty prayer.

Adrianna lived in an apartment above her son's shoemaking shop in one of the nicer tenement buildings. The rooms were clean and comfortable, although the heavy smoke from the charcoal brazier quickly made Mary's eyes hurt. John moved the brazier to the farthest corner of the room.

The old woman lay in bed, quite still, but as yet alive. Two family slaves stood near her, unsure about what to do. Her grief-stricken son sat in a corner, praying through his tears.

John spoke with the son. "He says that his mother has been ailing for a while, but she seemed to revive yesterday, and they thought she would recover."

"It often happens that way. Was she able to talk with her son when she was alert, tell him good-bye?"

"Yes," John said after a moment's conversation. "At least, he didn't think it was good-bye then. But now that he thinks on their words, he realizes it was."

"It's a good death then." Mary loosened the woman's headdress and gently stroked her forehead. "She doesn't seem to be in any pain, and she was able to tell her son good-bye. God has blessed this house."

John brought her a stool, and Mary sat by the woman's bed, holding her hand, praying. She said all the prayers she knew in Hebrew, then recited other Hebrew words—Psalms, Proverbs, even bits of stories she could remember in the original language. Adrianna was an old woman, and there was good chance she might know some of the old language, had perhaps heard it spoken when she was young, or maybe knew some of the prayers herself. At any rate, it could only be a blessing to fly into the arms of God with your ears still echoing the language of the Patriarchs. Several times Mary thought she saw the old woman smile, and once it seemed as though her lips moved in unison with Mary's prayer.

When Mary felt the end time nearing, she had John bring her the living water and oil, and she purified Adrianna for her last, greatest journey.

Sunset was just a couple of hours away when Mary and John finally left the dead woman to the care of her son and servants. John decided they should stop at the gem-cutters guild hall where the First Fruits festival was taking place, so that he could let his father and sister know of Adrianna's death, and they could then tell others. The synagogue would arrange the burial.

"She'll probably be buried near my mother," John said as they left the tenement and entered the street. "On the other side of the hill. I'll take you there sometime."

As they walked Mary noticed that many of the shops on the street had pictures of shoes painted or inscribed on the doors and walls.

"That's because we're in the shoemakers' street," John explained. "This is where most of the members of the shoemakers' guild live."

On the way to the gem-cutters guild hall John pointed out other guild streets, such as the fullers street and the street of the diviners, as well as guild halls like the small, plain meeting hall of the linen-workers' guild and the much grander doctors club, an impressive building heavily decorated with statues and plaques recording the great deeds of its members.

John explained that in Ephesus, everyone belonged to a guild and most people belonged to more than one.

"A guild is a group of people—usually friends, neighbors, or people in the same type of work—who decide to organize a club together," John said. "They write up a set of laws for their club and elect officers, find a place to meet—sometimes at the baths, or they might build a special guild hall or maybe meet at a temple—and they decide which gods they want to devote their guild to and then they have meetings."

"What do they do at their meetings?"

"Honor their gods with prayer and gifts. Socialize. Plan civic events and festivals. They also have burial committees, so that when people die they are given proper funerals and receive the proper prayers, and their graves and tombs are cared for."

"Why do they need to write up laws for that?" Back home, if a group of friends wanted to meet, they just did it.

"It's so they have a sacred and legal identity and rights. People respect guilds. Guild halls are considered as sacred as temples. If you look, you'll see they always have basins for purification outside the entry. The synagogue that meets at my father's house is a guild, and it's a committee from that guild that will attend to Adrianna's burial. My brother Enoch's Disciples of John the Baptist group is a guild. There might even be a Guild of Judean Widows that you could join."

"Women can join guilds?"

"Women, men, slaves, freeborn, freedmen—anyone can join the guilds. In fact, there are gentile God Fearers in some of the Judean guilds. It's one of the best ways for people to learn about us. See that building over there? That's a Judean guild hall. You can tell by the menorah on the column. I think it's the Association of Judean Dietary Workers."

Soon they reached the gem-cutters guild hall. "Is this a Judean guild?" she asked as they climbed the marble steps to the graceful portico that shaded two sets of doors, one open, one closed. They stopped by a stone wash basin near the open door, and John asked a slave standing near the door to go bring out one of his family slaves.

"Not entirely," John said after the slave left. "The gem-cutters guild is a very rich and powerful guild. A lot of Israelites belong, but also a lot of gentiles. They decided that rather than create two separate guilds, they'd just put in two doors. This is the door for the worshippers of God."

He pointed to the other door, and she noticed the familiar multi-breasted statue atop the wash basin.

"That's the door for the worshippers of Artemis Ephesia," John said.

Pelagios, a slave belonging to the family's head slave Epenetus, came over, and John gave him the message about Adrianna for his father. Pelagios gave John a message in return, which John shared with Mary as they left.

"Archisynagogos Lavi was here," he said as they hurried down the street, anxious to get back home before night set in and the Artemis festivities began in earnest. "He's ended my engagement to his daughter Martha."

Mary hadn't known John was engaged, but refrained from saying so. John had probably mentioned it sometime and she probably hadn't been listening. "How do you feel about that?" she asked instead. She thought he looked sad.

John shrugged. "I don't know. I kind of liked her, but I haven't seen her in five years. We've never spoken. I guess it doesn't matter. My father will find someone else for me." He pulled her back as a couple of drunken revelers passed them, chanting.

"What are they singing?" Mary asked.

"'Great is Artemis Ephesia,'" John said. "It's a popular song. You hear it a lot around here."

On the way back up the hill they talked about the mikvah, where Mary would serve and purify Hebrew women.

"The bath is new," John said. "Building hadn't even started when I left for Jerusalem, although all the contracts had been signed. We have a lease of the spring and the buildings for fifteen years. If the Artemisium agrees that we've been a good tenant then they'll let us renew the lease for fifty years."

"My house seems old, although the plaster and paint look new."

"It is an old building, yes. Since long ago, maybe a thousand years, the priests and priestesses of the temple of Artemis used to do their initiatory rituals at a spring in the caves near their temple precinct. But an earthquake a few hundred years ago closed off the spring, and they had to find a new spring for their initiations. They found the spring up on Mount Kouressos, and they built the stone building as a replacement for the cave. A few times a year a bunch of them would come up to the hill for a night or two, do whatever heathen things they do, and then they'd go back to the Artemisium. Then the earthquake a few years ago—the one that destroyed the synagogue—opened a new spring in the caves near their temple. So they no longer needed the mikvah site."

"And they leased the spring and the building to the Israelites?"

"Yes. I know it seems odd; we'd never lease one of our old sacred sites for gentiles to use, but my father and Artelia are friends, and he convinced her. The women have wanted a mikvah for a long time. They don't feel comfortable purifying at the public baths or in the sea like the men do. And after the synagogue was lost, there was a lot of discussion that maybe it was God's punishment because we weren't following the purity halakhah. I told you about that already."

"Yes."

"So my father knew that the Artemis worshippers had abandoned the spring on the hill, and it seemed like a gift from God. He convinced Archisynagogos Lavi that we could turn the old stone building into a proseuche, with the main room being devoted to prayer. The little side room could be a place where the mikvah attendant could sleep. 'Proseuche' means prayer, or house of prayer, in Greek. The building is made of stone, so it was fine for us to purify and use. We decided to focus on purity and prayer first before we build the rest of the synagogue."

"Do you plan to build the synagogue up there by the mikvah?"

"I think we would like to, but so far the Artemisium isn't willing to give up that much of their land. And my father says we're not really ready to build a synagogue yet—politics, he says—Ephesian politics, Roman politics, and even quarrels among the Israelites ourselves. Especially now…"

They were quiet for a while as each thought about the terrible quarrel they'd witnessed that day and its repercussions. The ripples of Enoch's sin caused a wave in John's own life, and now he and the young woman Martha must both find others to marry.

Mary found she had just enough strength to make it up the hill and back home, almost falling into her bed even before John left to hurry back to his own house. That night the music of the Artemis procession drifted once more through the window of the proseuche, but Mary was too deeply asleep to notice.

She thought: "My son, I'm finding this all so difficult. Why haven't you returned for me?"

3

"Has my son rejected me?"

On the walk back from the city yesterday, John had told Mary not to expect him at the proseuche today. With so much furor in the house over Rebekkah and Aspasia and now the severing of his engagement to Martha, he thought he should stay at home to be available for his family. Slaves would bring her meals up to the proseuche, and he'd come up the next day to take her into the city to shop at the harbor agora.

No one would enter the proseuche for seven days because of her corpse contamination from her time yesterday with Adrianna. If anyone came up to use the mikvah she'd have to avoid them.

Today was the anniversary of her son's resurrection from the dead—a day of celebration, surely—and she was all alone.

The spring sun shone bright, and she felt good from her exercise yesterday. She decided that today she would walk to the temple of Artemis and get permission to gather wood here at the proseuche so that at least she could have a fire in the hearth to warm the women after mikvah. She considered waiting until John could go with her, but realized she wanted to do this herself, walk all alone to the temple of the idol and think about her strange new life.

She wasn't sure she'd find anyone who spoke Aramaic, but it seemed likely. Her husband Joseph had spent his annual priest duty as a Temple builder, and she and the children had always accompanied him to Jerusalem. She knew enough about the Hebrew Temple to guess there should be plenty of scholars around at this Greek place.

The morning was still cool as she started walking down the hill, but she knew it would warm up before too long and she'd begin to regret her heavy black gown and head covering. Very few of the Israelite women she'd met here dressed as she did, most having adopted the Greek style.

As she walked along the path she'd taken yesterday with John, down into the valley where the city was, she wondered what Joseph would have thought of all this. He would have been horrified, of course, but she thought he would also have been fascinated by the strangeness of it all. And no doubt he would have laughed, often. She still missed him, although he had been dead almost ten years now.

She also thought about her family back home. After Jesus' death, she and John had lived in the village for a while with her daughter Anna, but Anna didn't think John was a good influence on her children because John kept talking about the Parousia, the end times when Jesus would return, the dead would rise, and the armies of God would defeat the armies of Rome. Mary wasn't quite sure where all this army and war against Rome stuff came from. She had certainly never heard Jesus speak of such things. But like all of the disciples of Jesus, John believed that the Parousia was imminent and thought paying attention to anything else was a waste of time. After Jesus died, John refused to return to the Temple for school.

Anna had no patience with end-times prophecies, which she'd had to live with when her husband was a disciple of John the Baptist and had stopped farming his fields, almost bringing disaster on his family until she put an end to such nonsense. And now her own brother's death had started it up again. Not only did such talk get her children too excited to sleep, it also made them dismissive of doing their chores—"Why should I feed the chickens? The end of the world is coming today—I prophecy it!"

So Anna didn't appreciate Mary bringing John into her house, although she let them live there because she was a good daughter and loved her mother, and it hurt her to see the depth of her mother's grief over her brother's horrible death. Everyone except Anna expected Jesus' imminent return. They'd say: "Don't be sad, Mary, he'll probably be returning today. You should be preparing a meal for him, not watering the ground with your tears." But Anna, who was the brightest of her children, kept telling her Jesus was a hero but he was dead now and wasn't coming back. Mary didn't know whom to believe. She felt she was going mad.

She couldn't move in with her other daughter, Tirzah, because her husband was a high-ranking Pharisee who had enough trouble with the Sadducees as it was without his relationship to one of their enemies being brought to their attention. Poor Tirzah had broken off all ties to her brother, to protect her husband and children. Mary knew this hurt not only Tirzah and the children but also her husband, Aaron, who loved Jesus and his brothers and even agreed with most of what Jesus taught. But Temple politics were harsh and dangerous these days, with all the revolutionaries and talk in the streets about rebellion against Rome. The Sadducees had the beautiful new Temple to protect, and they would do anything to guard it and the pilgrims who worshipped there from the anger of the Roman authorities.

Mary had decided to ask either her son Simon or her son Joses for a home, because she got along quite well with both of her daughters-in-law and thought life with either of those families would be tolerable, when two things happened almost simultaneously: John received a letter from his father telling him it was time for him to return home to Ephesus, and her sons James and Judas in Jerusalem sent her a message that things had become very dangerous there and she should try to stay hidden if possible. There had been several revolutionary incidents, and a mob influenced by the Sanhedrin, the Temple court, had stoned to death one of Jesus' young followers, Stephen, after some pilgrims complained that he preached blasphemy and treason.

John, an admirer of Stephen's, wanted to go to Jerusalem where the action was, to join James and the twelve in preparation for the Parousia. Mary couldn't allow this. Even in the thickest hours of her sorrow, she knew that it was her responsibility to take care of him. She would not allow him to die as Stephen had done. As Jesus had done. She told him that as the mother of Jesus, Judea had become dangerous to her, and she wondered if he would allow her to accompany him to Ephesus.

He reluctantly agreed to go home, and she packed a small chest with clothes and a few things to remind her of her children, including a tunic that had belonged to Jesus that she sometimes slept with because the smell of it comforted her. She bade a tearful good-bye to the friends who had been so close to her over the last few difficult years—to her sister Salome and the sister of her heart, Mary, who was married to Joseph's brother Cleopas; to Jesus' disciples Joanna and Mary Magdalene; and to Mary, the mother of the two "sons of Thunder" disciples, James and John. The six of them—four were Marys, always much confusion there—had been through great sorrow together, and it was hard to let go, almost as hard as leaving her children and grandchildren. But Jesus had expected her to take care of John, so she made herself say good-bye to them all.

She didn't feel strong enough to travel by road to Ephesus, so they caught an early ship in Caesarea, one of the first to leave dock at the beginning of the shipping season. This proved to be a mistake. Headwinds forced the boat to anchor for days on end as they crawled their way along the southern coast of Asia.

John spent the long weeks fishing and talking with the crew, learning as much as he could about boats and shipping. He also talked to her, probably told her things about Ephesus, but her grief so consumed her she didn't remember anything he might have said. She had been grief-stricken before, but leaving her children and grandchildren and everyone and everything she had ever known had only plunged her deeper into the black sorrow. She had slept most of the way to Ephesus.

She realized now that John had changed during the trip. When they were in Judea, all he could think about or talk about was the Parousia. But as he got closer to Ephesus, the realities of coming home filled him, and his heart reopened to the world his father had established for him. He hardly ever mentioned the Parousia now.

Mary reached the bottom of Mount Kouressos and the fountain that stood outside the state agora and turned east to follow the sacred way back toward the temple of Artemis. Soon she left the city through the main city gate and walked around the countryside base of Mount Pion.

The sacred way was littered with remnants from the numerous processions of the festival month. These were mostly leaves, decorated boughs, flower petals, and the remains of torches, but Mary also saw broken bits from carts and musical instruments and odd pieces of clothing that she hoped didn't all come from the same person. She was grateful not to see piles of manure on the road and assumed that there were probably slaves who kept that sort of thing cleaned up for the benefit of the people who marched in the procession.

Grapevines covered the rocky crags of the hillside in vineyards that no doubt belonged to Artemis. The agricultural land on the flat side probably also belonged to the goddess. Mary didn't recognize the young crops just breaking through the dirt. She waved to the workers in the field and they waved back. Today was a lovely morning and at third hour still not too hot to be out walking.

She turned the curve of Mount Pion and stopped in her tracks at her first glimpse of the temple of Artemis. She was used to the Temple at Jerusalem, so had expected something big. But the size and overwhelming beauty of this alien sanctuary astonished her. From this view, the temple of Artemis seemed to be of similar design to most of the lovely Greek temples she'd seen, a rectangular marble building surrounded by a colonnade. But this temple was on a much more massive scale than anything she'd seen before. The temple rose high out of the ground, towering far above the buildings that surrounded it in the temple precinct, easily the largest and tallest building she'd seen since the Temple in Jerusalem. She couldn't make out details from here, but she could see the immense columns that held up the roof and squinted her eyes to count them.

She'd helped Joseph from time to time in his work and had grown pretty good at estimating size. She couldn't be sure because she was still so far away, but she could see tiny people walking around and thought this side of the building must be almost two hundred cubits in length. Not as large as the Temple Mount in Jerusalem, of course, but certainly much larger than the sacred inner courts area of the Temple, open to only priests and Hebrew men. The huge columns looked to be perhaps thirty or thirty-five cubits high, and she tried to count them. She thought she saw at least twenty of these columns holding up the roof on this side of the temple, but couldn't be sure because the morning sun's reflection on the building glared in her eyes, so harsh it almost hurt. She wondered if the roof was gilded.

Here in sight of the temple, people camped out in tents. The density of tents increased as she neared the temple precinct. But she didn't see much activity from the tents and assumed most people were still asleep after the late celebrations. The people she did see seemed friendly enough, and many of them waved at her. She couldn't help but smile and wave back.

The temple of the goddess rose high at the center of a temenos, a temple precinct. Beautiful gardens and orchards surrounded the temple itself, and other buildings circled around the periphery, none higher than one story lest they impede the view of the temple. Mary noticed a couple of streams flowing near and around the buildings as she approached and saw puffs of smoke floating into the air from various places in the temenos. She walked through a gate and into a garden then followed a path around until she reached the front of the temple.

She had been right about the size. The front of the temple, which could be reached by mounting an enormous platform of stairs, was nearly a hundred cubits wide. Everything was marble, and much of the marble was painted or gilded. Unfortunately she couldn't see the inside from the bottom of the platform of stairs, and she would not walk up the steps and enter for a better view inside.

Instead she sat on a bench in the rear of the garden that fronted the temple and looked up at the building, trying to understand what she saw. The triangular pediment above the front columns contained a painted frieze of Artemis surrounded by people who looked astonishingly like women holding weapons. The columns of the double colonnade were of white marble, in the Greek style. Because the building still rose so far above her even from this distance at the back of the garden, she couldn't see very far into the cella, or inner room, but she could see enough to realize that the door of the cella was open and an enormous black and gold statue of the idol Artemis stood within. She couldn't see the head or feet of the idol from where she sat, but the many orbs that stuck out from her torso were unmistakable. She could also see that the columns inside the cella were green, not white, surrounded by heavily decorated walls. Most of the people entering the temple were women.

It was only after she sat down that she realized how tired and thirsty she was from the walk. She could see several fountains, including a huge, elaborate fountain at the foot of the temple steps, and decided that after she rested a bit she'd go get a drink of water.

A woman sat down on the bench next to her. She was richly but modestly dressed in a white embroidered chiton with a blue shawl covering her head. A slave stood nearby, holding a parasol over her, which now also shaded Mary from the sun.

"Beautiful, isn't she?" the woman said in Greek.

Mary thought she understood what the woman said from the expression on her face, which seemed to indicate a reverence for the idol inside the cella, but she wasn't really sure. She shrugged her shoulders and smiled, indicating her inability to speak Greek.

The woman studied her for a moment then spoke in another language. When Mary shrugged again, she asked the question a third time, this time in

Aramaic. The accent was different, but Mary could understand most of her words.

"Imposing, I think, is a better word," Mary said. "It's a very imposing idol."

The woman smiled but said nothing.

"The temple, too, very imposing."

"Not beautiful?" the woman asked.

Mary laughed. "Yes," she admitted, "it's very beautiful. My Temple, back home, is also very imposing and also very beautiful. But the sanctuary is hidden, surrounded by inner and outer courts, and impossible for gentiles to glimpse except for the very top. But this one, right out in the open for everyone to see, with columns instead of walls and the interior space just open like that..." She shrugged. The idea that just anyone could come and sit in front of the Temple back home and look right into the depth of it was incomprehensible.

"There's usually a curtain in front of Artemis," the woman said, "and the doors to the cella are usually closed, but this is the festival month. You're welcome to enter the outer colonnade of the Temple, which is the largest temple in the world. You could see more of my Lady if you climbed the stairs."

Mary shook her head. "No, thank you." Non-Judeans were not allowed in the inner courts of the Temple in Jerusalem, although if they were purified, they could enter the outer court area to pray or conduct business. Judean women weren't allowed to walk through the Nicanor Gate into the inner Court of the Israelites, let alone enter the Court of the Priests where the sacrifices were made, and it would be the worst sort of blasphemy for a woman or gentile to ever enter the sanctuary of the Holy Place and the Holy of Holies. It would not be proper for her to enter the temple of this god, even if allowed, since the idol's worshippers would certainly never be allowed entrance into the Temple of God back home. "But I am curious about something," she said. "Why does the idol have so many..." Her voice trailed off and she waved her hands over her chest.

The woman sat in silence for a moment and then she spoke. "You're a Judean, yes? The new guardian of the sacred spring up on Mount Kouressos?"

Mary liked the title "guardian of the sacred spring," but thought it sounded too heathen to claim for herself. "I am an Israelite, yes," she said. "And I am the new mikvah attendant."

"Then I will tell you one or two of the mysteries of the Goddess, because you will understand. They're lesser mysteries, but still, you understand that they can't be shared with others?"

"I understand," Mary said. She knew it was allowed for her to hear the stories of the idols, so long as she did not believe them or teach them to other people.

"I trust you," the woman said. "There's something about you that makes me want to confide in you. Well, you are the guardian, after all. The name of the Goddess, whom you keep referring to as an 'idol,' is Artemis. Do you know anything about the Greek goddess Artemis?"

Mary shook her head.

"That's just as well, because this is not her. The Greeks think this is her and the Romans think it's her—she whom they call Diana—but it isn't. We let them think it is, because it's convenient for us to do so. It lets us keep our mysteries while seeming to be completely out in the open, as you said. The best place to hide a secret is where everyone can see it, but they don't know what they see."

"He who has ears to hear, let him hear," Mary said, her son's words.

"Exactly," the woman said. "To everyone else, it's just noise." They smiled at each other.

"So," Mary said, cocking her head, "I'm still not hearing anything."

The woman laughed, a light, pleasing sound. "I'm Artelia," she said.

"I'm Mary."

"Good name," the woman said. "It means the oceans, the deep. Very significant name."

"In Hebrew it means 'bitter.'"

"Oh surely not," Artelia said. "I'm sure it has another meaning. Something to do with water."

"What does Artelia mean?"

"Daughter of Artemis."

Mary nodded. Perhaps this woman would know someone here who could give her permission to glean the wood, or maybe she was High Priestess Artelia herself, although John had told her that many people in Ephesus were named after the goddess. "What does Artemis mean?" she asked.

Artelia laughed. "Again you bring us back to the mysteries."

Mary smiled.

Artelia took a deep breath. "I feel compelled to tell you, even though you're not an initiate. Unless...are you interested in becoming an initiate?" she asked hopefully.

Nothing was more unlikely. "No," Mary said. "But don't worry. It's safe to tell me."

"Yes. I know it is. Very well. There is only one true God and She is Artemis. 'Artemis' means 'Lord of Heaven, Mother of Us All.' The land, the oceans, the heavens—they were all born from Her, from Her body. You can't see much of them from down here, but all over Her body are carvings which tell the story of the creation of everything."

Mary craned her head up and then stood to try to get a better view, but she couldn't see much of the huge idol without climbing the temple steps. "I have an idea," Artelia said. She turned and spoke to the slave who held the sun parasol over them, and she ran off to speak to a guard who stood near. The guard walked over to them. Artelia gave him instructions, and he hurried away.

"Let's walk around while he gets things prepared," Artelia said. They stopped for a drink at the fountain, and then she gave Mary a tour of the temenos. As they walked, the slave with the large parasol followed behind them, shading their heads from the increasing heat of the sun.

Artelia refused to speak of Artemis or her temple statue. Instead, she showed Mary the wonders of the temenos. Mary saw the treasury where monies such as the Israelite Temple tax were stored and the art galleries where votive offerings not displayed in the temple were kept and sometimes put on view. Artelia pointed out the music hall, the zoo and stables, the baths and privies, the administrative buildings and workrooms, the artisan shops, the kitchens, the hostel for important visitors, and the grand living quarters for the priests and priestesses as well as the lesser quarters for the initiates and slaves. She pointed to hives out in the field, where the beekeepers worked. She said that free men and women such as artisans, clerks, gardeners, and guards lived in Ephesus or a nearby village and usually walked to the temple each day for work, though sometimes when it was very busy and they had to work late they would camp out in the field that Mary had noticed on her walk here, where pilgrims were now camped during the festival month.

The thing that most surprised Mary in the temenos was the presence of shrines and altars to gods other than Artemis. One emperor god even had his own temple attached to the temenos. Mary had seen altars and shrines to pagan gods before—even the outside walls of the Temple temenos back home were covered with them—but it would be the vilest blasphemy to bring any other god's presence inside the Lord's Temple area. Even emperor gods. It seemed so strange that Artemis or, rather, the priests and priestesses of

Artemis allowed all of these others here. At one shrine, Mary stopped in shock to see the most grossly obscene statue she'd ever encountered. "Is that a statue of what I think it is?" she asked, horrified. The grinning, naked man seemed to be holding his own enormous erect member, as large as one of his legs.

"That's the shrine of Priapus," her new friend said, "and yes, it's exactly what you think it is."

Mary shook her head. Of all the idols she could see, this one was easily the most foreign and offensive to her, even more than the idol with the legs of a goat. "If that statue was erected in Jerusalem, the priests would destroy it immediately."

Artelia shrugged. "He's a god of fertility. Very popular with men. And a lot of women too." More people stood in reverence at the shrine of the obscene Priapus than at any other, including the crowded shrine of Apollo, the Greek Artemis' twin brother. "Frankly, he's the most popular god in the place. Other than Artemis Ephesia, of course."

Mary was confused by the way Artelia talked about the "gods." Hadn't she said that she believed the only god was Artemis? She asked Artelia, who laughed.

"When I talk about 'gods,' I'm talking about these silly Greek and Roman things. Most of them aren't real, and the few real ones are only servants of the Great Goddess."

Mary was not going to debate this, so she commented on the fact that none of the buildings was over one story tall (except, she could see now, the temple of the emperor—but even that looked puny near the temple of Artemis). Artelia told Mary that the Artemisium had very strict ordinances controlling the size of the temenos buildings. The only thing as tall as the temple was the enormous sacred tree at the south side of the temenos area, as wide as the outstretched arms of a dozen people. Mary smiled to see the storks nesting in its topmost branches and then noticed stork nests also erected on the roof of the temple itself.

Flags and banners rippled in the breeze, as did the tinkling and clicking chimes of clever wood and metal toys hanging in trees and on buildings. Here and there people sang or played music, while good-natured devotees of different shrines competed with each other in declaiming the glories of their particular gods. The air was pungent with wood and charcoal smoke, flowers, spices, perfumes, incense, and burnt offerings. Everything was clean, painted and gilded, marble and richly varnished wood, and the gardens and flowers were lush and colorful.

Mary's new friend was an important person here: not only did everyone bow as she passed by, but when she walked to the head of a vendor's queue to get them some fruit and tea, no one complained about it, and Mary did not see money change hands. Mary recited a silent blessing as she took the dried grapes that Artelia handed her.

This Artelia was probably the woman who could give her permission to use the wood. "There is much wood wasted, rotting on the ground up at the spring," Mary said. "May I glean fallen wood for my own fire?"

"I think so," Artelia said. "But let me think about what you can do for us in exchange."

They continued to walk, and Mary craned her neck, looking around. She saw that one of the streams she'd noticed before fed the baths and the smoke she'd seen came from both the bath steam and smoke from burnt offerings. She watched a transaction occur between an altar priest and a food vendor, and then she watched another and another and realized that all the food being sold here was food that had been sacrificed to one of the gods. John had warned her of this. She was grateful she'd eaten only one dried grape and gave the rest to a beggar she passed a moment later.

While giving Mary the tour, Artelia shared some of the history of the temple. It was almost a thousand years old, she said, although it had been rebuilt several times, most recently a few hundred years ago after it was burned down by a madman.

She also told Mary that the temple was a sanctuary for the desperate and downtrodden, people such as slaves, debtors, and young women being forced into objectionable marriages. Mary remembered the story John had told her about the thieves who robbed the synagogue and how Artelia had pronounced that people who blasphemed the shrines of the gods would not be allowed sanctuary at the temple of Artemis.

When the guard returned to the front of the temple, he was followed by five men wheeling a large wooden step platform. The two women walked over to them, followed by the sun shade slave.

"We use it to work on things like the shrine curtains, to hang up some of the higher paintings, and to repair the lower parts of the columns," Artelia said. "We don't like to lean ladders against the walls or columns, and the workers hate to set up scaffolding for small jobs."

The men pushed the machine over to the temple ramp, as if to roll it up.

"No, no," Artelia said. "No repairs today. Today we're using it as a viewing platform." She had them move it into position on the pavement in front of the stairs, and then she began to climb the wooden steps.

"Climb up and see," she said to Mary. Mary followed her up the steps of the wooden construction.

A crowd of curious people massed around the platform. Artelia told the guards to shoo them away, which they did with swift efficiency.

Mary reached the top of the platform and gingerly sat, huffing with exertion, on the top step in imitation of her new friend.

She had full view of the huge idol from up here. It stood towering in the middle of the incredibly beautiful, brightly colored cella. Massive green marble columns held up the cella roof. The floor was a pattern of black and white marble. Paintings, statuary, and other artistic displays covered the walls of the cella. But the cella's beauty was overpowered by the astonishing black and gold statue of a standing woman, stiff arms down along her sides and bent up at the elbows, easily the height of ten men. Intricate carvings covered the statue's apparel, from the top of her tall crown to the bottom of her floor-length gown. Artelia said that the statue was made of wood. The ebon color wasn't from paint. The idol was black from age and covered with gold leaf.

A verse from the prophets floated into Mary's mind, almost as though it was whispered by a sultry female voice: "I am black and lovely, O daughter of Jerusalem; black like the tents of Kedar, black like the curtains of Solomon." She wondered for a moment if this is what the Queen of Sheba had looked like. Hadn't King Solomon said that the Queen of Sheba's breasts were like clusters of grapes on the vine?

"Is this the Queen of Sheba?" Mary asked.

Artelia frowned. "I don't know where Sheba is. Artemis is the Queen of Heaven and Earth."

"It's the largest idol I have ever seen," Mary said politely. She was actually awestruck at the immensity of it, but it wouldn't do to make too much fuss over an idol. "And it's so bright—why is the light on it so bright?"

"The roof is open above the Goddess, so that the sun shines down on Her," Artelia said. "The statue of Zeus at Olympia would be taller if it stood. But he's a lazy god and just sits on his throne."

Mary had heard of Zeus, but she knew little about him. Artelia pointed to a shrine in a corner of the temenos, where a few people stood in front as a priest performed a ceremony on an altar; Mary thought he was preparing to burn incense or perhaps make a small offering.

"That's his shrine," Artelia said. "He's the Greek father god. Actually, many of the Judeans I've met think Zeus is the same god as your god and also the same god as the Egyptian Ammon-Re. They call him Hypsistos, which means the Highest God. They view all the other Greek, Roman, and Egyptian gods as simply the angels of Hypsistos."

Mary remembered that in the old days before the Maccabean revolt, the Lord God had been known as Zeus even in the Temple. That had been a bad time for faithful followers of the Law, who were forbidden to observe the Sabbath and were forced to eat pork to show their loyalty to the Greeks. She could readily believe that the Israelites in Ephesus would continue to confuse the Greek gods with the Lord Most High and His angels.

Artelia pointed out other gods, emperors, and Amazons depicted in statues and paintings in the cella, explaining that Ephesus was founded by the Amazons (although it would be three years before Mary learned enough about the Amazons to understand who they were or connect them with the warrior women depicted with Artemis on the front pediment of the temple). All of the art had been given by worshippers as votive offerings to Artemis. Many, Artelia said, represented the best works ever made by the world's most famous sculptors and painters.

From this height, Mary could see the large altar that sat on the platform at the top of the stairs. No offering was being burnt on it now (unlike in Jerusalem, where burnt offerings to atone for the sins of the people were made all day, every day), but there was much activity going on inside the temple. She asked Artelia about the lack of burnt offerings.

"We no longer sacrifice animals to Artemis," Artelia said. "We do a grain sacrifice on holy days, but Artemis no longer hungers for animal blood."

Mary nodded, and then they quietly watched the temple suppliants for a while. After washing their hands in the fountain at the foot of the marble steps of the temple entrance, lines of white-clad women climbed the steps to stand in front of priests, who purified them one-by-one by anointing their heads with something and then walked ritually around them waving smoke or incense. After this purification, each worshipper would walk respectfully up to the statue, climb the steps of the pedestal on which it stood, and kiss the hem of its gilded wooden gown. Then they left, some with tears flowing, some smiling, but most solemn.

Mary watched one woman as she went through the ritual of purification and worship, then continued watching as she walked down the steps and hurried over to an artisan stand, perhaps to buy a statue of Artemis made of silver or ceramic to take home. Is this woman alone, Mary wondered, or is she with her family, all of whom are worshipping at the shrines of their own favorite gods?

Something puzzled her. "Are all of the worshippers of Artemis women?"

"Not at all," Artelia said. "But today is a special day. Today is the only day of the year when married women are permitted to see the face of Artemis or worship at Her Temple."

"Why is that?"

Artelia shook her head. "That's one of the mysteries I can't divulge to you. Ask me the right question on the right day and perhaps I will answer it. All I can tell you about this today is that those women are all either pregnant now or they're women who gave birth sometime during this last year, and they are here today to thank the Goddess for giving them their babies. But I was going to tell you about Her eggs," she said, changing the subject.

Mary looked at the tall statue again. Yes, those could be rows of eggs hanging above her waist.

"As I told you before, there is only one God and She is Artemis."

At this, Mary felt compelled to finally speak up. She was somewhat ashamed that she'd waited so long, but this was another country and another god's temple and she wanted to be polite. But still...

"The Lord God of Israel is the only God," she said gently.

Her friend nodded. "I understand that you feel that way and I know you understand how I feel."

"Yes."

"Because I honor your feelings, I have had this platform brought out so that you can see the body of my Goddess without entering Her Temple."

"I appreciate that."

"So you will let me tell you my truth, what I believe?"

"I will. But I had to speak up. The God Most High does not tolerate other gods."

"I understand. And who knows—you say there's only one God, I say there's only one God—do you know what your one God looks like?"

Mary had to admit she did not. "But only because graven images are forbidden to us."

"That's unfortunate for you. Thankfully we don't have that injunction. Do you want to hear about the eggs?"

Mary smiled. "Yes, thank you. I have ears to hear." If she was going to live in Ephesus, it would be good to understand why its goddess was so important to the citizens.

"Artemis made heaven and hell, the land and the sea. She made the divine spirits of the underworld, the fish and monsters that swim in the seas, the beasts that walk the earth, the birds that fly above, and the heavenly creatures that guide and protect us. In this guise She is the Goddess of the Sun, and She bears the twelve signs of the zodiac on Her breast.

"As the sun, in the beginning She crossed the sky through the body of the bull, the constellation Taurus. Thus the bull, as the first of Her animals, has always been particularly sacred to Her. During the years of the bull sign, Her worshippers sacrificed calves and bulls to Her glory and prayed for the bull's strength and endurance.

"Then for two thousand years She crossed the sky through the body of the ram. During those years, we sacrificed sheep and goats, and the priests and priestesses cared for Her people as the shepherd cares for his flock. The carvings you see on Her body depict all of that. Her torso is the heavens. You can see the zodiac on Her breast, circling around Her neck. You can see the bull and the ram depicted in Her garments.

"But She has left the ram now and is at present crossing the sky through the body of Pisces, the two fishes. This is a great change for Her and for us, and our astrologers and diviners read the auguries day and night, trying to determine Her wishes. Great changes are coming, and the future is cloudy. She no longer wants animal sacrifices. We're unsure about how best to honor Her as she moves through Pisces. We pray that She will tell us how to serve Her."

"And the eggs?"

"Those are star eggs, birthed out of Her body. The stars in the heavens are the eggs of Artemis the Sun Goddess, glowing in the night sky."

Mary thought about it. "We are taught that the God Most High created the heavens and earth, the beasts and birds and fish and plants and all that breathe and live and grow. But we don't have an egg story." Not eggs, perhaps, but she did remember that God had told Abraham that his descendants would be numbered as the stars in the heavens.

"Well, maybe you do and no one ever told you," Artelia said. "As I said, this is one of the mysteries of the Goddess. Not many people know it. Of course, it's only one of the mysteries and a lesser one at that. If you ask me on another day, I may be compelled to tell you one of Her other mysteries. But today's mystery is the egg story."

Mary doubted that the Lord God had an egg story, but she couldn't say for sure since she couldn't read, and even if she could, she wouldn't be allowed to read the Torah anyway. But she thought for sure someone would have mentioned it sometime.

"Do the worshippers of Artemis believe in life after death?" she asked.

"Of course, for some people. Don't your people believe in it?"

Mary shook her head. "It's a matter of great debate among the priests."

"How about you? How do you believe?"

"My son died last year. If I didn't believe that I would see him again someday, I think I would go completely mad."

Artelia patted her hand. "I'm sure you'll see him again."

Mary could feel the water in her eyes and the heaviness in her chest that always accompanied her tears. She pushed them back, but it was hard. She realized there was something she wanted to talk about, something she could not discuss with any of the women of the synagogue, even if they spoke her language. It was the thing that had weighed the heaviest on her heart these long months since Jesus died.

"He appeared to others after he died," she said quickly, before she could change her mind.

"He did?" Artelia said in surprise.

"He was a great teacher and a prophet," Mary said, "a healer and a miracle worker, with many disciples. Some say he is the Messiah, the savior of our people. One of the things that he preached was the resurrection of the dead. After he died, his body disappeared from its tomb. My sister went there to prepare it, but it was gone. And then for a while he began appearing to some of his students so they'd know he'd been resurrected. Then the appearances stopped. Some people said they saw him float into the clouds."

Artelia looked sympathetic but skeptical. "Did the clouds come down and lift him up into the sky?" she asked.

"I don't know. I didn't see it. Why do you ask?"

Artelia shrugged. "They say that happened when the heroes Romulus and Hercules changed from partly human to fully divine after they died."

Mary remembered suddenly that Enoch and Elijah had also been lifted into the sky at the end of their lives.

"My dear, I hate to ask this, but I must," Artelia said. "Are you sure he was really dead?"

Mary was surprised that her eyes felt dry. "Artelia, he was flogged and crucified. I held his pitiful, lifeless body in my arms. I could hardly breathe from the smell of his blood that covered me. Yes, I am sure he was dead."

Artelia let out a deep breath. Now she was the one in tears. "I am so, so sorry."

"But he never appeared to me afterwards," Mary said sadly and felt the tears well again. This was the greatest burden of her life. "He appeared to many others, but not to me."

Artelia put her arm around her new friend. "Well, let's think about why that might have been," she said. "You say you believe in life after death and believe that when you die you'll see him again."

"Yes. I believe that."

"You also said that he appeared to his students so that they would know he was resurrected."

"Yes."

"You're not one of his students."

"No."

"You didn't need proof."

Mary sighed. "No. But comfort would have been nice. It would have been nice to see him. It's hard, having the last sight of your child be the one I have. I don't dream very often, but when I do, that's the sight that torments me."

Artelia put her other arm around Mary and rocked her gently. "I know it's hard. If you'd like to change your dreams, we have good dream interpreters here. Or one of our seers could commune with your son's ghost for you."

"No, thank you," Mary said. "I'll keep the nightmares God has given me."

Artelia silently rocked her for a moment more, up on the high platform in front of the temple of Artemis, their faces warmed by the spring sun. Mary spoke again, whispering.

"You don't think that the reason he appeared to others but not to me was because he was angry at me or didn't love me?"

Artelia stopped rocking Mary and looked into her face. "Is that what's been worrying you? My dear, you have the pure, shining aura of a divine spirit, the brightest I've ever seen. Of course he loved you."

Mary did not understand all the words Artelia used, but took comfort in her assurance. Of course he loved her.

"Why would you think he was angry at you?"

"Because it was my fault he—"

A woman yelled up at them and started climbing the steps of the platform. A young woman, she vaulted up the wooden steps with ease. Soon she sat on the other side of Mary, and the squeeze of the three women on the top step was tight.

The woman was dressed in ornate purple robes and her hair was arranged to sit high on her head in an elaborate style. Gold jewelry and ornaments covered her body. Her face was painted white.

Artelia scolded the woman then explained the problem to Mary. "I just told her that she can't enter the Temple looking like that," Artelia said. "There are very strict rules about proper and respectful garb—no brightly colored clothing or purple garments, very little gold or jewelry, no white paint on the face. Hair is supposed to be worn down and the suppliant should be barefoot." Mary glanced at the woman's feet, clad in bright embroidered slippers. "She used to be a daughter of Artemis—she knows better."

"Yes, well, I'm a priestess of Isis now, and this is how we dress," the woman said in heavily accented Aramaic. "I'm Arsinoe," the woman said, addressing Mary. "Who are you?"

"This is Mary, the new guardian of the sacred spring," Artelia said.

"Oh, the new Judean guardian!" Arsinoe said. "I love Judeans! You know, it's become very fashionable in Rome these days to go to Judean synagogues and worship Theos Hypsistos. Did they rebuild the synagogue here yet? I'd love to attend."

Mary was flummoxed by this. Fashionable? Judeans? "No," she said. "They're holding synagogue in private houses now."

"Pity." Clearly house synagogues weren't fashionable. "But I hope you'll tell me when you get your real synagogue built."

"I'll do that," Mary said, unable to imagine this colorful, fluttering woman sitting patiently through a synagogue service. "But I'm confused. You used to worship Artemis, but now you're a priestess for a different god?"

"Isis," Arsinoe said. "She has a pretty little shrine over there—see it in the corner? The one with the beautiful statue of the winged woman? But Her real

Temple is in Ephesus, near the Prytaneion. You should come by and worship sometime. It's very elegant."

Mary wondered if John had mentioned the Isis temple when they walked through the town. She vaguely remembered seeing a plaque near the state agora with a winged woman carved in ivory, and she mentioned this.

"That's not Isis," Artelia said. "That's winged Artemis, the Artemis of Persia."

"But most of the time when you see a winged goddess in Ephesus, it's usually Nike, the goddess of victory," Arsinoe said. "She's the goddess of the mint, and so people who worship money worship her."

At that moment Mary knew with absolute certainty that she would never come to understand the complete pantheon of gods in Ephesus.

"Arsinoe was a daughter of Artemis," Artelia started, but Arsinoe interrupted her.

"That means I was an orphan, abandoned as a baby by my parents or by my mother's master at the temple of Artemis," Arsinoe said dramatically. "Left to be raised at the temple or thrown away at the garbage dump. Luckily for us all, the priestesses decided to raise me."

Artelia sighed, but didn't rise to the bait.

"And then later I was sold to the Temple of Isis, because only the most beautiful women can be Her priestesses, and I was the most beautiful woman in the land."

Mary wasn't quite sure how to respond to this. "Um, you are very beautiful," she said politely, although actually she thought the white paint and towering hair looked rather odd.

"Why are you here, since obviously it's not to show respect to Artemis?" Artelia asked.

Arsinoe let out a loud, complaining sigh. "It's that new Dionysus priest you put behind me in the procession," she said. "I will not have him around me anymore! There I was, carrying the statue of Isis and Her little baby Harpokrates, very poignant, very tender, and that lecherous cretin kept running up to me, grabbing at me and humping at me and making everyone laugh. I almost clobbered him with the statue, which would have been quite irreverent of me. The Temple of Isis will not participate in any more processions if we are to be treated like that."

"I'm sorry, Arsinoe," Artelia said. "I thought you'd be able to handle him. But you're right— he's even worse than the last one, and I had to ban him from the processions permanently. For tonight, I'll move the emperor statue in between Dionysus and you. That should subdue him—he won't dare any misbehavior toward Tiberius Augustus. And if that doesn't work, I'll ban him like I did the last one. The Katagogia festival is bad enough—I won't have him profaning the Artemisia."

"The Katagogia festival is the big Dionysus festival," Arsinoe confided to Mary. "It starts as soon as the Artemisia is over. You will want to stay locked in your house during that festival, because it's just an excuse for the most obscene behavior. The devotees have a phallic procession and then they run wild through town with ritual beatings, androgynous behavior, orgies and wild theater, and everywhere you see people drunk on wine and even eating human flesh as part of their communion with their god. It's disgraceful."

"I don't think it's real human flesh they're eating," Artelia said mildly. "I think they're pretending to be eating the body of Dionysus. And you've been trained in the Eleusinian mysteries, not to mention the mysteries of Isis and even some of the lesser mysteries of Artemis. You know better than to sit in judgment on the rituals of any god."

"Bah," Arsinoe said. "We're Greeks, not barbarian cannibals. To even pretend they're eating flesh, god or human, is monstrous," she asserted.

Mary couldn't imagine such a thing. "I'll be sure to stay away from them." She made a confession. "I'd always heard that the goddess of the Greeks was involved in all sorts of sexual perversions in her temple. I'm glad to know that's not true."

"Well, it depends on the goddess and the temple," Artelia admitted. "The temple of Aphrodite in Corinth is notorious. But certainly there's no sexual intercourse allowed at the Temple of Artemis."

"Or the Temple of Isis," Arsinoe added.

"Or the temple of Isis," Artelia agreed, nodding. "Artemis and Isis are both virgin goddesses."

Mary remembered what Arsinoe had said about carrying a statue of Isis and her baby in the procession. "Who is baby Harpokrates then?" she asked.

Arsinoe explained about Isis and her brother-husband Serapis, how Serapis was killed and his corpse dismembered by the dragon Typhon, and how Isis had found all the pieces but one and had brought Serapis back to life. Unfortunately the one piece she couldn't find was the one necessary for procreation, but she had found a way to make herself pregnant anyway. "Isis is not the only virgin goddess with a child," Arsinoe said with a malicious look at Artelia. "Cybele, the old mother goddess who was worshipped here before Artemis, is also a virgin mother."

"Cybele is not a virgin," Artelia said wearily. Evidently this was an old argument.

"Yes, she is. You know as well as I do that her priests had the—" she looked at Mary, then said, "well, I can't say, but you know that's only done to priests who serve a virgin goddess." She pointed to a small shrine in the garden, away from all of the traffic. "That's Cybele over there, Mary, that little chunk of broken stone. She used to be the great goddess here. Artemis will want to watch out, lest someday another Great Goddess usurps her and Artemis finds herself relegated to just a little spot in Isis' garden."

Mary looked down at the old shrine. She had thought it just an old broken rock, but now she saw the worn engraving of a woman, a baby sitting on her knee.

"Isis will never reign here," Artelia said. "She will have to be content with her pretty little temple near the Prytaneion, which Artemis in Her great generosity is gracious enough to allow."

The women's sniping made Mary uncomfortable. "Who is the baby on Cybele's knee?" she asked.

"Oh, that's her son Attis," Arsinoe said. "He's one of the resurrection gods."

"Resurrection gods?" Mary asked, distressed.

Artelia put an arm around her. "Arsinoe, I really don't think—" she began hesitantly, but Arsinoe rambled on.

"Yes, you know—gods who die and then come back to life. Like Serapis, Dionysus and Mithras. Usually it's something to do with the renewal of crops in the spring. However, I can't share those mysteries with the uninitiated." She smiled spitefully at Artelia but no one had heard her last sentence because Mary had collapsed and Artelia was calling to the guards to come up and help her friend down from the platform.

Mary revived after she was back on the ground, a cup of water held to her lips.

"It's all that black she's wearing," Arsinoe was saying. "She must be terribly hot."

"Mary, how are you feeling?" Artelia asked.

"I'm all right," Mary said and started to stand. "I should be getting back home," she said, although she didn't know if she'd be able to make the long walk back without fainting.

"I'm having a cart brought around for you," Artelia said. "So just relax."

Mary smiled in gratitude. She knew she should demur, but just now that was beyond her.

"Have you walked in the sacred grove yet?"

After a moment's confusion Mary realized Artelia spoke of the grove of trees near the proseuche. "No, I never have."

"Well, take a walk back there. Visit the labyrinth."

Mary frowned. "I don't know what that means."

"It's a shape on the ground," Artelia said. "You'll know it when you see it. Anyway, I'll send some people up to clear it off, and what I'd like for you to do is keep it clear afterward—remove any brush or weeds that come up. In exchange for that, you can glean all the wood you need for your own purposes. Just don't let anyone else take wood home with them."

Mary nodded. "Thank you. I'll look at this shape and let you know if I can accept your terms."

Artelia smiled. "There's nothing about the labyrinth that your god can complain about," she said.

Mary couldn't be sure without making her own assessment. Her God had many rules.

During the luxurious cart ride home, Mary thought about all the things she'd seen and heard today, all the stories about the different gods and about the star eggs of Artemis. She'd never paid much attention to astrology and hadn't heard that the sun was now going through the body of the two fishes. She shivered as she remembered the story she'd heard from John, about how her son had miraculously fed a multitude with only two fishes and some bread.

When she got home, as tired as she was, she nevertheless headed straight for the mikvah. She lay for a long time in the cool and purifying water, thinking about the astonishing day.

She thought: "My son, I know the beloved voice that whispers to me belongs to God. But whose voice do the false-god worshippers hear in their hearts?"

CHAPTER 4

"Wondrous Babel sings to me, perfumed, exotic, appalling."

When John arrived with her breakfast the next morning he was impressed and amused to hear of Mary's visit to the idol's temple. "So you actually saw the goddess of the moon?" he asked.

Mary frowned. "I think she's the goddess of the sun," she said hesitantly, remembering the egg story of the day before. They washed and then carried a rug outside near the trees to enjoy the morning sun as they ate.

John shook his head. "Nope. Artemis is well known as the moon goddess."

Mary shrugged. It didn't matter to her. "The good thing is that I'm able to gather the wood that falls in the grove."

They blessed their food then hurried through their breakfast so that they could walk down the hill to the city before the day got too hot. They were still suffering corpse pollution and thus had the whole day to themselves. No one was expected here today. Aspasia's baptism had been postponed until next week, when Mary could participate. John wanted to take her to the harbor agora today because although they had to stay away from Hebrews, there was no concern about them polluting gentiles with their impurity.

Back in Judea, being around gentiles was itself considered a pollutant. But Mary could see the difficulty of following that stricture here. And she was curious about the town.

They walked the same route as before, stopping again for water at the state agora fountain. But this time after drinking the water they walked west, toward the harbor.

They'd taken just a few steps when John turned her around to face the entrance of the state agora. From here she could see the enormous open area behind elaborate entrance columns and the stoa columns at the other end.

"I don't think you've seen the inside of the agora before. My father meets with other city leaders here. It will be crowded with people late tonight, when the Artemis festival really gets wild, but right now most people are at the hippodrome or the theater, watching the athletic and theatrical competitions." Even now she could see food and souvenir vendors inside the state agora, doing a brisk business. "Those arches on the other side are the walls of the Basilica, where the law courts and stock exchange meet, and past that is the Prytaneion, where the city magistrates meet."

He turned her back around and they continued their walk down the street. She asked John to point out the temple of Isis, which Arsinoe had mentioned was located near the Prytaneion. He did, and added, "This street is called the Embolos. That means it's the place where all the other streets meet." He tried to speak loudly because of the noise of the crowd. "It's part of the sacred way that runs from the temple of Artemis around Mount Pion, through the city and back to the temple."

Then John started reading the names of people inscribed on the buildings, and she realized to her horror that most of the lavish buildings on this street were tombs. And in some of them, people seemed to be picnicking. She saw live people laughing with their families while they ate a meal in the tombs of the dead. Children drank water from the fountains of the dead.

"Is this a cemetery, John?" She was stunned. Corpse pollution was one of the worst forms of pollution, requiring a full seven days of purification.

"They think differently here, Mother. In Ephesus, people will pack a picnic and take the family to a temple to eat it. They do that to socialize with the god—it's as though the god is the host of the meal. And the same thing here with the tombs, in the city of the dead—when they eat in the tomb, it's like they're attending a dinner party given by the dead person. "

She glanced in another tomb and saw two people having sex. What did this mean, were they having sex with the dead person too?

John pulled her away. "I'm sorry, Mother," he said, "but I told you before we came that this is a very immoral city."

"I'm never going to get used to this place," she said, shaking her head. Before she came to Ephesus, she had thought of herself as a fairly observant Hebrew. But no truly observant Hebrew would be able to survive seeing half the things she'd seen in the last few days. She thought of her mother and knew the dear woman would have fainted dead away at the sight of the first naked and uncircumcised statue. She couldn't imagine her response to the temple of Artemis or the shrine of Priapus.

In Judea, the Israelites of the Greek dispersion had a bad reputation for dissolute living, for failing to keep the commandments. But how could anyone possibly keep all the commandments living in a place like this?

John pointed to a strange octagonal building with a pointy roof. She was grateful to have her thoughts interrupted. "That's the tomb of a queen of Egypt who was killed by her enemies when she sought asylum at the Artemisium."

"I've never seen a building with a roof pointed in that way," Mary said.

"All the buildings in Egypt have pointy roofs," John said authoritatively.

Mary didn't remember seeing pointy buildings on her one trip to Egypt, early in her marriage, but that was a long time ago and she hadn't been paying attention to architecture. "It must rain a lot there, to need that kind of run-off for their houses," the carpenter's widow said, frowning because she remembered Egypt as being quite hot.

"No, I think it has something to do with their gods."

Mary nodded. This was one thing she had learned in her short time in Ephesus. People did strange things for their gods.

They neared the harbor. The smell of the sea and sound of the sea birds sharpened. They passed the wholesale and retail fish market, and John pointed out a particular stand where she could find properly prepared fish, split while alive with their blood poured out.

The harbor agora was a large, square market where just about every exotic item produced in the world could be found. Souvenir shops squeezed together, stuffed with terra-cotta, bronze, stone and lead images, reliefs, and statues of Artemis Ephesia and her temple—these were particularly popular with pilgrims now, during her festival. But many items were sold in the agora that had nothing to do with the image of Artemis and everything to do with her city's reputation as one of the most cosmopolitan cities in the Greco-Roman world, an import and export center as renowned as Alexandria or Antioch and much more sophisticated than Rome.

This was where importers and exporters of goods and merchandise showed off selections of their most beautiful and desirable products for the world's traders. An Ephesian citizen interested in a new rug might look around at the harbor agora to see the latest styles from exotic locales, but when it came time to actually buy a rug they would go to the rug merchants' alley hidden deep in a less expensive part of town. But if he or she was a rug merchant from Smyrna interested in the latest goods from Arabia—why, the harbor market of Ephesus held all a merchant could hope to find.

Mary was fascinated to see people of every possible skin shade from the palest white to the deepest black; people with round faces and narrow eyes and others with narrow faces and round eyes; hair that was black and brown and white and yellow, straight and wavy and tightly curly, and even some people with bright sunset-red hair that she thought surely must be false. She'd had no idea there were so many different types of people in the world, and it was extraordinary to see them all here together, talking, laughing, and doing business with one another. Many of them had exotic animals with them, monkeys and colorful birds and large striped or spotted cats. Often the animals would shriek or growl, but none of them emitted sounds like the strange cries she heard most mornings from the grove up by her house.

Mary and John walked slowly around the square, peering into shops and kiosks and tents, permanent structures and handcarts, all filled to overflowing with amazing wares and magical services. She stared at the glorious pottery and glassware she saw—shops stocked with incredible glass lamps in the shapes of animals and flowers; glass-blowers making stunning clear blue glass vessels, vases, candlesticks, and tableware; carts with delicately painted dainty ceramic and carved bone and ivory objects like buckles, toiletry boxes, and jewelry boxes; and nearby these were the metal smiths, who sold the same types of items as the glass, pottery, and ivory merchants, only made out of gold, silver, copper, lead, and bronze.

Many of the merchants were women, and much of what these women sold had been selected with an eye to what women would find particularly pleasing. Cloth merchants in beautifully styled and embroidered outfits displayed gorgeously dyed lightweight cloth in bright colors such as purple, red, and yellow, much of it woven through with alternating colors. They sold pre-sewn garments from exotic locales such as Persia and Africa, and for heavier clothes they offered soft naturally black woolen cloth imported from Laodicea and Hierapolis, as well as other precious wools from Galatia and beyond. To complement their goods, these women displayed examples of jewelry sold by other merchants—earrings, necklaces, bracelets, hair clasps, rings, armbands. There was hardly a part of the human body that didn't have an exquisite gold-and-gem trinket available here at the market ready to take home, just perfect to show the body off.

Mary also noticed a few Roman soldiers here and there, but they seemed very different from the soldiers in Jerusalem. For one thing, there were far fewer of them in this city. And for another, the Roman soldiers in Ephesus seemed relaxed and happy. They joked around with citizens. They seemed glad to be here, very different from the angry occupiers in Jerusalem. Still, just the sight of a Roman soldier—even a smiling one—made Mary shudder, and she thought she would probably always feel that way about them.

With particular pride, John walked Mary through a large shop stocked with cinnabar from one of his father's mines. Ephesus was a center for cin-nabar mining, and there were many cinnabar merchants haggling with traders interested in the raw crystals and the crushed ore that was used to produce quicksilver and vermilion. John explained that the rich red beauty of the raw crystals was used in decoration, that quicksilver was used in gilding silver and bronze as well as an important component of many medicines, and that ver-milion was an orange-red pigment used for painting.

Herbalists sold prepared medicines, powders, and herbs from around the world—universal standards like opium, hemp, saffron, and rose oil, plus hundreds of more exotic treatments. A few of the medicines she recognized, such as mountain tea, used for head congestion, and dried sea onions, used in poultices, but most were strange to her. She saw several places where fresh, dried, and seed hyssop could be purchased and had John figure out the stand-ard price for haggling purposes when they went shopping later in the Judean market, after the holiday ended.

Barkers shouted, sang, and danced to entice buyers into their shops, although since Mary couldn't understand any of the languages, there was no chance of anyone convincing her to enter if their shop didn't look attractive or interesting. But one merchant's unusual wares did compel her because they looked like ordinary gray clumps of stone, which seemed a strange thing to be selling even in as odd a place as Ephesus.

John addressed the merchant in Greek then said to Mary: "They're imported from Gaul. They have something to do with purification."

The man, seeing an opportunity for a sale, spoke hurriedly in broken Aramaic. "They're a solid magic potion called 'soap.' Here, let me show you how they work."

He poured clean water into a basin then dirtied his hands in some mud set aside for demonstration purposes and used the soap to wash his hands. "See? Magic. You Judeans are fanatic for cleanliness—I know you'll find these potions invaluable."

Fascinated by the bubbles, Mary saw an immediate application. "Does it work to clean clothes?"

"Oh, quite well. Makes cloth look like new again. And you don't have to wear the fabric down by pounding it on rocks or subjecting it to the harshness of a urine wash. Think of the money you'll save by not buying new cloth so often."

Mary held one of the stones of magic soap in her hand and smelled it. "Oh, very pretty!"

"Scented with lavender, that one."

"Very nice." She loved the smell that just holding the soap left in her hand.

"How much do you want for it?" asked John.

"Four denarii for one, a box of fifty for seventy denarii."

Although John's father was quite rich and John knew him to be generous, four denarii was almost the equivalent of a week's pay for an average man. John only had one denarius with him (plus some small coin, a few dupondii and a couple of sestertii), but even if he'd had the entire price, he doubted that Alexander would want him to spend that much on something he'd never even seen before. He told the merchant that they couldn't afford a tenth of that so there was no point in even bothering to haggle, and Mary carefully replaced the soap stone on the table.

"I think those would be nice to have at the mikvah," Mary sighed as they left, although she knew she'd never dare to use such a thing without knowing how they were made.

John agreed. "I think it would be a pleasant thing to have at the baths." He promised himself to mention the soap to his father. If nothing else, perhaps they could buy a stone as a gift sometime for Mary, assuming the merchant was able to sell enough soap from this shipment to consider it a worthwhile product to keep in stock.

"John, I know we were going to wait until we could visit the Judean shops, but since Deborah is baptizing Aspasia soon, we should probably get a few things here today for that."

"What do you think she'll need?"

She wanted to be able to purify and to provide comfort. "Hyssop, certainly. I'd like to have hyssop available, for sprinkling, and I know Deborah will like to use it in the baptism ritual. Also cushions for the women to sit on after their prayers. And we will want to make them some hyssop tea and maybe have a little bit of food to offer. I don't even have a lamp there, nor oil." She wondered at herself—she had been so completely wrapped in her sadness that she hadn't noticed before now that she didn't have a lamp, because she was always asleep before dark.

John felt ashamed that he hadn't remembered to provide Mary with more of the basics she needed for comfort. He'd brought her some blankets and each day brought over some food, but he hadn't thought much about what she would need to really make a home for herself: things like dishes or lamps or maybe a small table and stool for her room. Normally Deborah or his father would have thought of such things, but everything was so confused at the house, first with preparing for Passover and now Enoch's divorce and wedding and Adrianna's burial. No one had remembered Mary. But he should have.

"I am so sorry, Mother. Tomorrow I will have some slaves bring you everything you need—cushions, lamps, oil, dishes, food, blankets, everything. I'll talk with Deborah, see what we need to bring over. But I don't think we have any hyssop at the house, so we should buy some of that here."

They walked back toward the spices and herbs section. The market was so loud—not just because of all the business people hawking their wares and Ephesians and tourists trying to be heard above the din, but also because of the many people standing around giving speeches to anyone and everyone who'd listen. Mary, of course, could understand none of the speakers. She asked John what they were saying.

He pointed to a man standing on a plinth, holding a scroll. "That's a city herald. Right now he's announcing today's gifts to the goddess, things like statues and money, and also listing the names of the donors. He just said that a freedman named Hercules is providing a meal for all visitors from Athens in honor of Artemis Ephesia."

He listened for a while to a stately man expounding something in a mellifluous voice. "That one is a Pythagorean. He's talking about nature and harmony and divine knowledge. And something about purification. I start at gymnasium next week, so I'll be able to tell you all about that when I learn more."

He pointed to another one. "That's someone you'll probably get to know, Ezra the Judean. He sometimes participates in festivals. He's prophesying about the Messiah and the end of the world. He's been doing that since I was a child."

"And they let him?" she asked in astonishment, staring at the Israelite man declaiming loudly in Greek.

"He's very careful to never say anything bad about Rome. I should tell him that the messianic age has already begun, that the Messiah has died and been resurrected and that now we're waiting for the Parousia."

Mary nodded, wondering again if the Parousia would happen today. Tears threatened. She welcomed the distraction of a shop selling pearls and shells.

There were so many different kinds and shapes and colors. They overflowed from jars and bins and entranced her with their shimmering swirls of color: greens and blues, purples and pinks, grays and whites and yellows. She stared at a pile of pearls tied together in strands, in awe of their beauty and sheen. She watched as a woman picked up a shell and held it to her ear and was fascinated when John told her that the sound of the sea was magically trapped inside. She'd had no idea such beautiful and wondrous things lived in the sea. She wanted to touch them but didn't dare once John told her what they were. She didn't know if it was allowed—it was hard to imagine that things that lived in the purifying sea could be polluted, but shellfish, which lacked fins and scales, were forbidden to eat, and the bodies of unclean animals were forbidden to be touched. She knew that many rich Hebrew women wore pearls as ornaments, so probably it was all right to enjoy their beauty. She'd ask someone at the synagogue if it was all right to touch them.

She realized suddenly that she knew the woman listening to the shell.

"Arsinoe, isn't it?"

"Judean guardian lady!" the Isis priestess said with delight. She set the shell down and embraced Mary, wrapping her in her exotic perfume and powder scent.

John stared at the colorful vision holding his black-clad mother in her bangled arms.

"Arsinoe, this is my son John," Mary said.

The priestess stared at the boy with critical interest. "Very handsome. But he doesn't look much like you."

"He's the son of my heart. You may know his father, Alexander."

"Alexander the Judean! You are the son of Alexander the Judean? He is very rich."

John had no idea how to respond, but Arsinoe wasn't waiting for him to answer anyway.

"Judean guardian lady—I think I've forgotten your name!"

"Mary."

"Yes, Mary, yes, of course. What have you bought today, Mary? Such a beautiful day to shop. Show me what you've bought!"

"We haven't bought anything yet."

"With all the beautiful things in all the beautiful shops in the most beautiful agora in the world, there isn't anything to tempt a Judean guardian lady?"

"Oh, everything is very lovely," Mary assured her, hoping the woman wasn't really offended that Mary hadn't bought anything. "The glassware and the cloth. And these beautiful shells. And the soap."

"But you must have something," Arsinoe insisted, and as she moved away Mary noticed the two slaves following after her, laden with her purchases.

"Come, come," Arsinoe called back to Mary and John. "Come with me. I want to buy a gift for you. Your first gift from the famous agora at Ephesus!"

Protesting, they followed her out of the seashell shop. Mary noticed people staring at them and thought they must look like some kind of entertainment, the laughing, sparkling, bejeweled woman in brilliantly colored clothes rushing through the crowd followed by a black-enshrouded Judean, a boy, and two heavily laden slaves.

They passed a little shop selling sundials and water clocks and a stall with pre-carved tombstones from Galatia (just add inscription), and a whole display of panoply—helmets, armor, swords, shields and other warrior equipment. They hurried past sculptors with pre-chiseled bodies of men and women on display (just add head) and a man with leviathan-puppet hands juggling fruit in front of a colorful cart featuring amusing and magical trinkets from around the world.

They stopped finally at a shop selling souvenirs of a winged idol in a variety of poses, the most predominant being a mother and child.

"It's Isis," John said.

"Yes." Mary recognized the image.

Shrieks of delighted welcome greeted Arsinoe from the inside of the shop. "Come in, Mary and John, and meet my friends," she said, pulling Mary through the door and introducing her to several people. Mary was confused by the press of the people squeezed between the shelves and the rapid, unintelligible conversation, but thought one or two of the people were shopkeepers and the others probably customers.

John was able to converse with everyone in Greek, but Arsinoe was the only one of the others who spoke Aramaic. She gossiped for a while with her friends, sometimes translating a particularly outrageous thing to Mary, who didn't know the people involved or understand the reasons for the laughter.

Eventually shopping ensued. Arsinoe or one of the shopkeepers or customers would pick up a figurine or medallion or picture, and then they'd discuss the selection. Occasionally Arsinoe asked Mary: "What do you think?" to which Mary would always say: "It's lovely" because really, what else could she say? She protested against Arsinoe's generosity, but Arsinoe swept all arguments aside.

Arsinoe finally kissed Mary and John good-bye outside the shop entrance, happy about her largesse, promising to visit them at the proseuche very soon. She fluttered away, followed by her slaves and their burdens.

Mary stared down morosely at the figure in her hand, a small, exquisite, utterly forbidden golden pendant figurine of a winged goddess and her child, and sighed. "I begin to understand your father."

John took the idolatrous graven image from her. "It was very expensive. Arsinoe must really like you," he said, amused sympathy in his voice. He slipped the thing into his bag. "Do you still want to buy hyssop?"

The shop that had the freshest selection of hyssop was run by a Samaritan, who assured her that the harvesting of the hyssop had been done in a way that was not inconsistent with any purity laws. After her sojourn in the Isis shop, having a civil conversation with a Samaritan didn't seem so extraordinary. A kind man named Abraham, he reminded her of a friend from back home, a jovial butcher named Daniel—he seemed so familiar, in fact, that talking with Abraham almost made her feel homesick.

He seemed to enjoy her company as well, although that may have been the manner he adopted with all potential customers. He said that his wife had been delighted to hear that a mikvah was being built in Ephesus, and now that he had met the attendant he would feel quite comfortable allowing her to use it.

"Her name is Rachel," he said.

"I look forward to meeting her," Mary said solemnly. She was glad that John had told her already about the agreement with the Samaritans, otherwise in her shock she might have said something unkind. She felt guilty about speaking with this decent man in her polluted state.

"Please forgive my impertinence," Abraham added as he handed the wrapped hyssop to John and received a small coin in payment, "but that lavender perfume you wear is quite lovely. May I inquire if you obtained it here in the agora?"

Mary explained about the soap. The odor still lingered on her skin. She was grateful it had not been overpowered by Arsinoe's perfume.

"Oh yes, I've seen those before," Abraham said. "They're manufactured in Gaul and Germania. Quite a nice item, though costly." He turned and scrounged around in a pile of bags behind him, then handed her a sheaf of dried leaves tied in red wool. "My wife and I will be honored if you would accept this from us, as our gift to welcome you to our city."

Mary received the leaves from him, breathing in the lovely lavender scent of them. What a generous gift! Her eyes threatened to fill with tears again, but she quickly blinked them away. She was determined that no tears would flow down her cheeks today. Abraham noticed her wet eyes and beamed. He liked having his gifts appreciated. "One more thing we'd like to give you," he said, taking two rocks out of bowls hidden in the back of a crowded shelf and handing them to her. "Flint and iron," he said. "If your fire goes out you should have some way to start one again, since up on the hill you don't have any neighbors living nearby to borrow fire from."

Mary didn't mention that she didn't yet have a fire to maintain. She knew that John would certainly make sure she always had one now. She handed the two rocks and the lavender to John to put in the bag with the hyssop and the chunk of Isis gold. "Thank you, Abraham," she said. "You're very kind. I am glad to meet you and I look forward to meeting your wife as well. I know we are going to be good friends."

"I feel that as well. I did not plan to be here at all today—a holy week, you know—but one of my most important customers is in the city today and wished to meet with me. He just left, just moments before you entered my shop. If you had come even an hour later, I would not be here. So God must have meant for us to meet here today." He bowed to her. She and John returned his bow and said good-bye.

Later back home, John showed Alexander the tiny Isis figure. His father burst into laughter. "Thank you for accepting it," he said to Mary. "I know that was hard for you." He gave her an approving smile.

She thought: "My son, the market holds an abundance of treasures and magic. But most remarkable of all is the dance of the different peoples of the world as they try to forge friendships with strangers."

5

"What is a Hebrew, outside of the Land of God?"

A lexander's slaves spent the next few days helping Mary to settle into her new home. Mary's family had never owned slaves. The only slave she'd ever known personally was a freed woman who'd been a slave in Rome and moved back to her family's farm near Galilee after she'd been granted manumission. Mary could not approve of slavery and was not entirely comfortable having so many people looking to her to tell them what to do. In the end, she called on the only related experience she had and pretended that they were her children as she gave them instructions.

The slaves placed rugs on the floor and small pieces of furniture around the two rooms, hung colorful lengths of cloth on the walls and over the window, set up a dressing tent adjacent to the mikvah, and prepared a small plot for vegetables, herbs, and flowers in a sunlit spot uphill of the outhouse. They left her some barley bread, a few jars of preserved food, and some salted fish, but Mary would seldom make a real meal for herself during her years in Ephesus as John or his family's slaves would always come by a few times a day, bringing her food from Alexander's table.

She thought Aspasia's baptism went well, considering the language differences. Deborah did most of the talking, and Mary performed the purification and cleansing ceremonies. She made some of Abraham the Samaritan's lavender into incense, which she wafted over Aspasia, Deborah, and the six other attendees, and created a ritual out of tying the red-dyed wool strands from the lavender bundle around the hyssop before she dipped it in spring water for purification sprinkling over Aspasia. Both of these new rites went over well with the women present at the baptism. Deborah's slaves brought bread and oil, dried fruit, olives, nuts, and a nice dried berry tea for the after-ceremony visit, which they prepared in the old hearth, now comfortably heating the stone building with a large supply of wood gathered from the ground around the grove.

The ceremony began with prayers, then Deborah did her teaching, then came the purification and immersion, and then they sat on comfortable pallets, cushions, and lush rugs in the warm proseuche. Oil lamps sitting in lamp stands on small tables now lit up the corners of the room. The women enjoyed the light meal and friendly company. After closing prayers they left, but Deborah's people left the large tea urn and cups behind so that Mary would have them available the next time a group met at the proseuche for prayers and socializing.

The afternoon prior to Sabbath sunset, Mary began a pattern she would continue for two days out of the seven for many years to come. She walked to Alexander's house with John in the afternoon, had Sabbath evening dinner, and spent the night. During the Sabbath daylight hours she attended the house synagogue that met at Alexander's house. After sunset she had dinner with the family and spent the night again (usually along with numerous others; Alexander's house was large and his hospitality great) and then the next morning she joined John, Enoch, Aspasia, Deborah, and Enoch's Disciples of John the Baptist guild for an early meal and meeting before everyone left for their daily work.

Before entering Alexander's house, she would always walk past the centerpiece of his front doorway, an elaborate fountain with dozens of spouts of bubbling water, to wash instead at an old pitted stone basin where rain water collected, near the mezuzah fastened to the right front doorpost and the lampstand where the Sabbath lamp was lit each week. She would wash her hands, feet, and face in the old basin and then enter the house, taking comfort through the years in knowing that in this, at any rate, she continued to keep the commandments—she never began her Sabbath prayers or meal without first washing herself in living water.

There were many times, especially in later years, when it seemed as though every little ritual or belief or religious practice from her early life was altered or influenced by her time among the gentiles, and she would be grateful for the few moments of nostalgic peace she felt each Sabbath when she turned her back on the beautiful man-made fountain, gushing with water carried from man-made pipes through the man-made city, and washed her hands in the still-but-living rain water contained in the old stone basin, chiseled out by man but made, as all stone was, by God Himself.

She was also glad that after that first Sabbath, John too began using the stone basin instead of the fountain for his Sabbath washing.

Mary spent most of that first synagogue watching and learning. Since she couldn't understand the words, she tried to understand the hearts of the people by the manner in which they treated one another and the level of devotion they seemed to have for the Sabbath and its rituals.

After a trumpet sounded, announcing assembly, they met in the exhedra, men sitting on one side of the room and women on the other. The room was crowded, with at least thirty people in attendance. Many people had to sit out in the peristyle. She was glad to see that everyone kept their heads covered during worship, even though they met in a private home. John sat next to Mary, near the door; they sat apart from everyone else so that his continuous translation of the Greek words wouldn't disturb anyone.

They began with prayers and then had the readings from the Torah and the prophets. Two of the men responsible for the Torah reading were clearly uncomfortable with Hebrew, and even Mary found herself smiling once at the abysmal pronunciation. John told her apologetically that the replacement scrolls, quickly prepared, weren't as beautiful as the old Torah had been, but Mary felt it was the words that mattered, not the beauty of the parchment or copying skill of the scribe.

"That'll be me one day," John said gloomily after they listened to one man struggling through the Hebrew story of Joseph and the Pharaoh. "Everyone's going to laugh at me. I should have studied harder at the Temple. I hope Jesus returns soon."

Mary amazed herself by almost smiling at this. She patted John's hand. "Never mind, dear," she whispered, "we'll find someone for you to study with."

Greek interpretations were provided for all of the spoken Hebrew, both prayer and scripture. Some prayers were offered only in Greek. The homilies and discussion were completely in Greek. As John carefully translated everything for her, Mary was grateful that although he may have neglected his Hebrew studies when he was in Jerusalem, he had been an excellent student of Aramaic.

Today's texts and dialogue focused on relationship with gentiles. Mary was glad to learn that she was not the only person troubled by the loosening of traditional practices in Ephesus. She discovered that there were some people here who had not attended the First Fruits festival in town because it was held on the afternoon of the Passover High Sabbath, and she decided that in the future she too would refrain from breaking Sabbath merely for festivals. She agreed with the person who said that they should have held the First Fruits festival on the following afternoon. She frequently found herself nodding, often in agreement with someone who was in debate against Alexander, then remembered that he was John's father and that it was disrespectful of her to allow her disagreement to be shown to the man's son.

The conversation shifted from discussion of First Fruits gifts to complaints about the heavy tax burden. Some people felt that after they sent their gifts and tithes to Jerusalem and paid their taxes to the city of Ephesus, that it was expecting too much of them to also be taxed by Rome, especially when most Roman citizens were exempt from taxes. The provinces paid most of the taxes that kept Rome afloat.

A woman rose to speak. Mary stared.

"That's Hannah," John said. "She's a Mother of the Synagogue, very highly regarded."

"I have never known a woman to speak in synagogue," Mary said. Back home, any woman who dared to do such a thing would have been rebuked, removed from the building, and maybe even permanently expelled.

"That's one of the things that my father and Lavi argue about," John said. "Women don't speak in the synagogue that meets at Lavi's house."

Mary wasn't sure how to feel about this. Clearly this was another Ephesian novelty. But she'd often wanted to speak up herself during assembly, had often thought that she had important things to say if only someone was interested enough to listen.

"What's she saying?"

"She believes that we have a responsibility to pay taxes to Rome because Rome keeps us safe and protects our rights as Israelites."

Mary remembered something she'd heard her son say, and she whispered to John. But she must have been louder than she'd thought, because Hannah turned to address her.

John translated Mary's words to Hannah.

Alexander spoke up, addressing Mary in Aramaic. "Go on," he encouraged her. "What were you saying?"

Mary was acutely embarrassed, but forced herself to speak. "I said 'Give to Caesar that which is Caesar's and to God that which is God's.' It's something my son said once about taxes, when he was in discussion with some Pharisees."

"He was a great man," John piped up then said it again in Greek.

Alexander translated her words for the crowd then asked, "What did he mean by that?"

Mary asked John to give her a coin and he took a couple of them from his purse.

She held up one of the coins and asked, "Whose image is this?"

The people looked at the coin. "Artemis Ephesia," they said.

She nodded, trying not to be thrown by the answer. She glanced at the coin, recognizing the idol from the beautiful temple. She set it down quickly, troubled to be holding an idol's image in her hand for the second time in a few short days, then selected one of the other coins John had given her. "And who is this a picture of?"

"Caesar," they said.

"When asked about the paying of taxes, my son showed the crowd a coin, asked them the question I've asked you, and when they told him it was Caesar he said, 'Give to Caesar that which is Caesar's and to God that which is God's.' In this case, in this town, I think he would also say, 'Give Artemis that which is hers,'—meaning the city, of course, not the idol. My son believed that the rulers were owed their due, whoever they were."

Alexander translated her words and another heated discussion began.

After synagogue ended, Hannah came up to Mary and tried to make conversation, but Mary did not feel comfortable talking with the woman with only a fifteen-year-old boy to translate her words.

At dinner that evening the men joked about the lack of skilled Hebrew scholars in the younger generation. Evidently Enoch's Hebrew was also disappointing.

"I don't understand," Alexander said, helping himself to more fish from a serving dish near his couch. "Both of my sons studied with Rabbi Gamaliel. He and I were students at the same time under his grandfather Hillel, so I know him well and know that he's a great scholar. And both of my boys are bright. But their Hebrew and scripture knowledge wasn't much better when they returned from Jerusalem than it was when they left home. I thank God that I was able to spend time teaching them before they left, or they'd be completely ignorant. As it is, John's going to have to go back to synagogue school with Samuel."

John translated this for her and then asked his father a question in Greek. Mary knew that the only reason John hadn't learned much from Rabbi Gamaliel was because he'd spent all his time with Jesus and his disciples, who were more interested in discussing what scriptures meant than in helping a boy memorize texts. It was because of his attention to these conversations that his Aramaic was so good. And she suspected Enoch's experience with John the Baptist had been similar.

John's father responded to his son and the men laughed. One made a friendly comment to John, and he smiled wanly in return.

"I asked my father how I can attend both gymnasium and synagogue school, and he said that he was confident that I'll find a way. But I'm not going to have much time to spend with you, Mother. We'll have to find someone else to teach you Greek."

Mary nodded. "That's fine, son. At gymnasium you'll learn everything you need to know to be a Greek and Roman citizen and a leader like your father. That will be important for you, when you're a man."

"I'm lucky to be able to attend gymnasium. At least that's what my father says. Enoch couldn't be a member because they didn't admit Israelites ten years ago. But my father was a member of the gymnasium guild when he was young, and he petitioned the gymnasiarch to get the right of membership returned to us." He sighed. "These men here will tease me about that too. Theokritos just made a joke about my taking up the books of Homer—that's what they call all Greek and Roman literature and philosophy, the 'books of Homer.'"

Mary didn't understand.

"Homer was a Greek poet," John explained.

"Oh."

John changed the subject by telling the group about the strange shrieking sound they'd sometimes heard coming from the grove near the proseuche. No one knew what it might be, but all were happy to guess.

"They think it must be some kind of demon, left there by worshippers of Artemis Ephesia to guard the trees," John told Mary after much discussion. "But they don't think it will bother you in the mikvah or proseuche, because demons hate sacred places. My father will talk with Artelia about taking it away."

Enoch addressed her. His Aramaic was almost as good as John's. "Will you be attending our meeting in the morning?" he asked.

Mary looked at John. "Enoch means the meeting of the Disciples of John the Baptist," he said. "They meet early in the morning, before people start their work."

"John has promised to give us more details about the death of our teacher and the impact his death had in Jerusalem," Enoch said. He reclined on a couch, as did most of the men. Most women sat on raised pallets, separate from the men and the main table. Aspasia sat close to Deborah. Mary had noticed many women looking coldly at Enoch's new wife and thought it was kind of her former mistress/new sister-in-law to offer her protection and support.

"Yes, and I will tell you all about Jesus, who became the teacher after John died and who many say was more important than John," John said.

"We'll make up our own minds about that," said Enoch and then turned to Mary. "This Jesus—he was your son, the one with the coins?"

"Yes."

"Did he have many disciples? As many as John?"

"Hundreds."

"And the priests—how well did he get along with them?"

"They argued with him a lot," Mary said.

Enoch smiled. "He sounds like a true teacher to me. We'll be happy to hear about him."

The next morning's meeting was held in the exhedra, after a very early breakfast. Sunrise was just barely lighting the sky when the ten people joined together for prayers and discussion.

They discussed the teachings of John the Baptist. Mary was glad to see that Enoch blushed and looked sheepishly at newly baptized Aspasia when he spoke of the importance of exercising virtue and of behaving toward each other in righteousness. The conversation was actually very similar in content to what she'd heard Jesus discuss with his disciples—an expectation of the coming new age, a final judgment and the resurrection of the righteous, although the Disciples of John the Baptist seemed to place a much greater emphasis on the importance of purification than Jesus and his followers had.

John spoke about the riots that had broken out in Jerusalem and all over Judea after the execution of John the Baptist and said that many of John's disciples had become followers of Jesus after John's death. The group seemed open to hearing about Jesus, and Mary thought that John, though young, did a good job in his teaching. During this first meeting, he told the group about the things Jesus had said about John, including his statement that among all people ever born, no one was greater than John the Baptist. When they said their closing prayer and left for their day's work, many of them still had tears in their eyes after hearing Jesus' loving words about their master.

That night Mary heard the music from another procession and again she walked down the hill to the lookout place, this time taking a blanket with her to help keep the cold out of her bones. It was slightly darker now, the moon no longer full, and she realized as she carefully made her way to the spot that if she was to have a new moon celebration at the proseuche this next month, something the synagogue women had requested, she would need to begin planning it right away and announce it at the next synagogue meeting.

The songs of the procession were different this time, more melodic and less wild, and she wondered what that signified. Presumably there were stories being told in the music, but all she could hear was the tenderness. Above her in the trees, the storks settled, occasionally clicking to one another, and she smiled, feeling their protection and regard.

When the procession entered the city, she imagined the buildings they passed as they danced along the same route as before, the route she'd followed with John on their visits. There, that was the state agora they were passing. And now the procession had reached the octagon tomb. And now, yes, now just past where they turned in the road—that was the big square merchant agora at the harbor, where they sold pearls and soap and little golden graven images.

There was something so magical about being up here near the stars, listening to the clicking of the storks and the crickets and enjoying the music and the procession of lights. She was grateful that she was far enough away not to be troubled by the words of the songs, no doubt praises sung to Artelia's imposing idol.

She thought: "My son, this place is strange, but I think I could make it my home."

6

"Secrets lay hidden all around, waiting to be uncovered."

When John brought her breakfast the next day he said, "We've found a teacher for you. Someone to teach you Greek."

"Oh, John, that's wonderful," Mary said with a big smile. "Who is it?"

"His name is Adonis, which is a very funny name for him, as you'll soon see. He's quite old and nearly blind."

"Oh, poor man!"

"He was a great philosopher and a teacher at the gymnasium when he was young, one of my father's favorite teachers, but now he's a weak and sick old man. My father found him begging near the theater. Deborah's caring for him at the house now, but my father thinks that in a few days he should be well enough to come up here to give you lessons. A couple of slaves will be along directly to set up a tent for him to sleep in at night."

"All right," Mary said hesitantly.

John frowned. "That's all right with you, isn't it, Mother?"

"I suppose. It just seems odd that you should want to bring a strange man up here to stay with me, that's all."

John laughed. "Mother, don't worry. He can barely see and can hardly walk. He's perfectly harmless. And if you don't like him, he can always go back to begging at the theater."

Mary couldn't imagine herself disliking someone so much that she'd wish that sort of life for him. She smiled wanly. "I'm sure it will be fine." They settled back on their rug in the warm sunshine to enjoy their breakfast.

They heard someone walking up the hill. "Perhaps someone wishes to use the mikvah," John said.

"Perhaps."

The large woman who approached the proseuche carried a pack as big as another person on her back.

"Oh, that's Gilana," John said happily. He stood and waved, shouting to the woman in Greek. "I asked her if she remembers me," he said.

The big woman came over to them and sat her pack down on the ground. Mary realized that it was an enormous pile of clothes, tied in a bundle.

"Little Johnny, all grown up!" the woman said with a laugh. "You're big enough to marry me now! When shall we set the date?"

John was embarrassed at being teased, but smiled anyway and interpreted her words for Mary. "Gilana, this is Mary, who is like my mother."

The two women smiled at each other. "I came up here today to meet you," Gilana said, "so I'm glad little Johnny is here to introduce us. You'll be seeing me a lot."

"You purify often at the mikvah?"

Gilana burst out laughing when John translated Mary's question. "I don't bother with the mikvah. I'm a laundress. I clean clothes in the stream that runs off from your spring." She pursed her lips together and made a demure face. "I spend ten hours a day in that water, so I'm always pure," she said primly.

"I'm honored to meet such a holy person," Mary said with a grin.

Gilana laughed again. "I think I'm going to like you."

"Would you like to join us for breakfast?" Mary asked.

"Now I know I'm going to like you," Gilana said and sat down on the rug beside them. As she helped herself to their food, Mary noticed that Gilana's hands were red and rough but very, very clean.

Their conversation was awkward due to the language restrictions, but Mary realized quickly that she would enjoy having Gilana as a friend. She looked forward to learning Greek so that they could visit even in John's absence.

Later in the morning after John and Gilana left, two women came up the hill to use the mikvah. Mary hadn't met them before and thought they might be from Lavi's synagogue. After putting on her water robe (a gift from Deborah), she showed them to the new tent that Alexander's slaves had set up next to the mikvah entrance and waited while the women disrobed.

She had lit lamps down in the bath this morning, but it was still fairly dark down there. The darkness was necessary for modesty but could be dangerous while walking up or down wet stone steps. This mikvah was much larger than any village mikvah she'd ever seen—more the size of the mikvot built for pilgrims in Jerusalem, where a constant stream of people into the large stone baths required a separation of the steps going down into the water from the steps coming back up. Mary helped the women as they walked the entrance side of the double steps down into the water.

She purified them by sprinkling them with hyssop dipped in the spring water, and then one at a time they walked into the bath where she assisted them in their cleansing by helping them to go under the water once, twice, three times, careful to make sure that their entire bodies, including their hair, were completely covered by the cold, living water. After their immersions, she led them up the exit side of the steps back to the dressing tent and motioned for them to join her when ready in the warm proseuche, cozy from bits of burning wood that she and John had gathered earlier.

She quickly changed into dry clothes in her own room and prepared hyssop tea while the women dressed in the tent. After they joined her, she led them in prayers, and then the two women enjoyed their tea and chatted in Greek with each other as they warmed up and dried their hair in the comfortable room.

They seemed happy when they left, effusive with compliments she couldn't understand, and Mary was still smiling while she hung their wet toweling and her own wet robe up to dry on hooks set up near the hearth. She realized that she liked this life as a mikvah attendant. She liked being part of this sacred ritual and wondered what else she could do to make it more pleasant or more meaningful for people. She wished she could have spoken with the women to tell them about the new moon ceremonies she planned. Well, one day soon that would be possible too.

She realized she hadn't cried even once today. Helping others did it, she decided. She couldn't focus on her own sadness while her mind was on the needs of other people.

At midday, she heard the sound of wagons and voices coming up from the road on the other side of the hill, the road used by Artelia's slave when he'd brought her home from the idol's temple. When the cart had stopped to let her out, the driver had pointed to a walking path that she had followed in some trepidation until she realized it led directly to the proseuche.

Mary was not surprised to see workers from the temple walk up the path today, because Artelia had mentioned she would send someone to do some work in the grove. She was, however, quite taken aback to see Artelia herself, carried aloft on a litter. Behind the litter, other slaves hauled food and bundles of cloth. They carried these directly into the proseuche. The litter bearers let Artelia down, and Mary's friend embraced her as the women slaves scurried around in the little building.

Artelia laughed at Mary's confused frown. "Don't worry, my dear, we didn't bring any sacrificial food or wine. I sent some of my people down to the Judean market this morning to make some purchases. So let me show you the labyrinth in the grove and explain what needs to be done, and afterwards we can just sit and have a nice visit together."

"May I show you the mikvah first?" Mary asked. She thought it would be nice for Artelia to see how the Israelites used the spring.

"I came to see the cold bath after it was built, but no one has ever explained the purification rituals to me. So thank you, I would like that." She gave the male workers some instructions and they went off into the woods while Mary and Artelia walked over to the mikvah.

Mary explained the reasons and rituals of purification, some of which astonished Artelia. "Are you telling me that your god considers women's moon blood to be filth?" she asked indignantly.

"Yes," Mary said, unsure how to respond to Artelia's offended tone.

"Well, in that regard he could not be more different from Artemis," Artelia said decisively. "Artemis treasures moon blood as a particularly sacred fluid." She said that she would like to see the purification ritual in practice sometime, and Mary felt grateful the ladies from this morning had already left and wouldn't be made embarrassed by Artelia's questions.

After the mikvah tour, Mary and Artelia walked into the woods, following an old path. Both women smiled at the clicking sounds made by the storks up in the trees, annoyed that humans disturbed the ground beneath them. Mary told Artelia about the meaning of the Hebrew word for "stork" and about how much she enjoyed having them here.

The symphony of birdsong and stork and cicada clicks was suddenly interrupted by the loud and frightening demon shriek that Mary had heard so often coming from these woods. She looked at her new friend to see if she could explain.

Artelia grinned broadly at the dread sound. "There are still peacocks here! I thought we'd gathered up all of them when we abandoned the labyrinth. How blessed you are!" She told Mary about the wondrous birds, brought from India as a votive offering to Artemis long ago. They were considered holy birds by the worshippers of the goddess. Only the highest priests and priestesses could use their plumage in regalia, and the birds were not allowed out of their enclosed garden at the temenos. However, some birds had once been brought up here as part of a ceremony, and when they immediately began making nests on the ground and hunting for food on the thick-leaved floor of the woods it was decided to let a few of them roam free up here in the sacred grove, since there were so many of them back at the temenos they had actually become pests.

"They're still sacred birds, and we don't want them to get loose in town. Those barbaric Romans eat peafowl, so that's made us particularly careful. We don't allow the sale of peacocks in Ephesus, and ownership of the feathers is illegal to all but temple personnel for ritual use. When we still used the laby-rinth, we kept watch on the ones living in the grove up here, and whenever the flock grew too large we would take most of them back to their garden at the temenos, where we can control the population. When we stopped using this place, I gave strict orders to have them all gathered up. Now that you're here to enjoy them, I'm glad to know that some escaped capture." As they walked she scanned the ground and now she spotted a couple of long feathers and picked them up. She handed them to Mary.

"Here, have these. Feel free to gather them for your own enjoyment. But please do not give them away or use them to decorate yourself."

Mary took the two feathers with a trembling hand. "This comes from a bird?" she asked in a whisper. She was awestruck at the beauty of the green and blue eyes at the tips and couldn't stop stroking them.

"Only the males have those plumes," Artelia said. "The females are pretty birds but look quite dull next to their mates."

"We thought they must be demons to be making such sounds," Mary said. "But I see now that they're like the storks—God put so much beauty into their bodies that He didn't have any left for their voices." She was eager to see what they looked like with their feathers intact.

"Well, they do behave demonically sometimes," Artelia admitted. "If you see one, don't get too close. They're especially bad during mating time, which is the only time of year you should be troubled by the shrieks."

They soon entered a large clearing in the trees, and Mary could see a circular shape formed on the ground, outlined by stones. A curving pathway had been created between the stones, round and round, often reversing direction. Workers were clearing up limbs and leaves that had fallen on the ground, while others pulled up plants that had grown up inside the space. There were no graven images around, but there were several plinths, including one in the center of the shape, which certainly must once have held statues.

"Once they get this work done, you should be able to keep it clear without too much effort," Artelia said.

"What is it used for?" Mary stroked the peacock feather across her cheek.

"This labyrinth? It's not used for anything now. But we used to use it in a ritual dance, tracing the path of the sun across the sky. As a young initiate, I often used to dance the sun dance here."

"What does that mean?"

"There used to be a statue of a bull in the center of the labyrinth," Artelia said, "but we moved it to the labyrinth near the sacred cave when the spring reopened. You remember what I told you about how Artemis the sun used to cross the sky through the body of the bull?"

"I remember."

"The dance, which is very old, commemorates that time. The dancers go through the seven circuits, then reach and circle the bull, which we call the 'Asterion,' meaning 'star.' The seven circuits represent the seven planetary circulations. Then they dance their way back out again, stopping at each turning to contemplate the twists and turns in the paths and patterns of their own lives.

"You see, the secret of the labyrinth is that there is only one way in and there is only one way out. The Lady of Heaven has put us each on a particular path, and whether we think the way we're going is the right way or not, so long as we keep putting one foot in front of the other, going forward, eventually we will reach our destiny, no matter how roundabout it seems. Just as the sun has its one path it follows each day, so too our life, from the dawn of our birth to the dusk of our death, has but one path to follow."

"Amen," said Mary. The two friends smiled at each other in perfect harmony.

Artelia noticed a worker moving the center plinth and called out to him. After he answered, she thought for a moment then gave him additional instructions. The other workers went over and helped him to lift the plinth and carry it out of the center of the labyrinth and set it to the side. After some consultation, they began rearranging all of the plinths, moving them from their separate spots to locations next to others, so as to form connected structures of stone.

"You won't be putting up any statues, so I thought you might prefer to use the plinths as benches and tables," Artelia said.

Mary looked at the bases doubtfully. "Some of them are pretty tall to be used as benches."

Artelia shrugged and yelled to the workers. They set one of the plinths on its side. "Better?"

"Yes, actually that would probably make a nice bench."

"Good. I'll have them move a couple of them out near your buildings, so that you can sit on them when you're outside."

When Mary thanked her, Artelia said, "I hadn't thought to move them at all. But there's a beech tree growing in the exact center of the labyrinth, up under the old Asterion plinth, so obviously that tree should now be the new center marker. Artemis is particularly fond of the beech—you'll notice this grove is primarily beech trees. You may glean from these trees as much as you wish, by the way. The leaves, bark, and nuts are good in various medicines, and beechnut oil is quite nice. Some people even eat the nuts, I'm told."

Mary bent down to pick up a beechnut from the ground and examined it.

"Some of my women can tell you more about them, I'm sure. Oh, but you don't speak Greek…"

"I'm getting a teacher. They've hired an elderly Greek man named Adonis to come teach me the language."

"Adonis?" Artelia frowned. "Do you know anything about him?"

"He's blind and lame now." Mary recalled John's words. "He used to teach at the gymnasium and was one of Alexander's teachers. Alexander found him begging near the theater and thought that if he became my teacher, he wouldn't need to beg anymore." Mary hadn't thought about it before, but she now realized what a profoundly kind man Alexander must be.

"Oh, of course," Artelia said, nodding. "I know him. I hadn't realized he had fallen on such hard times. He will make an excellent teacher for you."

They sat on one of the plinths and watched the workers for a while, and then Artelia said, "I'm feeling thirsty. Are you thirsty?" They walked back through the path to the proseuche, Mary with her head down, looking for more of the wondrous peacock feathers.

Artelia's slaves waited for them at the door of the proseuche, toweling held in their arms. Two small benches were now placed outside of the door, near copper kettles filled with water. Artelia sat on one of the benches, and Mary smiled to herself to see her friend's head positioned next to the mezuzah. A slave beckoned to Mary to sit on the other bench.

Mary sat and watched as two slaves approached Artelia with water and toweling. One held out a basin for Artelia to dip her hands in, while the other kneeled at her feet. Mary stood and gently pushed away the woman at Artelia's feet, then hurried to pull the stone wash basin over to where her friend sat. When the slaves saw what she was doing, they rushed to help her with the heavy thing.

Mary washed Artelia's feet with the living water then nodded to a slave for a towel. She dried her friend's feet carefully then glanced up to see Artelia looking at her quizzically.

"Why did you do that? You are not my servant."

"No. I am your hostess."

Artelia nodded then spoke quietly to the slaves. They emptied the stone basin then carried it over to the mikvah to refill it, an act Mary was never able to perform due to its weight. The basin always took her ages to refill with repeated trips to the spring carrying a small stone bowl.

"Sit," Artelia said. "They will be back soon."

Mary sat, and when the slaves returned with the water she held her hands out to dip them in the water before the basin was placed at her feet.

Artelia then knelt on the ground to wash Mary's feet, an act Mary was confident she had never performed for any person before. She sat in silence while her friend performed the ritual, enjoying a comfort she had not experienced since leaving Judea—the pleasure of having someone else wash her feet.

When her feet were dry, she stood, and the two women walked into the proseuche.

"Why did you do that?" Mary asked. "You are not my hostess."

"No," Artelia said. "I am your friend."

They sat on cushions placed around a small table laden with bread, vegetable relishes, fish, and eggs. "My slaves aren't conversant with Judean food customs, so this food is very simple. I hope you don't mind."

Mary was quite certain that one Judean food custom was: Do not eat anything prepared by idol worshippers at their temple, whether it was prepared for idol sacrifice or not. But she was so touched by the sweetness of the high priestess's gesture—and particularly by her effort to honor Mary's God by purchasing the food at the Judean market—that Mary decided she would eat every little bit, with gratitude. She remembered hearing her son Jesus once say that you are to eat whatever you're given: if someone cares for you enough to provide you with food, you should respect their kindness enough to eat it. She promised herself that from then on, throughout her life, she would do exactly this, in respect of Artelia's kindness to her today.

But one thing she must do. "I would like to offer the blessing," she said. Artelia nodded her assent, and Mary recited the Shema in Hebrew, then followed with her normal mealtime blessing, recited in Aramaic.

"That's a lovely prayer," Artelia said as they began to eat together. "At the beginning you spoke a different language, I think—one I do not know. Is that Hebrew?"

"Yes." Mary translated it: "Hear, O Israel! Adonai is our God! Adonai is One!"

"Is Adonai the name of your god?" Artelia asked.

"No," Mary said. "'Adonai' is what we say in place of the Name, in our prayers. Or sometimes when we're talking together, we'll just say 'Hashem,' which means 'The Name.' The Name of our God is too holy to be spoken aloud."

Artelia nodded. "That's what I had heard. A god with a name so holy it cannot be spoken aloud is a very powerful god."

"Yes."

"Are you enjoying Ephesus? It must be very different from Judea."

"It could hardly be more different. Besides the worship of all of the idols here, the morality of the people is so different."

"How so?"

"When I walked in the town, I saw people having sex in a tomb, which is so profoundly immoral that I hardly know which thing offends me most—the fact that people would have sex in a tomb or the fact that they would have sex out where other people could see or the fact that the tombs of the dead are right there in the middle of the town."

"Well, I don't see anything immoral about the tombs being in town, but then I don't understand many of the beliefs of the Judeans. I agree that having sex in the open where people can see, whether it's in a tomb or not, is an immoral thing. Unless it was part of a Dionysian or Aphroditian ritual?"

"I don't have any idea about that, but I don't think so. It was in the middle of the day, and it was during your Artemis festival."

"Well, it was certainly not part of an Artemisian rite. We'll assume it was just regular fornication. You don't often see that sort of thing in public in Ephesus. Ephesus is no less moral than any other city in the empire, and it's a lot more moral than Rome. The Greeks have always held higher standards than the Romans. In Rome, everyone does everything in the streets, in public. It's practically the law." She thought for a moment then conceded, "Although in Corinth, I must admit that the rituals at the temple of Aphrodite encourage all sorts of licentious behavior even outside of the temenos."

Mary had been thinking about something and decided to ask. "Artelia, you're the high priestess, aren't you?"

"Yes, I am."

"Then I've been wondering—when I was at the temple, why did someone of your, well, status stop to talk with someone like me—a strange woman and by herself? I'm sure there were many more important people you should have been spending your time with, especially during your festival month."

"Mary, dear, the reason I stopped to speak with you was, frankly, because you were dressed all in black like some kind of demon. Everyone else in the Temple was wearing white, except for Arsinoe in her crazy purple robes. I needed to see if you were there to perform some evil sorcery. Of course, I realized quickly that you were just ignorant of the proper way to dress in the presence of Artemis." Then she added: "That reminds me..." and she spoke with one of her attendants.

The woman picked up the pile of cloth and brought it over to set between Artelia and Mary.

"Most of this is ordinary linen," Artelia said. "You can use it to make a couple of nice summer chitons. But this is my real gift to you." She picked up a beautiful length of shimmering blue cloth and handed it to Mary.

Mary took it with trembling hands. "It's so soft and beautiful—it's like the peacock feather," she gasped.

"It's silk, a cloth from a land at the farthest end of the world. Put it on."

Mary stood and replaced her old black head covering with the beautiful blue cloth. Artelia smiled. "It's stunning. You should always wear blue." She nodded to an attendant, who brought a shiny silver mirror over to Mary. "Take that over to the light and look."

Mary took the mirror with nervous hands and walked over to the door. She hadn't held a mirror more than a half-dozen times in her life and certainly not in the years since her children had grown. She occasionally noticed her reflection as she bent over a wash basin, but a face floating in rippling water was not a true image.

But when she looked at her face in the mirror she was glad to see she didn't look bad. And the blue cloth on her head was gorgeous. She had never seen any cloth this beautiful before.

"Artelia, I don't have the words—"

"You're welcome. You won't want to wear it every day, but on special occasions I think you'll enjoy having something nice."

"Oh, I will."

"And now that I know blue is your color, I'll have some ordinary blue cloth sent over to you so that you can wear it every day."

"Oh, I don't think—"

"Don't argue. I don't want to see you wear that awful black anymore."

Mary smiled. "Everyone dresses like this back home."

"Do you want everyone who sees you to stare at you because you look so strange?" Artelia scolded.

"No," Mary said solemnly, remembering the child who'd mistaken her for a Judean fortune teller. "I do not. Thank you, Artelia. You are very kind. I wish I had something to give you."

"You have given me your friendship, Mary; that's a great gift indeed. Because of my position, there aren't many people I can speak with frankly and openly. I'm grateful to know you. You won't believe this, I know, but I think your presence here is a gift from the Queen of Heaven."

Mary removed the precious cloth from her head and refolded it, replacing it with a length of simple linen held out to her by one of Artelia's attendants. She would take all of these fabrics to the synagogue to examine for shatnez before she made any of them into garments, but she didn't need to mention that to Artelia "You know, I know of another goddess who's called the 'Queen of Heaven.'"

"Oh?"

"Yes. Women back home use that name to refer to a goddess named Asherah. Some women in my hometown used to put up Asherah poles in secret and have figures of Asherah in their homes, but they would never discuss it with me. I think she used to be the wife of the God Most High, but I don't really know anything else. The priests say terrible things about her, so she must have been very powerful."

"I've never heard the name Asherah," Artelia said, "but poles, or trees, are often used in worship of the Heavenly Goddess in Her guise as Creator of Nature. This is another of the mysteries that I think I can tell you, because you mentioned the Asherah poles, and, of course, you are the guardian of the sacred spring." Artelia spoke to her slaves, and they all left the proseuche, closing the door behind them. Mary and Artelia sat alone together in the darkened room, lit only by lamps and the sunlight that peeped through the open window.

"This Asherah—did she have anything to do with bees?" Artelia asked.

Mary thought for a moment. "I don't know," she said finally. "I never heard it mentioned."

"I'm sure she did. It's another part of the mysteries. Like the zodiac and the star eggs, it's another way to look at the body of Artemis. You see, Artemis is also a tree god. She lives in Her body like a bird lives in a tree. Think about Her statue—how straight She stands; Her crown, like new growth on the top of a palm tree; Her arms, held out at Her waist like limbs on a tree."

Mary thought about the statue and realized that yes the idol did stand like a tree would stand. "Yes, I can see it."

"Some people see Her tree body and think the eggs are bird eggs, but that's not true. In this guise, She is the Queen Bee. She is covered with bee eggs, popping out from the beehive held inside Her trunk. Her headdress looks like a beehive—bees are associated with palm trees, you know. The gold we paint on Her reflects the fact that She streams with honey. One of our most sacred dances is the bee dance, and the bee keeper, the Melissa, is one of the most important priestesses at the Temple. The next time you look on Artemis, you'll notice that another of the creatures you'll see decorated all over Her body is the bee. And when you look at Her plaques, statues, and fountains in town or at the clothing worn by Her priestesses and attendants, you'll begin to notice the bee motif." Artelia pointed to her own chiton, and Mary noticed for the first time that the lovely embroidery around the collar of her dress was a depiction of bees in flight.

"So the eggs are star eggs and they're also bee eggs?" Mary found this very confusing.

"The eggs of Artemis have several other important meanings as well, but I can't speak of them today. Maybe never. But one thing you should know: from the smallest to the largest, all is the same. The bee egg is the same as the star egg. Things on the earth are in sympathy with those up above. And that's as much as I should say on this for now."

Mary remembered something John had said. "I've been told that Artemis is a moon goddess, but you told me before that she's the goddess of the sun."

Artelia sighed. "Yes, that's one of the ways our Artemis gets confused with the Greek Artemis and Roman Diana. Diana is the goddess of the moon and of the hunt—that's who she is, and as I said, we allow people to confuse Artemis Ephesia with this foreign goddess. And Artemis Ephesia may seem like a moon goddess, for two reasons. First, Earth's twin planet, which we never see because it's on the other side of the sun, is sometimes depicted by a crescent, which people confuse with the moon. The mystery of the twin planets is another thing I can't discuss with you, unfortunately, but it's essential to having full understanding of Artemis Ephesia. And second, many of our most common rituals are connected with the cycles of a woman's flow, which are regulated by the moon."

"We have a new moon ceremony every month. It's just for women."

Artelia nodded. "I'll bet the tradition was started when your people still worshipped Asherah."

"It's all very interesting. But I'm not sure if Asherah is also a queen bee. All I know is that she was supposed to be the wife of God."

"You should always focus on what a god does, not what a god is, because once you start saying what the god is, you put limits on them," Artelia said. "For example, the moon symbolizes our physical self and the sun symbolizes our spirit. If we say Artemis is the Goddess of the Moon—our body—does that mean she can't also be the Goddess of the Sun—our spirit? And vice versa: since Artemis is the Goddess of the Sun, doesn't that imply She is not also the Goddess of the Moon, the Stars, or the Earth? Because of course She is the Queen of the Cosmos, the Lord of all that is. She is the Totality. And even calling Artemis a 'she' and the god of Judea a 'he' limits them, because if you think of a god as being male or female, you deny him or her the attributes of the other. If you say that Asherah is the wife of your god, doesn't that mean your god is simply a man and does not have the essential qualities of woman—the ability to create, to give birth, to nurture?"

Mary thought about all the verses she'd heard in her life describing God. "He's often described as vengeful, angry, jealous, and punishing, a loving father but stern. But the wisdom of God is a woman, who invites all who love simplicity to eat at her table. Her house is the world and her pillars are the pillars of heaven."

Artelia grinned with delight. "I didn't tell you why bees are important to Artemis. The bees of the Holy Mother represent wisdom, which can be extracted from the experiences of daily life in the same way that pollen is extracted from the flowers. And the beehive itself shows the great bee wisdom: even the finest architect cannot design a building as complex as a beehive. So when we say Artemis is the Queen Bee, we mean she is the Queen of Wisdom. I think it's very interesting that the wisdom of your God is a woman."

"She came out of God's mouth and existed before the beginning of creation," Mary said. "And sometimes God is described like a woman. For example, when King David spoke about how wonderfully he had been made, he said that when God created his inmost being He knit him together in his mother's womb."

"That's lovely," Artelia said. "In fact, I think that's the prettiest thing I've ever heard about your god."

Then she stood and walked to the door, speaking loudly in Greek, and her slaves returned inside to pack the things away for the trip back to the temple.

After hugging Mary good-bye, Artelia stepped into her litter and was lifted up by the bearers. "You should never come to the Temple unaccompanied again, because there are many criminals around. They come to seek sanctuary and stay to cause mischief. I'll send someone up here regularly to check on you, and if you want to visit me you should return with him."

Mary smiled. "All right." She watched the small procession as it took the path leading to the road downhill. Then she went to her room to put her lovely new things away.

She thought: "My son, if the wisdom of God is a woman, why cannot women study the Word of God?"

7

"Everything has its season, its joy and its sorrow."

Six months later

"John, will you please have someone take Adonis down to the baths?" Mary asked. "He's a dear man, but his stench is unbearable, and Rebekkah told me that some of the women are avoiding the proseuche because they can't stand to be near him. He refuses to bathe in the mikvah because the water's so cold."

John laughed. "I'll see to it today, Mother."

Mary felt sorry about having to make this request. The only reason that she was able to understand the women when they complained to her about Adonis was because he was such an excellent language teacher. But he had responded to the loss of his eyesight, hearing, and sense of smell in his old age by behaving as though everyone else also lacked those capabilities. She had the feeling, from some things he'd mentioned, that long ago he'd been a vain and handsome man, worthy of the name Adonis, but now that he couldn't see himself he no longer cared how he looked to others. He'd completely lost his sense of smell and had become oblivious to the odor of his own body. Some nights when she lay down to sleep she found her ears still ringing from the loudness of his voice as he shouted his lessons at her all day. And she worried that some of the stench he emitted might be due to an illness inside—but until the outside of his body was completely clean, she hesitated to ask a doctor to examine him.

Adonis was a philosopher, a Skeptic. He believed that it was impossible to know absolute truth or absolute falseness—denied, in fact, the very existence of "knowledge," because there was always information that was presently unknown that would make the thing "known" today to be false. Therefore he questioned everything and trusted nothing. He said that the deterioration of his own body was the best example he could give to the legitimacy of this approach—if you couldn't trust the truth of your own experience, then what could you trust? Mary said he smelled bad, but he couldn't detect any objectionable odor, so what was the real truth?

Skepticism had gone out of fashion in the gymnasia of Ephesus, where most of the teachers were Stoics or Epicureans. Adonis despised both of these schools, but particularly the Stoics. The Stoics, he said, believed in fate, gods, and virtue—which they believed they had sufficient knowledge to define. He said that the Epicureans, who focused on the attainment of happiness through simple pleasures, at least knew how to enjoy life. But the Stoics not only denied pleasure to themselves, they also denied it to others, judging others by their own standards of virtue.

The most insulting word Adonis had for a person was "Stoic."

Mary could hardly believe she had lived most of her life without ever hearing any of these terms. She now felt she could almost teach at the gymnasium herself, so thoroughly schooled did she feel in Greek philosophy.

She disagreed with the Skeptic view, not that Adonis ever heard her when she argued with him. She thought his intermittent deafness was suspiciously convenient because it meant he didn't need to listen to her when she talked about the Lord God or the Temple or the various rituals of purification that structured her—and now his—life. He completely ignored all Judean elements of his life here at the mikvah. He never attended synagogue or the First Day meetings of the Disciples of John the Baptist, held in the mornings at Alexander's house, or even the dinner meetings John had started to hold here in the proseuche at the end of First Day, where he taught about the signs that showed Jesus was the Messiah. Adonis was happy to attend festivals as long as people fed him, but he certainly never participated in the prayers or worship.

But Mary had to admit he was consistent. He despised worship of all gods and would say the most dreadful things about the gods of Greece and Rome—even about Artemis Ephesia. He would quote an old Ephesian philosopher named Heraclitus, who said that praying to a statue was like talking to a house. At least Adonis was polite enough to never say anything derogatory about the Lord God of the Hebrews. He simply ignored everything to do with Him.

Adonis believed that the search for wisdom was the most important thing people could do in their lives and that believing you had accomplished your search was the most foolish. He had no time for the so-called great thinkers and leaders of his day, and he claimed to despise politics. His favorite saying was: "When the tyrants govern, man is ruled by fear; when the priests are in charge, he is ruled by superstition; and when the people rule, he is ruled by ignorance."

Luckily Alexander and Artelia found him amusing and never seemed offended by his insults about the local, regional, or Roman political foibles of the day, many of which they were both embroiled in. He was always remarkably well-informed—a fact that constantly astonished Mary, since he was half deaf and almost blind and spent his days and nights up on a hill at a Judean mikvah, where most of the visitors were women who did their best to ignore him. Yet somehow he always seemed to know what was going on in the city below. Mary did not practice Skepticism, but she admitted to being skeptical about someone who claimed to despise politics yet seemed always to know so much about it.

"What month is it?" Adonis yelled at her suddenly, interrupting John who had been trying to reason with him.

"Mar Cheshvan," she yelled back, giving the Hebrew name for the month.

"Don't try to hex me with your heathen words!" he yelled. "What month is it?"

"October," she yelled back, giving the Latin name.

"Bah! You'll never be anything but a barbarian!" he yelled. "What month is it?"

"Do you mean Karneios?" she yelled back sweetly, giving the local Greek name for the month.

"Is it Karneios already?" he bellowed. "How quickly a year passes! I guess you're right!" he yelled at John. "It is time for me to take a bath!"

John laughed and helped the old man to his feet, trying not to grimace as the man's stench surrounded him. "I'll either take him to a bath in town or let him use the bath at the house, Mother," John yelled at Mary. "Whichever one he wants. Either way, I'll keep him at home tonight and bring him back in the morning."

"John, you don't need to yell at me. I can hear just fine. And don't hurry back—this will give me a chance to get his tent cleaned up and his bedding washed. In fact, just keep him there tomorrow, since I'll be coming over in the afternoon for Sabbath anyway."

"Don't worry too much about cleaning up his tent, Mother. Father said Adonis should stay at our house through the winter so you won't be always worrying about whether or not he's warm enough during the cold nights."

"Still, I'm going to give his tent a good airing. It looks like a rat's been nesting in there—and no doubt many have been. And please do something about his teeth."

"Eh?" Adonis yelled, blasting John with his dreadful breath. "Are you two talking about me again?"

"I'll borrow Deborah's toothpowder," John promised Mary. "And maybe even her soap." Deborah had fallen in love with the lavender soap and had no qualms about spending inordinate amounts of money to purchase it.

Mary grinned at the thought of Adonis smelling of lavender. "Excellent idea."

John and Adonis made their slow and creaky walk down the hill. Just before they reached the break in the wall to the city, they were passed by a small group of women coming uphill toward the mikvah. Mary knew all three of the women, members of Lavi's synagogue.

The woman in front was Esther, a mikvah regular. She had a recurring skin disease in which her skin became rough and scaly and flaked off in little patches. She came to be purified every time the skin on her face and arms cleared up. Each time Mary sprinkled Esther with hyssop before immersing her in water, she noticed small patches of the disease still remaining on parts of the woman's body—her back sometimes or sometimes her legs. As the priestly substitute on purification matters for the Hebrew women in Ephesus, Mary was supposed to examine the woman and pronounce her cured and clean or still diseased and impure. If she named her cured, the woman could go back to her regular life. But if she was still diseased, she would be expected to remain in the leper's tent her family had constructed for her, repenting in solitude for whatever moral failing had caused her to receive this punishment from God.

Mary had spent enough time with Esther by now to know she was a kind, sensitive, timid, and devoted soul, incapable of any grievous sin. When she came up to the mikvah she was always so sincere and sorrowful, so saddened by the latest rebuke from God that Mary never mentioned the remaining lesions she noticed, even though she knew that was precisely what she was expected to do. Those parts of the woman's skin would be covered by her clothes anyway.

Jesus had healed lepers of their disease. Mary often wished she could do that, but she didn't have the gift of healing the body. She could, however, help to ease a sorrowful heart.

When Esther came to the mikvah, the other women with her always purified first. Mary had Esther purify last so that she could flush out the bath after they left. She didn't really believe anyone could catch the woman's skin disease, especially in the pure living water of the mikvah, but she felt she would be doing her other visitors an injustice if she didn't take this small act of prevention. Everyone loved Esther and no doubt her family and friends were happy not to question when Mary always pronounced her clean, so long as the water she bathed in was refreshed afterwards.

She saw that Myia was one of the women with Esther. This surprised Mary, because Myia was heavy with child, expecting to give birth in just a couple of months more. The trek uphill to the mikvah was hard work for someone so pregnant. Mary realized that something was terribly wrong.

The other woman with Esther was Mary's friend Judith. Judith was Lavi's wife, a fashionable, genial, talkative woman a few years older than Mary. She had no sense of decorum, and consequently Mary now knew much more about Lavi than she had ever wanted to know about any man she wasn't herself married to.

Judith always stayed in the proseuche while the others bathed, enjoying the food and company. In all her visits, she had never once used the mikvah bath herself. She told Mary that she didn't need to subject herself to the cold water of the mikvah because she no longer had her moon and she was no longer having sexual relations with her husband. She came to the proseuche frequently, though, because she liked the company and the pretty walk up the hill. She had been here just a few days ago with her daughter Rebekkah.

Hearing the explanation from Judith about why she didn't need to purify anymore had provided a flash of enlightenment for Mary, who had previously not understood why married women were not allowed in the temple of Artemis. But now she wondered if it was a purity issue, and the last time she saw Artelia she had asked her about it. Artelia reminded her that, to Artemis, moon blood was sacred, not impure. But she said that Mary was right about the other—married women were polluted because of their sexual activity with their husbands and were therefore not permitted in the temple of Artemis. "No man can lift the veil of Artemis," she said, and Mary understood this to be one of their commandments. Once women were widowed and no longer engaging in sexual relations, they were allowed to return to the temple to worship.

Of course this didn't explain why married men were allowed in the temple. But when asked, Artelia told Mary that this was one of the things she couldn't talk about.

Mary hurriedly checked to ensure there was adequate toweling in the dressing tent in case her visitors had forgotten to bring their own, changed into her water robe, and then set water on the hearth fire in the proseuche in preparation for her guests.

Judith led the other two inside. "Brr, it's getting cold," she said, walking over to warm her hands at the fire. Judith always complained about the cold, even during the summer. Mary set a couple of warm furs on the floor near her friend's favorite cushion, then welcomed her other visitors. She was concerned to see that Myia's face was pale and sorrowful.

"Sit down everyone, and we'll have tefilah, our prayers," Mary said.

"Time for the tevilah tefilah!" Judith said jovially. They had developed the practice of sitting for their pre-immersion prayers and standing for the prayers after the tevilah bath. Judith, who knew very few Hebrew words, enjoyed referring to these prayers as the "tevilah tefilah."

After prayers, Judith started the tea preparations while Mary escorted Myia to the dressing room. After she unclothed, Mary helped the pregnant woman carefully walk the stone steps down to the bath. Before she performed the hyssop purification, she asked the question she had wondered about ever since she saw Myia pass through the break in the city wall today.

"Myia, why are you here?" she asked gently. "Why are you seeking purification?"

The woman, who had been on the edge of tears the entire time, finally released them. "There's something wrong with the baby," she said, sobbing.

Mary, frowning, bent down to place her hand on the rounded belly. She felt no movement. She felt all over Myia's belly with both hands. It felt hard and lumpy, as a belly full of baby should. The baby was there—she could practically outline its shape with her hands. But the baby, who should be moving around kicking his mother, was perfectly still.

"Oh my dear," Mary said. "What does the midwife say?"

"She's the one who sent me here today. She said that perhaps the exercise and the cold water of the bath would wake the baby up." Her heavy breasts leaked fluid, and her eyes were drenched with tears.

"Well then, let's hope she's right," Mary said, although she knew this was false hope. There was no life in Myia's womb.

Mary performed the short hyssop purification and then helped the weeping woman into the chilly water, allowing herself to become completely soaked as she very carefully assisted Myia in three complete immersions.

Afterwards she stood outside while Myia changed, shivering slightly in her wet robe as she pondered the truth of Myia's dreadful situation. She wouldn't change into dry clothes until after Esther's skin inspection and immersion was completed.

When she entered the proseuche after Esther's tevilah, she saw that Gilana the laundress was there, visiting with Judith while Myia stood warming herself at the fire. Seeing Myia, Mary wondered again what comfort she could give the poor woman.

"I'll be right out," Mary said, entering her room to change her clothes while the others waited in the proseuche room. Everyone in the community continued to call the building the "proseuche," even though they'd all finally realized it would never be a true place of prayer. The building was a place where women met to pray, but it was impossible to have a real prayer service without a minyan of at least ten men. Even the Friends of Jesus guild meetings that were held here never included that many men.

"Where's that old fool got to?" Gilana yelled at her. She and Adonis loved to torment each other.

Judith answered. "We passed him and John on our way here. John helped him walk, but I don't know where they were going." Judith deeply regretted that her husband, Lavi, had broken the engagement between John and her daughter Martha, and she was always interested in his comings and goings, worried that he might become engaged to another woman.

"Adonis is staying at John's house for a few days," Mary said tactfully from her room, not wanting to gossip about Adonis' hygiene. She finished dressing and walked back into the larger room, smiling to see that Esther had joined Myia at the fire. The fire in the hearth at the proseuche was a popular feature of the mikvah.

"Let's pray," Mary said. Her friends were in the mood to chat, and she wanted to complete the purification ceremony before the conversation became mundane. The women obediently stood for closing prayers.

Afterwards Judith walked over to a side table, returning with full hands. "The peacock feathers are gorgeous in your new vase," she said, setting the tall blue glass vase down on the tea table centered between the cushions.

"It's a very beautiful vase," Mary said. "It was a gift from Judith," she added to the others.

"What a generous gift!" Gilana said, admiring it.

"It certainly was." Mary smiled at Judith.

"You needed something very special to hold the beautiful feathers." Judith was an elegant woman—her bright wigs, cosmetics, and rich, colorful clothes were always in the highest style. She wanted desperately for Mary to let her take some peacock feathers home with her, and Mary would have been glad to do so, but Artelia's strictures were quite clear. No one but Mary could have them.

"The eyes on those feathers are incredible," Gilana said.

"When I look at them, I always think about the eyes of God," Mary said. This was the reason she felt so blessed to have the peacock feathers—they'd awakened her to a new awareness of the eyes of God. Now she saw God's eyes everywhere: in the wings of butterflies, in knotholes in trees, in ripples in water; even the sky above she now saw as God's eye, with the sun a bright yellow pupil. In town recently she had noticed depictions of a sacred eye built into architecture, drawn on doors and hanging in windows, and had learned that people in Ephesus used this image to repel evil. Although she did not know which god they honored, she certainly understood the inspiration for the image.

It seemed so fantastic that it would be here, so far away from God's Temple, right in the heart of idol worship, where she should find herself the most aware of the presence of God, most aware of His eyes watching her.

Esther frowned. "Are the peacock feathers a graven image then?"

"A symbol, maybe," Gilana said. "One made by God, so who can complain?"

"When I look at the peacock feathers, I don't see God," Judith said. "I see necklaces and earrings and mantle clasps. I see beautiful jewelry that I will never be able to make, because Mary says I cannot have any of these feathers. So instead I come here and look at the feathers and dream of my wonderful jewelry that will never be born."

She caught herself, appalled at her own words as she saw Myia staring down at her big belly, her protruding navel yet another eye of god. "Did the cold tevilah help, my dear?" Judith asked gently. "Did that lazy baby of yours wake up yet?"

Myia shook her head. "I don't think so," she said quietly, her voice thick with sorrow.

"I think we need some special prayers," Mary said. She moved next to Myia and gathered her big, bulky body into her arms. The other women huddled around them, tears flowing as Mary rocked Myia and prayed in Aramaic, a language the other women did not know. Mary knew that the baby inside Myia was dead. She prayed that God would allow her to pass the dead baby in peace, without pain, and that Myia would become pregnant again soon with a strong and healthy child. Then she prayed to the angel spirit of the baby, asking him to help his mother through this terrible time.

And then she prayed to her own dead child, her own sweet baby Jesus. She asked her son to be with Myia and her family, to bring them strength, comfort, and peace. "Let them feel you with them," she asked. "Let them know they are not alone."

When the women stood to leave, Mary pulled Myia to the side and said, "Please let me know how you go on and if there's anything I can do to help you." She hugged each of the women and they left, and then Mary put on the water robe again, damp but warm from the heat of the hearth, and she went down into the mikvah to flush out any impurity left from the improper immersion of the woman with skin disease lesions still remaining on the backs of her knees.

Later that afternoon, after it was clear the visitors were done for the day and after one of Alexander's slaves had dropped off her evening meal, Mary walked the path through the trees to the labyrinth.

The sky was darkening, and she held a lamp in her hand as she slowly walked the circuits. She walked the labyrinth every day, morning and evening. She walked very slowly, with great intention, feeling every movement of every muscle, every beat of her heart, and every breath in and out, sometimes taking as long as a summer hour to reach the center.

In the mornings, as the sun rose and the birds sang their wake-up songs, she thought about her Jesus as she walked, each circuit of the path representing a different aspect of his life and death. During the morning ritual into the center, Mary focused all of her attention on her son. This once-daily concentration unleashed her from the obsessive reflections that had so tortured her in the past. She never found herself crying for no reason during the course of the day any more. Her weeping was restricted now to these morning walks, when sometimes her body would release so much water through her tears that she would later emerge from the woods parched with thirst, her eyes sore and red and her lips chapped and dry. When her tearful shuffles finally reached the center of the labyrinth each morning she would pause to rest and settle her emotions at the beech tree. When her soul felt calm she walked the circuit away from the center, letting her heart fill with gratitude at the great blessing God had given her in allowing her to have Jesus as her son.

In the evenings when she had to hold a lantern against the darkening sky, she thought about the presence of God in the experiences of the day. She thought about each of her interactions and how she could have been kinder or more helpful to others. She thought about the unexpected blessings the day brought and gave thanks. The evening walk through the labyrinth was when she allowed herself to fully feel her connection with God.

Walking the labyrinth at night was very different from the walk in the mornings. She felt as one being with the dark sky, as though the light from her lantern and the stars twinkling above her were one and the same thing. As she walked the twists and turns of the circuits, going back and forth yet always ahead, she felt like one of the constellations—the Pisces, perhaps—and felt in her body an awareness and connection with her God that she knew was the same connection that the priestesses of Artemis must have felt when they performed their sun dances up here.

Tonight she reflected on Adonis, praying that the old man was suffering from nothing more serious than a dirty body. She thanked God for John, expressing her deep gratitude for the love she had for the young man, a prayer she made every night. She thought about Esther, able to enjoy a meal with her family tonight, and prayed that her disease would remain in abatement for a long time.

She thought about Judith, making the best she could of her life with a difficult husband, and of Gilana, the arthritic fingers of her hands swollen with cold water pain. She thought, as always, about her family back home in Judea and prayed that they were safe and happy and that she would see them again someday.

And most of all, tonight, she thought and prayed about Myia. She felt a huge weight wrapped around her heart and knew that Myia's burden and sorrow had only just begun. Mary had never heard about a baby that died inside the mother without being born and prayed that the poor dead thing would release its hold on Myia's womb very soon. Mary knew that as soon as Lavi and the other leaders of Myia's synagogue became aware of her condition, she might be cast out of the assembly as the ultimate in impurity: a living, walking tomb. As long as Myia carried a dead baby inside her, everyone who came into contact with her would be made impure and would remain impure for seven days after the contact.

The proper thing today would have been for Mary to announce the baby's death and pronounce Myia, herself, and the three other women who'd been near Myia polluted. And perhaps that would have also been the kindest thing she could have done—kinder perhaps than letting the midwife make the announcement back home where Myia's presence would render her entire family impure.

But somehow this didn't feel right to Mary. She didn't believe God wanted her to pronounce anyone unclean. Her role was to provide comfort and compassion, not to facilitate anyone's ostracism or isolation.

And as she thought about this, drifting with infinitesimal slowness around the twisting circuits of the dark night labyrinth like a human constellation, she felt God move in her heart and knew that she was right. She knew too that as long as she remained here in this place, doing this work, she would never cause anyone pain if it was in her power to give them comfort instead.

She stood for a few moments in the center, praying, and then she slowly followed the ciruits away from the center back to her life, her heart filled with gratitude at the blessings of the day.

She thought: "My son, if the eyes of God watch from every part of His creation, then He is both watcher and watched. Are the sorrows He witnesses His? Is He both comforter and comforted? Bereaver and bereaved?"

CHAPTER 8

"Can God's embrace enfold all the clashing hearts?"

Mary served as hostess at the Sabbath meal at Alexander's home the next night. She had assumed this role because Aspasia, Enoch's wife, was too timid to take on such responsibilities and Deborah had married and left home to run her own household. John wanted Mary and his father to wed, and Mary knew that Alexander would have been amenable if she had ever given him the slightest encouragement. But Mary had no desire to remarry. Alexander had the good sense to recognize this and not pressure her about it. She would be his hostess when necessary, and both were satisfied with that.

She found Adonis sitting happily in the kitchen, waiting for food to be served. He would not be joining the others at dinner, not only because he was a gentile but also because there would be non-family members present and he couldn't be trusted not to say anything blasphemous. She sat down next to him and was glad to realize that being near him wasn't an unpleasant experience anymore. Only a slight sickly odor remained.

"Are you having a nice visit?" she asked.

"Food's good. But the hospitality needs some improvement."

"How so?"

"Well, it's been years since I entertained anyone, so my ideas might be out of date, but I must say I don't approve of this new fashion of chucking your guests into a bath the instant they enter your house."

"And making them wear new clothes too, I see."

"And rubbing their gums raw with a bristly twig. I'm surprised there's a tooth left in my head."

She sniffed. "And they made you chew some mint too, I think."

"Pah! Nasty stuff that."

"Did you like the lavender soap?"

"That was the only good part about it. Now all the pretty young things keep looking for an excuse to sniff my neck."

He smiled at her and she slapped at him.

"I hope you weren't too attached to the vermin in your tent, because I evicted them."

He shrugged. "There's more where they came from."

"Adonis, it's getting colder now, and Alexander wants you to stay here for the winter. Did you want to just remain here now or do you want to spend another month or so up at the proseuche?"

He thought for a moment then said, "There aren't as many pretty girls here. I'll go back with you on First Day."

Mary smiled at his use of the Greek words depicting a Judean concept—the day after Sabbath, which the Israelites called "First Day"—instead of using the Greek name "Day of the Sun." She clasped a hand to his shoulder, then left to supervise the meal.

After dinner she spoke with Jacob, a doctor. She asked him if he would examine Adonis to see if there was something serious causing the faint sour odor that remained.

"After sunset tomorrow, I will," he promised. "Before I leave to go home."

"You won't stay tomorrow night?"

"I have to spend all day Sunday preparing for the big medical competition," he said, using the Greek word for First Day. She smiled at the incongruity.

"Well, I hope your visit with Adonis won't take too long."

"You must know that anything that's wrong with him is caused by sin. I might be able to relieve a little pain, but no true healing can occur unless he repents of his sin."

Mary sighed. "Adonis doesn't believe in sin. He certainly won't repent of it."

Jacob shrugged. "I'll see what I can do."

But when he examined the annoyed old man after sunset the next evening, he discovered that there was very little that he could do.

"He has a tumor in his belly," Jacob told Mary and Alexander in private. "He won't live long. If he was a young man, devout, otherwise healthy, I would say an operation might save his life. But he's old and unrepentant, and the operation would no doubt kill him. Keep him comfortable. Encourage him to eat, because pretty soon he's going to lose his appetite."

"I'm surprised he's not in pain, if he's that sick," Mary said.

"He's in terrible pain," Jacob said, surprised. "Why would you think he wasn't?"

"He has never said a single word about it," she said quietly. "Not one word of complaint, ever."

"He's an amazing man," Alexander said.

"Very brave, if what you say is true," Jacob said.

"Is there anything we can do for the pain?"

Jacob shrugged. "You could feed him opium. I have a little with me, and you can get more from any herbalist. If he hesitates to take it, you should mix it in his wine."

"I'll have opium and wine sent up with you in the morning," Alexander told Mary.

Mary felt terrible. "For months he's been complaining because I don't keep wine up at the proseuche. I've made him drink water, like the women do. But wine might have given him a little relief."

Alexander gave her a slight, compassionate smile. "Mary, he's an adult. It's his pride that kept him from relief, not you. If he had even once told you that he was in pain, you would have given him anything to alleviate it."

"His simple request for wine should have been enough for me. Who am I to deny someone their pleasure just because it isn't mine?" She knew this was an important lesson for her, but she was sorry it came at Adonis' expense.

"Now you sound like him, railing against the judgmental Stoics," Alexander said. "Thank you, Jacob, we appreciate your help." He handed the doctor a couple of coins and the physician left.

Mary and Alexander walked to the triclinium, where the First Day guests waited to dine before spending the night and attending the Disciples of John the Baptist guild meeting in the morning. She saw that there were two new people here tonight—God Fearers who had attended synagogue for a few weeks and had now decided they would like to attend the First Day assembly as well.

God Fearers were Greeks who recognized that the Lord God of the Hebrews was the one true God. The Hebrews, who believed the Messiah was coming soon, bringing the worship of the God Most High to all people, were happy to welcome the God Fearers into the assembly as long as they followed the commandments. For the most part this wasn't a hardship, and most God Fearers were willing to adopt most Laws including the dietary rules and commandments about worship. Only one commandment presented a true stumbling block: the commandment of circumcision. Greeks had a horror of bodily mutilation and few Greek men had sufficient faith to subject their bodies to this most essential requirement.

The Israelites allowed God Fearers to attend their assemblies and most festivals even without circumcision, but they made it clear that unless a man was circumcised, he would not be found acceptable by God and would not be allowed to be schooled in the Torah. Consequently most God Fearers were women and several had become regular attendees at the mikvah and the monthly new moon ceremonies that Mary held at the proseuche.

However, both members of this new couple were devout in their adoption of Judean ways. Narcissus had been circumcised and now received private Hebrew instruction. His wife, Calandra, had accompanied Deborah to the mikvah last week, and she seemed to appreciate the purification rituals. Enoch had baptized both of them at the mikvah, as he did all God Fearer converts after circumcision.

After the blessing, Mary walked over to them. "Welcome, Calandra! Welcome, Narcissus!" she said to the couple who reclined a bit apart from the rest of the gathering. Eating a common meal with gentiles defiled Hebrews, and someone thus defiled was not supposed to participate in other religious observances until purified. God Fearers who converted were accepted into the assembly, but their presence still made the Israelites uncomfortable. "May I join you?" she asked, sitting down on a cushion near Calandra's head. Immediately other people moved nearer to join them. Aspasia, nursing Seth, her baby son, engaged Calandra in conversation.

Mary smiled gratefully at the young mother then nodded to Epenetus, the head slave, to begin serving.

Hannah, revered as Mother of the Synagogue, sat nearby. She did not attend the Disciples of John the Baptist meetings, but she often spent the First Day night at Alexander's anyway so that she wouldn't have to walk home in the dark. Mary decided to speak with her about an idea she'd been considering ever since Jacob's examination of Adonis.

"Hannah, I seek your advice about something," she said respectfully. Mary did not know Hannah well, since she did not use the mikvah (no doubt for the same reasons as Judith) and did not visit the proseuche.

"Yes, Mary?" the older woman said.

"Do you know Adonis, my teacher?"

Hannah smiled slightly. "We have never met, but I have heard a great deal about him," she said.

Mary nodded. No doubt everyone here knew a great deal about Adonis. Well, that should make things easier. "I have been concerned about his health and asked Jacob to examine him."

Hannah smiled more broadly, and Mary remembered that Jacob was the woman's son. That could only help.

"Unfortunately, Jacob found that Adonis has a tumor in his belly. He said that my teacher does not have long to live. He also said that he is in considerable pain, even though he has never once complained to me about it."

"Oh, that's very sad. I am so sorry."

"Yes, so am I. I am quite fond of the old man. And I'm concerned about how to care for him. He's all alone in the world, you know. Except for me. And Alexander, of course, who's been a good friend to him."

Most of the table now listened to the conversation, which was good because she wanted everyone's acceptance of her plan.

"Hannah, I want to put a cot for Adonis in the proseuche. I want him to be able to spend the rest of his life sleeping next to the fire at night, near enough to me that I can care for him if he takes a bad turn. But the proseuche belongs to the community, and I don't want to do anything to cause concern or show disrespect or dishonor. I am a woman alone and Adonis is a Greek. What would you advise?"

Hannah thought for a moment, the center of attention as all waited to hear her words. "Could Adonis not be cared for here?" she asked.

"Yes, of course. But I think he would be happier with me. He enjoys living at the proseuche. I would prefer to not take that away from him. But if you think it necessary, we will of course move him to Alexander's home, where he would be well cared for." She glanced at Alexander, reclining at the front of the room, and was glad to see his smile of approval.

Hannah nodded. "It's kind of you to consider the poor man's wishes in this. It's unfortunate, really, that he's a Greek citizen. If he were your slave, it would be your duty to care for him. You could let him sleep wherever you wanted."

Mary was not familiar with all the rules of slave ownership. "I don't think he would allow himself to be enslaved," she said doubtfully, "even under these circumstances."

"No, of course not. Nor should he have to. He's been a good friend to all the Israelites in Ephesus. We owe him a great debt."

"How so?" Mary asked in surprise.

"He taught you to speak our language, my dear," Hannah said gently. "Because of him, we can all communicate with you. I don't think you know how important you've become to all of us. I often hear your name invoked, people saying 'I'll need to ask Mary about this' or 'I wonder what Mary would think about that.' We've become dependent upon your kindness, your wisdom, and your generosity. No one would ever question your motive for doing anything. You could move any number of Greek men into the proseuche and nobody would dare say a thing against it."

Several people cheered in agreement. But Mary noticed a few people frowning.

She put her hands to her embarrassed face. "Oh, how very kind you are, Hannah! All of you are. I'm so touched."

There were more cheers. She picked up a napkin from the table to wipe her damp eyes. "So you won't mind if I move Adonis indoors. How about Lavi's synagogue? Will they mind, do you think?" The few frowns she saw told her that some people here did mind. She would meet with them one by one, try to assuage their concerns.

"I'll visit tomorrow with Sarah, their Mother of the Synagogue, just to make sure they're fully informed of the situation," Hannah said.

"Thank you. And the Samaritans—you don't think they'll mind either?"

"I don't know why you should care if they do, but no, I'm sure they won't."

"I'll speak with old Isaac the Samaritan tomorrow," Theokritos volunteered from the end of the cushions across from her. "We have a gem-cutters guild meeting."

"Thank you. All of you, thank you." She looked around at these people who had been strangers to her only six short months ago. Her heart felt full to bursting now with love for them. What a blessing Ephesus had become to her.

"Alexander, I'm feeling so grateful. Would you please lead us in a prayer of thanksgiving?"

Alexander nodded, and they all rose as he recited one of the psalms of David.

After the Disciples of John the Baptist meeting the next morning, Mary and Adonis climbed into a mule cart for the ride back uphill to the proseuche. John walked alongside and a slave walked in front leading the mule. Carefully packed in the back of the cart were three amphorae of wine and a large plug of opium, plus a new bed pad and furs. Alexander had realized that although Mary might have gotten rid of the rats when she cleaned out his tent, Adonis' old bedclothes were no doubt still riddled with fleas, which she would not want to bring into her home.

"You'll have to come to synagogue with us every week," Mary teased Adonis. "They never send me home by cart when I come by myself—I always have to walk."

"Hmm?" Adonis said vaguely. A kitchen slave had shown Mary how to mix the opium and wine, and she had tried the concoction out on Adonis before they left. Opium was expensive and exotic and not something she had used before. She wondered if she had made it too strong.

John's weekly meeting of the Friends of Jesus guild was held at the proseuche late that afternoon. This guild had had a rocky start. For one thing, the name seemed weak. John's first choice of name was Disciples of Jesus, but he knew that name might alienate the Disciples of John the Baptist members who would otherwise be the most likely people to join this new guild. The most ideal name, of course, would have been Disciples of Jesus the Messiah, but John's father strongly opposed the use of that word to describe Mary's son.

"Jesus is the Messiah, Father," John had insisted. "The messianic age has begun."

"I'll believe the messianic age has begun when Hebrews rule the world and all people worship the one God," Alexander had said. "In the meantime, I'd prefer you not go around fomenting rebellion against the empire."

So they called themselves Friends of Jesus, a name which Mary secretly liked very much.

The second difficulty was choosing the time and place for meetings. Meetings that included meals always attracted a larger attendance than meetings without food. But Alexander, who already hosted large Sabbath and First Day dinners as well as Sabbath and First Day breakfasts for people who'd spent the night, was opposed to sponsoring a fifth community meal in his home every week.

There was really only one sensible place left—the home of Jesus' mother. The best day for the meeting, all agreed, was the afternoon of First Day, because then they could have the left-over food from the First Day meal of the night before, supplemented by dishes brought by members of the guild. They tried to finish their meeting in time for most people to walk home before dark because Mary's home was not large enough for people to sleep there—although she did keep pallets available for emergencies and for children who tired early. Unfortunately, having the meetings this early meant that often people couldn't attend because of other duties.

Several of Alexander's slaves came to the proseuche shortly after midday carrying food and extra cushions for seating. At the edge of the room, they set tables up with bread, bowls of food to dip or slather on the bread, olive oil, and pastes made of fish, barley, and dried vegetables such as chickpeas, cabbage, and garlic. They arranged pallets and cushions in a circle in the center of the room so that people could see each other while they ate and talked, and they set a few small tables in the center to hold plates of food and drink.

"Everything looks fine," Mary said to Epenetus, Alexander's chief slave, who had supervised the preparations. "Especially the stone basins of water and towels at the front bench—thank you for setting that up for me." John had told Mary about a dinner where Jesus had washed the feet of everyone who attended, and Mary was so moved by this that she had implemented a ritual at the guild meetings: she washed the feet of the first person who arrived and that person washed the feet of the next and so on. In this way, everyone both gave and received this loving attention.

"You're welcome, mistress," the man said. "We'll stay around and clean up for you afterwards."

Mary nodded. "Thank you, Epenetus." A sudden thought struck her. Epenetus was the head slave at Alexander's house, a slave of such high rank that he even owned slaves of his own. He certainly did not have to be here doing this menial work for her.

"Epenetus, why do you come here?" she asked.

He looked at her in surprise. "To serve you, mistress."

"Yes, but you could send anyone to do this work. Why do you come yourself?"

He looked down at the ground, embarrassed. "I like to hear Master John tell the stories about your son Jesus, mistress. I hope you do not mind."

She nodded. "And the others who come with you? Are they also interested in the stories?"

"Yes. The slaves who come here are all interested in hearing about your son and his miracles and teachings and his loving kindness to everyone. So much like you, mistress. We all wish we could have known him."

She glanced over at Adonis, snoring by the hearth, still under the influence of the opium she'd fed him that morning. He would no doubt have much to say later about what she was about to do.

"Epenetus, if you and the other slaves come to hear about Jesus, then you are members of this guild."

"Yes, mistress."

"And so from now on, during guild meetings, I expect you to behave as members."

"Mistress?"

"You may make the preparations for the meeting and clean up afterwards, because that is your duty. But while we are meeting—while we are eating together, listening to John, enjoying our 'love feast' as Adonis sarcastically calls it—I expect you and the others to join us as members of the guild. I believe slaves are allowed to join guilds?"

He sucked in his breath. "Yes, but I'm not sure Master Alexander would agree to this."

"I'll speak with him about it," Mary said firmly. Alexander had allowed his own son to marry a slave. She did not think there would be any difficulty about this.

"But mistress—most of us are not Judeans. Only Heron—he's the only one who's been circumcised."

"We allow the God Fearers to attend synagogue. All friends of Jesus are welcome here." She led Epenetus and the other slaves outside to the bench by the door and began their initiation as guild members by washing Epenetus' feet. When Enoch, Aspasia, and the other members arrived and moved to lineup by the door, Heron stood waiting to wash the feet of the first one in line.

The God Fearers Calandra, Narcissus, and their slave arrived. This was their first time at a Friends of Jesus meeting and the first time Narcissus had come to the proseuche. Their slave carried a covered dish, and while her owners stood in line for foot washing, she went into the proseuche to set the dish on the table with the rest of the food. Mary was grateful to see one of Alexander's slaves welcome the slave and lead her over to the cushions where the other slaves waited.

Calandra came over to Mary, beaming. "I love coming here," she said to Mary. "I told my husband how comfortable it is. I don't think he believed me when I told him you keep a real fire in the hearth."

"I see you brought a dish of food."

"Yes," Calandra said. "It's Narcissus' favorite dish, chicken with honey and fish sauce. I used to use pork when I made it, but of course not anymore. Now we use chicken, and although it's good, I must confess that it really does taste better with pork. I hope you like it."

"Let's join hands together in prayer," John said, stopping all conversation. But as they prayed, Mary knew that only half the attention of the guild members was on the prayer. The other half of their thoughts were: There's no pork in the dish Calandra brought, but the food was cooked in a pan that might have been used to cook pork. The bowl sitting on the table has probably held pork. The spoon in the bowl has been used in the past to serve many unclean things.

The fish sauce probably contains shellfish.

"Did she bring the utensils to the mikvah to be cleansed?" Junia whispered to Mary immediately after the prayer ended. Junia and her family were the members of the Disciples of John the Baptist guild who had been the most interested in joining the Friends of Jesus guild. Most people were dismissive of the Friends of Jesus because John, their leader, was so young and lacked authority. But Junia's family believed John's message that Jesus was the Messiah.

"No," Mary whispered back. Since Mary did not allow the slaves to serve, it was time for everyone to fill their own plates. But no one did. Calandra's bowl of chicken sat on the table like a turd, the room silent as people stared at the noxious dish, the only sound in the room the snores from the insensate Adonis curled up near the hearth.

"How was the chicken killed?" Enoch's wife Aspasia asked Calandra.

The woman was confused by the question. "My slave bought it in the market, fresh today. I don't know how it was killed."

Mary thought about all of the chickens she'd seen in the gentile market, hanging from their feet, their broken necks dangling; strangled, every one. Then she thought about the time, right here in this room, when Artelia's idol-worshipping slaves had served her food purchased from the Judean market and the promise she had made to herself then to always respect the intention behind the gift.

She carried her plate over to the food tables and gave herself a large serving of Calandra's chicken-with-fish-sauce. Like most people she usually ate meat only as a condiment, a flavoring for vegetables and grains, but now she loaded her plate with the chicken in Calandra's bowl. John followed and then Gilana. When finally the slaves served themselves, the bowl of chicken was quite empty and they were able to fill up on delicacies that would normally have been the first to go.

Mary was troubled that the slaves all waited until last to eat. She wanted them to feel they were full members of the guild, equal to everyone else in the sight of God and the love of Jesus. She decided that in future she would wait until they were served before she took her own food. Perhaps others would do the same.

She asked John if she could give the lesson today. This was the first time she had made such a request. She was not comfortable with public speaking, but she remembered some sayings of Jesus that she thought were important for people to hear.

She told them that her son had said that what went into a person's mouth did not defile them; rather, it was what came out of their mouth that could be defiling. She also related the story of the time Jesus told the twelve that they were to eat whatever God put in front of them.

This led to a spirited discussion in which even Epenetus participated, although the rest of the slaves remained silent. Mary felt gratitude toward everyone for their openness in considering the new ideas and was compassionate toward those who were still uncomfortable about eating polluted food. She reminded everyone at the end of the meal that there would be a new moon ceremony the following night, knowing this would give the women, at least, an opportunity to purify if they so chose.

After the closing prayer, Mary pulled Calandra aside and told her of the things she would need to do if she ever took food to Alexander's house or fed Israelites in her own house. Enoch's wife joined them.

"Will you take Calandra to the Judean food market and introduce her to our butcher?" Mary asked Aspasia.

Aspasia looked at Calandra with compassion. She knew what it was like to want to be a member of the community but not be fully accepted. Some people still treated her as though she were a slave instead of a beloved member of an important family. "I will be happy to do that."

The days were getting shorter. Dusk was nearing as the people left. Several people had brought napkins to pack up leftovers, so Epenetus and his assistants took only empty dishes home with them. The people left in groups, carrying torches since there was no moon to light the way. As Calandra, Narcissus, and their slave stood at the door to leave, Mary told them how glad she was that they had decided to join the Friends of Jesus guild. "And thank you for bringing the chicken," Mary said sincerely. "It was quite delicious."

She thought: "My son, may I always remember to honor the pure heart."

CHAPTER 19

"I must respect how others want to be treated, lest my assistance become another's burden."

When Adonis woke the next morning he complained loudly about his opium headache.

"I'm sorry, Adonis," Mary said. "But the doctor told me you're in great pain and that the opium would alleviate your distress."

"Did I ever ask you to alleviate my pain?"

"No, you've been very brave."

He brushed that aside. "Living with pain is my choice. You should not simply assume that your job is to alleviate the suffering of others, because you can never know what's best for another person."

"But you asked me for wine. I know that was for your pain."

"I asked you for wine because I like wine. But I don't like opium. At least not yet. Maybe at the end when the pain is unbearable, I'll ask you for opium. But I don't want it now."

"But I can't bear to think of you in pain," she protested.

"Find a way to bear it. The only thing in my life I can control now is my mind. I've lost my family, my friends, my home, my reputation, and my possessions. And now my body is going. I actually consider myself lucky—blessed, to use one of your words—because I still have my mind, the ability to think, to question, to reason. It's the most valuable of all my possessions and one which many other people in my age and condition lose straight away. In alleviating my pain, you stole one of my few remaining days of awareness."

Although he didn't use the hated word, she realized that again she had behaved as a Stoic, thinking she knew what was best for other people. She was horrified. "If I can't trust my own judgment, how can I know the best way to treat others?"

"You should do unto others as they would have you do unto them," he said, quoting a teacher from long ago. "Treat others in the manner they wish to be treated."

"How can I know what that is?"

"Very simple. Just ask them."

Deborah led that evening's new moon ceremony, Rosh Chadesh. She enjoyed ritual and had created many beautiful dances and chants, and Mary always let her take the lead when she wished. Only once had Mary made a suggestion for Rosh Chadesh—she had suggested the labyrinth could be used as a location for the ceremony. But the women all found the labyrinth strange and idolatrous, and they chose instead to hold their ceremonies in an open space near the mikvah, where several old plinths now formed a circle of benches with a fire pit in the middle, used only for these monthly events.

Adonis and the women's slaves stayed inside the proseuche while the women gathered around the fire under a dark sky lit only by stars and the thin silver crescent of the new moon. Deborah led them in their chanting as they blessed God, praising Him for renewing the moon and renewing the covenant with His people. After the standing chants they danced around the fire singing songs of praise to God, and then Deborah recited from psalms and prophets, verses that spoke of God's protection in the night. They closed the ceremony by embracing one another and offering each other the peace of God. Afterwards, a complaining Adonis moved to his old tent outdoors for an hour while the women retired to the proseuche to warm up with berry tea and light food before walking the dark path downhill to their homes.

Women who participated in Rosh Chadesh were allowed to make the day a festival day, free of work. Consequently the new moon observances brought together women from both synagogues, happy to put away their disputes and worship together this one night of the month. However Aspasia and Rebekkah never showed up at the same ceremony and Mary thought that Deborah and Judith probably coordinated this to ensure that embarrassment never occurred.

The main topic of conversation in the proseuche that evening was Myia and her dead baby.

"She and her family are farmers," Deborah said. "They pick olives, figs, and grapes to sell in the Judean market. Her impurity makes the entire family, their slaves, and all of their products impure. Everything is harvested now, but none of the people in her household dare touch any of the jars of olive oil or dried figs or any of the other foods they usually sell during the winter, lest they defile their entire crop."

"What is she going to do?" Gilana asked.

"She's moved into a woman's tent out in a field," a woman from Lavi's synagogue said. "In seven days her household can be cleansed and then they can go back to work."

"But what about Myia?"

No one knew what would happen to Myia, whose dead baby remained entrenched in her womb. The midwife had given her a strong abortifacient, normally forbidden to Judean women. But even that hadn't worked; it had only made her very sick.

"The auguries are bad," Judith said. "Her family consulted the psalms, the bones, and the stars. Not one fortune teller could offer anything but sorrow. I'm afraid she's going to die out there, all alone with her dead baby."

"Send her to me," Mary said, then remembered her conversation earlier with Adonis. "If she wants to come. Ask her if that's what she wants."

"What will you do?" Judith asked.

"I don't know. I'll think of something."

"No one will come to the proseuche or mikvah while she's here," one woman warned.

"She and I will stay away from the mikvah," Mary said. "If people want to come for immersion, the bath and the changing tent will remain undefiled by us. You all know where the branches of dried hyssop are if you wish to perform your own rituals."

"I am willing to come to the mikvah to perform purification, if needed," Deborah said.

The women all left soon afterward, too sad to stay and gossip together. They left together, torches lit, accompanied by slaves carrying stone vessels filled with water from the spring, used in their houses to keep ritual impurity from spreading.

Judith held back to speak with Mary. "Thank you, Mary. Expect to see Myia here sometime tomorrow. If she's still alive."

"All right." Mary waved good-bye and then went to bring Adonis in to sleep by the hearth.

"Is your prayer room to be a healing temple now, a dormitory for the sick? Is it your intention to turn your proseuche into an asclepeion?" Adonis asked in aggravation when she told him about Myia. "First me and now this dead baby woman—where is it going to stop? Should I expect to start seeing snakes let loose on the floors in honor of the great healer Asclepius and his revered daughter the goddess Hygeia or whoever the Judean equivalents are?"

"Adonis, what would you have me do?" Mary asked in frustration. "The poor woman is isolated in a tent, in a field, her dead baby still inside her womb. You expect me to do nothing?"

"I expect you to recognize that you cannot fix everyone's pain."

Mary shook her head. "I know that. I know. But I can't just leave her all alone."

Adonis poured himself a glass of wine. "I know you can't," he said sadly.

Mary lit a beechnut oil lamp. "I'm going to go walk the labyrinth. I have a lot to pray about."

"Well, leave me out of your prayers."

"Sorry, old man. Being prayed for is the price you pay in exchange for living here." She heard his faint chuckle as she closed the door behind her.

Myia was delivered to her the next morning, carried in a small donkey cart and accompanied by a single slave who helped Mary bring her into the proseuche and lay her down on a pallet thrown quickly to the floor. The poor woman was fevered and delirious.

"Demons," the slave said. "Mistress is filled with demons."

"Thank you for bringing her. You may leave now." The slave quickly and gladly obeyed, running back downhill and pulling the reins of the donkey cart behind him.

"What, don't you believe in demons?" Adonis asked.

"When I was a young person, I had visions," Mary said. "People used to say I was filled with demons."

"Were you?"

"No. I was filled with God."

Adonis wisely chose not to respond.

Mary heard a sound at the door. John had brought breakfast for Adonis.

"You probably don't want to come in here," Mary said before he could enter. "We're polluted."

"So I heard. Deborah was over this morning telling us about Myia. Is there anything I can do for you?"

"I need a lot of water, clean living water. But I promised I wouldn't go into the mikvah myself. Can you fill some stone bowls and urns at the spring for me?"

John did so and promised to come back up at least twice a day to see if they needed anything, saying he didn't care if he did get polluted.

"He's a good boy," Adonis said, eating his breakfast after John left.

"John is the delight of my heart," she agreed. Mary was fasting. Back home, the second day of the week was a fasting day, along with the fifth day. This was convenient for everyone, because Second Day was a market day and so most people were too busy to prepare food anyway. But every day was a market day in Ephesus, so each family here chose their own best days to fast.

Mary had adopted Third Day as a fast day because sometimes there was food left at the proseuche on Second Day after the Friends of Jesus meetings and she could not let food be wasted. But Adonis expected to be fed every day, saying he refused to be starved just because of Mary's superstitions. He had even demanded food a couple of weeks ago on Yom Kippur.

She sat down beside Myia on the floor and began to wipe her fevered head with a cool, wet cloth. Myia's gown was damp with the liquid lightly seeping from her hard breasts.

"Aren't you concerned that being near this impure woman will pollute me?" Adonis asked after a while.

Mary set the cloth down and stared at him. "Adonis, you are a gentile and a sinner. Everything about you is impure. Being near this poor woman will in no way harm you."

"I can accept that. But do you really believe that being near her harms you?"

She sighed. "What I think about it doesn't matter. It's a commandment. I have to obey."

"I find many of your beliefs incomprehensible and unreasonable."

"I know you do."

Someone knocked at the door, and Mary got up to answer it. She stood back as she opened the door so that she wouldn't pollute the person at the doorstep.

It was Okeanos, one of the curetes from the temple of Artemis. Artelia sent him up to the proseuche every week or two to see if Mary needed anything and to see if she was free to visit.

"Okeanos!" Mary said, tears of relief welling in her eyes. "I am so glad to see you!"

"Lady, what is wrong?" he asked, alarmed. "What do you need of me?"

"Did you bring a cart with you?"

"I have one, yes. The oxcart. Did you want to come to the Temple today?"

"I want to take my sick friend there." Surely someone at the temple would be able to help Myia.

"And me," Adonis said. "I want to go too. I haven't been to the temple in a long while."

"Why would you want to go to the temple?" Mary asked. "You don't worship Artemis."

"I enjoy the art."

Okeanos entered the room. "I can take all of you in the cart," he said. He glanced with compassion down at Myia then bent to lift her carefully in his arms. "I'll carry her to the cart and then come back to carry you too, old man."

"You will not," Adonis snapped. "I can walk to the cart myself."

Mary covered her head with one of her blue shawls while Adonis filled his wineskin for the trip, then she helped him walk the path to the road where an oxcart waited. There would be blankets and water already in the cart, enough to ensure a comfortable trip for all three of them.

Okeanos drove them to an area far back of the temenos, to a lovely temple Mary had never seen before.

"Well, look at that," Adonis said, pointing to a large statue of a man holding a serpent-entwined staff. "It's Asclepius. You actually brought her to an asclepeion." He gave Mary a sharp look. "I hope you don't expect to leave me here too."

Okeanos shouted instructions to a couple of slaves. One ran off to inform Artelia of their arrival, and the other came over to help Okeanos carry Myia into the healing temple.

Mary hurried to follow Okeanos. "I'll wait here for you," Adonis said. "I can't stand to be around sick people."

The priests and priestesses at the Artemis temple were known as "spondopoi." Two white-clad female spondopoi came over to confer with Okeanos and then led them to a room with several beds for the sick. Okeanos and the slave gently set Myia down on an empty bed. "I'll leave you now," he said to Mary. "These women will help you."

Mary told the women everything she knew about Myia and her condition. "I think it's the medicine the midwife gave her that's made her so sick."

The women nodded. "I know what she used," a spondopoios said. "It's very powerful—I can still smell it on her breath. I would have tried the same thing myself. But it didn't work, and now we need to help her get strong again. As weak as she is now, her body couldn't expel the baby even if the medicine did work."

After a while Artelia joined them, affectionately slipping her arm through Mary's. "I understand we're curing Judeans now."

Mary told her about Myia and that she didn't know how to help her but couldn't leave her alone in a tent to die.

"You did the right thing bringing her here. This is the week of our annual medical competition, which brings in doctors from all over to compete in surgery, medical recipes, new instruments, and new techniques. All the world's best doctors are here. Your friend could not be in better hands."

Mary remembered that Jacob had mentioned a medical competition when he treated Adonis. "Oh, that's wonderful. Thank you, Artelia." She tried to speak with Myia, but the woman was still delirious.

"We have a few things we can do for her fever," one of the healer priestesses said. "If you come back in a few hours, she may be able to speak with you."

Mary thanked them, and then she and Artelia left to join Adonis, still waiting for Mary in the oxcart.

"Have you finally come to the Temple to show obeisance to the Queen of Heaven, you old reprobate?" Artelia greeted Adonis.

"Just wanted to see some new girls' faces," the old man said. "I'm getting a little tired of the same old ones up on the hill."

"He told me he came for the art," Mary said.

"Oh, I've heard that one before," Artelia said. She waved her litter bearers over. "I feel like walking to the Temple," she said to Adonis, "so that I can visit with Mary. Would you mind riding in the litter for me?"

"Oh, I suppose," he said, forcing a sigh. The litter bearers helped him out of the oxcart and into the litter then lifted him up. They left the asclepeion grounds and entered the temple precinct for the temple of Artemis, Mary and Artelia walking alongside the litter.

Mary told Artelia about the tumor in Adonis' belly and her decision to let him stay in the proseuche.

"He's welcome to live here, if you'd like," Artelia said. "We're happy to offer him our hospitium. We provide food, shelter, and clothing to many indigent people. And of course he would be near to the doctors."

"I'll let him know that, but I think he'd prefer to stay with me."

"No doubt, but are you sure you want the burden of caring for a sick old man?"

"It wouldn't be the first time. I cared for my husband when he died. He wasn't as old as Adonis, of course, but he was very, very sick."

"What was his affliction?"

"Lockjaw," Mary said. "He was a carpenter and stone cutter. One day his tools slipped and he was badly cut. He was terribly sick for a long time before he died, his muscles rigid and spasming, his jaw and hands tightly clenched. He was in great pain. Alexander's physician gave me a pain medicine for Adonis called opium. Do you know it?"

"I do know it," Artelia said.

"I gather it works quite well. I would have done anything to have had something that strong to give my Joseph for his pain. And Adonis has it available to him but doesn't want to use it."

"Everyone's different."

The litter bearers halted in front of the temple steps. Artelia stopped them before they could let Adonis step out. "Take him up into the temple entrance. He's not going to want to walk those stairs. And remain up there so that you can bring him back down when he's ready to leave."

Mary watched the litter bearers carry Adonis up the ramp to the temple.

"You are a very nice woman, Artelia."

"I'm simply a reflection of the Goddess, a vessel of Her goodness," Artelia said, repeating a common temple axiom, and then the two friends walked arm-in-arm around the garden, catching up on news.

A few hours later, Mary and Artelia accompanied Adonis and the litter bearers on the walk back to the temple of Asclepius. Artelia excused the men after they let Adonis down, saying she would walk back to the temenos when she was ready.

"Nice young men, those," Adonis said, watching the litter bearers walk away. "Did they have the penectomy?"

Mary stared at him. "I don't think I know that word."

"No," Artelia told him coldly. "They did not."

"Penectomy," Adonis repeated to Mary. "It means the surgical removal of the penis."

"What are you talking about?" Mary asked.

"The penis. Removed." He made a slicing action with his hand. "You know. You are aware that's what they do to the men here, aren't you?"

Mary gave a dismissive laugh. "It is not, it—" She saw Artelia glaring at Adonis.

"Is he right?" she asked in shock. "Do you make the men cut off their—"

"It's one of the mysteries," Artelia said. "I cannot discuss it with you. But it only applies to certain priests, the Megabysos and the highest rank of the male spondopoi. It's part of a sacred ritual and is certainly not performed on litter bearers."

"I don't know why you look so shocked," Adonis said to Mary. "Your people do the same thing."

"If you mean circumcision, it is not the same thing. Only a bit of skin is cut off."

"It's exactly the same thing. It's just a matter of degree."

Artelia took Mary's arm again to lead her up the steps. "You wait out here," she told Adonis in a scolding voice, and the two women entered the asclepeion to check on Myia.

"Don't be angry," Mary said. "Adonis didn't mean to offend you."

"Of course he did. He's a trouble-making old fool who gets great pleasure out of annoying people."

"Well yes, but he's also very amusing. And he has a good heart."

"I suppose so," Artelia conceded. "I hope you aren't alarmed by what he said."

Mary shrugged. "If it's only done to high priests, I presume it's by their choice."

"Of course it is."

"Then there's nothing to alarm me about it," Mary said as they entered Myia's room. What she thought was: The high priests of Artemis must truly be devoted to their goddess to subject themselves to something like that.

Myia's fever had gone down and she appeared comfortable. "Myia, are you able to wake up and talk to me?" Mary asked.

Myia opened her eyes. "Mary, where am I?" she asked weakly.

Artelia answered. "You're at the Temple of Asclepius. They're going to do everything they can to help you."

Myia stared at Mary. "You brought me to an idol's temple?" she whispered in horror.

Mary shrugged. "You're already polluted, Myia. At least maybe they can help you get better."

The two healer priestesses came in. Each carried a small baby. Myia and Mary stared and then Myia's eyes welled with tears.

"Why have you brought those babies in here?" Mary asked sharply. She couldn't believe anyone could be so cruel as to parade living babies in front of a woman whose own baby was dead in her womb.

"These babies were left at the Temple of Artemis today," one replied. "They need milk. Myia's breasts are bursting with milk, straining to flow. If she would consent to feed these babies, they would all three be better off."

"Myia, are you willing to feed them?" Mary asked the sick woman.

Myia's face showed her distress at the idea. "I guess I could. But I don't think I'm strong enough to hold them." She struggled to lift her arm, and Mary watched it shake.

"She doesn't have to do anything," a spondopoios said. She handed her baby to Mary, and Mary found herself swaying to comfort the crying infant while the woman untied Myia's robe and opened it to free her breasts. At first sight of the two full breasts an unbidden thought flashed into Mary's mind: the eyes of God.

The two women sat on each side of Myia, each holding a baby to a breast and helping it begin to suckle. After a few moments both babies had caught on, and Mary saw an expression of huge relief settle on Myia's face as her hard breasts began to empty.

"Later we'll massage her and treat her with magnetized stones," one of the women told Mary. "If she still can't expel the baby, we'll consult with the doctors."

Artelia led Mary away. "I think she'll be fine. You can come back tomorrow to see how she's doing."

"I'd like that."

"You can even bring that old coot with you, if you want."

"If he wants to come."

"Oh, he will, if only to have another chance to annoy me."

"You're generous to invite him."

"Well, it's as you said. He's amusing."

On the way home, riding in the oxcart, Adonis jabbered on about exquisite statuary and paintings in the cella and about other pieces he'd seen by these same artists in his travels in his youth. His favorite painting was an ancient panel by Apelles called "Alexander the Great Holding a Thunderbolt." Although it was mildewed and beginning to rot with age, it still impressed the viewer with optical effects that made it stand out like a statue rather than a flat-surface painting. They'd let him go right up to it, to see it as best he could. He also heaped lavish and lecherous praise on the five bronze statues of Amazons created by the great Greek sculptors Phidias, Polycleitus, Cresilas, Cydon, and Phradmon—the guards had helped him to climb on the plinths and feel the statues with his hands because he was a poor blind man.

But Mary only half-listened. Her mind kept returning to that brief instant when she had seen the eyes of God in Myia's breasts, and she wondered if a bouquet of sacred eyes might be another thing the devotees of Artemis saw when they looked upon the strange orbs that hung from their idol's chest.

"You know, the Amazons used to cut off their right breasts so that they could fire arrows with more speed and accuracy," Adonis said. "That's where all those tits on Artemis come from—the Amazons sacrificed their breasts to her. But the Amazon statues at the temple all have both breasts. I checked."

He chortled, and Mary stopped to look at him, realizing what he had just said.

The orbs on Artemis were breasts sacrificed by the Amazons? She thought about the spondopoios' decision to let Myia nurse the foundlings. Mary realized that her own decision to save the woman's life by taking her to the temple had resulted in the sacrifice of another woman's breasts to Artemis.

Undelivered, Myia remained at the temple of Artemis for five years.

Mary thought: "My son, how can I best serve those who are beyond my help?"

10

"Everyone loves the man who promises a better future."

Summer, four years after the crucifixion of Jesus

Now that a new emperor ruled in Rome, Mary hoped there would finally be peace in Jerusalem and she could return home. Perhaps he would be a friend to the Israelites, like his revered ancestors Julius Caesar and Caesar Augustus had been. The many statues that had been erected in Ephesus in the last few months showed a good face, noble and kind. He was Gaius Julius Caesar Augustus Germanicus, but everyone called him Caligula, a nickname from his childhood.

The empire was lit with joy that summer, with feasts, sacrifices, and celebrations from one corner of the world to the next, because the old emperor Tiberius was much despised and the new emperor much loved. In Ephesus, there was talk that Caligula would finish building the temple of Didymaean Apollo, and the city leaders were thrilled at the idea of Ephesus being home to such an important oracular temple, paid for by Rome.

Mary avoided public events as much as possible because she didn't like crowds or the type of wild behavior that could explode in an instant whenever a mob gathered. She never attended the races at the hippodrome or ventured into town on any of the festival days. But she had agreed to attend two events in celebration of the new emperor: the opening of a new play at the theater and a festival at the Basilica sponsored by the temple of Artemis.

On the day of the play, she followed her normal routine in the morning. She fed the goats and walked the labyrinth. She weeded her herb garden and cut some hyssop that she'd planted as a garden hedge. She ate her breakfast outside, watching David and Bathsheba, her favorite of the many pairs of storks that returned to nest in her trees year after year, as they tried to convince their fledglings to flap their wings hard enough to lift out of the nest. At fourth hour she dressed in her best linen chiton and a lightweight blue shawl that covered her head and shoulders and walked down the Mount Kouressos road to the state agora to wait for John, who was to meet her at the agora fountain. She carried a new sun parasol in the heat, and not just for the walk into town. The play started in the afternoon at sixth hour, and she needed the parasol to ensure she didn't burn her face while watching it.

John was already at the fountain when she arrived, standing tall and handsome in new clothes, his cheeks sparsely covered with a young man's beard. He was eighteen years old now, a dedicated scholar at the gymnasium and a rising leader in the synagogue. He was engaged again, to one of Theokritos' daughters, and they would marry in two years when he turned twenty. Judith had cried when Mary told her, sad to lose the dream of John as her son-in-law.

"I'm glad you brought a parasol," he said as they began the walk down the Embolos. "If you hadn't, I was going to suggest we stop at the harbor agora on the way to the theater."

"It was a gift from Isaac the Samaritan, for caring for his wife when she was ill," she said, admiring it as she swirled it around.

"Will any of the Samaritans be attending the theater today?"

"I have no idea," she said. The Samaritans in Ephesus trusted Mary because back home in Israel the Samaritans had been subjected to the worst of Pontius Pilate's brutality, and they knew her son had been executed by that procurator. She now acted as an intermediary between the Samaritans and the Judeans in Ephesus. "Why do you ask?"

"The playwright, Damonikos, is an Israelite. This new play he's written in honor of the emperor uses an Israelite story instead of a Greek or Roman one. My father talked him into it because he thinks that if the Greeks knew our stories, they wouldn't be so fearful of us. We're all very proud."

"Really? What story is it?"

"It's 'The Testament of Abraham.' Samaritans should enjoy it too."

"It sounds very interesting," she said, though she privately doubted that any gentile concerns about the strange ways of the Judeans would be assuaged by the story of a man so devoted to God that he was willing to place his own son on an altar for sacrifice.

They walked past the tombs, and as usual Mary noticed people out picnicking with their dead. She had never again seen anyone having sex in a tomb, however. In the four years she'd been here, she'd learned a lot about Greek, Roman, and Ephesian customs. She now understood eusebeia, the devotion and allegiance that the people felt toward their city and their city's goddess, and she now believed the city of Ephesus wasn't as immoral as she'd originally thought. Most of the people she met were kind and generous, conscientious and hard-working, and were even quite devout according to their own traditions.

She didn't know any of the deceased entombed along this road, because most of these monuments were old, and only the very rich and important could arrange a gravesite in the heart of town these days. Most entombments now were at the cemetery on the back side of Mount Pion. Her friend and teacher Adonis was there, his sepulcher next to that of John's mother, Leah, who'd died in the great earthquake. This was another thing that she had to get used to: Hebrews and gentiles shared the same cemeteries. Adonis had been the first person buried by the Friends of Jesus guild. Guild members who tended his grave tended Leah's grave as well, in respect of John. Mary knew the Disciples of John the Baptist guild also tended Leah's grave, as did the synagogue guild, so her tomb and the area around it was always clean and well-kept.

They turned at the end of the Embolos and walked past the harbor agora to the enormous theater. As they entered through one of the entrance gates, they heard a loud roar from the hippodrome nearby, where a race or other athletic contest was being held. Mary wondered if the actors would need to shout in order to be heard over the crowd at the other event.

"The races will probably be over when the play starts," John assured her, and he helped her to pick her way around people, steps, and seats to the Judean block located in the ima cavea, the desirable seating area near the front of the stage, purchased by one of Alexander's ancestors when the theater was last remodeled. This block of seats had been maintained by the family with annual contributions ever since. Menorahs, now old and worn, were carved into the side of the seats at each end of the row.

Mary greeted the family as she sat down—Enoch, Aspasia, and little Seth; Deborah and her husband, Daniel, who'd left their baby daughters Tamar and Ruth at home. Alexander had invited a couple of asiarchs, delegates from cities in Asia to the provincial council, to join them in their row, but he and they had not yet arrived.

"I'm so glad you finally agreed to come!" Deborah said, leaning over her brother and his family to speak to Mary. She'd been asking Mary for years to come to the theater. "I hope that you'll enjoy this enough to attend the theater again!"

"I hope so," Mary said politely, although she was already wishing the play was over so that she could go home. It was very hot today. She was grateful that Alexander had had a slave sitting in her spot since morning, keeping the marble seat from getting too hot.

The theater filled up, Alexander and his visitors among the last to arrive. Alexander sat next to John, so Mary couldn't help overhearing his conversation.

"So you've seen other plays by Damonikos of Ephesus?" Alexander said to his guests.

"Oh, yes," said one of the men, introduced to her when they arrived as Lucius Gratius Cinna. "I saw his 'Twelve Labors of Hercules' in Smyrna last year."

"I saw that in Corinth," said the other man, Vibius Atius Iullus. "Very entertaining."

"Well, you'll find this a special treat," said Alexander. "This is the premier staging of his newest play. And it's the first play he's written with a Judean theme."

"Well, that should be interesting," Vibius Atius Iullus said. Mary thought he sounded doubtful.

"I was unaware that he was Judean," Lucius Gratius Cinna said thoughtfully, and then the audience began to clap as the curtain was lowered into the stage to reveal the first scene.

The two main characters in "The Testament of Abraham" were Abraham and the archangel Michael. Other characters that Mary could identify and recognize were Abraham's son Isaac, his wife, Sarah, and, of course, God, represented by a booming voice. All familiarity ended there. The play was a comedy, based on no story she'd ever heard.

Abraham was an old man, God's favorite, and it was time for him to die. Because of God's affection for the old man, he sent Michael to Earth to give the bad news.

Michael, dressed as a Roman soldier, repeatedly referred to himself as God's commander-in-chief. He was a rough, tough general who turned soft when confronting the righteous Abraham. Over and over he tried to tell the old man that his time was up, but he kept being tripped up by events and misunderstandings. And when he finally managed to tell Abraham his life was over, time for him to die, Abraham said no. He refused to go.

So then God sent Death to convince Abraham to let go of life. In order to not frighten Abraham too much, Death wore the costume of a simple peasant when he came to his door. But Abraham wasn't at all intimidated by a peasant, and again he refused. Finally Death had to show his true monstrous self before Abraham paid any attention to him.

And then the play really went wild, with Abraham traveling around the world in a flying chariot, smiting sinners, sassing angels, and sending criminals and fornicators to a fiery judgment. It ended with Abraham being reconciled with Michael, rescuing the people he'd condemned to punishment, and finally being tricked into accepting an escort into paradise.

For five hours Mary sat enrapt, shocked, and thrilled. All around her people roared with laughter and screamed with terror. No experience in her life had prepared her for either this story or the adventure of the stage.

"What did you think, Mother?" John asked her. His eyes were shining, his face aglow with laughter.

"It was amazing," she said, her voice still shaking from all the excitement.

Alexander addressed his family. "I'm taking our guests to the stage house to meet Damonikos. You're welcome to join us if you'd like."

Mary held tight to John's hand as he pushed their way through the crowd to the hidden rooms behind the stage, sometimes using Mary's parasol as a wedge. Over the next hour she stayed close to one or another of the family as they explored the maze of rooms, congratulated actors, and saw stage magic secrets revealed. Eventually she found herself standing on the stage itself, as the stage house became too crowded to hold all of the people who wanted to meet the actors and talk about the play.

When she was introduced to Damonikos, the playwright, he immediately asked her: "What was your favorite part?"

This was easy. "When Death opened his peasant robe and all the hideous monster faces popped out. I leaped from my seat in fright."

"That was a nice effect," Damonikos said proudly. "Playwrights all over Rome will be copying it in no time at all. By this time next year, every play you see will have monsters popping out of people's clothing."

"I don't remember ever hearing that story about Abraham before," she said hesitantly.

"No? 'The Testament of Abraham' is popular all over the empire. Aren't there any Judeans where you come from?"

"Well, yes. I'm from Jerusalem."

"That backwater," he said dismissively. "There's nothing there. No culture. No art. The temple in Jerusalem is just a bunch of blocks stuffed inside one another, like a large children's toy. Have you seen the temple of Artemis here? The open marble columns, the friezes, the art, the beauty? Jerusalem has nothing to compare."

"It has God."

He shrugged. "Well, yes, there is that," he conceded and shifted his attention to John.

Damonikos was interested to hear that John was attending gymnasium and asked him if he was uncomfortable participating in athletic events.

Mary had no idea what that meant, but John understood immediately what Damonikos was referring to, and he blushed. "It is awkward."

"I had an operation to disguise it, and now I can exercise naked with no problem," the playwright said. "If you want the name of a surgeon, just let me know." He moved away to speak with some other people.

Mary stared at him as he walked away and then looked at John inquiringly.

"He means circumcision," John said. "Greeks are horrified by it, and whenever they see one of us, they just, well, they just stare. And sometimes they say things."

"Oh," she said and then changed the subject as they searched around to tell the family good-bye. "Did you ever hear the Testament of Abraham story before?"

"Sure. It's very popular in the community here. They used to read it to the kids in the old synagogue sometimes. There are a lot of other funny stories like it, stories about Job, Moses, Joseph, and the other prophets and patriarchs.

I never thought about it before, but I guess I never did hear anyone tell those stories when I was living in Jerusalem. I'll bet Jesus never heard them."

"Probably not."

"Do you think he would have liked those kinds of stories?"

"I think this play would have made him laugh," she said, smiling to herself at the thought.

The event at the Basilica was held a couple of days later, on the Sabbath. Alexander, ever the politician, entreated Mary to go with him because many women and wives would be there, and it would look odd if he came by himself, the lone Judean. She agreed to it because she owed him so much and also because Artelia had asked her to attend. Mary and Alexander would of course be the only Hebrews there, the only children of God spending the Sabbath at a festival honoring Caligula and Artemis. She hadn't spent the night at the villa or attended synagogue today because she hadn't wanted to try to explain her impiety to anyone.

Alexander sent a cart to the proseuche to fetch her because it was important that she not be dusty or tired from the walk downhill into town. The Basilica was located between the Prytaneion and the state agora, a walk she was very used to by now, but she was glad to accept the ride because she wore her beautiful blue silk shawl today and would hate for it to be dirtied. She also wore various bits of jewelry, gifts she rarely had opportunity to display, and thought she might not look too out of place with the prominent and elegant women who would be in attendance.

The Basilica was a long, beautiful, two-storied public building. Made of marble with a wooden roof, it was supported by an impressive series of columns and arches around the exterior. Its primary use was for official and commercial gatherings such as courts of law, the stock exchange, and commercial business, but it was also used for public meetings and events.

Only important people like the leaders of temples, business, and government had been invited to today's festivities at the Basilica, sponsored by the temple of Artemis in partnership with the temple of Hestia Boulaia. Artelia, who had recently been elected head magistrate at the Prytaneion, was the hostess of the event, and the new Roman proconsul, the representative of the new emperor, was the guest of honor.

Alexander had been unable to accompany the cart that brought her down from the proseuche, but he was careful to meet it when it arrived at the agora and to walk alongside of Mary as they climbed the east entrance steps into the Basilica.

"Have you ever been here before?" he asked her.

"No, I haven't." She blinked her eyes as they entered, moving from the bright sunlight to the cool, darkened space within. She glanced around at the mosaic and marble floors, the friezes high on the walls, and the impressive marble colonnades. "It's a beautiful building."

"Those statues are the emperor Caesar Augustus and his wife Julia Augusta." Alexander pointed to the prominent statues near the entrance. "The last major renovation of the Basilica was during his rule, although there was also a little bit of work that had to be done after the big earthquake. If you look around carefully you can still see cracks in some of the stone and marble."

Mary walked over to stare up into the face of the man who'd been such a good friend to the Israelites. The face in this statue looked a little older than the face on the altar at Alexander's house, but she could still recognize the emperor's features. Then she looked at the plain but noble face of his wife.

"I've never heard of her before."

"She died not long ago," Alexander said. "She was very old. Her name was Livia Drusilla, but when Augustus died he changed her name in his will."

"Really?" Mary thought Roman names were needlessly confusing, most people having at least three and some, like the emperor, having twice as many as that. The idea that even those names could be changed by a clause in someone else's will made no sense to her.

"Yes. In his will he adopted her into the Julian family—Julius Caesar, you know, Augustus' adopted father—and he also granted her the title Augusta in recognition of her majesty. She was the great-grandmother of our new emperor."

Some other people came by to look at the statues, and Mary and Alexander turned to follow the crowd of elegant people entering the center nave of the Basilica.

Artelia stood talking with some people near the rows of seats set up at the end of the nave beneath the gallery, but when she saw Mary and Alexander standing near a fountain at the corner she excused herself to come greet them.

She embraced Mary. "Alexander will want to sit with the new proconsul's people so that they can get to know him. But I've reserved a place for you beside Arsinoe because you always seem to enjoy her chatter."

"Thank you," Mary began, but she stopped speaking as she saw the expression on Alexander's face when Artelia greeted him. His face glowed as though a lamp was lit behind his eyes, and a tender smile danced around his lips. Artelia clasped his hands in hers, and Mary saw Alexander's fond expression mirrored in the face of her friend.

It lasted only a moment and then Artelia moved away to greet other guests. Alexander touched Mary's elbow to guide her toward Arsinoe.

The priestess of Isis was always easy to spot, with her rich purple gowns, piles of jewelry, and outrageous hair and makeup. But she had added an element to her outfit today that held Mary speechless when she first saw her.

She was wearing a fish on the top of her head, perched on a metal stand.

Alexander gave Arsinoe a quick greeting, then said, "I'll meet you later, Mary," choking out his words through suppressed laughter. He sped away, and Mary found herself enfolded in the loving, heavily perfumed arms of her friend.

"Is that a real fish?" Mary blurted out after Arsinoe released her.

"Do you like it?" Arsinoe reached up to pat the elaborate structure into place. "It's a real fish, but stuffed with straw. It's the new look of Isis, to honor the age of Pisces."

"What did Artelia say when she saw it?"

"She didn't say anything because she wishes she thought of it first."

Arsinoe led Mary to the seats that had been reserved for them.

"Oh, I wanted to show you this," Arsinoe said after they sat down. She raised her arm to show Mary an amulet she wore on her wrist. "It was made by a Judean sorcerer."

Mary peered at it. "Is it a magical thing?" A few Hebrew letters were inscribed on the cover, but she was unable to read.

"Very magical. There are Judean incantations sealed inside, written in your secret language, that the sorcerer told me to recite every day." She recited the first one, and Mary smiled at the pronunciation.

"You understood it!" Arsinoe was delighted. "What did I say?"

"'I will love the Lord my God with all my heart and all my soul and all my might.' It's part of the Shema, our most sacred prayer."

Arsinoe nodded. "And this is the second one," she said and recited it.

Mary had heard these Hebrew words spoken all her life and knew what they meant too. "Let all who take refuge in you be glad and let them sing songs of joy forever. Spread the cloak of your protection over them, so that those who love your name may rejoice in you," she said. "It's one of our hymns, written by a great prophet."

Arsinoe nodded. "And then I finish the incantation with 'our great Mother Isis'. I know that part, because it's in Greek."

Mary had never heard of the sacred writings being used in idol worship before and had no idea how to respond.

"The Judean who made this for me also exorcises demons," Arsinoe said. "Can you perform exorcisms?"

"No. I'm afraid I can't." She shrugged apologetically.

Arsinoe frowned at Mary's apparel. "Why aren't you wearing the beautiful gold Isis pendant I gave you?"

A bell chimed, announcing the program was about to begin. Mary escaped the tricky question as Arsinoe started gossiping about the important people now hurriedly being seated.

Artelia addressed the crowd, her speech followed by speeches from other dignitaries, then the proconsul. The speeches were long and dull, repetitions on the theme of how wonderful life in the empire would be now that the great Caligula was emperor. But finally everyone finished talking, and Mary whispered, "Is it done now?"

"It hasn't even begun yet," Arsinoe answered.

Musicians began playing and a number of men and women walked out onto the floor.

"Those are spondopoi from the temple of Artemis. They're going to perform some songs and sacred dances."

The first part of the program was a song rendered by the himnodoi, the temple singers.

"I am the power emanated.
      And I am present to those who reflect on me,
      And I am found by those who yearn for me.
Look upon me, you devoted ones who reflect on me, and you listeners. Hear me.
You who are waiting for me: I am here for you.
And do not close your eyes to me.
And do not speak evil of me, nor hear it.
Do not lose your awareness of me, not for a moment. Pay attention and remember!
      Do not lose your grip upon me in your heart."

Arsinoe whispered to Mary: "They stole that song from us. That's Isis' song."

Mary nodded absently. She recognized the tune. They used it in the synagogue.

> "I am the incomprehensible silence,
>> And the ever-present thought.
> I am the voice that eternally resounds,
>> And the word that continually repeats.
> I am the utterance of my name.
>> Is. Is."

"See? See?" Arsinoe said.

Mary nodded again, but her mind was resounding with another name: I AM.

The long song finally ended. Several groups of dancers took the place of the singers. "Those girls there are dancing out the creation of the deer and stags," Arsinoe pointed out. "And over there they're dancing out the creation of the dolphins. These are just a few of the sacred dances from the Thargelion, Artemis' birthday festival. The priestesses dance continually through the festival so that by the end, all of the creatures of the planet have been made by Artemis Ephesia."

She watched the dancers, occasionally shaking her head or sighing. "Look at that sloppy quail. She's supposed to stay low, keep hidden, not prance out in the open like that. The quail is a modest bird, that's why she's precious to Artemis. Artemis would be ashamed of that quail."

Mary didn't see anything wrong with the quail, but all this was new to her. She quite enjoyed watching the girls doing the bee dance, their wings moving rapidly as they flitted from flower to flower. "Do you know all these dances?"

"I was the best dancer that temple ever had. They'll never be able to replace me."

Mary was unsure how to reply. She wondered if Arsinoe regretted leaving Artemis for the service of Isis and then remembered that she hadn't had a choice in the matter because she was sold to the other temple. "I'm sure the Isis temple is glad to have you," she said gently.

"They certainly are," Arsinoe said emphatically.

And then a new dance began, one that included priests and priestesses together. "This is the main part of the program," Arsinoe said. "This is the part that really honors the new emperor. It's the story of the hero Parnassus."

Mary watched the dance carefully but could make little sense of it. She did figure out that the priestesses swooping around with their arms held out were birds and that their flight was being controlled or directed by the priest portraying the hero.

"How does this honor the emperor?" she asked finally.

"Parnassus was the founder of Delphi, where the Greek Artemis' brother Apollo has his great oracle. Parnassus invented the art of reading the future in the flights of birds."

"Why does that matter to Caligula?"

"Parnassus was the son of a nymph, Cleodora. But like many heroes, he had both a human father, Cleopompos, and a father who was a god, Poseidon. Our new emperor believes that he also had two fathers—Germanicus, a human, and Jupiter, the king of the gods. So this dance honoring the hero Parnassus is really a dance honoring the hero Caligula."

Mary was grateful to hear the explanation; she had wondered about the two men circling a woman at the beginning of the dance, one a big man with bulky muscles and peasant clothes, the other a tall, slender man dressed in gold and wearing a crown. "Do all emperors think they have two fathers?"

"I don't think so," Arsinoe said. "This is the first time I've heard of it."

The program ended with a very old dance created by the ancient Queen Hippolyta and her Amazons. The mellieras, the female initiates, danced while circling one another with weapons and shields. It looked very dangerous, and the audience was held spellbound as the girls frequently seemed near to killing one another. Only their shield skills and nimble feet helped them evade death.

"We always perform the Amazon dance for the Romans," Arsinoe said. "It reminds them that we are strong and can protect ourselves."

Alexander came to find her after the program was over, and Arsinoe left them to join the rest of her contingent from the temple of Isis. "There's a banquet next," Alexander said to Mary, "over at the Prytaneion. We'll be sitting with the asiarchs and their wives."

Mary looked at him. "Who cooked the food?" she asked warily.

He had the grace to look embarrassed. "They'll be serving meat sacrificed by the priests at the temple of Hestia Boulaia, next to the Prytaneion."

"Alexander, the Sabbath hasn't even ended yet."

"I know."

She sighed, deciding finally that it was more important to honor Alexander than to follow the Law. "All right," she said, forcing a smile to her lips. "Lead me to the Roman banquet."

"I assure you, it won't be an orgy," he said lightly.

"A what?"

He realized she was unfamiliar with the unsavory reputation attached to Roman banquets. "Never mind," he said, taking her arm and leading her to the Prytaneion.

At dinner she shared a couch with Alexander, who thoughtfully chose her food for her, careful not to select any shellfish or pork from the array of unfamiliar dishes continually refreshed on the table in front of them. The banquet lasted over four hours, making it the longest meal of her life, although Alexander said he'd been to many that lasted longer. The food was good, the wives of the asiarchs quite friendly, and the jugglers, acrobats, and mimes superbly entertaining.

When she and Alexander returned to the villa that night and he asked her if she would be willing to accompany him to similar events in the future, she told him that perhaps she would. She'd remembered that her son was known for eating with sinners, although probably not so many of them at the same time. And she doubted he'd ever attended a four-hour meal.

Before going to bed they stopped in the atrium to pray. Alexander prayed to God that Emperor Caligula would prove to be as good an emperor as they all hoped and that he would be as kind to the Israelites as his great ancestors had been. Mary prayed that Jerusalem would be safe now, at last.

She thought: "My son, is this man the King of Peace that Jerusalem's been waiting for?"

11

"My son the Rabbi teaches us how to live."

Winter, six years after the crucifixion of Jesus

Mary thanked Heron, the slave bringing in the last bowl of fresh goat milk, and watched as he carried the heavy jar over to Thales, the slave responsible for pouring the milk into the small bowls of honey. She walked over to check on the table of honey, gathered with Artelia's permission from beehives in the orchard, and smiled at Pelagios, the slave who'd done such a nice job arranging the honeycombs in a large bowl for display. He would place the chunks in the small individual serving bowls when the people were ready to be fed; then the people would carry their bowls over to be filled with milk. In today's baptism, John was using a special verse from the Torah: "Lo, thus says the Lord God: enter into the good land, a land flowing with milk and honey." Feeding milk and honey to the convert and his friends afterward would be a nice touch, she thought.

This was John's first baptism. Epenetus, a man who'd been a slave in the home of Alexander all his life, was so drawn to the message of Jesus that he'd decided to convert to Judaism. He'd been circumcised two weeks ago and today was his baptism. Usually when God Fearers were baptized, they were baptized by Enoch, after the teachings of John the Baptist. But Epenetus wanted to be baptized by John, because he said it was Jesus who led him to the truth of God, not John the Baptist or Moses or any of the prophets.

The women of the Friends of Jesus guild hurried in. They'd washed their feet when they first arrived, then waited outside the proseuche while the men accompanied John and Epenetus into the mikvah for the baptism. The Festival of Lights had just ended and the sun had barely risen on what would be a very short day. It was quite chilly so early in the morning, but the women didn't think it fair that they wait in the warm proseuche while Epenetus was immersing in the icy water of the mikvah.

"They're ready?" asked Mary.

"They're coming now," said Theodora, and she hurried over to take her favorite seat near the hearth. She would marry John in a few days. She was much beloved by Mary.

"Do you think there are enough lamps lit?" Mary asked. It was daylight, but still dark and gloomy. This was a special day and it needed to feel festive. She'd always loved the Festival of Lights and wanted to continue the season's sense of hope and renewal into today's event.

"Everything's beautiful, Mother," Theodora said. Mary gave her a quick hug and then greeted the other women.

Epenetus came in, followed by the rest. Mary kissed him on both cheeks then urged everyone to sit. After John led them in opening prayers, Mary said, "I have something special I'd like to share with you. I don't take it out often because it's very precious to me. But I'd like Epenetus—I'd like all of you—to have a chance to hold it."

She went into her room and came back with a folded cloth held tightly to her chest. "This is a tunic that belonged to my son Jesus," she said softly, and she placed the precious thing into Epenetus' trembling hands.

Epenetus held the tunic to his face, breathing it in. When he finally released it to pass on to the next person, Mary saw his face was wet with tears. From one person to another the tunic was reverently passed, to be held to a face or clutched tightly to a heart. When John, the last person, finally handed it back to her, his hands were shaking badly and his eyes were wet and anguished.

Mary took the now tear-soaked tunic in her arms and spoke gently to the people. "If you walk over to Pelagios now, he'll give you a bowl of honey, and if you take that bowl over to Thales, he'll fill it with milk. Then while you enjoy your milk and honey, I'll tell you a story about how we used to celebrate the Festival of Lights back home, when Jesus was a child."

This would give John time to recover so that he could give his baptismal sermon without choking up with tears. This was a special day, and he'd worked on it all week.

Later after everyone left, John remained to visit with Mary. "How do you think that went?" he asked.

"I thought it was a good meeting. Epenetus seemed happy. I wasn't present for his baptism, of course, but I'm sure that went well too."

"It was kind of you to let everyone hold his tunic, Mother."

She shrugged. "I'm glad that I have it to share. I'm delighted that people who never met Jesus should be so drawn to him. You're a wonderful teacher, John. He would be very proud of you."

"Thank you, Mother. Epenetus' slave Pelagios has asked me if he can be baptized too. I think there will be more people wanting it, now that we've done this first one."

"I think so too."

"I'd like to do something really special for them, Mother. Something besides the baptism, something that differentiates the Friends of Jesus guild from the other Judean guilds."

"Well, the worshippers of Artemis initiate their priests and priestesses in a cave," she said. "Going into the dark then re-emerging is like being reborn, or resurrected. During the ritual, the leader asks initiates to give up their old wicked ways and devote themselves to Artemis. An initiate refuses three times and then 'caves in,' or acquiesces. You might try something like that."

John stared at her. "I think that's an excellent idea, Mother. But I'm a little afraid to ask you how you can know all that."

Mary laughed. "Not from personal experience, I assure you."

"So we take the converts to a cave," John said, thinking. "And talk about resurrection as a disciple of Jesus."

"Before or after the baptism, do you think?"

"I think before. I like finishing with the milk and honey in the proseuche, after the baptism."

"I agree. So before we have the baptism, we'll have a ritual in a cave."

"Yes. I think initiates should be anointed with oil, as a sign of their being chosen by God."

"Great idea. Take them to a cave, anoint them with oil. Daytime or nighttime, do you think?"

"Nighttime. Definitely. We'll set out torches and lanterns to guide us there. I'll find a cave around here that's not too hard to walk to at night. Initiates should probably fast for a few days first."

"Yes," said Mary. "And pray."

"And pray. They fast for a few days and then we take them to a cave at night and talk about their renewal as a follower of Jesus. They stay there all night praying, and just before dawn we go back, anoint them with oil, then bring them to the mikvah for baptism. Then we celebrate in the proseuche with milk and honey."

"John, I think that's lovely. Your sister Deborah couldn't have designed a more sacred or meaningful ritual."

"Our mother was always good at things like that. She always thought of the little details that would turn an event into something festive."

"Well, you certainly have her talent. How often should we do these ceremonies? Every time someone converts?"

"No, I don't think we should do them too often," John said thoughtfully. "We want them to be very special. How about annually, during Passover?"

"That's when Jesus died," Mary said quietly.

"I know. I've been thinking I'd like to start doing something to commemorate his death and resurrection. I think this annual resurrection ceremony would be a nice way to do that. Just until the Parousia, you understand." It hadn't been necessary to commemorate Jesus' death when they were expecting him to return immediately. But it had been six years now and they were still waiting. If they waited much longer, people might begin to forget him.

Mary walked over to John and stood on her toes to give him a big hug. "Thank you, John. I'd like that."

Someone knocked on the door, and John walked over to answer it. It was Okeanos with a message from Artelia.

"Your friend Myia is dying," he said in a rush. "You may wish to come see her."

"Go tell Myia's family," Mary told John. "I'll bring her back and prepare her for burial." She would have liked John to accompany her, but she wanted to limit the number of people who would suffer corpse contamination—and she particularly did not want John polluted, since he was to be married in a few days. It saddened her to realize that now she would not be witness to his wedding. She hurried to collect a warm cloak and then ran to follow Okeanos to the horse-drawn cart waiting down on the road.

Things had been difficult for Mary five years ago after she took Myia to the healers at the temple of Aesclepius. Myia's family had been profoundly distressed about it, and Mary was required to come before the full gerousia, the Judean council of elders, to explain her actions to the twelve archontes.

The council meeting was held in the stone-cutters guild hall near the temple of Dionysus. Mary knew many of the archontes, but certainly not all—many of them did not attend either Alexander's or Lavi's house synagogues but were still highly respected members of the Judean community in Ephesus. She suspected she was acquainted with most of their wives, but since they did not introduce themselves, she could not connect any faces to any of the stories she knew. Other than the four archontes from Alexander's synagogue, she knew only Archon David and Archisynagogos Lavi. Of course Alexander was also one of the archontes, but even he seemed troubled by her actions.

The leader of the gerousia, whose title was Politarch, was a man named Aaron. He was a carpenter by trade. She took that as a good sign.

"How can Myia observe the commandments while living at the idol's temple?" he asked her.

"Does she pray every day?"

"Does she have proper food that hasn't been sacrificed to the idol?"

"Does she purify?"

"Does she avoid unnecessary contact with gentiles?"

Mary did her best to answer all questions honestly even when she knew the answers reflected badly on herself: "How did you know the healers at the idol's temple would care for Myia?" and its follow-up question: "How do you cleanse from your own pollution after you visit your friend at the idol's temple?" The fact that she had decided to allow an elderly gentile man to live in her house only added fuel to the fire. The archontes didn't question her motivation, they said, but they had great concern about her ability to make the right choices.

In the end, they decided that although it would be impossible for a man to live in the temenos of an idol under any circumstance, women weren't held to such high standards. They told her that if Myia decided to repent and if God chose to release the baby from her womb, she would be allowed to return home to her family. The elders also chastised the family, whose observance of corpse contamination halakhot was unreasonably strict for people living outside of Jerusalem and would have resulted in the death of the woman.

But they told Mary that if a situation like this arose again, she should allow the gerousia to decide what to do. They said she shouldn't take on that responsibility herself.

She worried for a while that the gerousia might decide she was unfit to be their mikvah attendant, but this never happened. She suspected there had been much discussion about it in her absence. If so, she was never informed.

She continued to purify, counsel, and care for women and their children in the same ways she had before, sometimes putting the needs of the women ahead of the Law. She never took any issue before the gerousia to decide. And old Adonis spent the remainder of his life in the comfort of the proseuche, under Mary's unquestioned care.

Myia never repented, and God never released the baby from her womb. She had continued through all these years as a wet nurse for the sons and daughters of Artemis, the children abandoned to be raised at the temple. Occasionally a doctor would visit the temple of Aesclepius and would want to try out a new surgical tool on Myia, an embryo crusher or a womb scraper, but the healer priestesses who were now her friends advised against it because her baby was large in her body and the bleeding would be too great.

And after a while, Myia herself didn't want to lose the baby. It was the only child of her body, and she took comfort in the fact that it would always remain part of her. She enjoyed feeding the children of Artemis, but those babies cried, made messes, got older, learned to talk and run away. The baby in her body would do none of that. It would always remain with her, always be part of her, always be there for her to love.

Mary had been expecting today's news. Myia had been quite ill for about a month, and the healer spondopoios at the temple had told Mary that carrying the stone baby for all these years had weakened Myia's heart. Myia's family had not been willing to go to the temple to say good-bye, but they had agreed that if Mary prepared her body, they would see that she was buried according to Judean custom. The Friends of Jesus guild had privately agreed to look after her grave if her family did not make other arrangements.

Artelia had sent Okeanos to her by horse-cart so that she could reach the temple quickly. Mary hurried into Myia's room as soon as he halted the horse at the steps of the asclepeion.

The smell of burning incense permeated the candle-lit room. Myia opened her eyes and seemed glad to see her, so Mary forced her face into a smile.

"My dear, how are you feeling? Are you in much pain?" She smoothed Myia's hair away from her face.

"No, not really," Myia whispered, trying to breathe. "They've given me medicine. But I think it won't be long now."

"No, perhaps not."

"I've named the baby."

"You have?" Mary said in surprise. Myia had always insisted that the baby could not have a name until it was born and always referred to it simply as "my baby."

"Yes. I've named him Jesus, after your son who died and then came back to life. Do you mind?"

"No," Mary whispered, her eyes filling with tears. "That's fine."

"Because I'd like my baby to come back to life, to have another chance to be born, maybe to another woman. Like the potter's clay, in the scriptures."

"Yes." Mary leaned her face next to Myia's and kissed her.

"Will you baptize us?"

"What?"

"You told me that the Friends of Jesus were baptizing Alexander's slave," Myia said. "I haven't been purified in so long, Mary. I feel so unclean. I'd like to be purified and baptized before I die. And I'd like my Jesus to be baptized into God's covenant as well."

Mary took a deep breath. It was one thing to purify and baptize a dying Hebrew woman, to give her the comfort of knowing she would enter paradise clean in the eyes of God. But it was another thing entirely to baptize a baby who'd been dead for five years.

Then she looked into Myia's face and her heart melted. "Of course, Myia. I'll purify and baptize you both. Just give me a few moments to get everything together."

She wished she had known of this before, because she could have brought hyssop from the mikvah. But Israelites were not the only people who practiced purification. Mary turned to Lila, a young initiate crying softly near the bed. Myia and Lila had grown close in the last few years, and Mary had been glad that Myia had a friend in this alien place. She gave Lila a few instructions, and in less than an hour everything was ready.

The spondopoios removed Myia's loose gown from her body, and she now lay on the bed on clean blankets, another clean blanket covering her.

Mary took Myia's hands in her own. "Let's pray." Mary said the full Shema, in Hebrew because she knew it would comfort Myia to hear the words of the Torah in the language of the Patriarchs. She followed this with other prayers in Hebrew and then with some Aramaic prayers including the one she had taught her own children when they were young, the one that began "Our Father, eternal within us, hallowed be Thy Name." She finished with prayers in Greek that Myia would know. Myia smiled to hear them and joined her whispering voice to Mary's.

Mary dipped her finger in a small bowl containing oil of spikenard that Lila held out to her. She gently marked Myia's forehead with the cross shape that was used by the Hebrews to represent the Messiah and she said, "'Fear not,' says the Lord, 'for I have redeemed you. I have called you by name and you are Mine. I will be with you when you pass through the oceans and through the rivers and you will not be overwhelmed. When you walk through fire you will not be burned, nor will you be consumed by the flames. For I am the Lord your God and the Holy One of Israel. I am your Savior.'" She moved the blanket aside to make the same mark on Myia's belly and said the same words.

She placed her fingers in a stone bowl of spring water that was brought to her and sprinkled a few drops on Myia's hair, her face, her body, and her belly. She said the words that John had spoken that morning at Epenetus' baptism: "Lo, thus says the Lord God: enter into the good land, a land flowing with milk and honey."

She nodded to Lila to bring her the next bowl, and she took a bit of honeycomb dipped in milk and rubbed it against Myia's chapped lips. The woman opened her lips enough to touch her tongue against the comb, and then her mouth closed and her head relaxed into the pillow.

"Thank you," she whispered, her eyes closed.

"You're welcome, my dear," Mary whispered back, but she doubted that she was heard.

She sat praying quietly by Myia's bedside, listening to the sound of her breathing as it became more strained. After a while Artelia came over, setting her hand on Mary's shoulder.

"That was a lovely ritual."

"Oh, were you there?"

"I stood by the door."

Mary nodded. "It won't be long now."

"No. It won't be long."

"Do you know, when I first brought her here, years ago, just before she was given those first babies to feed, I had the strangest thought."

"Oh?"

"I saw her breasts, and I thought they looked like the eyes of God. I wondered if that was another of the things your people see when they look at the image of Artemis. And then Adonis told me that the Amazons used to sacrifice their breasts to Artemis, and I realized that in leaving Myia here to be a wet nurse to the children of the idol I was also offering that sacrifice."

Artelia addressed Lila and the other spondopoios. "Could you leave us for a little while?"

The women left the room.

"First of all, the tale about the breasts sacrificed by the Amazons is just a children's story, told by people who see the eggs of Artemis and don't understand what they mean. No one cuts off their breasts for Her," Artelia said as they continued to watch over Myia in her last breaths.

"Your priests cut off their penises."

"That's entirely different, and you know I can't discuss it with you. But I can discuss sacrifice, or gifts, rather. Not what we give to the Goddess, but what She provides to us. The Great Goddess is the source of spiritual food for all who devote their lives to contemplation of our essential being, just like a mother's breast is the source of all nourishment for her baby. But one of the great mysteries is the fact that you don't have to know the ritual worship of Artemis—or even Her Name—to partake of that food. Like the many spokes on the same wheel, or the many roads that all lead to the same city, the many breasts of Artemis show that there are many ways to find that same sustenance. Both of the incantations you spoke today—they could either one have been spoken here in our Temple rituals. There are many ways to gain that same spiritual nourishment."

Mary didn't reply.

"Have I ever told you about our sacred stone?" Artelia asked.

"I don't think so."

"Very long ago, Artemis hurled a stone from the heavens to this place, telling us that this was where Her Temple was to be built."

"Do you still have that stone?"

"We certainly do. It's the most sacred item at the Temple, held inside the body of the great statue of Artemis Herself."

Both women stared at the body of Myia and the belly straining with the stone baby she held within.

"We believe that sacred stone is the navel of the earth. It connects the baby earth with its mother, the Holy Queen of Heaven."

Myia's breathing was shallower now. She made an odd sound and then her breath faded completely away.

"The oxcart is out front," Artelia said. "There are blankets inside to hold her. I'll send some of the spondopoi in to carry her."

"Only women. But wait a while."

"Of course."

"Thank you for being here," Mary said.

Artelia patted her shoulder and then she left.

Spring, five months later

Mary was happy to see Theodora walking up the path. An unknown young woman accompanied her. Mary hadn't seen Theodora as often as she had in the winter, when the girl had come up to the mikvah to purify after every intimate relation with her new husband, John. The frequency of her visits became a point of hilarity among the other women, and even Judith had gotten over her resentment over losing John as a prospective son-in-law enough to make jokes on the rare occasions when she came to the proseuche and Theodora wasn't there. The girl didn't come up so often now that she was expecting a child, but the speed at which she had become pregnant was itself a source of amusement among the other women.

Mary walked out to meet the women on the path.

"Theodora, my dear, how are you?" She gave her a careful hug. "Are you feeling well?"

"I'm doing very well, Mother, thank you. I want you to meet my cousin, Quartillia. Her father, Philip, sent her and her three sisters from Jerusalem to live at my father's house for a while. Things have become very dangerous in Jerusalem, and Ephesus seems like the safest place in the world to be."

"Welcome, Quartillia. Did you want to purify?"

"Another day perhaps, Mary. Mostly I just wanted to meet you." The girl was staring at her, almost in awe.

"Oh?" Mary opened the door and showed them to cushions in the proseuche. She busied herself with making hyssop tea and setting out a few things to eat while they settled in.

"Quartillia has something she wants to show you, Mother," Theodora said. She sounded excited.

"All right." Mary came over to sit down next to them. She looked inquiringly at Quartillia, who was still staring at her.

"I can't believe I'm talking to the Master's mother," Quartillia said finally. "May I call you Mother too?"

"Quartillia is a follower of the Way," Theodora said. "That's what they call it in Jerusalem. The people who are disciples of Jesus are called Nazorenes, and the belief that he's the Messiah is called the Way."

"Did you know my son?" Mary asked doubtfully. Jesus had been dead for seven years now. Quartillia would have been very young when he died.

"Not in the flesh. But I know him in my heart."

"Show her what you brought, Quartillia," Theodora urged her cousin.

Quartillia set the bag of cloth she had been carrying onto the table. She reached in, pulled out a scroll, and unrolled it.

"See what I brought for you?" Her hand on the page was trembling.

"My dear, I'm afraid I can't read," Mary said apologetically.

"Read it to her, Quartillia," Theodora said.

Mary stood and walked to a corner table to pick up a lamp. She brought it over to the girls and set it down by the scroll. "There. Now you can read it to me."

Quartillia began. "John would say to the crowds going their way out to be baptized by him, 'Children of vipers—who told you how to flee from the wrath that is coming?'"

Theodora interrupted her. "No, don't start there. Start later, when Jesus is teaching."

Quartillia rolled through the scroll a bit and started again. "This is what he said to his disciples. 'Happy are those who are poor in spirit, because yours is the kingdom of God. Happy are those who hunger for righteousness, because you will be filled. Happy are you when you are hated and persecuted by men, when they exclude you and reproach you and call you wicked on account of me. Leap and rejoice on that day, for look! You have much reward in Heaven, for their fathers did the same things to the prophets.'"

"What is this?" Mary said, her voice shaking.

"Quartillia collected the sayings of Jesus and wrote them down," Theodora said with excitement. "Here are the stories that the twelve share when they meet together and when they preach to the people."

"How did you hear them, child?" Mary asked Quartillia.

"My father is one of the seven who administers the distribution of food in the church so that the Apostles can focus on the ministry."

"The Twelve are now called the Apostles, Mother," Theodora said, interrupting, "because they're the teachers of the Way."

"I hear them speaking all the time," Quartillia continued. "I thought it was important to write their stories down so others could hear the stories even in their absence."

"What do you mean administer the distribution of food?" Mary said, frowning.

"Everyone who hears and believes in Jesus must sell everything they own," Quartillia explained. "Then they give the money to us so that we can care for the widows and buy food to distribute to the hungry."

"Why do they have to sell everything?"

Quartillia looked at her in surprise. "So that they're ready for the Parousia, Mother. Nothing else matters."

"Don't they earn money?" Mary asked. "I knew the Twelve—they were fishermen and carpenters and tax collectors. How do they feed their families?"

"We take care of the families. I told you—with the money we get when people sell everything they own."

"And my sons James and Judas? They agree to this?" Mary often received letters from her sons, because any time they met a pilgrim from Ephesus in the Temple, they asked him about her and requested that he take a message back with him. The letters told her how the family was doing, all her sons and daughters, with much detail about the grandchildren. They told her Jerusalem was still dangerous and she should stay in Ephesus where it sounded like she had a good, safe life. They never mentioned the Nazorenes or the Way. Perhaps they thought it was unsafe to write such things in letters given to strangers to carry.

"James is our leader, the head of the church," Quartillia said. "He's the one who tells us what to do. He decides which disciples should work together and where pairs of disciples should travel to teach people the Way. He and Peter are responsible for everything that's done." The tone of her voice showed her puzzlement that Mary didn't know this.

"And my son Judas?"

"He doesn't go by the name Judas anymore," Quartillia said. "Neither he nor the other Judas use that name because they don't want to be confused with the betrayer. We usually call him Thomas, or sometimes Didymus, which means the same thing in Greek."

Mary smiled slightly. They had often called Judas "Thomas" when he was young. "Thomas" meant "twin" in Aramaic, and Judas had always been Jesus' shadow, always trailed him everywhere he went. He had even been one of Jesus' first disciples, one of the Twelve. James hadn't become a disciple of his brother's until after his death, when Jesus appeared to him after his resurrection from the tomb.

"Thomas is in Syria now, teaching about the Master," Quartillia said.

Mary shook her head and tried to smile reassuringly at the girls. "Clearly I have a lot to learn about what my children have been doing and about the wonderful work you've done, my dear."

She remembered something Theodora had said when she introduced Quartillia to Mary. "Why did you say things are more dangerous now in Jerusalem? What's happened?"

She knew life had become very dangerous for Israelites in other parts of the world. In Alexandria, Egypt, for example, where Israelites had lived for hundreds of years and were very powerful, thousands of them had been slaughtered in a devastating pogrom and the rest forced to experience terrible atrocities because they refused to worship the emperor. Emperor Caligula had decided he was divine, a living god, and had demanded that his statue be installed in all of the synagogues in the empire so that he could be worshipped alongside the Judean God.

Alexander's ancestors had been slaves in Alexandria. After manumission, his grandfather had emigrated to Ephesus where his children could live as freemen and Roman citizens. Alexander still kept in touch with some of his cousins back in Egypt. When he had heard about the pogrom, he quietly purchased a bust of Caligula and set it on his family altar with the busts of Julius Caesar, Caesar Augustus, and Artemis Ephesia. He invited the Roman proconsul over for dinner and showed him the altar, and the Jews in Ephesus never faced any harassment over not worshipping Caligula.

"The emperor Caligula has ordered that his statue be erected inside the Temple in Jerusalem, in the Holy of Holies," Quartillia said. "The priests absolutely refuse, of course. Everyone is afraid there will be a great war now. We believe that this is what Jesus has been waiting for. He will return now and will lead us to victory against the Romans and their blasphemous emperor, and the kingdom of heaven will finally be ours."

This was the war-like Messiah image of Jesus that had been discussed so much among his followers in the year after his death, resulting in the death of Stephen, the young man who had been stoned for inciting unrest among the pilgrims to Jerusalem. It was difficult for Mary to reconcile this with her own memory of her son as peace-loving, gentle, and kind.

"Why don't you read me your scroll?" she said to Quartillia. "You can start at the beginning. I'd like to hear all of it."

Quartillia and Theodora stayed with her the rest of the day while Quartillia read through her scroll. Mary was grateful that nowhere in the words that had been collected did Jesus say anything about leading his followers into a war. Almost all of the sayings Quartillia had written down, in fact, were similar to things Mary herself had heard her son say—mostly lessons on being a loving and righteous person. He made reference to the female Wisdom several times, and Mary took note to mention this to Artelia. She was delighted to learn that he taught his disciples to pray the simple prayer that she had taught him as a child. She was troubled by his statement that his followers should sell their belongings and donate them to charity, because she thought the disciples in Jerusalem had taken these words too far, giving up everything including their occupations and ability to support their families. But there were only two things she heard that gave her real disquiet.

Quartillia read that Jesus said anyone who came to him and did not hate his own mother and father and brothers and sisters and wife and children could not be his disciple. This truly hurt Mary, and she couldn't understand why her son would say such a thing. But Quartillia told her that several of the disciples had heard him say these words—and that in fact these comments were the source of much discussion, because no one could agree on exactly what he meant by them.

The other thing that distressed her—that distressed her so much that she actually argued with Quartillia about it—was when the girl read that Jesus said, "He who isn't for me is against me, and he who doesn't gather with me scatters."

Mary remembered him saying the opposite. She remembered him saying: "He who is not against us is on our side, and the one who is far away from us today will be near to us tomorrow."

"So are you saying he didn't say 'He who isn't for me is against me?'" asked Quartillia.

"I don't know," Mary said in distress. "I'm not one of his students or his disciples. I'm not one of the Twelve. I'm his mother. I wasn't always there when he was teaching."

But privately she thought: I hope he didn't say such a thing. It's not a very loving thing to say. And she worried that in the years since his death, people might have started to misremember his words.

"I never heard him say that," she repeated.

Theodora asked her to let Quartillia hold Jesus' tunic. Mary did so and stood by helplessly as Quartillia sobbed into it for a very long time, releasing it only when John came to the proseuche to escort the women home.

She thought: "My son, I'm in awe that your loving message continues to be cherished by so many people who never met you."

12

"The limits of my body frustrate me."

Autumn, eight years after the crucifixion of Jesus

"You don't want to walk all the way to the cesspit to dump that," Junia said in her weak voice. "Just empty the chamber pot out the window. Everybody does it. But don't get caught, because you could be arrested."

Mary looked toward the window. Junia's beautiful wool cloak, the one that Mary had admired so at synagogue, was pinned to the frame to keep out the worst of the cold wind. At the edges between the cloak and the window frame, Mary could see into the window of the tenement building next door, only inches away.

She hated to think what that ground was like, in the space between the two buildings.

"No, that's all right," Mary said in her most cheerful voice. "I need to go outside anyway. I'll be right back, and then I'll go get some clean water for you." She smiled at the sick woman and lifted the chamber pot in her two hands, hoping the lid would stay on. She walked steadily over to the door, careful to keep the contents from lapping out, and set the pot on the floor, pulled the door open, set the pot outside in the corridor, closed the door behind her, lifted the pot again, and walked down the filthy, reeking corridor to the stairway. She climbed carefully down the rickety wooden stairs to the ground four floors below, the chamber pot splashing ordure onto her gown with her every shifting step.

The stench outside was foul, but it wasn't as noisome as the smell inside Junia's closed house. Mary walked down the crowded, narrow street to the dung pit, dodging around garbage, carrion, and excreta, trying her best to keep her balance so that she wouldn't splash any further noxious discharge onto herself. The street was filled with smoke from a thousand charcoal braziers, making it difficult to see; everywhere people were yelling, crying, laughing, and fighting, making it hard to think. It was almost impossible not to bump into other people as she walked, and they swore angrily at her as their own clothes were splashed by the contents of the full chamber pot.

When she finally reached the dung pit she was repelled to realize that there was no way she would be able to walk to the hole to empty out the pot without getting filth all over her feet. She sighed, made the noxious walk to the hole, and then walked back up the street with the empty pot, coughing from the smoke and apologizing when she tripped on a drunken vagrant lying in a doorway. When she neared the stairs, she let her caution relax and then she slipped in vomit. She swore as she almost fell on her face into the muck that covered the ground.

Mary squared her shoulders and walked back up the stairs and back down the corridor. She made herself push open the door, this time ready when the closed and fetid stench of urine, feces, vomit, sweat, and decay hit her like a wave. At least summer was over so that the flies and bugs weren't as bad as they might have been. She itched all the same.

"I'm going to get some water now, Junia," she said. "We'll clean you up and get you something to eat, and then we'll clean up this room. You'll feel ever so much better when your room is clean again."

"Thank you, Mary," the poor woman said. "I'm so glad you're here."

Mary went downstairs again, this time carrying a wooden bucket that she filled at the nearest fountain. The fountain featured a statue of Priapus; Mary tried very hard not to look at the source of the stream filling her bucket. Up and down the stairs she went, carrying clean water up and dirty water down, although the water she carried up was not as clean as all that, green and somewhat smelly. She was careful to boil it on the brazier before she gave any to Junia to drink.

Junia had lost control of her bowels, and there was hardly a clean blanket, towel, or piece of clothing in the house. As best as she could, Mary washed the smaller pieces in a basin, hanging them out the window to dry as she had seen other people do. She tied the larger pieces together in a bundle to take back up the hill with her. She knew Gilana would wash them for her.

Junia's husband, Andronicus, and her brother, Herodion, were working in the cinnabar warehouse at the dock, but Elah, her son, should have been here to help. He had come up to the proseuche at dawn this morning to tell Mary that his mother was sick and needed help, but then he disappeared the moment Mary reached the door of their house.

Mary understood why he wouldn't want to be around to see his mother this way. But still, she really could have used the help. Mary wasn't young, and going up and down these stairs was hard.

She needed to get Junia some food. She spent a few moments standing in the room trying to decide the best thing to do. It was a long way to the Judean market. After all this work, it would be impossible for Mary to walk there from Junia's apartment, buy food, walk back, and then have enough strength to walk uphill to her own house, especially carrying a bundle of filthy clothes.

She walked over to the bed. "Junia, I'm going to go get you some food now," she said gently.

Junia turned to look up at her. Looking into her sad brown eyes, Mary was surprised by a sudden recognition: These are the eyes of God.

Mary shook her head, wondering where that strange thought had come from. She often thought she saw the eyes of God in the beauty and purity of nature, but never before had she thought she saw God in the eyes of another person, especially a person surrounded by filth. Was it blasphemous to see God in such circumstances?

She climbed down the stairs again, this time carrying a clean bowl, and went to a food stand near the fountain. She purchased a large bowl of meat and vegetables that had been sacrificed to the god Dionysus and then she climbed back up the stairs to help Junia sit up and eat.

It was mid-afternoon when Elah finally came home, just in time to enjoy the food that Junia had been unable to finish. As Junia fell asleep, Mary addressed the boy. "I'm going to leave now and see if I can get these clothes and blankets washed yet today. I'll be back tomorrow. If your mother isn't any better then, I'll go get a doctor for her."

"We don't have enough money for a doctor."

"I'll take care of it," Mary said. She was a pretty good healer with basic things, but there could be any number of reasons for runny bowels. Sometimes they caused people to die. She wouldn't hesitate to call a doctor for Junia if necessary. "You stay here with your mother. Don't leave her, except to get food or water or someone to help if she gets worse. You're a big boy, old enough to help your mother. You can keep the chamber pot emptied for her. And don't let her drink water that hasn't been boiled. Give her the water in the ewer on that table."

He wrinkled his nose but agreed to stay and help. As she left, Mary looked again at the beautiful wool cloak being used to shutter the window. She now knew this cloak was Junia's most prized possession. Mary hoped the weather wouldn't change to rain, because she was afraid that water would ruin it.

Gilana the laundress was just finishing up her washing when Mary reached her, but after making a few comments about the state of Mary's own clothes, she agreed good-naturedly to wash all of Junia's things and then bring them up to the proseuche to dry near the hearth tonight. Grateful, Mary even managed a weak laugh when Gilana begged her not to show her thanks with a hug.

When Mary reached the mikvah, she stripped off her filthy clothes, intent on immersing herself in the cold, clean water. But at the last moment, she decided that some things were too noxious even for a mikvah to cleanse, so she rushed naked to the spring's runoff to stand shivering while the icy, flowing water washed away the filth from her body.

Naked, she hurried back to the proseuche then banked up the fire in the hearth, put on her warmest old gown, and at last luxuriated in the warm, clean beauty of her simple place, watching the familiar glowing eyes of God dance around the embers in the hearth, thinking about Junia's eyes.

She was too tired to eat or to walk the labyrinth. After Gilana brought Junia's wet clothes in to dry, Mary curled up in a couple of furs near the hearth and went to sleep. She did not even wake up when Gilana brought in Mary's own freshly washed clothes to dry at the hearth.

The next day she dressed in her oldest gown and head covering and filled a small stone jar with water from the spring. The pure living water could be used to purify the noxious fountain water before Junia drank it or bathed in it. Carrying the jar, a few herbs, and the clean clothes, Mary walked down the hill to Junia's tenement neighborhood.

The poor woman wasn't any better, and today she had a terrible fever as well. Mary boiled water and made hyssop tea. She told Elah to help his mother to drink it and left to find a doctor.

The only doctor Mary knew was Jacob, Hannah's son, who had a family surgery near the doctor's guild hall. She asked a person at the guild hall for directions to the right house.

"It's down that street," the man said. "Look for the menorah on the lamp post."

But when Mary finally found Jacob, he declined to help. "We're practicing up our entry for the Aesclepius competition. It starts in just a couple of weeks and we're at a crucial stage with our recipes."

"Please, Jacob—Junia's bowels are running like water. I don't know what to do."

"Where do they live? What fountain do they use?"

Mary told him the neighborhood and then, embarrassed, told him they used the Priapus fountain.

He nodded. "We've had trouble with that fountain before. Dead things are always getting trapped in the pipes from the aqueduct. I'll talk with the city council about it. In the meantime, have the family use a different source of water. And I'll send my daughter Tirzah with you, to see what she can do to help."

Mary smiled. "I also have a daughter named Tirzah."

"Well, that's a good sign then," the doctor said, and he went to call Tirzah in.

Before Mary and Tirzah left, the doctor spoke with his daughter about his preliminary diagnosis. "The best thing for her would be to consume a portion of gladiator liver, but that's very expensive treatment. Try the usual concoction first."

Tirzah agreed, and she and Mary left.

"What was that about gladiator liver?" Mary hoped she had misheard.

"Our presentation in the medical convention will be on the uses of gladiator liver in the treatment of various illnesses," Tirzah said. "But don't tell anyone. We don't want anyone to steal our ideas."

"I won't say a word." Mary was thoroughly appalled by the whole concept and sickened that Israelite doctors would include such a thing in their practice.

She vowed that no matter how ill Junia was, not one bite of gladiator liver would touch her lips.

Once they arrived at the tenement, Tirzah's competence and professionalism reassured Mary. Tirzah did a complete examination and assessment of the patient and agreed with her father that the disease was caused by the water the woman drank rather than any sin she might have committed.

"That will be a relief to her family," Mary said.

"Let me put together a concoction to kill the demons of disease that have taken up abode inside her bowels." Tirzah made Junia drink a small glass of hart's horn, myrrh, pepper, and wine. "Give her some of that to drink every hour. Don't let her drink any more of that water. She should be feeling better by tomorrow."

"Thank you so much!"

"And you should also remove everything that's colored red from the room," Tirzah said. "Red draws the blood out of the body, and she has already lost enough blood through her bowels."

"Of course, doctor. I'll hide everything that's red." Mary took comfort in the doctor's expertise.

Mary didn't want to leave Junia until her husband or brother arrived to take over her care. When finally her husband Andronicus arrived, it seemed as though Junia felt better. At almost dark, Mary left the tenement and began her walk back, her way lit only by the stars and the lamps burning in the windows of the houses she passed.

In all the time Mary had lived in Ephesus, she had never worried about her personal safety. She seldom went into town; when she did, it was usually during the day and in the company of others. She never went to the Artemisium alone or at night. She lived alone up at the proseuche, but she had the reputation of Artemis' sacred grove to protect her. She never thought that anyone would harm her.

So she was taken completely by surprise when the man grabbed her, threw her against a wall, and started fumbling at her clothing. Her head hit the wall hard, and for those first few moments she was too dizzy to even scream for help.

And then it wasn't necessary to scream, because someone pulled the assailant away from her and threw him to the ground.

"I can beat you up or you can run away," growled a deep young masculine voice.

In the dark, Mary saw the shape on the ground scramble up, stand for a moment assessing his chances, and then run quickly away.

"Lady, are you all right?" her rescuer asked gently.

"Um, my head hurts." Her legs wobbled and didn't want to hold her up.

"I can help you walk. Do you live far away?"

"Very far," she said sadly.

"Do you have any friends nearby?"

There was Junia's place, but she'd rather walk uphill to the proseuche. "I have a friend up on Mount Pion," she said. She thought she could make it to Alexander's house.

"Hold onto my arm and tell me which way to go."

Alexander's villa wasn't close, and Mary was exhausted when they reached it. The young man had to practically carry her the last part of the way.

The front door was closed for the night, so her rescuer pounded on it. The slave Thales opened it; shocked by Mary's appearance, he began yelling for assistance from the household.

"Oh lady, oh my dear, dear lady." His voice shook and frightened tears ran down his face.

"What's going on?" Alexander cried, running into the vestibulum.

"Help me get her into the house," the young man said. "Then I'll tell you what happened."

Alexander lifted Mary and carried her into the atrium, her least favorite room in the house. She opened her eyes as he set her down, glancing at the family altar.

"Where's the bust of Caligula?" she asked.

Alexander shook his head. "I was in a meeting at the baths when I heard the herald announce that the emperor had been assassinated. I rushed home, smashed the bust into a million bits, and ordered Epenetus to burn the pieces in the hottest fire in the villa. I thought everyone in the city knew."

"No one mentioned it to me. I'm glad it's gone." Her voice was weak.

"What happened to you?" he asked insistently. He took a glass of water from a slave and held it to her lips. She drank thirstily, and the young man answered.

"She was attacked in the tenements. Her head's bleeding and there's a bump, but she wasn't badly hurt. The man didn't have time to do anything to her."

"Are you sure?"

"I saw it happen. I reached them right away."

"Where is the man?" Alexander asked, his voice cold with anger.

"Gone," the young man said. "I have no idea who he was."

"Mary, do you know who attacked you?"

"No," she said, and then she looked at her young hero. "I don't know who he is either."

"Sorry," the young man said. "My name is Apollos."

"Well, young Apollos, the entire Judean community is in your debt," Alexander said.

"No need," Apollos said. "I'm an Israelite too. I'm glad I was there to help."

Aspasia and her women took Mary to a bedroom to help her clean up and rest. Apollos stayed in the atrium to speak further with Alexander.

Though she found that she couldn't bear to eat, Mary joined Alexander for breakfast the next morning, assuring him that she was well enough to return home. As he ate, he told her the boy's story. Apollos was one of the Israelites from Egypt who had immigrated to Ephesus after the pogrom in Alexandria.

"He's highly educated in Greek philosophy," Alexander said, "but he knows very little about the Torah. Doesn't speak a word of Hebrew. I gather his family were apostates but kept some of the practices. He's circumcised, at least."

"Is his family here?"

"No," Alexander said. "He lost everyone back in Alexandria. He's actually a relative of mine, a part of my family that stayed in Alexandria when my grandfather emigrated from Egypt to Ephesus."

"Poor boy," Mary said. "What has he been doing since he arrived in Ephesus?"

"Very little, from what I can gather. He works as a scribe occasionally. But that doesn't matter now, because he has a new occupation."

She smiled fondly at her friend. "You've given him a task?"

"I have. He's going to take care of you."

"What do you mean by that?"

"You need a servant anyway. Better to have one who's young and strong and can protect you."

"He's going to live at the proseuche with me?"

"He is," Alexander said firmly. "He'll be back here shortly to escort you up the hill."

Alexander insisted that Mary and Apollos be driven up the hill by donkey cart. "I don't like the bump on the back of Mary's head. Apollos, you're to watch and make sure she doesn't do anything strenuous."

"I need to check on Junia," Mary said.

"I'll send someone to take care of Junia," Alexander said. "If she's not better, I'll have her brought back here, and I'll make Jacob leave his idiotic recipes long enough to check on her. Anything else?"

"No," Mary said. "Thank you." She was grateful that she didn't have to walk up the hill and also grateful that someone else would take care of Junia. Her head really hurt.

The cart ride up the hill was agony, and she leaned over the side several times to vomit. When the cart finally reached the proseuche, Theodora and Quartillia sat on the benches outside, waiting for her.

"Mother, where were you?" Theodora asked. "And who is this?"

"This is Apollos, who is going to be my new helper."

"Mother, I have very bad news," Quartillia said. Mary saw that her eyes were red and swollen. She hurried to get out of the cart and took the girl in her arms, ignoring the sharp pains in her head.

"My dear, what has happened?"

"It's James, the son of Zebedee," Quartillia said, crying. "He's been executed. I got a letter from my father."

Mary felt dizzy. Apollos grabbed her and helped her into the proseuche. He eased her onto a cushion and poured her a glass of water.

"Speak," he ordered Quartillia.

"I don't know much. Just that the Nazorenes are being persecuted, and Agrippa had James put to death by the sword."

"He was always a wild boy, but very dear," Mary said sadly. "Jesus called him and his brother John the 'sons of Thunder.' I'll have to write a letter to his mother." Her heart hurt, thinking about her friend Mary's pain.

"I can write it for you," Apollos said.

"And I can take it to Jerusalem for you," Quartillia said.

"You're not going back there!" Mary said in alarm.

"I am," Quartillia said firmly. "My father needs me."

Mary stood up to go to the girl, then almost fainted when her head pounded again. She just couldn't do this now. "Excuse me, but I need to lie down for a while." She wobbled into her room, lay down on her bed, and cried.

She fell asleep and woke up at midday when Apollos stuck his head in her door. "Mary—say, can I just call you 'Mother' too?"

"Go ahead."

"Mother, there's a priestess from the temple of Artemis here to see you."

Mary sat up quickly, and the excruciating pain almost split her head open. "Apollos, have you ever mixed opium in a glass of wine?"

"No, I never have."

She told him how to do it, and while he hunted for the bit of opium left from the last days of Adonis' life, Mary forced herself up to greet her guest.

Artelia was sitting on one of the benches outside. When Mary neared her, she saw that her friend looked almost as bad as she herself felt.

"What happened to you?" they both said at almost the same time.

"I got hit on the head," Mary said. "You?" Her words were slurred.

"My story is longer than that," Artelia said, "so you should sit down. Do you remember Lila?"

Mary frowned and sat down on a bench.

"She was an initiate when Myia was at the temple of Aesclepius. They were friends. She helped you with Myia's baptism."

"Oh, that's right," Mary said. She felt dizzy again.

"She was chosen as one of the select, one of my twelve priestesses. Then she got married a year or so ago."

"Well, that's a good thing. Isn't it? They can get married if they want, can't they?"

"Oh, certainly. They can get married. But if they do they can't return to the Temple to worship or to serve."

"Right." Mary vaguely remembered Artelia telling her that before. But she could hardly concentrate. Where was that boy with her drink?

"There are a lot of other things she could have done," Artelia continued. "She could have joined the Demeter cult—they have their own festival, the Thesmophoria, that's just for married women. Or she could have approached the temple of Isis and asked for permission to enter. Followers of Isis have many of the same rituals and beliefs we have, but they aren't so invested in chastity. They would have been glad to welcome a sister priestess from Artemis. Or she could have left her husband, waited ten years, and then undergone ritual purification. She could have worshipped at shrines to Artemis in the meantime. But the Temple and the sacred Mysteries—these are forbidden to married women." There was anguish in her voice.

"Artelia, what happened?"

"She was caught. Right there in the Temple. Right in the middle of the most sacred ritual. I don't know how she thought she wouldn't be caught."

"Artelia, what has happened?" Mary asked again.

"What would happen if someone blasphemed at your great temple in Jerusalem?" Artelia asked, looking her friend directly in the face.

"She was stoned?" Mary said, aghast.

"No. Not stoned. Artemis doesn't want human blood, except for moon blood. No torture. Her violators take poison."

"She was poisoned?"

"Indeed. By her own hand. She even knew the old ritual to use, which she could have only discovered by reading some of the secret books. She planned for her death. She must have been very unhappy."

"She must have truly missed worshipping Artemis," Mary said. She remembered the young girl who had been so kind to Myia. One more tragedy.

"What do you mean?"

"Well, what would you do if someone told you that you couldn't worship your goddess anymore?"

"Lila could still worship," Artelia insisted.

"But not in the temple. Not there at the statue, near your sacred stone. She couldn't serve her goddess in the way that mattered to her. What would you do if someone took that away from you?"

"I'd want to die. But she didn't have to get married."

Mary shook her head, then immediately regretted it as the pain struck. "All young women want to have families. It's a natural desire that God gives us. I'll bet even you were tempted, when you were her age." The glaring sun hurt her eyes, and she turned her head away from her friend so she could shade them.

"I suppose I thought about it," Artelia admitted.

"I wouldn't say this if I didn't feel so ill, because I usually try to only say kind things, but I think it's cruel that your halakhah makes you choose between having a family and serving your god."

"What does that word mean?"

"Halakhah. It means the path that you walk in your relationship with God. The beliefs and the traditions. The commandments that God has given His people."

"Well, it's as you said. It's a commandment our Goddess has given us. The simple fact is, we can't serve Her fully in our heart if our mind is occupied thinking about people. We can't give our complete allegiance to Her and also give it to a husband or children."

"Well, Lila wanted to have both, or maybe she changed her mind about the husband. But either way, I guess she'd rather be dead than live without serving your goddess."

"I'm sorry she felt that way. But it makes more sense now. Thank you for your unkind comment. It helps."

"You're welcome."

The friends sat in silence for a few moments.

"There's too much death today," Mary said.

Artelia looked at her. "Did someone else die?"

"A boy from back home. One of my son's disciples. Executed."

"Oh my dear, I'm so sorry."

"And now my poor little Quartillia is going to go back to Jerusalem, and it's so dangerous there I can't bear to even think of it."

"Young people make foolish choices," Artelia said. Mary knew she was thinking about Lila again.

"So what happens now?" Mary asked.

"Hmm?"

"At the temple. What happens next?"

"The Temple is polluted. We have to close it down and purify everything. Well, you know how that goes."

"Yes, I do," Mary said. She saw Apollos coming toward them, a glass in his hand. She said a silent grateful blessing. "Do you want a glass of opium?" she asked her friend.

Artelia stared at her. "Mary, I think you better tell me how you hit your head."

Apollos told her about the attack, and Artelia took charge of Mary. Her litter bearers helped Apollos carry Mary to her bed, and then one of them ran back to the aesclepeion for a couple of doctors. Until a doctor could see her, Artelia refused to allow Mary to drink any opium.

"But my head hurts," Mary moaned.

"I know, dear. We'll give you some nice willow bark tea very soon, which will help ease the pain in your head. In the meantime, perhaps you'd like to hear some prayers to your god." She looked inquiringly at Apollos.

He shrugged. "I don't really know any," he said.

"Aren't you a Judean? You look like a Judean."

"Sorry."

"Well, we need some divine help here. If you can't call on the Judean god, I'm calling on Artemis."

As Artelia and Apollos squabbled about prayer, Mary lost consciousness.

She woke to the reverent mumbling of someone praying. She struggled to clear the cloudiness from her eyes, and the whispered words stopped. Mary turned her head toward their direction and saw Artelia staring at her, smiling broadly.

"Bless the Goddess—you're awake."

But Mary couldn't say anything, because as she looked at the face of Artelia, she saw God staring back through her eyes. And more than that: she saw Artelia's familiar features subtly shift into the features of a different face and then a different one and then a different one. Mary stared in awe at Artelia's face as her features continued to change, a new face sweeping over the last one, over and over and over, some young, some old, some light-skinned, some dark, but all of them, every one, a woman's face and all of them the face of compassion.

"How do you feel?" Artelia asked.

"I see God in your eyes," Mary whispered.

Artelia laughed gently. "My dear, I've seen God in your eyes since the first time we met."

Mary smiled and fell back asleep.

When she woke the second time, it was to hear one of the spondopoi urging her to take her medicine. Mary obediently opened her mouth, and because she was thirsty she swallowed the bitter liquid without complaint. She looked over the woman's shoulder and saw Theodora and Quartillia. Their faces were blotchy with tears.

"I'll be all right," Mary said to them, her voice shaky and faint.

"I told them you were going to live, but they insisted on staying," the healer priestess said. "Now tell them to go away so that I can clean you up."

Mary did feel sticky, and there was a bad smell in the room that she feared might be her own body. "Go get some rest, girls. I'll be fine."

Theodora and Quartillia came over to kiss her first. "We'll be back later," Theodora promised.

Mary smiled at her then looked up at Quartillia. "I'm glad you're still here."

Quartillia caressed Mary's cheek. "I won't leave for Jerusalem until you're better, Mother. So don't worry."

They left the room, and Mary heard them reassuring other people that she would be well. Then she smiled to hear a room full of voices reciting prayers of thanksgiving to God. Judging by the many deep voices, there might even be a minyan in the room. For the first time, her house was a real proseuche.

The next time she woke up, she actually felt pretty good. She lifted her head and realized it felt very light. She put her hand to her head and discovered to her horror that she was bald. Someone had shaved her scalp. She frantically moved her hands over her head. Most of it was wrapped in a large bandage.

"There was swelling," Artelia said. She was the only other person in the room. "They had to do surgery."

"What does that mean?"

"They drilled a hole into your head, to release the bad humors."

"Did they get them all?"

"We think so." Artelia poured her a glass of water and helped her drink.

"That tastes so good," Mary said.

Artelia smiled. "Your sacred spring has the best water in Ephesus."

"Who did you and Apollos finally pray to?"

Artelia sobered and pulled her stool close to Mary. She took Mary's cold hand between her own two warm ones. "I have an interesting story to tell about that. I sent him down the hill to gather some Judeans to pray for you while I prayed to Artemis. Did I ever tell you about the great mystery of Artemis, the Mother Earth?"

"No."

"As Mother Earth, She is the center of the web of creation. The stars and the zodiac all circle Her body, drawing sustenance from Her, because everything is ultimately part of Her body—we come from Her body, we live on Her body, and we return to It. Everything we need comes from Her—all nourishment, all healing, all purity, all goodness. I was calling on Artemis to nourish you with Her healing presence, and She was here—I felt Her—but Her presence was just a shadow behind the stronger presence of another. A masculine presence."

"Masculine?"

"Yes. I ordered him to show himself to me, because I could not allow any evil demons to interfere with your healing."

"My son used to order evil demons out of people."

"I'm not surprised. It was your son who appeared."

Mary stared at Artelia. "My son appeared?"

"I think it must have been him. There was a quality about him that reminded me of you."

"Did he speak?"

"No. He just stood here looking at you."

"Did he smile?" She'd loved her son's smile.

"No. His face was very serious, almost like a statue. But he emanated light—and a fierce love. And when he was here, I felt heat coming off you. He was healing you."

"And he didn't say anything?"

"Just at the very end. Just before he left."

"What did he say?" For years Mary had yearned to see her son, and now when he finally appeared she had been unawake and unable to see him. It just wasn't fair.

"He looked at me for the first time," Artelia said. "And he said: 'Thank you for being her friend.' And then he left."

"He thanked you for being my friend?"

"Yes."

Mary didn't know how to respond. Tears leaked from her eyes. Finally she said, "Well, I too thank you for being my friend."

Artelia squeezed her hand, and then she raised it to her lips and kissed it. "It is my honor."

Mary thought: "My son, I've received so many blessings since my attack. Forgive and bless the man who hurt me."

"God blesses and punishes righteous and unrighteous alike."

Summer, eleven years after the crucifixion of Jesus

A t first she couldn't see him, there in the dark, filthy cell. But when the jailer thrust his torch around she heard chains rattling and then she saw the filthy skeleton of a wincing man, his head turned against the harsh light. "Who are you?" he asked in anguish.

"Move the torch away, please," Mary said to the jailer. The man stepped back to place it in a ring in the wall. Mary bent down to address the prisoner. "I'm Mary. I came here to visit someone else, but when I heard you here in the dark I asked the jailer if I could visit with you for a while." She had been visiting Tychicus, son of the God Fearers Narcissus and Calandra. Tychicus had arrested after getting into a drunken brawl with some pilgrims from Rome, visitors to the temple of Artemis. Calandra had begged her fellow guild members at John's church to visit her son in jail because he was terribly scared and lonely.

Apollos and Mary had walked here together, but prisoners were only allowed one visitor, and Apollos had stayed outside. Mary had brought Tychicus food and water from the spring. Happily, he had frequent visitors, enough to keep him clean, clothed, and well-fed, and even more happily he would be released in a few days. She had found him chained to a soldier, kneeling on the ground and playing merels, a game with black and white balls that her own children had played sometimes. He didn't seem distressed by his confinement.

But after she left him, hurrying with the jailer toward the clean light of day, she felt moved to glance into a dark cell. And then she heard the sound of a person truly alone and scared.

"Who is that crying?" she asked the jailer. The utter anguish of the sound tied knots in her heart.

"Just a wretch scheduled for execution," the man said.

"I'd like to visit him, please."

And now she was here with the poor man and she didn't know what to do. She heard scurrying in the rushes on the floor and knew there were rats. She glanced around the small cell, now flickering with torch-lit shadows, and did not see even a small stool to sit on. She grimaced and forced herself to sit on the ground next to the man.

"Careful," the jailer said.

"He's in chains, manacled to the wall."

"And he has nothing to lose if he hurts you."

"What do you want?" the man asked her. She could hear the tears choking his deep voice. She could see he had once been a big man, but now he was skeletal, held together by strips of filth.

"I don't know what I want," she said honestly. "I just wanted to see you, to give you comfort if you need it."

"Why?"

She realized why she was here. "My son was executed."

There was silence for a few moments and then he spoke. "Tell me about him."

And so she did. She told him the entire story, about her visions and her son's birth; his childhood and his brothers and sisters. And then she told him about Jesus the man and teacher. Because of Quartillia's scroll, read so many times now in the church that all knew it by heart, she was able to speak about her son the way his disciples spoke about him. She told the man about the healings and the miracles; the teachings about how a person should live and treat others; about his death and resurrection and the hope of the Parousia. She told him about the Nazorenes in Jerusalem and the Friends of Jesus church here in Ephesus; about their meetings and their baptismal rituals, and finally about the son of two members whose imprisonment had caused her to be here today. She told him how the death of her son had broken her heart, but she didn't relate the true horrors of that day until the prisoner asked.

"How was your son executed? Tell me how they killed him."

So she shared with him the images that were seared into her soul: the metal tips of the whip, shredding his precious skin; the anguished screams of her son; the nails pounded through his flesh; the splintered wood, painted red with his blood; the very worst of her nightmares. By the end she was crying heavily, her tears falling down the man's iron collar onto his bony shoulders.

Eventually she fell silent. All was quiet in the cell for a long time except for the rats and the occasional tearful sniff from the corner where the jailer still stood.

"Thank you for telling me about Jesus," the imprisoned man said. "And thank you for baptizing me with your tears. Would you pray with me?"

"Oh yes." She took his poor chained and battered hands in hers. She taught him the simple words and they prayed together.

"Will you see to my burial?"

"What is your name, my son?"

"I am Nikolaos," he said.

"Nikolaos, I will see to your burial, and I will say prayers over your grave."

"Thank you."

As she and the jailer left, they heard him praying. His prayers were addressed to Jesus, a fellow criminal and victim to the executioner. His voice was softer even than the sound of the rats, but Mary knew God wept when he heard it.

"What did Nikolaos do?" Mary asked the jailer as he was opening the outside door. The sunlight knifed into her eyes, and Apollos hurried over to help her.

The jailer shrugged. "Killed someone, I think, or maybe stole from someone important. I don't remember. Does it matter?"

"No. I'd like to bring him some food and clothes. Will he still be here tomorrow?"

"He won't be executed for another few days."

"How will they do it?"

"Sword," he said, and she remembered that was how James the son of Zebedee had lost his life.

"I'll see you tomorrow then," she said.

"Lady?"

"Yes?"

"Do you think I could come to your Friends of Jesus meetings?"

She told him that of course he would be welcome, and they left. It was a long walk home because she kept stopping along the way to vomit.

After Nikolaos' corpse, the head severed from the body, had been on display for a few weeks as an example to others, the executioner released it to Mary. Mary prayed while John and Apollos buried him in a small space at the edge of the cemetery at the back of Mount Pion. After much discussion, she had agreed to a temporary grave as prelude to placing his bones in an ossuary, a practice used when burial space and funds for entombment were limited. John and Apollos thought even this respectful treatment to be excessive. The corpses of most criminals and poor people were simply thrown into great holes outside the city, along with dead animals and the overflow from the city's dung pits.

The burial over, the three of them stopped to show their respect to Adonis and Leah at their tombs and then they walked back to town. Mary listened as John and Apollos fell into their favorite occupation, talking about the Logos, the energy that created the world. John now equated Jesus with the Logos. He had started using the word after hearing it from Apollos, who had learned it from Philo, his Judean teacher back in Alexandria.

Apollos had not been particularly interested in the teachings of Jesus, although he was always present at the Friends of Jesus church, since it met in the room where he slept. But one day at the church, John mentioned that Jesus sometimes referred to himself as the "son of man" or the "son of Adam," and Apollos, astonished, said that those were two of the phrases Philo used to describe the Logos.

He told John that Philo said that the Logos was the creative principle of God, an intermediary, necessary because God himself could not come into contact with imperfect material things. God used the Logos as a model for the human mind: it was the connection between God and man.

John had heard the term Logos used by the Sophists and Stoics in his lessons at the gymnasium, but he hadn't paid much attention. He delighted in being able now to connect the Greek philosophy he had learned at the gymnasium with his comprehension of Jesus and his mission. Particularly as time went on and the Parousia did not occur, his understanding of the importance of Jesus' life had changed. Now he and Apollos spent all of their time together discussing it. Mary, who knew Theodora worried, sometimes had to shoo John away from the proseuche late at night when her two sons were still in front of the hearth, deep in discussion of their philosophies, lost in time.

Mary did not have an opinion about the Logos. It did not fit in with anything she had ever heard Jesus say, although she tried to keep an open mind when she listened to John and Apollos talk. She had been taught Greek philosophy by a Skeptic, and she could just imagine the scathing comments her old teacher Adonis would make if he were here—especially since John said that the Stoics considered the Logos to be the divine energetic principle of the universe. Adonis had loathed the Stoics. However, she vaguely remembered him quoting the old Ephesian philosopher Heraclitus from time to time, and John quoted Heraclitus as saying "all things come to pass in accordance with the Logos." She wished she'd paid more attention so she could share in the boys' conversation.

The three of them had been walking in the city for a while, moving through tenement area to public area to tenement area on their way to Alexander's villa, when Mary noticed that the smell of smoke was stronger than usual. They stopped, alert, and then the screaming began.

Flames shot out of a window in the building next to them, and then they heard the horrible sound of a child screaming in agony. John hardly hesitated before running up the stairs of the tenement, fighting the crowd of people hurrying down. A moment later he was standing at the window of the burning room, screaming "Apollos!" Apollos ran under the window and caught the child that John threw down, and then a moment later John himself fell screaming out of the window.

Apollos quickly threw the small child to Mary. The child's gown was aflame, and Mary ran to the nearby fountain to drop the screaming baby into the water, fighting other burning people to reach the water. Moments later she was joined by Apollos, carrying the larger John across his back. The fire in John's clothes was out, but he was covered with smoke and blood and his face was contorted with agony. "I think he broke some bones in the fall, Mother," Apollos said.

"We need to get out of here," Mary said.

They squeezed along with the screaming crowd away from the tenements, but the fire moved even faster. Mary carried the burned baby and Apollos carried the broken John.

They ran, goods and furniture showering them, flung desperately from the windows of burning apartments. Houses fell, crushing all unfortunates running nearby. Burning people screamed, and others screamed just as desperately trying to find their loved ones. The unbearable heat and strong smoke meant that they could hardly breathe or see. Mary, one hand clutching Apollos' tunic, continued to move with the crowd, unable even to see the ground below her, aware sometimes that the soft impediment she tripped over was a human body, fallen and crushed beneath the frightened mob.

The fire was the worst in the tenements, where everything was made of wood, straw, pitch, and cloth. So they headed toward the public spaces, where the large marble buildings, temples, and fountains would be less susceptible to the flames.

Mary realized that they had neared the state agora. Most people who had got this far collapsed at the large fountain outside the agora, but Mary knew where the air would be less smoky. "The Basilica," she said to Apollos. "It's made of marble, and there's a fountain inside."

They climbed the marble steps to the Basilica, passing the statues of Emperor Augustus and his wife, to set John and the child on the cool marble ground near the fountain inside the nave. John was moaning, but the baby had long since ceased to make any sound, although Mary knew it was still alive.

"Can you take care of them, Mother?" Apollos asked. "I have to go out there and help."

She stared at him wretchedly. "We'll be fine, dear. Please try to be careful."

He bent down, kissed her, and ran back out into the inferno.

Mary removed her scorched shawl, dipped it into the water of the fountain, and began to care for her two patients. John's hip was broken and he had minor burns. The child—a little girl—had worse burns, but she was blessedly unconscious most of the time. Mary herself had burns, but all of her limbs worked, and she would worry about treating her skin later, after the emergency was over.

She settled the baby in John's arms and moved to help another injured person who lay crying on the floor nearby. The floor space between the colonnades of the Basilica became more and more crowded with injured people as the fire spread through the city. The marble temples of the gods, which once

Mary had considered so foolish, now became true sanctuaries, safe havens for those whose wooden homes were ablaze. The state agora became a place where the dead lay dumped in piles and the frightened homeless huddled together. The cool marble floors of the Basilica beside it became an asclepeion, where injured people were treated and comforted by Mary and the priestesses of the nearby temple of Hestia Boulaia.

The devastating fire blazed through the city for hours, destroying half the wooden tenements in the city and making a large percentage of the population homeless and without food, shelter, or wherewithal. In the horrors of the fire, God did not distinguish Judeans from gentiles. Mary would never again view pollution and purification in the same way as she had before the fire. She would never be able to smell a burnt offering without remembering the smell of burning human flesh.

She was impressed by the tenacity and bravery of the Roman soldiers. Ephesus did not have the organized Vigiles Urbani, watchmen of the city such as existed in Rome and Alexandria, to police crime and fight fires. Instead, Roman soldiers, joined by citizens such as Apollos, took on the role of fire fighters, using pumps, buckets, quilts soaked in water, and other equipment to fight the flames and knocking down buildings with hooks and levers as needed to create fire breaks. They formed bucket brigades and worked with citizens to catch people as they jumped from burning buildings. Army doctors came to the Basilica the morning after the fire, bringing medicines, pain killers and skilled hands to assist with the care of the injured. A Roman bone setter treated John's hip injury.

Mary received enough opium to keep the burned child sedated for a month, and the doctor even told her what to expect when it came time to wean the child off the medicine.

"Look at Mary's hands," said one of her patients, an astrologer and sorcerer named Sceva. He was the first person Mary had treated after John and the little girl, and he felt protective of her.

Mary demurred, but the doctor ignored this, taking her hands gently in his. He frowned to see the raw flesh on the palms and backs of her hands and pushed the cloth on her arms aside to examine the blistered skin there.

"How far up do these burns go?" he asked.

"Just my hands and arms. I'm not hurt anywhere else."

"Why haven't you done anything to treat these?"

"I've been busy."

"If you don't get these treated, you could lose your hands. As it is, you'll be badly scarred and probably crippled. I hope you don't rely on weaving or embroidery for your livelihood, because you'll never do any kind of detailed work like that again."

Having scared Mary into taking care of herself, he moved on to his next patient, and she went to find one of the priestesses to treat her burns.

After the fire danger was over, Apollos returned to the Basilica, bringing slaves from Alexander's villa to take John, Mary, and the baby back to the house. The houses of the rich, up on the hills, were made of stone and brick and were less susceptible to fire. Buckets of water always sat in corners of Alexander's house, and his slaves were trained in fire fighting. His house, like most of the houses of the wealthy, still stood intact. Deborah lost her house, but she, her husband, and her children survived and moved into her father's place. Everyone who lived with Alexander and who had been home when the fire began remained unscathed; this included Theodora and all of the children. Alexander and Enoch, who had been at the baths, were uninjured.

But Enoch's sweet wife Aspasia, the former slave and mother of his children, had been shopping in the crowded Judean market when the fire spread into that part of the city. She died along with one of her women and a dozen other Israelites.

John's wife Theodora proved to be strong and capable. She took over the running of the house and caring for the grieving and injured. She and Deborah prepared Aspasia's body for burial, and she made sure all the prayers were said and rites were followed, missing nothing even in the confusion of the week. Mary would never think of her as a child again.

Mary and the injured baby, whom she called Salome after her sister, stayed at Alexander's house for two weeks receiving care for their burns. At the end of the first week after the fire, the head slave Epenetus came to ask Mary if she could attend Alexander in the atrium. She allowed a slave to cover her head with a shawl and hurried to the room.

In the atrium, Alexander and Artelia sat together enjoying a fruit drink. Artelia set her glass down and rushed to hug Mary.

"Oh my dear, I just heard about your injuries. Okeanos went up to the proseuche several times to check on you, and when you didn't return there, I decided to come here. I needed to consult with Alexander anyway."

"How are you doing? Was the temple damaged?"

Artelia shook her head. "No, we're very good at preventing fires. The last great Temple was destroyed by a fire long ago and now we take strong precautions."

"I'm glad."

"It may be safe from fire, but Artelia was just saying that the temple is facing another danger," Alexander said. He seemed to have aged ten years in the last week. He was burdened by the devastation felt by the members of his synagogue. He grieved for Aspasia, who had grown up in this house and been a loving wife to his son and a good mother to his grandchildren.

"We're facing the depletion of our treasury," Artelia explained to Mary.

"Why?"

"Because Ephesus is the Temple Keeper of Artemis, and in times of peril Artemis must feed and house Her people. That will be expensive. The fire destroyed all commerce in the city, and I doubt that there will be any tourists at the Temple for a long time and so there will be no taxes this year. That will further drain the treasury. And just this week we discovered that the Temple income was already dangerously low. Some unscrupulous city officials who were supposed to manage our income have misused Temple monies to fund excessive and unnecessary celebrations. That's what I wanted to consult with you about, Alexander. I want to renew our request to the governor to put the management of the treasury and Temple income back into our hands. I'd like your advice about that."

Mary learned then that it had been a long time since the spondopoi of the temple of Artemis had been in control of the great treasury that bore her name. Long ago the city government decided that it could better manage the temple funds. Emperor Augustus had agreed and had granted the temple a separate and generous income to cover temple expenses. Unfortunately, even this income was managed by others. The people who gave votive offerings to the temple, the people whose taxes were paid to the temple, and the people who worked for the various temple fishing, agricultural, and commercial enterprises, all thought that Artemis, through her spondopoi, was responsible for the money. So did most people who relied on the temple treasury for banking purposes, as a place to save or borrow money. But in fact, civil administrators managed those funds, and often these people were not good guardians of Artemis' treasury.

"There's hardly enough money for the fall processions, nor enough to arrange and care for this year's dedications. There's not enough income left to feed and shelter masses of homeless and starving people as well."

"If it's a choice between feeding and sheltering the people or paying for festivals, processions, and dedications," Mary said, "I think your choice is clear. I've always wondered if Artemis loves her people. Because if she does, she will care for them in their time of despair, even if it means limited celebrations for a while."

"You don't believe She exists at all," Artelia said.

Mary looked at her friend and saw the eyes of God looking back at her. She looked next at Alexander and saw God shining through his eyes as well. She shrugged. There was no way to describe what she believed.

"The Judeans will make a donation to the temple of Artemis," Alexander said. "We haven't taken our sacred Temple tax to Jerusalem in two years. We will donate all the money we have banked at the temple, with the strict proscription that it's to be used by the high priestess of Artemis for the care of the citizens of Ephesus during this emergency. I'll need to discuss it with the gerousia, but I'm sure they'll agree eventually. This is their city too. And the Judean community doesn't have the organization to manage a charity of this size."

When Alexander made his request to the gerousia, they remembered their anger some years before when Pontius Pilate had used Temple funds to build an aqueduct into Jerusalem. For many of them Alexander's request seemed like a similar blasphemy. But the following week, after much anguished debate at the gerousia, the city heralds announced that the Judeans had made a substantial donation to Artemis, in gratitude for her protection of her city. The Israelites squirmed at the way this was worded, but their fellow Ephesians recognized and appreciated their generosity, and later when Israelite homes and businesses were being rebuilt they found their gentile neighbors as helpful and supportive as their synagogue brethren.

But it was a long time before everyone had permanent shelters again. In the meantime, even with Artemis' help, people were desperate for housing, and food became increasingly difficult to obtain. Mary realized this when she returned home two weeks after the fire and discovered that two Hebrew families and their slaves had moved inside the proseuche.

Every blanket, fur, piece of clothing, and cloth in her house had been appropriated by someone, everything except for the few things from back home that she kept in a small trunk in her room. Fortunately Jesus' tunic was kept in this trunk, so she didn't really mind losing everything else, not even the beautiful length of blue silk Artelia had given to her long ago, which was now torn in half and used as swaddling for one baby and a tunic for another.

Apollos took charge as soon as he and Mary arrived. He moved the family out of Mary's bedroom and helped them to reconstruct Adonis' old tent to move into. He allowed the other family to stay in the proseuche for the time being, but told them that they would need to make other arrangements soon, they would need to go somewhere else if people came up to use the mikvah, and they must either join the Friends of Jesus church or leave the building during the First Day meetings.

The squatters had been milking the goat, and Apollos told them they could continue doing so. He showed them where to find honey in the grove. He showed the women and children how to gather beechnuts that had fallen to the ground and how to make beechnut paste and oil. He put two of the older children in charge of the garden and showed them how to weed and cultivate the vegetables and herbs. He impressed on them that the only fire allowed on the hill was the one he himself maintained, the one in the hearth.

Someone from Alexander's house continued to bring food every day for Mary and Apollos, though only once a day now and not as much or as varied as before. They did not bring enough to feed the squatter families. The tragedy had strained even Alexander's resources.

"We're going to have to let the families eat the peacocks," Apollos said to Mary. "I'll do the killing. At least one a week. And if I can catch a few of the peahens, we can see if they'll lay eggs for us."

"Let me tell Artelia first," Mary said. She knew her friend would sadly agree, but she wanted her to know about it before the sacred birds became food.

"When Okeanos comes up, I also want to ask him about guards," Apollos said.

"What do you mean?"

"Mother, people are starving down in the city. It's going to get worse this winter. We won't be able to keep them from coming up here and taking our wood and our food if we don't have help from the temple."

"Apollos, first of all, it's not our wood. It's Artemis'. If the Artemisium wants to send guards to protect their grove, that's their business. But we worship God. And God tells us to feed the hungry and to clothe the naked. Do you remember what Jesus said, in that scroll of Quartillia's? If someone asks you for your cloak, give them your tunic as well. This is a test of us, of our hearts and our faith."

"Mother, they already have all our cloaks and our tunics. We don't have anything left to give."

"We still have Jesus' own tunic," she said with sad determination.

Apollos looked at the bandages covering Mary's hands, damp and discolored from the fluids still seeping out even though new skin had begun to grow. He knew she would hand over her own heart to a stranger if he or she needed it. "Don't fret, Mother," he said, sighing. "Jesus' tunic is safe. If more squatters come up, we'll figure out how to make clothes out of peacock feathers for them."

"And talk to Okeanos anyway," she said. "I'm sure the Artemisium won't want to send guards. But if things start to get really crowded up here, they'll probably be willing to assist us with food and blankets."

That winter, an epidemic raced through the homeless, hungry people of the city, killing thousands. Salome's family, if they survived the fire, were likely among the people lost in the epidemic, because even though Alexander's slaves searched for months, no one ever appeared at Mary's door to claim her.

She thought: "My son, help me always to provide rescue when possible and hope and comfort when it's not."

CHAPTER

14

"Heaven and hell are born from within."

Spring, fifteen years after the crucifixion of Jesus

Mary lay back on a blanket on the ground, her attention drifting. One ear listened to John speak, but the other listened for storks. Passover had ended over a week ago. The birds were late this year.

"We have some guild business we need to conduct today," John said. It was a beautiful day and over a dozen people attended the church meeting. After the Great Fire, when the Friends of Jesus meetings became very crowded, meetings had moved outside to the old marble plinths now used as benches. If it was very cold outside, the Friends would light a small fire in the fire pit that had been originally used for the new moon ceremonies, but everyone was still nervous about fire and usually did without one. They certainly didn't need one on a gorgeous spring afternoon like this.

Not as many people attended the church now as they had during the Winter of Despair, when the First Day and Fourth Day meals at the Friends of Jesus meetings became crucial to the survival of many people. During those awful times, Mary and John had gratefully accepted food and clothing donated by the temple of Artemis to augment other donations. "Better an empty belly than food sacrificed to an idol" was fine in theory, but Mary was unwilling to watch children starve when she had resources available to feed them. They didn't need the donations anymore because most people again earned money, and food and clothing were more plentiful. The church was once again able to focus its meetings on the signs and teachings of Jesus the Messiah.

She heard hammering and other noise from a home being constructed on the hill between the proseuche and the city wall. She had neighbors now. Many of the people who had found shelter up here after the fire had decided they liked living up on the hill, where the air was clear and the water was clean. First they set up tents. Then they started to build houses, and the temple of Artemis was too concerned with other matters at the time to stop them. The grove was almost gone before temple guards began taking punitive action against people cutting down the trees. Building of permanent residences up here had slowed once wood had to be purchased from merchants at the harbor and then hauled up the hill. But people continued to work on the houses they had started.

Mary was worried that the storks wouldn't return at all because most of their nests were gone, their trees cut down. Only a few pair had showed up last year, and there were even fewer trees for them now.

"We need to decide how best to help Agathon's wife and children," John said.

"We buried him," one man said. "That helped." There was a sharp, shocked burst of laughter and then he said, "No, I didn't mean that the way it sounded. I just meant that I don't understand what else we can do for them."

"He left a widow and orphans who have no income, no business, and no way to live," John said. "I believe it's our responsibility to care for them. Suggestions?"

Mary let the waves of conversation float over her as she rested her face in the sun. After a while she turned her half-attention from the earnest voices discussing charity and responsibility to Salome's bright, clear laughter floating through the air. Mary's daughter was playing, searching for beechnuts with other children in the sparse grove, her constant pain bravely ignored.

Then Mary heard a peacock's loud screech. She grinned, realizing that one, at least, had survived. Perhaps the storks would return as well.

She had almost fallen asleep when Apollos whispered to her. "Mother, look who's at the mikvah."

She opened her eyes and allowed Apollos to help her stand. Two people, a woman and her slave, were waiting near the dressing tent. Mary recognized both of them, because they'd been here a few days before Passover. The woman was Eugeneia, wife of Politarch Aaron, leader of the gerousia; her slave was a man named Sophos. Mary was surprised to see them because last time they were here she had chastised Eugeneia. In fact she'd been expecting repercussions from the incident.

Mary had been troubled by the fact that Eugeneia brought a male slave to assist her with undressing and dressing, something that had never happened at the mikvah before. Mary had told the man to wait in the proseuche for them, saying she would help Eugeneia with her clothes herself.

Eugeneia had laughed. "Sophos helps me dress at home. What difference does it make here?"

"You're here to purify. There's not much point if you pollute yourself before and after the tevilah."

"But he's not even a real man. You think my husband would let a real man dress me? He's been castrated. He doesn't have any testicles."

"I don't care if he doesn't have a penis," Mary said. "He's to wait in the proseuche." She immediately felt bad about talking this way in front of the man and glanced at him in apology. He didn't notice. He simply stood there, expression detached, eyes on his mistress, waiting for the next order.

Eugeneia shrugged and ordered him to wait in the proseuche. He left, and Mary helped Eugeneia to undress, her hands clumsy because of the scarring from her burns.

"I usually purify in the baths, during the women's morning hours. But Aaron's been wanting me to come up here and purify according to tradition."

Mary nodded and helped Eugeneia to walk down the stone stairs. She picked up a small branch of hyssop, prepared that morning by Apollos because her own hands couldn't clutch anything tightly anymore. Before she wet the hyssop for sprinkling she said ritually, "Why are you seeking purification?"

"My moon has ended. My husband wishes to have relations with me."

Mary purified Eugeneia with the hyssop sprinkle, then helped her to cleanse through immersion in the cold water of the mikvah.

Eugeneia complained about the cold water during the walk up the stairs, through her dressing, and as they hurried to the proseuche. She was still complaining as she stood warming her hands in front of the hearth while Mary went into her room to change into a dry gown.

Suddenly Mary heard Eugeneia yell. Then she heard a loud slap and Eugeneia screaming at her slave. Mary rushed out of her room and, incredibly, saw the man handing a thin whip to Eugeneia. The woman lashed once at the slave's shoulders before Mary, screaming "Apollos!" was able to grab the woman's upraised arm.

Sophos pulled Mary away from his mistress and might have done her harm if Apollos hadn't run in and stopped him. Little Salome entered behind Apollos and began to cry.

"Mother, are you all right?" Apollos said in angry distress. He had the slave's arms pinned behind him but released them when the man's muscles relaxed.

"I'm fine," Mary said.

"Well, I'm not," Eugeneia snapped. "My mouth is burnt!"

Mary looked down at the wet floor. A cup lay broken on the stone.

"The tea was boiling!" Eugeneia said.

"You whipped a man because your tea was too hot?" Mary was filled with a rare and energizing anger.

"He knows how to make it for me! He knows I can't drink things that are too hot!"

"I think you are one of the wickedest people I have ever met," Mary said fiercely, and then she saw God's eyes staring back at her from Eugeneia's shocked face.

"Why would you say such a horrible thing? Everyone said you were so kind!"

"Why would you think you have the right to whip this poor man?" Mary asked, calmer now. "Especially in a place of prayer?"

"He's just a slave!" Eugeneia said in irritation. "He doesn't have any feelings. He doesn't have a soul. He doesn't matter."

"You have lived too long among the Greeks if you have forgotten that we were once slaves in Egypt. To God, there is no difference between us, free or slave, rich or poor, young or old, male or female—we are all the same in the eyes of God." Her voice almost faltered as she looked at Sophos then and saw the eyes of God watching her from the slave's indifferent mask of a face.

"Are you all right, Sophos?" she asked gently. "Do you need treatment?" She remembered her son being whipped, and again she found herself filling with anger, but it was tinged with weary sadness now.

Sophos didn't answer Mary. He stood by Apollos, eyes on his mistress, waiting for her orders.

Eugeneia didn't speak again. She pushed past them all and left. Sophos trailed behind her.

So Mary was surprised to see them back again today. She walked up to them where they stood at the dressing tent.

"I was leaving the baths this morning and I slipped," Eugeneia said. "There was a dead body lying in the street and I touched it when I fell. I need to be purified."

"Corpse pollution lasts seven days. Come back in a week," Mary said.

"What?"

"You're going to be polluted for seven days. I can purify you after that." Privately she thought: Why are you here? You can't possibly care about corpse pollution. Even I don't care about corpse pollution anymore. There've been too many deaths.

"She didn't tell me that," Eugeneia said with a frown.

"Who?"

"Judith. She saw me fall. She saw me touch the corpse. She said I needed to come up here for purification, or I'd be shunned like that poor woman with the stone baby long ago. She said she was going to tell everybody."

"She might," Mary said. She hadn't ever discussed Eugeneia with Judith, but she knew the characters of both women well enough to guess they'd be bitter enemies. And they both attended the same synagogue, one the wife of the archisynagogos and mistress of the synagogue house, the other the wife of the politarch of the gerousia. The politarch's wife seemed abysmally ignorant of the proper way to behave. This probably also annoyed Judith.

Mary could imagine Judith's spiteful laughter over Eugeneia's corpse pollution. Mary softened.

"You don't need to purify today unless you want to. If you would like, we could pray together for a while in the proseuche. But you'll want to come back here to purify seven days from now, because Judith will check to make sure you do. In fact, she probably plans to be here."

"Why does Judith care if I purify or not?"

Mary sighed. She hated to be put in the middle of quarrels. "I don't think she really does care, although if you don't purify, she will probably make a fuss about it. But what interests her is the fact that, in the meantime, you're polluted."

"What do you mean?"

"I mean that you're supposed to stay away from everybody for a week. You say Judith said that she was going to tell everybody. That means she's going to make sure everyone avoids you this week."

"But what about my friends? We meet every day at the baths."

"Are they Hebrews?"

"Of course."

Mary shook her head. "You probably won't see them this week. And you should stay home on the Sabbath, not go to synagogue." Judith would be especially brutal if Eugeneia brought her corpse contamination into Judith's house.

"What can I do in the meantime? I always spend my mornings at the baths."

"Well, it's spring. You could work in your garden."

"I don't garden," Eugeneia snapped. "The slaves do that."

"You could come up here then," Mary said, sacrificing herself. "You can spend the week visiting with me."

Eugeneia stared at Mary, and then she and Sophos left without another word. Mary sighed as she realized that the woman and her slave would be back next week and no doubt Judith too, anxious for an update on Eugeneia's purification.

Apollos came up to her, and they stood together watching the two people walk away. "What was that all about?" he asked.

"Nothing important."

"I'm going to take Salome down to the harbor agora tomorrow. Would you like to come along with us?"

"I'd like that." They walked back together to the Friends of Jesus church meeting.

When she finished her labyrinth walk in the morning, she found Apollos and Salome already waiting at the proseuche although the sun had barely lit the sky. "We're going to go see the jugglers," Salome said.

"I know," Mary said with a smile.

"So cover your head so we can go," the child insisted, holding the cloth out for her. Mary gave Apollos a quizzical look, but he just shrugged and smiled.

Mary enjoyed walking through town these days because everything looked so new and fresh, even the tenements. No doubt before long these tenements would be as awful as the old ones had been, but for now they seemed clean and full of hope.

The priests at the various temples were performing their morning rituals as the three Judeans passed. Mary heard a hymn to Dionysus being sung at one shrine and then heard the same hymn sung down the road at a different temple, with Demeter's name instead of Dionysus'. It was a catchy tune, and she found herself singing the hymn as they walked, conscientiously replacing the idol's name with "Lord God."

They reached the market at the harbor. The first fishing boats of the morning were coming in with their catches, and sea birds flew shrieking overhead. She saw the captains of the boats walk up to the customs house to pay the tolls while their crews unloaded the fish to sell at the fish market. The fishermen's guild managed the customs house dedicated to Isis; the tolls were their association dues. Although a dangerous business, few burials occurred because most fishermen were lost at sea. Nevertheless, the guild of fishermen spent a great deal of money on dedications, inscriptions, and funerary offerings to the gods.

There was a new statue of Isis near the customs house. Mary noticed that she wore a fish on the top of her head.

Salome shrieked with laughter and ran off chasing something. "I'll watch her, Mother," Apollos said, and he hurried after the child. Mary smiled as she watched them. Apollos and Salome, both orphans, were family together now, Apollos a brother/father to the little girl. Getting older, Mary knew that her years left were few. She was glad these orphans would have each other after she was gone.

She walked slowly through the harbor agora. She didn't examine the items in the stalls and carts as closely as she had in previous years, although she did still stop to smell the soap and look at the pearls and shells. But these days when she came to the harbor agora, she spent most of her time listening to the people, enjoying the barkers, poets, heralds, philosophers, and preachers who fought for the attention of the public.

She waved at Ezra the Judean, still preaching the coming of the Messiah and the end of the world. He had actually stayed up at the proseuche for a month or so during the Winter of Despair. He'd politely attended the Friends of Jesus church while he was there, but clearly he remained unconvinced about Jesus and the Parousia. He wasn't the only Israelite declaiming today. She heard the voices of Jewish magicians reciting what the Greeks no doubt thought were powerful incantations. Mary recognized the Hebrew words of the Shema.

The popularity of astrology, sorcery, and fortune-telling had only increased since the fire. People who had lost everything hungered to know why the gods had allowed such things to happen, if more such tragedies lay in store, and what they could do to avoid them. The number of prophets, astrologers, sorcerers, dream-interpreters, clairvoyants, and soothsayers seemed to have tripled since the fire, and their section of the agora now spilled out into the street even past the theater.

Such people often tried to engage Mary in conversation. This morning one sibyl saw her as she was passing and immediately started pointing at her and praising the gods. "You will be known as the Mother of All," she said loudly. Mary smiled, nodded, and hurried past the curious people who were now gawking at her.

"Her shadow passed over me!" one of them said as Mary walked by. "I have been blessed! Praise Artemis!"

Mary ducked quickly into a wool importer's shop and watched a woman weaving a rug as she waited for the sibyl's customers to move on to something new.

After a while she walked past the block of souvenir shops catering to pilgrims honoring Artemis Ephesia, then over to her favorite spot at the agora, a fountain featuring three calm and peaceful women, their arms around each other's shoulders, peaceful faces glowing. They were naked, but she was used to naked statues now.

She sat on a bench watching the children playing in the water of the fountain, listening to the sea birds as they circled the harbor looking for food. It was a beautiful day, a day that was truly a gift from God. She felt content.

A long line of people danced through the harbor agora and passed by Mary as they wound around the fountain. "Great is Artemis Ephesia!" they chanted over and over again, their voices cracked and hoarse but the tune recognizable nonetheless. Most of them looked tired, but they gamely kept singing and dancing. Mary realized these people had probably been celebrating all night—had perhaps even been part of the procession that she and Salome had watched last night from up on the hill.

A woman sat down near her, of about her same age. A slave accompanied the woman, and Mary listened as the woman complained to the slave about everything in her world—the paucity of selection in the shops, the rudeness of her husband this morning, the soreness of her feet. The dancers had bumped her as they passed. The birds circling above had given her a headache with their screeching. The children playing in the fountain splashed her and now her chiton was soaked and ruined. The bowl of food the slave brought her was tasteless garbage and she wasn't going to eat it.

Mary had met a lot of people in her time in Ephesus. Many of the people who lived here had come from farms or small villages, as she had. Some of these people would tell her how much better things were back home on the farm or in the old village, while other people who'd lived almost the same lives would say the opposite, how much better things were in Ephesus. Mary listened to the woman complain to her slave and wondered what sort of life experiences could have engendered such misery in a person with so much obvious wealth.

There were two groups of priests back home with starkly different ideas about heaven and hell. The Sadducees didn't believe in the existence of either one. The Pharisees believed that heaven and hell both existed as places where the dead were rewarded or punished for their behavior during life. But listening to the woman, Mary thought: What if both the Sadducees and Pharisees are wrong? Maybe there is a heaven and hell, but they aren't places where you go after you die. What if heaven and hell are here and now, both together, and the only difference between the two is in each person's own heart? She thought: Wouldn't that be the worst possible type of hell—to be living in heaven and not even be aware of it?

She walked over to the woman and gently asked her if there was anything she could do to help her. The woman burst into tears.

That night she added the name of Lucia Capito to her prayers as she walked the labyrinth. Afterward, she took Salome with her to the overlook spot as she did every procession night, and they sat entranced, watching the parade of music and lights from the temple of Artemis snake around the hill and into the city of Ephesus.

A new spondopoios arrived the next day to see if she would like to visit Artelia at the temple.

"Where is Okeanos?" she asked.

The priest shrugged. He didn't know or perhaps he couldn't say.

"Go on, Mother," Apollos said. "You haven't seen Artelia in a while. Go visit your friend."

Mary decided against taking Salome with her to the temple. The child was still too young to understand the difference between God and Artemis. And Mary especially liked her talks with Artelia during the month of Artemision, because Artelia had greater freedom then to talk about the mysteries of the temple.

Mary found Artelia in her luxurious quarters, relaxing after the long night. They walked out to the peristyle, where they could sit under a tree sipping berry tea and chatting in the dappled sun, enjoying the flowers and the birds.

The temple was nearby, close enough to add beauty to the vista but not so close as to crowd out everything else. Mary smiled in relief to see many storks' nests on the top of the temple roof and in the upper branches of the huge sacred tree behind the temple.

"There haven't been any storks on the hill yet this year," Mary said. "Maybe they couldn't find the grove, since most of the trees are gone."

"The storks are still arriving. You may get some yet."

"Oh, I hope so. I enjoy them so much."

"How is little Salome doing?" They caught up on news, on friends, on births and deaths, on illnesses and healings. Mary told Artelia about the Roman woman she'd met at the fountain yesterday. When Mary had asked her if she could help her, the woman had poured her heart out about her father and mother, both long dead, and confessed how much she had hated them both.

"How dreadful to carry such hatred in your heart for an entire lifetime," Artelia said.

"Did you love your parents?" Mary asked. She realized she had known Artelia for fourteen years but had never heard her mention her parents.

"I never knew my parents. I was a child of Artemis."

"Now why didn't I know that?" exclaimed Mary.

Artelia shrugged. "I thought everybody knew."

"You've never said anything about your childhood."

"I don't think I ever was a child."

Mary had no idea how to respond to such a sad statement. "I was lucky," she said finally. "I had wonderful parents, and I loved them very much. I hope my children feel the same way about their parents."

"I'm sure they do," Artelia said with a smile.

Mary remembered something that had been bothering her for years and decided to ask Artelia what she thought. "Some of my son Jesus' disciples remember him saying something that I find very strange."

"Oh?"

"According to them, he said anyone who came to him and did not hate his own mother and father and brothers and sisters and wife and children could not be his disciple." Every time Mary thought of this, her stomach churned in rejection of the words.

But Artelia's face lit up. "Oh my dear Heavenly Goddess!" she exclaimed. "Your son was teaching the people to build the double-hulled ship. 'He who has ears to hear, let him hear,' I think you once told me?"

"Yes," Mary said, confused.

"Remarkable. Artemis says 'I am the voice heard by the breath; I am the words shouted in silence.' But I thought it was just a coincidence that your son said something similar. I had no idea the Judeans had such advanced teachings. Do you think Alexander has received these teachings? I would enjoy talking with him about it."

"I-I don't know. I don't understand what you're talking about."

"It's one of the mysteries, but I'll talk it through with you. Tell me: what is a double-hulled ship?"

"I don't know anything about ships. I would imagine it would be especially strong. No water would get in. It wouldn't sink. I think it would be harder to destroy in battle. A double-hulled ship would have a greater chance of reaching its destination."

"Exactly. Your son got all this from you, you know. You know all this."

"I don't know anything," Mary said with exasperation. "What does that have to do with Jesus hating me?"

"He didn't hate you, dear. I met him, remember? I know he loved you very much. But he couldn't let his love for you or for anyone hold him back on his journey across the waters to the spirit, to becoming one with the essence of God. He had to build a ship strong enough to keep all the forces out that would tie him to the shore or sink him before he reached the other side. You can't be tied to anything, you know. Not people. Not possessions. Not to anything."

Mary looked around at the beautiful peristyle. "But you own many beautiful things."

"I don't own anything. Even the combs in my hair belong to Artemis."

"He told people that if they wanted to follow him, they had to sell all of their possessions," Mary said thoughtfully.

"That's it; you understand this. You have the right kind of ears." Artelia smiled.

"No, I'm still very confused."

"I could teach you more, but you'd have to become an initiate of Artemis," Artelia said, laughing at the thought.

Though she'd never said so, Mary found herself from time to time actually considering this once unimaginable thing. She loved the peace of the temple and yearned to possess the wisdom of the spondopoios. But the Lord God did not accept any other gods. She couldn't be a child of God and also an initiate of Artemis.

"But you have the skills to figure it out yourself," Artelia continued. "You might think for a while about what the ship in this story stands for and then what that second hull represents. Think about the nature of the water in which it floats, and consider the creatures that live in the water. What might be waiting on the other side of the shore? Let me give you one hint that will help you: When you pray to your god, stop talking. Listen to what he has to say instead. Let everything else inside you be empty. Wait for the sound of his voice to guide you."

Mary nodded. "I can do that. Thank you." Perhaps God Himself would teach her His mysteries.

"When I pray to Artemis, I almost never speak," Artelia said. "I listen. I feel the Holy Queen in my heart. She guides my hands and directs my feet. She comes to me in dreams. Everything I am and everything I do is divinely directed by my Goddess. I am merely Her vessel."

"God has come to me in dreams," Mary said thoughtfully.

"I would be surprised if he hadn't."

They spoke of other things for a while, and then Mary remembered to mention that a new priest had brought her to the temple today. "I missed Okeanos today. I hope he's not ill."

"He's not ill," Artelia said slowly. "But he won't be the person who comes to check on you anymore. He has new duties at the Temple."

"Oh?" Mary began to frown. She remembered the procedure Adonis had mentioned long ago, that Artelia said was only done to special priests. "Did Okeanos have his penis removed?"

Artelia sighed. "You must know I can't talk with you about that."

"So he did."

"He's fine, Mary. It was his choice. He will be happy."

"I don't understand why they have to go through that." Perhaps if she was an initiate, this too would be made clear.

"It's all about purity," Artelia said. "You should certainly understand that. And it's also about the covenant that Artemis has with each individual priest. It's very personal for them."

"I'm sure," Mary said. She changed the subject. She was not quite ready to probe into practices that were explained with the words "covenant" and "purity."

Every god had mysteries.

She thought: "My son, if owning everything can bring dissatisfaction and owning nothing can bring bliss, what does 'ownership' mean?"

15

"My son the Logos shows us why we live."

Spring, nineteen years after the crucifixion of Jesus

M ary took her morning walk through the labyrinth, cried her morning tears, and ended the walk as she usually did, reaching the center of the labyrinth at sunrise. She looked up and saw, to her utter amazement, three suns rise in the sky. She wiped at her eyes, thinking that perhaps her tears were causing reflections, but all three remained.

"Apollos! Apollos!" she yelled. She knew he was up, because she'd heard him go out to milk the goats.

He came running through the trees and into the labyrinth. "What is it, Mother?"

She pointed to the sky.

"Oh my God." He fell to his knees and began praying. She hurried over to kneel beside him, and the two prayed together for a long time. When they finished their prayers and stood, only one sun was left.

Mary knew this was a miracle, but she wondered: what kind of miracle? Did it presage a blessing or a curse? She thought it was a blessing. This belief was reinforced when a few pairs of storks arrived at the grove a short while later and began to make nests in two of the remaining trees. She thought these were storks she'd known from years past, David and Bathsheba and Adam and Eve. It had been quite a few years since any storks had nested here at the proseuche, and the appearance of the kind mothers filled her with joy.

"I think it's the Parousia," she said to Apollos.

"Praise God," Apollos said.

But the morning went on and Jesus did not appear. Women came to the mikvah for purification. Their children played with Salome. Gilana came by to do laundry. Pelagios brought breakfast. Apollos studied the Torah, using the Greek Septuagint copy that Artelia had had made for him as a gift.

Mary mentioned the three suns to everyone she saw. No one had a good explanation; all agreed they were certainly a miracle. The first person to speak knowledgably about the three suns was Hieronymos, the spondopoios from the temple of Artemis who came up to the proseuche every few weeks.

She told him she couldn't go to the temple today because Sabbath began tonight and she needed to walk to Alexander's house this afternoon. When she was younger, it was no trouble for her to go to the temple of Artemis in the morning and walk over to Alexander's villa upon her return in the afternoon, but she no longer had the strength to make two long trips in one day. She told Hieronymos that if he returned for her in a few days, she would like to visit Artelia.

And then she asked him if he had any thoughts about the three suns. She said she knew that Artemis was worshipped as the sun, so she thought that a thing like three suns would have meaning at the Artemision.

"Oh yes," he said. "This morning the three-fold face of our Heavenly Queen appeared."

"Oh?" She realized that he might think she was more familiar with their mysteries than she really was.

"Yes. The regular sun was joined by the sun of the spirit and the sun of the mind. The three-fold face is very portentous. The astrologers, oracles, and soothsayers will be quite busy today trying to read the other auguries."

"So it's a blessing?"

"Not always."

Later she was playing with Salome, singing the same songs of the Patriarchs that she had sung to her children to teach them the old stories, when Apollos came to find her.

"They're here, Mother. My friends are here."

Mary stood up and told Salome to go play for a while. "I'm glad they've arrived." She followed Apollos into the proseuche.

For the last year Apollos had been a member of another church guild in Ephesus as well as the Friends of Jesus guild. This new church met in the home of a tent-making couple named Prisca and Aquila, and although they recognized Jesus as the Messiah and waited for the Parousia, in most other respects they were very different from the Friends of Jesus. They weren't associated with a synagogue. They were Israelites, of course, but the traditional practices of the faith were of little interest to them. They didn't discuss the Torah, the patriarchs, or the prophets. They didn't worry about things like polluted food or corpse contamination or ritual purification.

In addition, they didn't especially seem to care about the teachings of Jesus, his lessons about how to live a life pleasing to God, or the signs that showed he was the Messiah. Apollos had taken his copy of Quartillia's scroll with him to a few of their meetings, but they weren't particularly interested in hearing him read from it. Mary had a difficult time understanding what they did at their guild if they didn't talk about the Torah or the life and teachings of Jesus. She had asked Apollos to take her to one of the church meetings so she could see for herself.

Prisca and Aquila lived in a large tent located near the harbor, in the tent-makers district. It was a long walk for Mary, and she and Apollos arrived a little late because she'd had to stop at times to rest.

Prisca spoke as they walked in. Six or seven people sat on the floor listening to her. A skilled speaker, she enthralled and excited the people with her words and her energetic manner.

"I want to tell you all a story about Jesus," she was saying as they entered. A big smile filled Mary's face, and Apollos helped her find a comfortable place to sit.

But the story Prisca told wasn't really about Jesus. Instead she talked about a man named Saul, an Israelite who hated and persecuted the Nazorenes. One day, Prisca said, Saul was on his way to find and arrest the believers in Jesus when he was suddenly struck by a light from heaven, and he fell to the ground.

A voice came down from the heavens, saying: "Saul, Saul, why do you persecute me?"

"Who are you, Lord?" Saul asked.

"I am Jesus," the voice said, and suddenly Saul saw a vision of the crucified Jesus, emblazoned in light. "Now get up and go into the city, and you will be told what you must do."

The people hung on Prisca's words as she told a wondrous tale of blindness, healing, redemption, and dangerous escapes from soldiers and persecutors.

Mary didn't hear the rest of the story. She was thinking: So he appeared to yet another one after his death. The old pain resurfaced, and once again she felt bereft by her son, who had appeared to family and friends and strangers—even to Artelia and this Saul fellow—but never to her.

Prisca finished her story, and Apollos helped Mary to rise. "This is the mother of Jesus," Apollos said to the group.

Prisca rushed over, fell to the ground, and kissed Mary's feet. "What an honor, what a very great honor, to have the mother of the Savior here with us."

Aquila spoke up with the only words he would say that evening. "When did you know your child was the Son of God?"

And then the rush of questions came:

"When Jesus was a child, did he forgive the sins of all his little friends?"

"What was it like to have a child who was never naughty?"

"Did you ever see him wrestle Satan?"

"Did you always know he would be crucified to save us from our sins?"

"How did God appear to you when he gave you his son—as a swan? Or a golden shower?"

"When did you receive the Holy Spirit?"

"Were you at the crucifixion? Were you the first one to be washed in the blood of Jesus and granted eternal life?"

Horrified, Mary looked up at Apollos. He wrapped her protectively in his arms. "I'm sorry, but this is very distressing for her. We have to go." He helped her to walk to Alexander's house, where he borrowed a donkey cart to take her home.

He went back to the tent the next day. Although Mary and Apollos didn't discuss it, she knew he must have said something to discourage them from troubling her, because no one from the tent church—not even Prisca or Aquila themselves—had ever come up to the proseuche to see her.

Until now.

There were three people in the proseuche when she entered, Prisca, Aquila, and another man.

"Mother, I'd like you to meet Paul," Apollos said. Mary started to walk over to him, but the man did as Prisca had that first time. He fell on his face before her and reverently kissed her feet.

"Please get up," she said, her voice shaking.

"It's so good to see you again, Mother," Prisca said. Aquila just smiled and nodded.

Mary looked at Prisca. How could she tell this woman, this devotee of her son, that she didn't want her to call her "Mother"? She sighed. She knew Whose eyes she would see if she looked closely into Prisca's face. "It's good to see you again too, Prisca. Aquila."

Salome ran in. "Mother, look what I found." She held up a long stork feather.

Mary didn't look at Salome's find. She watched Prisca, who stared in revulsion at the child's scarred face.

Paul walked over to the girl and bent down. "That is a beautiful feather. Where did you find it?"

"Out in the trees. We have storks. They're building their nests. They're kind mothers."

Paul laughed. "Yes, they are. And I think you too have a kind mother."

"I have the kindest mother in the world," Salome said. "Are you here to purify?"

Paul kissed the child on her scarred cheek, and in that moment Mary's heart filled with love for him.

"I came here today to see Mary," he said, standing up again.

"Call me Mother."

"Thank you." He took her scarred and twisted hands in his and kissed them gently. "I am very glad to meet you."

"I'm glad to meet you too." She looked at Apollos for an explanation.

"Paul is an apostle, Mother. He travels all over, teaching about Jesus and founding churches. He's set up churches in Philippi, Syria, Cilicia, Galatia, Thessalonica, Corinth, and many other cities."

"But you're not one of the Twelve," she said to Paul. "Aren't they the apostles? Did you know my son?"

"There are a few other apostles besides the Twelve," Paul said. "I didn't know your son in his lifetime. But he appeared to me after his death."

Not another one, she thought in distress.

"You heard about Paul at the tent church," Apollos reminded her.

"No, that was someone else, I think." She tried to remember the name. "Saul," she said finally.

"Saul is my Hebrew name. I use my Roman name now. I'm afraid many of the followers of Jesus remember Saul as their persecutor, so I've stopped using that name." Paul reached into his bundle. "I have a letter for you from your son James." He handed it to her.

"I'll have Apollos read it to me later, when we're alone and I can concentrate on his words. Now I want to concentrate on my guests." She smiled at all of them.

"I hope you will let me visit you again," Paul said. "James told me that I mustn't bother you. Please tell me if I'm a nuisance."

"Oh my dear, I'm sure you won't be a nuisance. Will I see you at synagogue?"

"I'll be going to synagogue with my cousin Junia and her husband Andronicus," Paul said. "I'm staying with them. Do you know them?"

"I do. They're members of the Disciples of John the Baptist guild and our Friends of Jesus church. I hope you'll come with them to the church meeting, here in the proseuche on the afternoon of First Day."

"I will certainly be here," he said, smiling. "I'm looking forward to meeting John. Peter and the others remember him with great fondness, and I'm to tell him so."

"He'll be glad to hear news about them."

Apollos walked Mary and Salome to Alexander's house that afternoon. For the first time he didn't stay over for Sabbath.

"I'm going to Prisca and Aquila's tent. I may come back tonight or I may just stay there all night. I've been looking forward to talking with Paul."

"But Apollos, it'll be the Sabbath soon."

"Don't worry, Mother," he said, smiling. He kissed her and left.

She didn't see Apollos again until she and Salome arrived back at the proseuche on First Day after their weekly synagogue stay at Alexander's, accompanied by John, Theodora, and their children Leah, Joseph, and baby John, who was usually called Adonis because he was as demanding and opinionated as Mary's old tutor.

When they reached the grove they found Apollos waiting for them. "I came up for a while yesterday to milk the goats," he said as Mary kissed him.

"That was good of you." He always worried about the goats and rushed up every Sabbath morning after synagogue to milk them.

"I'm going to teach Salome how to milk them. But you'll have to find someone else to take care of them on the Sabbath."

"Apollos, what do you mean?"

"Let's all sit," he said. The adults walked over to the marble benches. Salome ran off to play in the grove with the children.

"I'm going to be an evangelist, Mother."

"Apollos, that's wonderful!" John said, embracing his friend.

"I don't understand," Mary said.

"I'm going to do what Paul does," Apollos said. "I'm going to preach the good news about Jesus."

Mary was silent.

"Mother, what is it? Aren't you glad for me?"

She sighed. "If this is what you want, then I am glad for you. I know you will be a wonderful evangelist—and I know you'll tell the people about Jesus' teachings, not about those strange things they talked about at the tent meeting. But I will miss you." She felt her chest fill with tears.

"I won't go far," Apollos said. "Just to Corinth to begin with, to help with Paul's church there. And I won't leave right away."

She refused to cry. She knew these were just foolish old woman tears. She didn't want to distress the boys. "I will miss you," she whispered.

"John will spend more time with you," Apollos said, looking in desperation at his friend.

"I certainly will, Mother," John said. "I'll come up here more often, and I'll bring you and Salome to stay with us more frequently as well."

"The children are always so happy to have Salome visit them," Theodora said. "And you know how much I treasure our time together."

"What about the goats?" Mary said, and then felt foolish over the question.

"I'll send over a slave to take care of the goats," John said. "Don't worry about the goats."

She made herself smile, and then she hugged the sons and daughter of her heart. "I love you all so much."

"We love you too, Mother," Apollos said.

She excused herself to go walk in the labyrinth. She wanted to have a calm and clear mind when the people arrived for the Friends of Jesus church meeting.

She walked for a while, stepping slowly, breathing slowly, following the twisting circuits, and she did finally find peace with the idea of losing Apollos. The sound of voices roused her from her meditations and she realized the members of the guild must be arriving. She started walking toward the proseuche and was about to holler a greeting to the people speaking when she heard her name mentioned.

"Mary may be very nice, and I'm sure she was a good mother to our Savior," a woman's voice said, "but she's an illiterate peasant, Paul." Mary recognized Prisca's voice.

"I don't think anyone cares about that," Paul said. The voices were getting closer, and Mary realized they were walking in the grove. She looked for a place to hide so that she wouldn't be embarrassed and they wouldn't be distressed by realizing she had overheard.

"Gentiles are used to the Greek gods and heroes," Prisca said. "They have certain expectations. They expect the mother of the divine Son of God to be more imposing, more impressive. Mary is no Leto."

Paul laughed softly. "No, she's not Leto."

"Well, that's the kind of thing that influences gentile converts," Prisca insisted.

"I don't think it's important," Paul said.

Mary ducked behind a tree as Paul and Prisca entered the labyrinth clearing.

"And here is another example of what's wrong with her," Prisca said. "Apollos says she spends hours in this idolatrous thing. We're trying to lead people away from the idols. And I've heard that her closest friend is the high priestess of Artemis, though I can hardly believe that's true. Mary is a decent woman, but she sets a bad example for the Nazorenes. I think we should just not mention anymore that she's living here in Ephesus. We'll do our preaching in the streets and the synagogues and just let her stay up here with her little church. She seems like a private person anyway. She'd probably prefer that."

"We'll see what Mary wants," Paul said. "If she wants a prominent place in our church, she shall have it." They walked back toward the proseuche, Prisca still arguing her case.

Mary took a side path out of the labyrinth so that Paul and Prisca wouldn't see her and be made uncomfortable.

The name Leto was familiar, but she couldn't place it. The next time she saw Artelia, she'd ask her who she was.

Members of the Friends of Jesus church were arriving. Paul stood with his cousin Junia and with John, who introduced him to other members of the church. Apollos introduced people to Prisca and Aquila. Children ran off to find Salome. Mary went over to visit with Epenetus, who was working with the other slaves to set out food.

John came over. "Mother, do we have any wine?"

"I don't know, John."

"There are four amphorae stored in the corner of your mother's room, Master John," Epenetus said. "But they've been there for a long time and may have turned to vinegar."

"There are?" Mary asked. "How did they get there?"

Epenetus shrugged. "People sometimes bring wine with them to Friends of Jesus meetings. We just never serve it, because the water is so good here and I know that is your preference."

"Well, Paul has a ritual he wants to perform," John said. "Before the meal. He will be serving everyone bread and wine, he says."

"I'll check the amphorae to see if any of them are good, Master John," Epenetus said. He came back carrying one amphora. "The others have all turned to vinegar. I'll take them back home to the kitchen. But this one is drinkable."

"That should be enough," John said. "I don't want anyone to get drunk anyway. After the ritual, they can drink water."

After giving Paul the items he needed, John began the meeting. After prayers he said, "I've asked our friend Paul, the apostle from Jerusalem, if he would lead the teaching today. He said that he would like to begin with a ritual that he brings to all of his churches."

Paul stood and spoke of his gladness at being here today, in this company of the beloved. He asked his assistants Prisca and Aquila to pass out cups to share and said that there would be a short ritual before and after the meal. As the cups were being distributed, he said that he was particularly pleased to be able to address them so soon after Passover, when Christ, the Passover Lamb, was sacrificed.

John's church did not generally refer to Jesus by the title "Christ," or "Messiah," but everyone certainly understood the reference. However, the view of Jesus as a sacrificed Passover Lamb was new, and everyone was very quiet and attentive as Paul continued to speak.

He spoke of the three suns that had appeared in the sky a few days before, describing them as the Father, the Son, and the Holy Spirit. This view of Jesus as the Son of God was also new to the church. They were used to considering him as the Logos because John and Apollos had discussed that many times, but most church followers equated the Logos to the Holy Spirit, the divine energetic principle of God mentioned by the Prophets, and so this explanation of the three suns was confusing.

Mary was struck by how similar Paul's explanation was to the explanation the temple priest Hieronymos had given her of the three-fold face of Artemis in which the regular sun, the goddess, was joined by the sun of the spirit and the sun of the mind.

Paul then nodded to Mary and John and said to the group, "Because you have been faithful to the Lord from the earliest days, I want to share with you the most holy and sacred mystery known to those who follow Jesus Christ, a mystery permitted and taught to only the most devoted of his saints, those who are ready to hear the revealed truth."

He took the pitcher of wine and said, "The Lord Jesus, on the night he was betrayed, took the cup he was given and gave thanks to God, and then he said to his disciples 'I will not drink again of the fruit of the vine until the time of the kingdom of God. Take this and divide it among you.'" Paul gave the pitcher to Prisca, who walked around the benches pouring wine into cups. The people drank.

Then Paul took a loaf of bread and broke it in half, saying, "The Lord Jesus, on the night he was betrayed, took bread, and when he had given thanks, he broke it and said to his disciples, 'This is my body, given to you. Take it and divide it among you. Do this in remembrance of me.'" He passed the two halves of the bread to the people near him, and they each took a part and passed the rest around.

Mary, sitting next to John, was surprised by this ritual, but she liked the idea of people sitting together, eating bread and drinking wine in memory of her son. It reminded her a bit of how the Greeks picnicked in tombs, sharing the meal with their deceased loved ones.

John was more disturbed. "I don't remember him saying that. Do you remember him saying that?" he whispered to Mary.

"I wasn't there."

"Paul wasn't there either, but maybe someone told him about it. I was there that night, and I didn't hear any of that, but maybe Jesus said it when he was alone with the Twelve. Maybe I was out of the room then."

"Maybe," Mary said.

"I don't understand about the bread being the body of Jesus," John said.

Mary frowned. This didn't make sense to her either.

Once the people had eaten the bread, Paul gave a blessing and then announced that the meal was ready. Everyone got up and helped themselves to food. While they ate, Paul gave a teaching on the temptations of Israel at the time of Moses, telling them how the Hebrews had failed to please God when they were in the desert. He said that the things that had happened to them then were written down in order to be warnings to the people now, so that the people now would know to flee from idolatry and be ready for the Parousia, the return of Christ Jesus.

When people had finished eating and it was time for the closing blessing, Paul took another pitcher of wine and said, "In the same way, after supper Christ took the cup and said, 'This cup is the new covenant in my blood, which is poured out for you. Drink it in remembrance of me.'" He gave the pitcher to Prisca to fill the cups again and said, "For whenever you eat this bread and drink this wine, you proclaim the Lord's death until he comes."

Mary stared at him then looked at John. "Did he just say that the blood of Jesus was poured out for the people?" She had lived for almost twenty years with the memory of the crucifixion of her beloved child as an atrocity, a monstrous, unbearable evil. Was Paul saying that the worst memory of her life—the blood of her savagely tortured son, drenching her, spilling into the dirt—was a gift to the people?

"I think that's what he said, and I think he also said to drink the blood," John said, frowning. Blood was one of the foremost pollutants. The gentiles, in worshipping idols, would often drink the blood of sacrificed animals. But for an Israelite, the idea of drinking blood was utterly abhorrent.

Mary got up quietly and left the meeting. She walked through the grove to the labyrinth, hoping to find the peace that usually came to her when she thought and prayed in this place.

She was staring at the ground, her feet barely moving in her deep concentration, when a voice jarred her out of her prayer.

"Mother, did I say something that distressed you?" Paul stood there alone, outside the circle.

She sighed. She was going to have to talk about this. "Were you there when my son was crucified?"

"I didn't see it in the flesh, but I've seen it in my dreams a thousand times."

"But you've seen crucifixions. You know what they're like."

"I've seen people who were crucified, yes, and I've walked along streets where crucified people were crying out in agony, but I have never been able to allow myself to witness an actual crucifixion from the hanging to the death."

"I will tell you what it was like," she said. She sat down on a plinth and looked at the ground. She described that horrible day in detail for Paul, hoping it would be the last time in her life she would need to speak these words. She didn't spare him and she didn't cry.

"Before that day, the Jesus in my dreams was always a small child. He had been so perfect when he was young, so beautiful. I loved my nighttime dreams then, the dreams of those days when he was my sweet baby boy. But he had lots of followers, people who came to listen to him, more and more of them every day, and that worried the Romans. And when the Romans got nervous the Sadducees got nervous, because they want to keep peace above all else. The Twelve blame the Sadducees for what happened, but I don't blame them for wanting to keep peace. They have God's Temple to protect, after all. I blame Rome.

"Prefect Pontius Pilate decided that my son was guilty of treason, of fomenting rebellion against Rome. Of wanting to claim the throne of Israel because his father was a descendant of King David. And of course his followers said he was the Messiah, anointed by God, which could mean the anointed king. The Sanhedrin went along with the prefect. I suppose the court thought of Jesus as a troublemaker anyway. He did argue with the priests sometimes.

"But the Sanhedrin didn't find him guilty of blasphemy. They didn't even give him the thirty-nine lashes. Instead they handed him to the Roman authorities, to sentence as they saw fit, since it was Rome that was so worried.

"The prefect had him brought out early in the morning to the palace for questioning.

"'Are you king of the Judeans?' he asked.

"The crowd cheered. I think they liked the idea of someone claiming to be king, although no doubt it scared them too. My son stood there, full of bravado. I think he must have known he was going to die anyway, or he wouldn't have provoked the prefect as he did.

"'If you say so,' he said. He wouldn't say anything else.

"That infuriated the prefect. He called to the guards to bring out majestic garments for the king of the Judeans. They put a dusty, tattered piece of purple over his shoulders and shoved a crown made of thorns on his head, so hard his head began to bleed and blood ran down his face. The prefect was trying to humiliate him, and it worked. Soon the people were jeering at him. The prefect continued asking: 'Are you the king of the Judeans?' But now Jesus wouldn't answer anything at all.

"The prefect ordered him scourged. Have you ever seen a scourging? They tied his arms around a post so his back was exposed, and a soldier whipped him using a lash with five thongs, each tipped with metal prongs. The metal bits raked deep over his skin, slicing open his back, and his back muscles convulsed with his screams, again and again and again, and I watched over and over as tiny beads of blood bloomed into flowing red streams. I remember noticing a scar on his back from when he'd fallen from a tree as a child—it had scared his father so—but it had healed well, leaving a scar that I now saw ripped in two and buried under blood and loose skin and flesh cut open to the bone.

"They'd stop the scourging from time to time so that the prefect could mock him. 'Are you king of the Judeans?' he'd ask.

"And when the prefect tired of those games, he had a cross patibulum brought out and ordered Jesus to carry it to the Place of the Skull, where they crucify the enemies of Rome. He could hardly even walk after the scourging, and he had to drag the heavy beam with his arms because he couldn't rest it on the broken flesh of his back. He didn't have strength to bear the weight. Someone from the crowd stepped out and helped him. I walked alongside so he'd know I was there. But I didn't cry because I knew my tears would hurt him even more. John was with me, and my sister and a couple of friends. Not the disciples or his brothers. It was too dangerous for them.

"When he arrived at the Place of the Skull, the Roman soldiers stripped him naked and tied him to the beam he'd carried. Then they took a mallet and some nails and nailed his wrists to the wood. I hadn't expected that, really. When they tied him to the wood with a rope, I remember I felt relief. But I guess that was just to make sure they had his arms firmly in place for the nails.

"As they set the first nail against his wrist, he wriggled his arm around, his hand clenched in a fist, but he couldn't escape the mallet because he was tied down. I still remember the way his flesh stretched in before the nail finally punctured through his arm. They hit a knothole with the first nail and had to do it again. Blood spurted out of his wrists. I remembered wrapping my fingers around those wrists when he was a baby. Such soft skin he had. I'd take his little wrists in my hands and cover his eyes with his hands, then put them over my eyes and pretend I couldn't see him. He'd giggle. He was such a good baby.

"They used ropes to pull the patibulum up to the top of the post, Jesus crying out with the weight pulling on his poor wrists as his blood dripped down to the ground, and then a soldier on a ladder secured the two beams together. Other soldiers held his feet up until he was high enough to rest his weight on the sedile, and then when the crossbeam was secured they took his feet and twisted them and nailed a long spike through his heels. I vomited then. I couldn't help it.

"When his body finally hung upright there, he screamed, even harsher than when he'd been scourged. There were big splinters in the wood, piercing his torn back. And of course his arms and feet hurt so. But his scream wasn't very loud. I think it was hard for him to breathe.

"He was always so modest. Very modest, even as a child. I know his nakedness up there was deeply shaming to him. And by then, he couldn't even control his bowels. Piss and shit dripped down his legs along with the blood. I know he would have preferred I didn't witness his shame, but I wasn't going to leave him. Flies settled on him, and the soldiers wouldn't even let me brush them away. They told me to leave, but I refused. I stood there and said: 'That's my son.' And they didn't press me. Toward the end, one of the soldiers offered him vinegar on a sponge to drink, which was kind of him, I suppose. But the whole thing was just a lark to the others. A couple of them even gambled over his poor ruined clothes.

"After a time they came and nailed a sign to the top of the cross. John read it to me. It said 'King of the Judeans.' It was Pilate's warning: 'We have crucified your king, and we will do the same to anyone else who dares revolt against Rome.' I think he really believed my son was the rightful king of the Israelites. But I never heard Jesus make that claim himself. Why would he? Half of Jerusalem and most of Bethlehem is descended from King David.

"John says that it was only third hour when the crucifixion began. Jesus remained up there on the cross for six hours, until the mid-afternoon, every moment utter agony. Plus the heat, the bugs, and the stench of his own body's fluids tormenting him. Often I thought he had died, and then I'd see his chest move or his body quiver. I stayed there the whole time. Finally he opened his eyes and saw John and me standing there. He told me to be John's mother. And I have been, from that moment until this. And John has been my son.

"Jesus was so brave, even when he despaired because he felt God had deserted him. He was a great man. His father would have been so proud of him.

"After he died, I let myself cry. I stood under the cross where he still hung crucified, my arms wrapped around his feet. A soldier came over and stuck a spear into his side; I suppose to make sure he was dead. Blood and water poured down over my head, drenching me, but I didn't release my boy. The soldiers took him down from the cross, pulled the nails out of his hands and feet, and I hung on to him the whole time. When he was released from the wood, his body fell on me, and I held him even more tightly. I have never cried so much. I ran out of tears, and my eyes began to weep blood.

"I can't possibly describe what it's like to be covered in the blood of your own child. The feel of it. The smell of it. I held his bloody, sticky body in my arms until the heat of his skin began to cool and the sweat of his body dried in the sun. One of his disciples had gotten permission from the prefect to bury him. It was hard to let him go, but I finally did. He had to be put into the tomb before sunset, because the next day was Passover."

When Mary finished speaking, she looked down at her hands. So vivid had the memory been, she was almost surprised to see they were clean of blood.

Paul listened quietly, and they sat together in silence for a long while. Finally he nodded and said, "I knew it had been like that." And then he told her of a time when he had witnessed a sacred ritual of the worshippers of the god Mithras. The ecstatic worshippers had sacrificed a bull and bathed in its blood.

"As I saw this, I thought about lambs sacrificed at the altar of the Temple in Jerusalem," Paul said. "Those sacrifices are made to ask God to forgive the sins of the people. Since my call, I've realized that the faith Jesus showed in accepting his death in Jerusalem was the ultimate sacrifice to God. Jesus was the sacrificial lamb provided by God like the ram He gave to Abraham in place of Isaac. He was like the Passover lamb whose blood saved the Hebrews in Egypt from God's wrathful judgment."

The comparison to Abraham and Isaac didn't make sense to Mary. "God doesn't want human sacrifice. He refused Abraham's sacrifice of his son Isaac. Why would God want my son sacrificed?"

"He is no longer your son, Mary—he is God's son. God redeemed us through the sacrifice of His son. Because of the grace of God, all we have to do is accept that sacrifice, accept God's righteousness. Jesus' blood was a gift for us. We should take more joy in the blood spilled by Jesus than the Mithras worshippers do when they bathe in the bull's blood, because the blood of Jesus brings eternal life to the saints." Paul always referred to the followers of Jesus as "saints."

Mary was too exhausted from her memories to argue with Paul about the gift of Jesus' blood. "I don't think that's how James and the Twelve view the crucifixion of my son," she said in a tired voice.

"Some of them do," he said. "The message I give to the saints is the truth that I received from the Lord. But many of them in Jerusalem think that what's important is that everyone obey the Law, that gentiles who want to be followers of Christ become circumcised and practice the dietary rules, and that we all just wait patiently until Jesus comes again. They completely ignore the importance of Jesus' faith, of his death. They keep sending people to confuse my churches by making them think that they need to focus on the Law. Half the letters I write are to try to rescue my poor people from the Judaizers who want to make them get circumcised and worry about what food to eat instead of simply embracing the sacrifice and faith of Jesus Christ."

"Paul, I don't know what to think about any of this. All I know is that my son died a monstrous death and I live with that memory every day and dream about it every night. If you can find anything positive about his death, I'm glad for you. If his death brings hope to your followers, I'm glad for them. But please don't ask me to attend meetings where everyone is talking about the cross and the blood and the sacrifice and all the rest of it. I can't do it. I just can't talk about this anymore."

She left him and walked to the proseuche. It was dark now. The people had all left. Salome waited for her.

She thought: "My son, help me to honor those devoted ones whose view of your life and death is so different from my own."

16

"Life is a series of connections and separations. We cannot prevent our loved ones from leaving us."

Three months later

M ary missed Apollos after he left Ephesus to preach about Jesus in the Achaean province. But she spent a lot of time with John and Theodora, and Paul came up to the proseuche to see her almost every morning. He often brought some of his followers with him, usually his young assistant Timothy but also sometimes converts from Ephesus and other assistant disciples who travelled to Ephesus to ask him for direction about where they should go to preach next or how they should resolve the various crises that afflicted his numerous churches in his absence.

Whenever she met any of Paul's followers for the first time, they would stare at her in awe and wonder while she sat drinking her morning hyssop tea in the sun, listening to Paul's accounting of the souls he'd saved and the hostile forces he'd faced the day before at the leather workers guild hall where he did most of his preaching. Eventually Paul's companions would all ask her the same question: "Can I see the tunic, please, Holy Mother?"

And she would go into her room and take Jesus' tunic out of the chest and bring it out to set in their hands. By this time the tunic had been held in so many hands and received so many adoring tears that it no longer smelled like Jesus. This saddened her. But she knew that as dear as the garment was to her, it was even dearer to the Nazorenes who had never met Jesus, who didn't have the memory of his face or his laughter or his embrace to cherish. So she was willing to share it with whoever asked.

Today Paul brought Epaphras and Trophimus with him. She had met Epaphras before; he had come from Philippi to bring Paul a letter from his church there. But this was her first time meeting Trophimus, a local Greek resident. He had gone to Prisca and Aquila's shop to buy leather goods and ended up crying prostrate on the ground, a convert to Jesus Christ. After Mary granted his request to see the tunic, she mentioned to the men that she had other plans today and could visit for only a little while. Before Paul could ask her about her plans, she asked him to tell her about James' church in Jerusalem.

"Well, they meet and pray and preach, all day and night, sleeping little and eating less. When they have a new convert, they tell him to sell all he has and give it to the church. Then they use that money to buy food and care for the poor and the widowed. Sometimes they have to beg for alms."

"I think it would be very difficult to feed everyone, every day. And I have a hard time imagining my sons begging for money."

Paul smiled. "James and Thomas preach, they don't beg. Other disciples take care of the people. And my churches take up collections for God's people in Jerusalem. Each week on the First Day, they set aside a sum of money and save it up for me to take to Jerusalem the next time I travel there."

"Your churches collect money for the Nazorenes in Jerusalem?"

"Yes. There was a council meeting in Jerusalem, where I met with James, Peter, and the others. They agreed that the gentiles who believe in Jesus do not need to be circumcised as long as they abstain from food polluted by idols, from sexual immorality, from the meat of strangled animals, and from blood. And I agreed to collect money from the churches I establish and send it to them to help in the care of the saints in Jerusalem. At least, James agreed to my converting gentiles without circumcision. Not all of the apostles concur. Peter disagrees, and a few others."

"Where do James and the apostles preach in Jerusalem?" she asked.

"In the Temple. Usually in the Court of the Israelites."

Only Israelite men were allowed in this area of the Temple. "So...the women lose their homes and their livelihood, they can't feed or clothe or house their children, and they can't even participate in the meetings?" she asked, indignant but not surprised.

"When Jesus returns, none of that will matter."

"Do you have many gentile converts?"

"Oh yes. Especially since I started preaching that circumcision is not a requirement."

"But Paul, how can a man become an Israelite without circumcision? That is the covenant with God."

"Belief in Jesus is the covenant with God," Paul said. "The old Laws are unnecessary. By God's grace, only the faith of Jesus Christ matters now."

She shook her head, not comfortable with how things were changing. There were certainly uncircumcised God Fearers in the Friends of Jesus church, gentiles who came to synagogue meetings and believed in the teachings of Jesus. But John would never baptize someone into the Friends of Jesus church who had not been circumcised. An uncircumcised man, no matter how devoted, could never be considered an Israelite.

"How did Jesus feel about circumcision?" Paul asked.

She was not sure how to answer this question. She remembered vividly when her son was circumcised. He was her tiny, precious baby, and though she was with the women when the mohel took the knife to him she heard his scream of pain as though he was right next to her. It was the first time she ever heard him scream. She thought that perhaps he would not be opposed to the elimination of this requirement.

And then she wondered to herself: If she was still in Jerusalem, where everyone was an Israelite, understood the covenant, and observed the Law, would she even be questioning this? Had she lost her proper sense of perspective, living among the gentiles so long?

"You'd have to ask his disciples about that. We never discussed it." She stood and looked at her shadow. It was nearing fifth hour.

"I need to say good-bye to you now," she said.

"What are you doing today?" Paul asked.

"A friend is coming to take me out for a while."

"A friend from the church?"

"No."

"From the synagogue?"

"No."

"Then perhaps your friend would like to hear the truth about Christ Jesus and the world to come," Paul said. "This could be Trophimus' opportunity to bring someone to the Lord."

"I'd like that," Trophimus said.

Mary shook her head. "I don't think so. But thank you for coming by." She stood and smiled at them, and then she walked into the proseuche, closing the door behind her.

She knew this frustrated Paul, knew he guessed that she was going to the temple of Artemis, and knew he wanted to forbid her to go. He just didn't dare give orders to the mother of Jesus and James. When she opened the door to let Hieronymos in a short while later, she glanced around outside. Paul, Trophimus, and Epaphras were gone.

"I'm taking my elderly maidservant with me today, Hieronymos." Mary went into her room and emerged with a woman hunched, slow-walking, and swathed in black. Salome walked with the woman, helping her to stand upright.

"Salome, I know you'll do a good job here while I'm gone," Mary said. "If anyone needs me to purify them, tell them to come back tomorrow. Otherwise show them where the towels and hyssop are."

"I know, Mother."

Mary kissed Salome, then she and the hunched woman left the proseuche. Mary was hoping that when Salome grew older the gerousia would allow her to be her replacement as the mikvah attendant, although she knew the girl's terrible scars might be an impediment. Actually even Mary's hands, defective since the Great Fire, made her less than perfectly clean.

Hieronymos led them to the oxcart, not asking any questions. He walked slowly for the sake of the elderly servant and gently helped her to climb into the cart, unusual courtesies toward a servant that Mary noticed and appreciated.

"You're a good man, Hieronymos," she murmured.

"Thank you, Lady, but all praise belongs to Artemis. I am merely a vessel of Her goodness."

Mary smiled, and they continued the rest of the trip in silence.

As they neared the temple, they saw a few Roman soldiers walking around, an unusual sight. Usually when soldiers came to worship at the temple, they wore non-military clothing in respect to the goddess.

The servant moved near to Mary. "Those are my husband's men," she whispered, with a slight nod at a group of men clustered near some of the soldiers.

"I think we should go to the asclepeion, Hieronymos," Mary said. "My maidservant isn't feeling very well."

"I don't think the asclepeion would be a good place for her, Lady," Hieronymos said, turning the cart down a different road outside of the temenos. "A very rich and powerful man, one of the Vedii, is looking for his insane wife. He has placed guards in front of the healing temple because he says she is injured and may seek medical attention. Your servant will not want to be near those rough men."

"No, she wouldn't," Mary said. "Do you have another suggestion?"

"High Priestess Artelia said that if you should bring someone with you today, you should await her at the Caves of Initiation. I'll take you there and then tell her of your arrival."

"Why did the woman's husband say she was insane?" the maid asked.

"Married women are not allowed sanctuary at the Temple of Artemis," Hieronymos said. "So any married woman who seeks sanctuary here must be mad."

The woman turned frightened eyes on Mary, who gave her a reassuring smile, shaking her head. "Don't worry, my dear."

The woman squeezed Mary's hand and nodded.

They arrived at the path leading uphill to the caves and climbed out of the cart. "You should take this path up the hill and wait just inside the first cave," Hieronymos said. "The high priestess will be along soon." He left, heading toward the temple.

The women looked in dismay at the steep, narrow, curving, rocky path that led up to the cave. It was the middle of a hot summer day. Mary assumed that walking up this path constituted part of the temple initiatory rites, a symbolic representation of something, since she couldn't offer any other explanation as to why the path wasn't smoother and straighter. She had never actually decided to seek initiation. But perhaps if she walked up this path today, they wouldn't make her do it again.

"We can do this, Marcellina," she said. "Just hold my hand."

The woman was thirty years younger than Mary, but she had been badly beaten. Although she had been healing and resting in Mary's room for the last three days, she was still weak. She had a broken arm and ribs. But there was no choice if she was to survive. Luckily the path, though difficult, wasn't very long. The women finally made it to the top of the hill, sweating, breathing heavily, and almost crawling at the very end.

Mary and Marcellina went into the first cave and collapsed on a couple of rocks, panting.

"I'm so thirsty," Marcellina said. "I wish there was some water."

"There's a spring in these caves somewhere, but we probably shouldn't go looking for it. I'm sure the high priestess will be here soon."

"I'm so grateful to you, Mother. I would be dead if I hadn't been able to come to you. Everything I've ever heard about you is true. You are a divine spirit and a blessing from the gods."

"Just the one God," Mary said, "but thank you. I'm glad that you knew you could come to me, although I was surprised to learn that even the Romans are familiar with my name."

"The women talk about you in the baths, Mother. About your goodness and your kindness to people in need."

"The high priestess is the truly kind person here. I didn't even have to ask her to help. She just knew to expect us."

"She must be an extraordinary woman."

"Are you talking about me?"

Mary and Marcellina turned and saw Artelia coming toward them from the back of the cave, lamp in hand and followed by two spondopoi.

Mary rose and embraced her friend. "We were talking about you, as a matter of fact. Hello, Ephesia, Phile," she said, addressing the spondopoi, two of the twelve select priestesses of Artemis. "This is—"

"Your maidservant, yes, Hieronymos told me," Artelia interrupted. "I understand she would like to join the pilgrims leaving for Corinth?"

"Um, yes," Marcellina said. "That would be good."

"Come with us," Phile said. "We'll shave your head and clothe you as an initiate. Will that be all right with you?"

"That will be fine," Marcellina said.

Mary embraced her and said, "When you get to Corinth, find the Judean synagogue and ask for Apollos, the evangelizer of Jesus. Tell him I sent you. He'll find people in Corinth to help you further."

"I'll never forget you," Marcellina said, grateful tears in her eyes.

"I won't forget you either, my dear," Mary said, smiling. Phile and Ephesia took Marcellina's hands and led her back into the cave.

"So your god gets this one too?" Artelia asked.

"God's will be done." Mary watched the lamplight disappear into the cave. This was not the first desperate person she had brought to the temple, though today's circumstances were more dramatic than usual. She turned to Artelia. "Where are they going? And how did you get in here?"

"There are secret initiatory passages that lead from the Temple to this cave. Your erstwhile maid and the spondopoi are going down to the barber so her head can be shaved and then to our dock at the river that leads to the harbor. She'll be with others and no one will notice her. She'll be safe."

"This is very kind of you, Artelia. I know that the temple does not offer sanctuary to married women."

"And we're not offering sanctuary now. That doesn't mean we will stand back and watch men beat their wives to death. But I do need to be careful. The Megabysos, the High Priest, has been trying to cause trouble for me lately, and he would be very happy to learn I aided the wife of one of Rome's leading citizens in Ephesus to escape from her lawful husband."

"Do we return to the temple through these passages or do I have to climb back down that hill?"

Mary's friend laughed. "I'm sorry you had to climb that awful hill, Mary. We'll walk a different passage from the others. We'll stop by the sacred spring so that you can have a drink of water."

The two women walked through the darkness, Artelia and her lamp leading the way. The passage curved and led downward. It was cool, but it stank of bats.

"The spring is over here," Artelia said finally, leading Mary into an open cavern. It was lighter in here, with hints of sunlight at the edge. Mary hurried over to the sound of splashing water.

"This is wonderful water," she said, filling her hands and her mouth with the sweet, clean taste.

Artelia joined her for a drink. "Yes, it's quite good."

After a while, thirst quenched, Mary wanted out of the darkness. She had never liked dark, enclosed spaces. "Is this the way out?" she asked, pointing to the light.

"Well, there is an opening there, but—" Artelia began, but Mary had gone ahead and left the cavern of the sacred spring. Artelia smiled as she heard the chimes that rang when Mary left the cave and entered the sunlight, and then she followed her friend.

Mary was standing on a platform built outside of the cave. Just inside the cave, unseen by the dozen or so people standing with mouths agape in front of the platform, a string of bells hung from the ceiling. Artelia walked expertly around the bells and joined her friend.

"She passed the test," Artelia announced to the small crowd. "Great is Artemis Ephesia!"

The people clapped, shouting ,"Great is Artemis Ephesia!" Artelia took Mary's arm and led her off the platform.

"What was that about?" Mary asked. She saw they were just outside of the temenos, near the sacred oak.

"You just passed the test of virginity. Congratulations."

"So how come you didn't make the bells ring?"

"Because only someone whose virginity has been questioned has to be tested," Artelia said. "The rest of us remember to walk around the bells."

Mary laughed, and the two friends walked toward the garden enclosure of the peacocks, where the male birds preened in full stunning array.

She returned to the proseuche late that afternoon to find Paul waiting for her.

"I want to talk with you about your visits to the idol's temple," he said solemnly, pacing in front of the hearth.

Mary began setting out the evening's food, left in the cupboard in her absence. She put an extra bowl on the table for Paul.

"Do you know where Salome is?" she asked.

"I asked her to wait outside when you returned so that I could speak with you alone for a few minutes."

Mary sat down at her normal dinner place and looked up at him inquiringly. He stared back at her. Finally he spoke.

"Why do you spend so much time at the temple of the idol?"

"They're kind people."

"There are kind people in the church and the synagogue too."

"Yes."

"So you don't have to go to the idol's temple to be around kind people."

"No."

"So you'll stop your visits."

"No."

She could feel his frustration and felt compassion for him. But she wasn't going to make this conversation easy for him. She was not under his guardianship.

"You shouldn't spend so much time around gentiles," he said finally.

"You spend most of your time around gentiles."

"Yes, but I'm trying to convert them to the worship of Jesus Christ."

"The members of the synagogue don't worship Jesus."

"But at least they're children of God."

"So am I."

His face had grown red. She could tell he was trying to stay patient with her. She realized she was enjoying this conversation and felt guilty. She let another wash of affection for him flow through her.

"Are you trying to convert the idol worshippers?" he asked finally. "Is that why you spend so much time there?"

"No."

"Then why?"

"Because they're kind people."

"Do they try to convert you?" He sounded anxious.

"No," she said. She wasn't about to tell him about the many times she had thought about becoming an initiate.

And now she realized for the first time how many people would be hurt if the mother of Jesus became an initiate of Artemis. She sighed. Well, she was too old to be climbing initiation hills and walking through caves blindfolded and all the rest of that silly stuff anyway.

He tried one last time. "I just don't think the priestess of Artemis is a proper friend for you, Mother."

"Jesus does."

"What?"

"Jesus appeared to her once. He thanked her for being my friend."

"How do you know?"

"She told me. Just like you told me that he appeared to you."

There wasn't much else he could say. Mary opened the door to call Salome in, and the three of them ate a quiet dinner together.

She thought: "My son, I pray for the frightened ones who try to control the behavior of others."

17

"I am swept up in a strange storm of devotion, tossed in a wild sea of belief. The thunder is getting louder and I cannot see over the waves."

M ary didn't see Paul the following day. The day after that, Judith came to the proseuche and informed her that Paul was in prison.
"Oh no," Mary said, distressed. "What happened?"
"He almost burnt down the city, that's what happened," Judith said, coughing. She did not feel well and had lost a great deal of weight. "The gerousia met and convicted him. My son David insisted that he be imprisoned while they decide whether or not to interrogate him with the proscribed forty

lashes minus one. As it is, he won't be allowed to step foot in any synagogue in this city again."

She told Mary that Paul, his cousin Junia, and her husband, Andronicus, had been preaching about Jesus Christ in the part of the city known as the sorcerers' area, a rebuilt part of town that had burnt to the ground during the Great Fire. A large crowd had gathered, and Paul had bested the renowned Judean sorcerer Sceva in a show of demonic exorcism. The people who witnessed Paul's triumph began to destroy the shop of Sceva and his sons, throwing all of their magical papers and scrolls into the street. Pleased at seeing people turn on these symbols of idolatry, Paul told the crowd to start a bonfire and to gather other magical and astrological scrolls and toss them into the flames too. The frenzy grew, and the mob destroyed the shops of several nearby astrologers and sorcerers as well, all of them Israelites.

It was midsummer now, the same time of year as the Great Fire. As the bonfire spread to neighboring property, the citizens realized the fun had gotten out of hand. Fire endangered several buildings before the concerned residents managed to put it out.

The proconsul called Alexander to his headquarters to discuss the fire. The province governor agreed with Alexander that since the victims and the perpetrators of the crime had all been Judeans, the Judean gerousia should decide the punishments.

"Alexander wanted to release them with just chastisement and expulsion from the synagogue," Judith said. "Of course, they're members of his house guild; therefore it reflects badly on him that they almost burned down the city. He says the gerousia has been trying for a long time to stop Israelites from practicing sorcery in Ephesus, since it's an abomination to the Lord and also makes all Hebrews look like superstitious fools, and that therefore the Nazorenes did us a favor. My son David insisted that they be imprisoned at the proconsul's palace while the gerousia continues its investigation."

"They? Do you mean Junia and Andronicus are also in prison?"

"All three of them."

"But Junia is expecting a child."

"Then she shouldn't have been out inciting the mob in the street with all of that Christ nonsense about the criminal Jesus," Judith said.

Mary stared at her friend. "You do know that Jesus was my son, don't you?"

"Yes, and I don't see you burning down the city over him, do I?"

Judith left soon after. Her cough was quite bad, and Mary was surprised that she had come to the proseuche at all, being so ill. No doubt she wanted to be the first to tell Mary of Paul's imprisonment, and in fact Mary saw a smile on her face when Deborah arrived just as she was leaving.

"Mother, did you hear about Junia and Andronicus?" Deborah asked.

"I just told her," Judith said, pausing at the door to see if Deborah had any additional news.

"You sound terrible," Deborah said to Judith. "I think you should be in bed." Judith's slave helped her into her donkey cart for her trip back home. Mary and Deborah walked together to the mikvah.

Mary asked Deborah if she would send a donkey cart to drive her to the prison the next day.

"I've never been to that prison," Mary said. "They must view Paul as a very important prisoner, to send him to the proconsul's palace."

"It's not Paul who's important," said Deborah. "It's a reflection of the status of my father and of the gerousia." Deborah didn't like Mary visiting a prison, but she finally agreed as long as she or John accompanied her on her visit.

Theodora and her children came up to the proseuche the next morning with Deborah. While Mary and Deborah went to the prison to see Junia, Andronicus, and Paul, Theodora would assist with the mikvah and Salome would spend time with the children.

On the way to the prison at the proconsul's palace, Mary and Deborah discussed Paul's disruptive behavior in the synagogue.

"My father was talking about expelling him anyway, even before this happened," Deborah said.

"Paul didn't attend synagogue that often," Mary objected.

"Yes, but when he did, he didn't allow anyone else to speak. And he was unwilling to allow discussion about anything except his beliefs about Jesus being the Messiah. You and John have been teaching that for years, but you do your teaching outside of the assembly meetings. You have your own First Day meetings, just like Enoch and the Disciples of John the Baptist have their First Day meetings. We don't mind Paul inviting people to attend his church. But we do mind his causing dissension in the assembly and his taking over our synagogue meetings to teach his own propaganda. And to teach that circumcision isn't necessary anymore—well, that is simply inexcusable. Even Father's affection for Junia and Andronicus wasn't enough for him to allow Paul to remain after he started saying that."

"Well, he won't be there to cause any more dissension in the synagogue," Mary said sadly. She knew it hurt Paul that he had been expelled from every synagogue he'd ever preached in. He'd told her the stories of his treatment, sometimes quite humiliating, in the various cities where he had founded churches. "I'm grateful that your father didn't permit the gerousia to whip him."

"Not yet, but it could still happen. They're still debating how many lashes are appropriate for Paul's behavior. I think that if they had any experience meting out this sort of punishment, Paul would have received the full forty lashes permitted in the Torah. Or if he was being punished for blasphemy instead of for fire-starting, he probably would have been whipped already. But because they've never beaten anyone for a civil offense before, they're uncomfortable about it. And I understand they also worry that they might by accident go over the forty lashes allowed by God, even if they tried to only give him thirty-nine, which my Father says is the standard practice to guarantee not going over forty."

"He told me he's received the forty lashes minus one on numerous occasions," Mary said.

"Then he certainly knows more about such punishment than anyone in Ephesus," Deborah said and then gave a weak smile. "Maybe they should invite him to serve on the gerousia, so he can share his expertise."

The two friends talked about Deborah's children and their studies at the synagogue school during the rest of the trip to the proconsul's palace. When they arrived they told the guards that they wanted to visit the Judean prisoners, and the guards took them to see the jailer.

The three Nazorenes were in a crowded cell together, along with Timothy and two other people. When Mary and Deborah arrived, the jailer said that there were too many visitors and that some of them would have to leave before these two new visitors would be admitted to the cell.

"Libo, Aculeo, this is Mary, the mother of our Lord, and Deborah, the sister of John, who was present at the crucifixion of our Lord," Paul told the two strangers in the room.

The two men fell to the ground near the women's feet. Mary was used to such response by this time, but this was a completely new experience for Deborah, who stared in astonishment at the men.

"Mother, Deborah—Libo and Aculeo are members of Caesar's household, in service to Caesar's relatives who live here in Ephesus," Paul said.

"Hello, Libo and Aculeo," Mary said. "God bless you both."

"Make them stand up, Mother," Deborah said nervously.

"Please stand now," Mary said to the men.

The two men stood. "We'll leave now so that you can visit with Paul," Libo said. "But we are honored to meet you both."

Mary smiled and moved aside so that the men could leave the room. After they'd gone, the jailer let Mary and Deborah enter.

"I know they believe your son was the Messiah," Deborah said, "but why did they say they were honored to meet me?"

"Because you're John's sister and John was a witness to Jesus' death." John, who had always been known in Ephesus as Alexander's second son and Enoch's younger brother, was as uncomfortable as Mary with his peculiar new status in the eyes of Paul's converts.

"John never talks about what it was like being at the death of your son. I had no idea it was so significant." Deborah was not a member of John's church, though she often attended the Disciples of John the Baptist meetings, which Enoch still held in Alexander's home.

"He talks about it quite a bit at the Friends of Jesus meetings," Mary said, hugging Junia, who had run into her arms the moment she entered the cell.

Mary spent a while with Junia, checking to see if she was healthy and asking if her son Elah was all right. Junia was the only prisoner not in chains, and she said this was because the jailer was treating her with gentleness due to her pregnancy. Everyone else wore manacles and was chained together.

"Elah is fine," Junia said. "He was working in the cinnabar mine with his uncle Herodion during the bonfire, so he wasn't arrested with Andronicus and me. And Andronicus is happy being here; he can listen to Paul talk about Jesus all day instead of crawling on his hands and knees through the mines, breathing that poisonous cinnabar dust." She told Mary that the baby she was carrying was strong and that she expected to be released long before it was born as the gerousia would realize she hadn't done anything wrong.

"I'll talk with Father about it," Deborah said. "I know they already decided not to beat you or Andronicus, so I don't see why you're in here at all. We'll get you out of here soon. Now tell me what we can bring for you."

Mary, reassured about Junia's health, left the two women and went over to see the men. Timothy, a visitor to the prison, acted as scribe for Paul, who was writing a letter to his church in Philippi. Andronicus listened intently as Paul dictated.

Mary listened too and found herself as fascinated as Andronicus. Paul was a splendid speaker and writer and his ways of expressing himself were very moving.

Always rejoice in the Lord. I repeat: Rejoice! Let your submission to God be known to all men. The Lord is near. Do not be anxious about anything, but in everything be prayerful. Make your supplications with thanksgiving. Make your needs known to God. And the peace of God, which passes all understanding, will guard your hearts and your minds in Christ Jesus. Finally, brothers, whatever there is that is true, whatever there is that is significant, whatever there is that is righteous, whatever there is that is pure, whatever there is that is endearing, whatever there is that is admirable, if there is any virtue and if there is anything worthy of praise, fill your thoughts with these things. Whatever you have learned or received or heard from me, or seen in me, do these same things yourself. And the God of peace will be with you.

The passion and kindness in his voice and the emotion of his words brought tears to her eyes, and she understood for the first time why her son could have revealed himself to this man, why Jesus might have chosen Paul to be his apostle.

"That is very beautiful, Paul," she said.

"Thank you, Mother. I'm glad you liked it. Shall I send your regards to the Philippi church?"

She thought about it, and then she had a vision of masses of people coming to Ephesus, wanting to stare at her and cry over Jesus' tunic.

"No, I would rather you not mention my presence here. I will pray for them of course."

"Even better. How blessed they are, to have the prayers of the mother of our Lord!" Paul was trying very hard to let her know their little spat was over.

Timothy spoke up. "Paul, you said that you were going to ask the Holy Mother if she would talk with Narcissus."

"Oh yes. Thank you, Timothy, for the reminder. Mother, your friend Narcissus troubles me. He is the father of our brother Tychicus. Narcissus is an important member of the leather workers guild and often comes into the guild hall while I'm preaching to argue with me about Jesus. Out of respect for the Friends of Jesus church, for Tychicus, and for your friendship with Narcissus I have not chastised him as I ought. Will you talk with him, please?"

She was horrified at the idea that Paul would want her to chastise someone for him. "If you have a problem with someone from the Friends of Jesus church, Paul, you should discuss it with John."

"But Narcissus argues with me in front of the gentiles, about circumcision and following the Law."

"Narcissus is a Greek, a God Fearer who converted to the Law. He has adopted all of our ways; he's even had himself circumcised, which I understand is a very painful procedure for a man. He is devoted to God and to Jesus. It is natural that he would have strong views about the Law when he sees you working to convert other gentiles with teachings that trouble him. I am grateful that you have treated him with respect, and I hope that you will continue to do so. But I really think you should discuss this with John."

Mary and Deborah left soon thereafter, comforted that their friends were healthy and in good spirits even though the issue of their punishment remained unresolved.

"Did that man call you 'Holy Mother?'" Deborah asked on the ride back home.

"Yes, he did," Mary said, sighing. "I've asked them not to do so, but I think they forget sometimes."

"They really do believe that Jesus was the Messiah, don't they?"

"It's more than that. They believe he is the son of God."

Deborah stared at her, and Mary realized that her friend was afraid to inquire what Mary herself believed. Mary was grateful for her reticence, because this was a question she did not know how to answer. The strength of emotion and belief that had built up around her son now seemed like a huge storm overwhelming the entire world. She felt battered on all sides and much too small to withstand the tumult raging around her.

Deborah succeeded in getting Junia and Andronicus released from prison before the next Sabbath. They were told that they were expelled from the synagogues in Ephesus and would not be welcome at any festivals in the future unless they repented and went on pilgrimage to the Temple to make atonement. Mary expected someone to tell her that she was not to allow Junia to use the mikvah after the birth of her child, and she dreaded the uproar that would result from her refusal to follow this stricture. Happily no one ever told her this.

One month after her first visit to the prison, someone pounded on the proseuche door, awakening Mary in the middle of the night. Salome opened the door, and when Mary entered the proseuche she saw Prisca and Aquila standing inside, breathing heavily. Aquila held his arm, which dripped blood. Prisca held onto Aquila, tears pouring down her face.

"Oh my dears!" Mary exclaimed and rushed to lead her visitors to comfortable cushions near the hearth. Salome made hyssop tea while Mary and Prisca helped Aquila to remove his tunic so that they could examine his wound.

"Salome, please fetch water, vinegar, and cloths so that we can clean and bind Aquila's arm," Mary said. She had never seen a wound from an arrow before, but she knew from the tear in his clothes what this was.

Mary washed the wound with water then dabbed vinegar into the hole, Salome helping her when her hands wouldn't bend enough. Aquila hissed through his teeth at the vinegar's sting, but Mary knew his pain meant that the demons of disease were being exorcised from his arm. She added honey to the wound to sweeten the skin as she'd been taught by the priestesses of Hestia Boulaia during the Great Fire, and then bound his arm tightly with a length of clean cloth.

They made up a nice bed for him in front of the hearth, which she kept lit but low during these summer months, and covered him with blankets. Throughout this entire process Prisca clutched at his hand, kissed him, and smoothed his brow, tears running continually down her face. Prisca's devotion to her husband, never apparent to Mary before, was tender to witness.

When Aquila was settled, Mary turned inquiring eyes on Prisca. "What happened, dear?" she asked.

"Oh, Mother, it's Paul! You have to do something to help Paul!"

Mary sighed. "What has he done now?"

"He's sick, Mother—he has the shivering fever. We think he's going to die. He thinks he's going to die. He's out of his mind most of the time, thinking that he's fighting the beasts of the idol or being crucified alongside Christ. We made petitions to the gerousia, but Archisynagogos David said that if Paul dies in prison, it's God's will."

"Did he really?" Ever since his advancement to archisynagogos after the death of his father Lavi, David had become quite rigid in his interpretation of the Law. She suspected that the gerousia would soon gain the beating experience they had previously lacked.

"So Aquila and I finally decided to break him out of prison ourselves. Unfortunately the guards saw us and fired arrows."

"You tried to break Paul out of jail?"

"Paul tells stories of times that God sent angels to release the apostles from prison. We'd hoped he'd do the same this time. But now we're thinking maybe you're the angel he needs."

Mary told Prisca she'd see what she could do in the morning. They made up a bed for the anxious woman next to Aquila's uninjured side. Mary brought Salome into her room to sleep, leaving the couple alone.

She had been to Archisynagogos Lavi's house before, after the fire. He'd asked her to visit with him privately so that he could examine her hands and they could talk about whether or not her scarring irredeemably polluted her. They had met in the atrium. There were no graven images in Archisynagogos Lavi's atrium or anywhere in his house that she could see. He was dead now and his son David ran the house and business.

When the slave saw Mary at the door, he gave a big smile. This man had accompanied Judith to the proseuche on several occasions and recognized her. Mary recognized him too and felt bad that she didn't remember his name.

"The mistress will be so glad to see you, Lady. She's been so sick and no one has come to visit her."

Mary felt terrible that she had never come to visit Judith, even though she'd known she was ailing. Her life had gotten so busy since she met Paul, and it seemed she never had time to visit the sick and needy in the way she used to. She vowed to do better.

The slave led her to the family bedrooms and showed her to Judith's room.

Judith lay in a curtained bed.

"Who's there?" she cried out in a weak voice.

But Mary hardly heard her. She was staring around at the room. It was swathed with peacock feathers.

The wall was frescoed with a peacock parade, the majestic birds circling the room in full painted array. The ceiling was painted in a circular peacock feather design.

But it was the real feathers that stole Mary's breath away. There were thousands of peacock feathers in this room. The rug, the window hangings, the curtain around the bed—all were made of peacock feathers. Even the chairs and tables were covered in peacock feathers, painted, embroidered, and real.

Real and illegal.

"It's me, Judith." Mary walked up to the bed so that her friend could see her.

A quick, guilty expression moved over Judith's face for just a moment and then gave way to a sly grin.

"What do you think of my room? Isn't it beautiful?"

"It's overwhelming."

"Don't you want to know where the feathers came from?"

"I'm curious, of course." Mary took her friend's hand. Her fingers were so thin. And although she was very clean, Mary recognized the slight sickly smell of disease that had accompanied Adonis in his last months of life.

"You know I always loved those feathers you had, from the first moment I saw them."

"I remember."

"It hurt that you wouldn't let me have them."

"It wasn't my decision."

"You chose the whims of the idol worshippers over your friendship with me."

"I'm sorry you feel that way."

"Well, the feathers were wasted up there, just lying on the ground, and you wouldn't let me have them, so I just took them."

"When?" Mary had never seen Judith carrying any feathers.

"I went up to the grove every First Day morning for years. I knew you stayed at Alexander's house after the Sabbath and that no one would be at the proseuche. My slaves and I scoured the woods every week, collecting feathers."

"Every week?"

"Until the Great Fire. After that, there were too many people up there."

"And we had to eat the peacocks."

Judith looked horrified. "I never knew you did that!"

Mary shrugged. During the Winter of Despair when they cared for the homeless, they had received food donations from Alexander and the temple of Artemis but never anything from Lavi's household. Perhaps that extra food would have been enough to spare the peacocks. "I never knew you were taking the feathers. But surely you didn't collect all of these from the sacred peacocks up at the grove." She waved at the multitudes of feathers. "There are just too many."

"I bought the rest." Judith's hands moved lovingly over the feathers on her bedcover.

"It's illegal to buy or sell peacock feathers in Ephesus."

"They were smuggled in. I'm glad you're here to see them. I've never been able to show this room to anyone. My pride and joy, and no one could see it, just because of that stupid law."

Mary remained talking with Judith, surrounded on all sides by the "eyes of God." But the feathers didn't feel like the eyes of God, not in here. In here, they felt like a lonely woman's pain. The room made Mary want to cry.

But she stayed for an hour visiting her friend, leaving only when it became clear that Judith was tired and needed sleep.

"I'll come back again tomorrow." Mary kissed Judith's cheek.

"I'd like that," her old friend said, closing her eyes. But just before she did, Mary caught a glimpse of God in Judith's tired eyes.

Mary left the room, closing the door softly behind her. A slave stood nearby. "Is the archisynagogos here?" she asked.

"I'll fetch him. You can wait in the atrium." He showed her the way and left to find David.

David did not make her wait long. She sat as she waited, but stood when he entered. He waved her back down. "I heard you visited with my mother." He took a seat nearby.

"Yes. But I also wanted to visit you."

"Why?"

"Because I'd like the gerousia to release Paul, and I understand you're the person who is insisting on his remaining in prison."

"We're still discussing what to do with him. It was grossly irresponsible to make a bonfire in that part of town. There are fire pits in town specifically designated for ritual purposes, or he could have had his bonfire out in the country, in an empty field near the marshy land. He needs to be punished."

"Yes, but in the meantime he's suffering from the shivering fever. He needs care."

"What do you want me to do about it?"

"I'd like you to release him from prison and let him stay with me." Until that moment she hadn't considered letting Paul stay at the proseuche. But having taken on the responsibility of getting him released from jail, it would be her responsibility to make sure he got well.

David looked at her face, then at her hands and grimaced. "What will you do if I don't release Paul?"

"I don't understand."

"Are you going to tell the temple of Artemis about my foolish mother and her peacock feathers?"

This question took Mary completely by surprise. "Of course not, David. Why would you ask me such a question?"

"Because it wouldn't be the first time you turned to them for assistance, would it?"

"I don't know what you mean."

He nodded at her hands. "When we were going to remove you from your position as mikvah attendant because of your defective hands. Father said that he received a visit from the high priestess. She told him that if you were removed from your position, the idol's temple wouldn't renew our lease on the mikvah."

Mary stared at him in shock, and he realized she had been unaware of Artelia's intercession.

"I'm sorry," he said. "I thought you knew."

"I had no idea. I discussed my hands with your father, here in this very room. I thought he was comfortable with the idea of my remaining the mikvah attendant." She almost said "guardian of the sacred spring," because she knew in her heart that was the title Artelia would have used in that long-ago conversation with Lavi.

"Should I expect to see worshippers of the idol here at my door demanding the release of Paul now?" David still sounded belligerent, but she could tell he was feeling embarrassed about his accusations.

"I shouldn't think so," she said mildly. She stood. "I'll be back to visit your mother again tomorrow, if you don't mind."

He stood and walked her to the vestibulum, frowning. "That would be kind of you. Only my sisters come to see her now. She's never had many friends."

Mary stopped and looked him in the eyes. "I've always been her friend," she said gently.

"I know," he said, half-whispering.

The slave opened the door, and David spoke up. "I'll speak with the gerousia. Paul will be released from the prison tomorrow, if you want to go fetch him."

She touched his arm. "You're a good man, David. Thank you."

She walked back to the proseuche. She wished she had the strength to walk to the proconsul's palace to see Paul, but she knew that would be too much for her. She would tell Prisca and Aquila of David's decision, and Prisca could go to the palace to let him know of his release.

Prisca and Aquila were sitting under a tree outside the mikvah when Mary got home. Prisca burst into grateful tears when she heard the news. "Oh, Mother, thank you! Thank you!" Aquila grinned and walked over to give Mary an embrace with his good arm.

"Children, it's all right. You go get him in the morning and bring him back here. I'll take care of him."

Prisca nodded. "I had thought to take him to our house, but I know he'd be happier here with you. And I really need to spend my time preaching, not nursing the sick."

"Let's go find Timothy," Aquila said. "He can go with you to pick up Paul, because I don't think it's a good idea if the palace guards get a look at my arm. They might ask questions about how I was injured."

"And then we'd have to figure out how to get you out of prison," Mary said with a smile.

"Exactly," Aquila said. "If we leave now, perhaps Prisca and Timothy will have time to go see Paul today."

The two of them went back into the proseuche to gather their things, then left.

Salome brought Mary a cup of tea. "Mother, how are you feeling?"

"A little tired, that's all." Mary gave her daughter a hug. The two of them walked outside to a bench in the shade and sat down. Mary drank her tea.

"Mother, I've made a decision about something."

"Yes?"

"I want to change my name."

"Don't you like the name Salome? It's my sister's name." Mary's sister Salome was now dead, she had learned in the letter Paul had brought her from James. She had loved her sister very much.

Salome kissed her. "It's a lovely name, Mother, and I hope you'll still call me by it. But when I grow up, I want to have a different name."

"What's that?" Mary brushed a lock of hair back from her daughter's face. Her daughter pulled it back to cover her cheek. She preferred to hide her scarred face with her hair.

"I want to change it to Mary," Salome said. "Because that's the most beautiful name in the world and because I want to be just like you."

"Why, thank you." Mary's voice was choked with emotion. "There are already a lot of Marys in the world, but I guess one more won't hurt. But I'll still call you Salome. All right?"

"You can call me anything you want. As long as you call me 'Daughter.'"

She thought: "My son, comfort the prisoners, including those punished within their own bodies and dreams."

18

"All actions have outcomes. The heedless wind destroys the nest."

The next day Timothy drove an oxcart up to the proseuche. Aquila walked alongside. In the back of the cart, Prisca sat with a delirious Paul, who shivered in the hot summer day.

"Bring him into my room," Mary said. She thought the privacy of her room would be the best place for him. She wouldn't have to expel him from the proseuche every time someone came to use the mikvah or when women came for the new moon ceremony.

Paul remained at the proseuche for several weeks. There would be hours when he was cogent and felt better, though he was still exhausted and his head hurt; then a sudden coldness would come on him, his body would tense up, and he'd become feverish and sweat for hours. He vomited frequently and had a difficult time keeping any food down. His head was in agony, and sometimes in the midst of his fever he'd see demons or visions of hell. As Prisca had said, sometimes he'd find himself fighting beasts or hanging crucified on the cross with Jesus.

He was utterly, unbearably crushed by his illness. He said it had struck him from time to time for years. Sometimes, in the midst of it, he despaired of life, wanted to die, wanted the constant misery to just end. Each time he came out of his fever, it was as though God had rescued him from the dead.

Paul had constant attention from visitors. Prisca and Aquila came by to visit every day, as did Timothy and disciples from churches in other cities who came to Ephesus to confer with Paul. John and Theodora came by every few days to see him. Alexander's slave Epenetus, who now attended both the Friends of Jesus meetings on First Day and Prisca and Aquila's tent church meetings on Fourth Day, took over the responsibility of bringing the daily meals from Alexander's villa to the proseuche himself so that he could spend time with Paul. Epaphras came to tell Paul good-bye before he left with the letter to the church at Philippi. Calandra and Narcissus' son Tychicus came by to get instructions before leaving with another disciple to go to Smyrna to preach in the baths and the streets and—it was hoped—to start a church there. Mary realized that this must be one of the reasons why Narcissus was so opposed to Paul—he had convinced Narcissus' own son to take up the difficult life of a travelling disciple of Jesus Christ.

But the person who spent the most time with Paul was Salome. During his bad times, she had no complaints about wiping his fevered brow, cleaning up his vomit, or emptying his slops. She loved to listen to him talk about Jesus and the Kingdom of God, and he patiently and lovingly shared his stories with her. He was also happy to help her with her reading and writing lessons, which had fallen by the wayside when Apollos left. Paul had no disgust at the child's scarred features. From the moment he met her, she was a much beloved child of God, perfect in his eyes.

"I think he sometimes misses not having a family of his own," Prisca said to Mary one day as they sat visiting together. They watched Salome, who was explaining the mikvah to Euphemia, a slave girl who usually accompanied her masters Helene and Aristobulus to the proseuche. Helene and Aristobulus were recent converts to Prisca and Aquila's church. They had walked up the hill every day this week to learn from Paul. While they visited him, their slave stayed with Salome. Salome enjoyed having a new friend, one who didn't look down on her because of her burns.

"He would have been a good father, I think," Mary said.

"Yes," Prisca said. "That's who he is to me. He's the loving father I never had as a child. I've told him so."

Mary patted her hand. "And you are a loving child to him, my dear. I know he's very fond of you. And very proud of you."

"Would you mind if we bring some people up to attend the Friends of Jesus meeting on Sunday?" Prisca asked. "Paul is feeling much better, and I know he plans on attending."

Mary appreciated the forewarning. "I'll let John know. You do know the Friends of Jesus church doesn't do things quite the same way as you do down at your tent, don't you?"

"Yes," Prisca said. "And Paul has told us that we are not to try to convert anyone else from your church."

Mary hadn't heard this before. "That's good of him. I'll thank him."

"Most of your members have already joined our church anyway."

"Yes, I had noticed that," Mary said with a rueful smile.

Mary did not attend synagogue while Paul was with her; she didn't want to leave him alone in the house in case his fever came back. On the morning of First Day, she walked the labyrinth, praying as usual, but when she left the grove to return to the house she was surprised to see that there were people already arriving for the Friends of Jesus meeting.

She walked up to Helene, sitting on a bench with her husband, Aristobulus, talking with another couple Mary didn't know. "I don't understand," Mary said. "Why are you all here now? The meeting won't start for another six hours." They were not members of the Friends of Jesus guild, but she remembered Prisca had asked her if the members of the tent church could attend John's meeting today.

"We thought we'd make a whole day of it up here," Helene said. "This is a beautiful place to spend the day together, singing, praying, and prophesying. You don't mind, do you, Holy Mother?"

"Oh no," Mary said, smiling weakly. "Of course not." She let herself be introduced to the other couple and tried not to grimace when the woman dropped to the ground and kissed her feet. She broke away as soon as she politely could and hurried over to Epenetus, who was directing a variety of slaves from different households in the setting up of tables and food.

"Epenetus, what is going on?"

"The Nazorenes decided to make this a festival day. They want to celebrate the healing of our beloved teacher Paul."

"Why didn't anyone tell me?"

"They just decided on it yesterday, at the tent. I told them I didn't think you'd mind." He looked at her nervously, and she patted him on the shoulder.

"Of course I don't mind, Epenetus. I was just surprised to see people here so early, that's all."

Paul walked out of the proseuche. Timothy and Trophimus hovered over him in case his legs were too weak. Their concern wasn't necessary. He hadn't had a shivering spell in several days and was getting stronger all the time. Today he seemed in good spirits.

"Mother, I hope you don't mind if there's a crowd up here today." He walked over to her and kissed her cheek.

"No, but I hope you will remember that John is the leader of the Friends of Jesus church and there are certain ways we do things that are different from your churches."

After much discussion, the people who had remained members of the Friends of Jesus church decided they weren't comfortable with many of Paul's teachings, including his rejection of the Law, the teaching to eat Jesus' body and drink his blood, and the idea that Jesus was the son of God. They accepted that Jesus was the Messiah and that he was the Logos—but they just weren't comfortable with the idea of worshipping him as divine.

"We will honor and respect John's meeting and teachings, Mother," Paul said. "I'll assure him of that when he gets here. But until the meeting starts, I hope you won't mind if the brothers and sisters gather together to pray and sing and talk about the Kingdom of God."

"Of course I don't mind, Paul."

A woman in beautiful, rich clothes came up to them and embraced Paul. "I am so glad to see you well, my dear friend," she said.

"And I you, sister," he said with a smile. He turned to Mary. "Mother, this is Chloe. We first met at our church in Corinth when she was visiting there, and now she's a devoted servant of our church here in Ephesus. She has been very generous in helping us to continue our work. Chloe, this is Mary, the mother of our Lord."

Mary saw the faint glimpse of dismay in Chloe's eyes as she contemplated getting her beautiful clothes dirty if she dropped to the ground in obeisance, and she rushed to embrace her before she tried. "My dear, I'm very happy to meet you."

"I am deeply honored to meet you, Holy Mother," Chloe said with a grateful smile.

Soon Sosthenes, another of Paul's followers, pulled him and Chloe away, and Mary found herself standing awkwardly with Timothy and Trophimus.

Nervous in her presence, Trophimus soon made an excuse to go talk to someone else. But Timothy was always very glad to be around Mary and wanted to have this opportunity to be alone with her. He spent the next hour telling her of his work with Paul in Thessalonica, Philippi, and Corinth.

"My son Apollos is in Corinth," she said when he mentioned that city.

"I know. We've heard very good reports of Apollos' work. In fact, I think some of the church members even prefer his preaching to Paul's!"

Mary laughed, glad to know that Apollos was finding success in his endeavors.

Over the course of the day, the crowd grew until there were fifty people or more sitting on the benches and grass and walking around the trees. Sometimes they'd sing hymns. Mary had the wonderful surprise of hearing Prisca sing. Prisca's voice was clear, strong, and incredibly pure, easily the most beautiful voice Mary had ever heard. Other times someone would start praying loudly and then others would join in. As the day progressed, more and more often someone would shout out a prophecy, and the first time she heard that it was a bit of a shock, but not nearly as shocking as when people started speaking in tongues.

She found herself staring at a woman whose head and hands were raised to heaven while strange sounds rushed rapidly out of her mouth. Then she noticed others were also speaking to heaven in this odd way.

"Would you like me to interpret for you?" Helene asked her shyly.

"Interpret? You mean you understand them?"

"Yes, that's my gift," Helene said. "Everyone has a gift. Some teach, some prophecy, some do miracles, some heal, some speak in tongues, and some, like me, interpret."

"So what are they saying?"

"They're talking about the Parousia and the resurrection of the dead."

"How do you know that? You understand those words?" What the people were saying didn't even sound like regular words to her.

"I don't understand the words. I feel the meanings in my heart. The Holy Spirit tells me what is being said."

"Oh." No one ever did anything like this in the Friends of Jesus church. Mary looked around, seeing all the people who were speaking in tongues.

Over by the food tables, Epenetus had his head and hands raised in the air as he spoke to the sky. And then to her surprise, she recognized the Judean playwright Damonikos in the crowd. He was also speaking in tongues.

Mary was relieved to see John, Theodora, and their children arrive. John walked with the limp that had slowed him down ever since he broke his hip falling after he saved Salome from the burning building. Mary hurried over to them.

"This is a big crowd," John said.

"You don't seem surprised."

"Epenetus told me about it last night."

"Paul said that he won't interfere in your meeting."

John smiled and kissed her. "Don't worry, Mother. Paul and I have talked about the different teachings of our churches. I'm not concerned about this."

"Oh, I'm so glad."

"Who's that girl with Salome?" Theodora asked.

Mary glanced over at her daughter, giggling on a bench with the slave Euphemia. The girls were both enjoying bread with honey, the only food Epenetus allowed anyone to have until the Friends of Jesus agape meal began.

"That's Euphemia. She's a slave who belongs to a couple of Paul's followers."

"She seems like a good girl," Theodora said, smiling to see Salome enjoying herself.

"She's very sweet," Mary said.

Soon John gathered everyone together and gave the blessing. He added to his prayers today his thanks that all of these people had gathered in this beautiful place on this lovely day to join the Friends of Jesus in their worship. After the blessing everyone went to the food tables to fill their plates and settle into places at the benches and on the ground, eating together while John gave his teaching.

Today he told the people about how he met Jesus. One day when Jesus was teaching at the Temple, John was supposed to go to class with his rabbi. Instead he stayed to listen to this holy man with his loving manner and his sweet words. Then he shared some of the miracles he had witnessed, which he considered to be signs that Jesus was the Messiah.

Mary was glad to see that the Friends of Jesus members did not seem distressed about the crowd of strangers. Narcissus and Calandra sat with a couple from the tent church who seemed to be friends of theirs, and Junia and Andronicus sat with Theodora instead of with their new tent church friends. Euphemia prepared her masters' plates for them then returned to sit by Salome.

Mary noticed two more people coming up the hill and walked over to welcome them. She realized as they came closer that these were not Nazorenes. The woman was Eugeneia, wife of the politarch; she was accompanied by a male slave. This wasn't the slave Sophos, whom Eugeneia had tried to whip in the proseuche years before. Mary had never seen Sophos again. He and Eugeneia remained in her prayers.

She met Eugeneia at the mikvah. "Would you like to go into the proseuche to pray before the tevilah?" she asked. She always asked Eugeneia this question, though the answer was always no. Often Eugeneia didn't even want to go into the proseuche to pray after her immersion. She only did so when it was cold outside and she wanted to warm up and dry her hair at the hearth.

"What's going on?" Eugeneia asked.

"It's a Friends of Jesus guild meeting. You've seen them before." Eugeneia often came to the mikvah on First Day.

"I've seen those little guild meetings that John has. But there's never been this many people up here before."

"No, they're having a festival today."

"Oh really?" Eugeneia said and started walking toward the food. "Can I join? I'm quite hungry, actually."

"Eugeneia, you're welcome to join, of course. But I think I should tell you that some of these people are gentiles." Most of them were, but she didn't say that.

"Gentiles?" Eugeneia stopped in her tracks and stared at Mary in horror. "Yes."

"Gentiles are up here eating?"

"Yes."

"With Hebrews?"

Mary sighed. "Yes." Mary understood the problem even better than Eugeneia did. This place was supposed to be a place of purity for Hebrews, and a crowd of unclean gentiles was polluting it.

Certainly few of the dishes had been prepared according to the Law. She wouldn't be surprised if pork and shellfish were among the foods being eaten here today—in the yard of the Judean mikvah and prayer house. Eugeneia didn't know that, of course.

"My husband is going to hear about this," Eugeneia said.

"Yes. Do you still want to use the mikvah?"

"I do, but I don't want you to sprinkle me. I can immerse by myself."

Mary nodded and waited with the slave while Eugeneia removed her clothes in the changing tent and wrapped herself in toweling, walked down the steps to the bath, dipped in the cold water, and came back up to dry and dress. When she was ready to leave, she spoke to Mary.

"I suggest you purify yourself, Mary."

Mary nodded. "I will. I do. Every day." She watched Eugeneia and her slave walk down the hill and then she returned to the meeting.

The meeting went well although several people from the tent church complained because they weren't served any wine.

The Friends of Jesus meetings usually ended before dusk so that people didn't have to walk home in the dark. John ended today's meeting at the usual time, then he and the other Friends of Jesus members left. The others were slower to go, which worried Mary. It was just past the new moon and very dark outside. But eventually most left, going in groups and carrying torches to light their way.

When she walked into the proseuche after waving good-bye to Epenetus and his slave Pelagios, nine people sat on cushions near the hearth with Paul: Timothy, Chloe, Helene, Aristobulus, Sosthenes, Trophimus, Damonikos, Prisca, and Aquila.

"Where's Salome?" she asked.

"She and Euphemia are checking on the goats," Helene said.

Mary nodded and sat down on a cushion to join the group. She hoped they wouldn't stay too late. Paul still slept in her room, so she and Salome slept out here. She usually fell asleep soon after sunset.

Paul spoke about love. Though still a bit tired, he now felt fully healed and had had a wonderful day in the company of the saints, which he said made him feel particularly inspired tonight. He said that of the three great gifts of the heart given by God, faith, hope, and love, the greatest of these was love.

Then he started talking about how God's great love for his people had caused him to give up his son to save the believers from their sins. At this point Salome and Euphemia came in and took cushions near Mary. Salome lay down with her head in Mary's lap and soon fell asleep.

When Paul started talking about Jesus' love for the world, a love which caused him to accept the agony of crucifixion and the spilling of his blood to save all the saints, Mary noticed that Euphemia had also fallen asleep.

Mary never liked listening to people talk about her son's blood. She wondered again when these people would go home. Paul noticed her frown and changed the topic to the Parousia and the resurrection of the dead. He reminded them that these events were imminent.

"Do you think Jesus will wait until after the next new moon before he returns?" Damonikos asked earnestly. "I'm planning to visit my mother in Corinth before the new moon and I've really been looking forward to it."

Mary shook the girls awake and stood. "Goodnight, everyone," she said. "Paul, the girls and I will sleep in the other room. You can sleep in here after everyone leaves." She turned to Helene. "Can Euphemia spend the night?"

Helene clearly thought it was odd that Mary would be worried about her slave's sleeping arrangements, but she wasn't going to say no to the Holy Mother.

Paul stood and walked over to kiss Mary and Salome goodnight. He nodded to Timothy to help Mary drag the sleepy girls and a couple of pallets and blankets into the bedroom.

Mary woke several hours later to the sound of people speaking in tongues, then fell asleep again. Much later, she woke to hear only Paul's voice speaking in the other room. Chloe was the only saint still awake, and she nodded frequently in agreement as Paul spoke on the importance of women keeping their heads covered in church.

Paul did not notice Mary as she closed the door and returned again to her bed. Outside the first cocks of the morning began to crow.

Euphemia arose first because she had to make sure Helene and Aristobulus had hot berry tea waiting for them when they got up. Mary got up with her, and the two of them went quietly into the proseuche.

Everyone was asleep, but Paul opened his eyes as soon as they entered.

"I'm sorry if we disturbed you last night, Mother," he whispered as Mary showed Euphemia where to find the tea, urn, and cups. Euphemia went outside to get fresh water to heat, and Mary rummaged in her small cabinet for bread, olives, and dried fish to feed her visitors breakfast. When Salome got up, they'd have fresh goat's milk as well.

"It doesn't seem like you got any sleep at all," Mary said to Paul.

"Sleep is a weakness I am blessed not to need. All I require is two or three hours a night, except when the shivering fever comes on me."

"Your friends don't share that gift." She nodded at the piles of people sleeping in the room. She hoped no one came up early this morning to use the mikvah, because this would look very bad.

"Among the Essenes, if someone falls asleep during assembly they have to do penance for thirty days," Paul said thoughtfully.

"If you practiced that, pretty soon your whole congregation would be doing penance," she said, laughing.

"The Essenes also inflict the same punishment on people who laugh foolishly," he retorted, and then he gave her a big smile.

When John, Theodora, and Deborah came up to the proseuche a few hours later, only Paul and Timothy remained. It had been years since Mary had seen John in the middle of an ordinary day. He looked very angry.

"The Friends of Jesus cannot meet up here anymore," he said after he kissed Mary's cheek in greeting.

"Why is that?" Timothy asked in concern.

"Politarch Aaron came to see my father last night. The gerousia is angry that Hebrews and gentiles are sharing meals up here."

"It's unclean according to the Law," Paul said.

"Yes," John said.

"But John, you've been having your meetings up here for almost twenty years," Mary said.

He put his arms around her and hugged her tightly. "I know, Mother. But we'll have to find somewhere else to meet now."

"Father says that the Friends of Jesus can't meet at our villa either," Deborah said. "He's very embarrassed about all this. He said that if he'd known gentiles and Judeans were eating together, he would have put a halt to the meetings years ago."

"Your people could join the tent church," Paul suggested.

"No," John said curtly.

"Then perhaps someone in your church could hold the meetings in their house," Paul suggested. "You might talk with Narcissus. He has a nice big house, in the heart of the city. It would be a perfect location for a house church."

Surprised, Mary asked, "How do you know that?" She knew that Paul and Narcissus did not get along. "Because his son Tychicus tried to talk him into letting us use it for a church. We've gotten too big for all of us to meet in the tent now and we need a second location. Last night Aristobulus agreed to host a church in his house."

John nodded reluctantly. "Narcissus would probably be willing to let us move the church to his house. But I hate to do it. Even though Narcissus and Calandra are God Fearers and converts, it still feels awkward having our meetings in a gentile's house. And too, the Friends of Jesus did a lot of good work up here on the hill." Mary knew he was remembering all of the people they had cared for here during the Winter of Despair. She also knew that with one word to Artelia, the Friends of Jesus could continue meeting here forever.

But she would respect the decision of the gerousia. She embraced John again. "It will be all right, Beloved Disciple. You'll do good work no matter where your church is."

Paul moved back to Junia and Andronicus' house that day. He knew that his presence in the proseuche only made things harder for Mary and John with the gerousia.

She thought: "My son, I feel a time of transition coming. May we face the changes with grace."

"If my son is divine, who am I?"

Spring, twenty years after the crucifixion of Jesus

Mary was extremely happy to have Apollos back home, and she was willing to agree to anything he wanted her to do, even to go to one of Paul's meetings. Salome milked the goats while it was still dark so that they could leave at first light in Apollos' rented donkey cart. They knew it was particularly important to Paul that Mary be there, so they wanted to reach Helene and Aristobulus' house in plenty of time.

Paul was having a special meeting this morning to celebrate the twentieth anniversary of the resurrection of Jesus. Mary never attended Paul's meetings because she didn't like all the talk about the blood; she had agreed to be present for this only because Apollos had asked her. John wouldn't be there; the Friends of Jesus church was having its own morning celebration at Narcissus and Calandra's house church. Although self-conscious among strangers, Salome wanted to go along with Mary and Apollos today. She wanted to see Euphemia, Helene and Aristobulus' slave, even though Mary told her the slave girl would probably be too busy to spend time with her. Salome hoped they could visit for at least a little while.

Afterward they would go to the First Fruits festival, these days held on the proper day, the day after Passover, in the afternoon.

They were not the last people to arrive at the house church, but it was already very crowded. People filled the peristyle, atrium, and exhedra rooms of the house. When they passed the triclinium, Mary saw that the tables overflowed with food. Salome noticed Euphemia carrying a heavy platter to the table and rushed over to help her friend. Euphemia shook her head vigorously at Salome, and Mary knew the girl had told Salome that she mustn't be interrupted in her work. A chief slave walked over to the girls and reiterated the message, a scowl on his face. Salome walked sadly back to Mary and Apollos.

Mary put her arm around her daughter. "Never mind, dear."

"Let's go find Paul," Apollos said. He shouldered his way through the crowd, Mary and Salome close behind him.

Paul was delighted that Mary had agreed to come today. He kept her close by his side the entire morning.

He began the meeting with a prayer to God that he ended by saying "in the name of Jesus we pray," the first time that Mary ever heard those words. Then everyone received their cups for the bread-and-wine/body-and-blood ceremony that would begin the meal. Mary did not participate. After it was over, the people got food from the table and settled in to listen to Paul preach.

Paul told the rest of the story of the last supper that Jesus had with his disciples. He told what had happened to Jesus after he shared the wine and bread with the Twelve. He told them about Judas the betrayer and the trial by the Sanhedrin and about Jesus being handed over to Pontius Pilate. He told them about the crucifixion, using much of Mary's description, she noticed. Then he told them about the burial and the resurrection of Jesus that was the reason for today's celebration.

Finally he spoke about what all of this meant for them, the saints, and their hopes for life everlasting in the kingdom of heaven. Paul spoke a great deal about Christ's holy blood.

Mary listened to it all, trying not to cry or even to show any expression on her face at all. Even after all these years, her pain, when prodded, was visceral. At one point Apollos, feeling her distress, took her hand in his, and she clung to it for the rest of the meeting.

After Paul finished his teaching, the people had a chance to speak. Some spoke of miracles and healings that had occurred after they prayed to Jesus, stories that ranged from someone who found a prized silver plate that had been lost to a family whose dead pig came back to life. "Praise Jesus!" the congregation would say after each miracle was told. Then people began to prophecy, most speaking of the imminence of the Parousia. Being the twentieth anniversary of Jesus' resurrection, people seemed hopeful that he would return today, right here this morning, in the presence of his mother and the community of saints.

People spoke in tongues for a while. Mary was proud of Salome, who sat through this quietly, hardly fidgeting at all.

Finally it was time for the second cup of wine/blood, the one they drank at the end of the meal. Some people hadn't waited; Mary had noticed several drinking while Paul preached.

After the wine/blood ritual, they sang a hymn, and Paul ended his meeting, saying: "As we leave today, let's greet one another with a holy kiss. The undeserved kindness of the Lord Jesus Christ and the love of God and the sharing in the Holy Spirit be with you all. Our Lord Come."

Mary realized he'd made this last pronouncement not in Greek but in her own language, Aramaic: "Marana tha." The way he said it sounded like an incantation, holy words that no one else could understand.

And then it seemed like everyone wanted to greet her with a holy kiss. Most chose to kiss her feet—people actually lined up to kiss her feet—and many of the ones who chose to kiss her lips used this intimacy as an opportunity to make personal or distressing comments to her.

One man who identified himself as a doctor said to her, "I've heard you take a cold bath every day; is that true?"

"Um, yes, but it's not a bath, really, it's for purification."

He took her face in his hands and turned it from side to side, examining her. "It's the reason you're so healthy at your advanced age. Cold baths tone the body, sharpen the senses, and preserve a good complexion even into old age."

"Um, thank you," she said hesitantly, appalled that a stranger would comment to her on the tone of her body.

Another man said, "Holy Mother, I've heard you still practice the Judean laws—is that true?"

"I try to."

"Do you really worship the head of an ass, back at your temple?"

She stared at him. "I have no idea what you're talking about."

Apollos put his arm around her. "That's a nasty lie, told by ignorant people. Judeans do not worship the head of an ass. They worship the One Holy God."

"Then do you still attend the orgies?" the man persisted.

"What?"

"The orgies that the Judeans have on their special day of the week."

Apollos pulled Mary away from the man. "Judeans don't have orgies," he said firmly.

"I'm talking about those celebrations they have every seven days," the man said earnestly. "You know, when they get drunk on wine and have orgies."

Mary stared at him in horror.

"You're confusing the Judeans with the Romans or perhaps with followers of Dionysus or Aphrodite," Apollos said. "Judeans follow a very strict moral code. No orgies. Ever."

"But everyone knows," the man insisted. "It's not like it's a secret. You can tell us."

Paul's assistant Sosthenes overheard the argument and pulled the man away.

"I'm sorry about that, Mother," Apollos said. "Sometimes people drink too much wine at these meetings. A few even attend just for the wine."

The next person in line dropped at Mary's feet, sobbing. Mary felt the wetness of tears and lips on her toes, and in her heart she felt the pain emanating from the woman.

"Holy Mother, my slave is pregnant with my husband's child. I cannot bear the shame of it, but Brother Paul says I cannot force the slave to abort the baby. What can I do? Can I expose the baby after it's born? Or should we raise it too, keep it as a slave in our home? I just don't think I can bear to have it there, flaunted in my face every day."

"Can the mother and child be freed?" asked Apollos.

"No. We rely too heavily on the slave. So heavily, in fact, that I don't think we can afford to let her care for the child after its birth."

Mary considered suggesting that they take it to the temple of Artemis because she knew the spondopoi would take good care of the baby. But she knew Paul would not appreciate her making this suggestion to one of his saints.

"What is your name?"

"My name is Julia, Holy Mother."

"Bring the child to me after it's born, Julia," Mary said.

"Oh, Holy Mother, thank you!" The woman slobbered kisses of gratitude on Mary's feet. Mary looked to Apollos, and he put his hands on the woman's shoulders to help her stand. Mary smiled at the woman, and she gave Mary a wet smile back.

"Mother, what are you going to do with another child?" Apollos asked with fond exasperation after the woman left.

"My worry is what am I going to do with a newborn child who needs to be fed?"

After the meeting she felt weary, unable to even contemplate attending First Fruits. But Salome, who was sad that she hadn't been able to spend time with Euphemia, looked forward to spending the afternoon at the festival with John and Theodora's three children.

Paul noticed Mary's pale face and suggested a solution. "Apollos, why don't you take Salome to First Fruits? Sosthenes and I can escort Mother home."

"How will you get her there?" Apollos asked. "Do you want to take my donkey cart?"

"I have a horse-drawn cart," Chloe said. "The Holy Mother can ride with me."

So Mary rode up to the proseuche in the cart with Chloe while Paul and Sosthenes walked alongside. Chloe saw to Mary's comfort with a blanket and water but didn't attempt conversation. Mary was grateful for the silence.

She went into her room to rest while the others settled into cushions in the proseuche to discuss today's meeting.

She awoke at mid-afternoon and went into the proseuche room. The three of them were still there, deep in conversation.

"Chloe's been updating us on the situation with our church in Corinth," Paul said to Mary. "Some of her workers just got back from making deliveries to the city, and they had some distressing stories to tell. Do you expect Apollos to return soon?"

It was Artemisia festival time. Salome never missed watching the procession of lights and music from up here on the hill. She'd been doing this for so long she knew all of the tunes of the Artemis hymns and which ones to listen for during the different days and weeks of the festival. She looked forward to singing along.

But Mary didn't explain that to Paul. "I'm sure he'll be back before sunset."

She spent the next few hours preparing her garden for seeds and cleaning out the beds where the year-round plants were awakening to the new spring.

Apollos and Salome arrived just before sunset. Mary and her daughter put together a meal for the six of them, using some food from her cupboards to supplement the food that Apollos and Salome brought back with them from the festival.

Over dinner, Paul and Chloe shared their concerns about the church at Corinth with Apollos. For one thing, the church had broken into factions, some preferring the teachings of Paul, some the teachings of Apollos, and some the teachings of Peter, who had stopped in Corinth on his way to Rome.

"I think you need to go back there, Apollos," Paul said. "They need to understand that we are united in our teachings."

"I am not going back there," Apollos said firmly. "I don't want to get embroiled again in their nonsense."

Paul turned to his assistant. "Don't look at me," Sosthenes said, just as firmly. "I've never liked Corinth. The whole city reeks of sin."

"Why don't you go back to Corinth yourself?" Chloe asked.

"I'll go later, but not now. I have too much work to do here in Ephesus," Paul said. "This is prime festival time for the idol worshippers, and Prisca, Aquila, and I reach a lot of people when they come to us to order tents and other leather goods. Also, Ephesus is a good central location for me, a good place to send workers out to start new churches. We have people preaching in Smyrna, Pergamum, Thyatira, Sardis, and Philadelphia now, all within a couple of days' walk from here. Perhaps Timothy will go to Corinth for me after he returns from Macedonia."

"If Timothy goes, I'll travel across with him but I won't stop in Corinth. I'll continue on to preach in the rest of the province," Apollos said. "Perhaps I'll spend time in Corinth later, before I return to Ephesus."

"I think you should just give up on Corinth," Sosthenes said. "It's not like with your churches in Antioch or Galatia, where Judaizers from the outside go in to confuse the people. In Corinth, the people don't need outside dissenters to cause trouble. They cause all their own mischief."

"The temple of Aphrodite is the source of the trouble," Paul said. "It encourages porneia, sexual impropriety, and once you have that raging through your city everything else goes rotten as well. That's why the people of Corinth are so different from the people of Ephesus. At least in Ephesus they worship a virgin goddess."

"What are the people in your church doing?" Mary asked. She couldn't imagine such a conversation as this about the members of the Friends of Jesus church.

"It's a constant madness over there," Chloe said. "They argue about everything—whether heads should be covered in church, whether women can wear cosmetics and fancy clothes, whether divorce is acceptable. There are factions fighting over Paul and Apollos, and people even brag over which one of them they were baptized by. And there's always some kind of porneia going on. Right now there's a man in the church who's sleeping with his father's widow, and there are others who regularly visit the temple prostitutes. Plus there are people in the church suing one another in the city courts. This makes us look like hypocrites."

"Why don't they just use the local gerousia to resolve their differences?" Mary asked.

"The synagogues there won't have anything to do with us," Paul said. "And they shouldn't be suing each other anyway. The church is one body of Christ, through the grace of God. If they fight with one another, it's a total failure of the church."

"There are other things as well," Apollos said. "They keep eating food sacrificed to idols. And they baptize dead people, thinking to give them eternal life, as though baptism were some kind of magical incantation."

"Actually, I don't have a problem with their eating food that's been sacrificed to idols, so long as they understand that the sacrifice was meaningless," Paul said. "I did promise James that we'd keep the people from eating the idols' food. But the saints have to get their food from somewhere. It's only a problem if they still believe the idols are real. If they believe that, they're defiled by it."

"I think it's a bad practice to eat the demons' food no matter what," Apollos said, and Mary remembered how troubled he'd been during the Winter of Despair when the Friends of Jesus church had accepted food donations from the Artemisium. "But it's not important enough for us to argue about."

"I agree. I'm more concerned about their boasting and their pride. They're puffed up over their spiritual powers, over their own knowledge and wisdom. Those who can speak in tongues think they're better than those who prophecy and vice versa. They're so prideful they think they can ignore my authority. This is a problem."

"You might want to tell them that Jesus said that anyone who seeks the kingdom of God must humble himself like a child," Mary said. She looked at Apollos, wondering if he had ever shared Quartillia's scroll with Paul.

"They're too childish already," Paul said, shaking his head.

"Well, I think that instead of worrying about whether or not their heads should be covered in church, you should tell them to just love one another," Mary said.

"They need to know both," Paul said.

"By the way, Holy Mother, we've decided to start a widow's fund in the church, to help women whose husbands didn't leave them enough money to support themselves," Chloe said to Mary. "People were horrified that you have to continue to work up here."

"I think it's a good idea to have a widow's fund," Mary said. "But you shouldn't take up a collection for me. I'm happy here, and I have everything I need. However, I know a number of needy widows who would be grateful for any assistance."

Paul decided to write a letter to the Corinthians, and Sosthenes agreed to assist him. Apollos escorted Chloe back home to protect her from the unruly crowds celebrating the festival of Artemis down in the city. While Paul and Sosthenes worked on their letter to the Corinthians, Mary and Salome slipped outside to settle in at their favorite spot on the hill and watch the Artemisia procession.

When Mary and Salome got up the next morning, Salome to milk the goats and Mary to walk the labyrinth, Apollos, Paul, and Sosthenes still slept in the proseuche. Mary smiled to see her son sleeping at his normal place near the hearth. She was glad to have him home, at least for a little while.

When she walked back to the house, humming a tune to herself, she saw Paul sitting on one of the benches outside.

"Beautiful day," he said.

"Yes, it is," she said with a big smile.

"That's a pretty song you're singing," he said. "What are the words?"

"You wouldn't like them."

"Why not?"

"The song is from the Artemis procession. I'm sure it's a song praising the idol. I don't know the words, just the tune. But they sing it in many of the processions, so I know it's an important song for them."

"Maybe we could write our own words to go with the tune," Paul said. "No reason to waste good music."

"I agree."

"You spend a lot of time with the idol worshippers, don't you?"

She shrugged. "Not so much time."

"I admire them," he said.

She stared at him, disbelieving. This was a different approach from before. "You what?"

"The temple of Artemis," he said. "I admire them. They do a lot of good work here in the city."

"Yes, they do," Mary said warily.

"And they're all virgins, aren't they? Like the Essenes, back home?"

"Yes, they are."

"The men and the women?"

"All the spondopoi, yes."

"Celibacy is more difficult when men and women associate together, which is why the Essenes don't allow women in their community. There are a thousand slave prostitutes at the temple of Aphrodite in Corinth."

"Oh my goodness. Well, there's nothing like that here." Actually, ever since the death of Lila, who had killed herself after polluting the temple, Mary had wondered if there might be some kind of sexual component to the secret mysteries. But if there was, it must be one of the great mysteries; the secret was well-kept.

"Timothy used to be an Essene. He complains about the Dionysus festival here. I understand it's quite barbaric, but I don't think even it can compare with happenings in Corinth."

"I must admit I don't go into the city during the Katagogia festival," she said. "I was warned against it my first year here. But I suspect you may be right, it probably isn't as bad here as in Corinth."

"I wish I could convince the saints in my church to adopt celibacy like the Essenes and the priests and priestesses of Artemis do."

"It's not just celibacy they adopt here. The priests of Artemis have a rather significant operation performed on themselves."

"I had heard that."

"You can't even convince your followers to be circumcised. If God's covenant is too difficult for them, I can't imagine them adopting the practice of the priests of Artemis."

"Followers of Jesus don't need an operation to keep themselves celibate," he said. "They have their faith."

"I don't really understand why you think celibacy is so important."

"It's important because people need to focus their time and attention on preparing for the return of the Lord."

"Paul, my son has been dead for twenty years. He hasn't returned yet. What if he doesn't return for another twenty years? Do you really expect all of the people of your churches to remain celibate for all those years? Even Peter is married."

"I'm sure Peter and his wife have a celibate marriage," he said.

It had been many years, but Mary had known Peter and his wife very well. "I doubt that."

Paul shrugged. "Be that as it may, you make a good point. If people cannot remain celibate they should marry, for the containment of their lusts. I'll include that in my letter."

"Why do you write so many letters?" She'd never met anyone else who wrote so much or so often.

"The gentiles don't have any written scrolls from their gods instructing them on how to live, as we Israelites do. Only the priests of the idols know all the stories and rituals—and they're usually unwritten and kept secret. It's important that the people have written instructions, telling them how to live, so that they can read them over and over again."

"So why don't you just teach them the Law?"

"Because most of the Law is unnecessary. The faith of Jesus has replaced the Law."

"But you just said that written rules are necessary."

"People have to live together," he said. "And they need to know how to do so in a good and loving way."

Mary still didn't understand why he rejected the Law if he only intended to replace it with other rules that sounded suspiciously like most of the old ones, but she wasn't going to argue about it.

"I just wish I could convert more Artemis worshippers," he said.

"There were a lot of people at your meeting yesterday. And they were almost all Greeks—I didn't see very many Israelites at all."

"They're Greeks, but very few of them were devotees of Artemis before they converted. And none of Artemis' women have converted at all. I haven't managed to crack that nut yet. But I will."

Mary mentioned this conversation to Artelia a few days later at the temple. She had finally remembered to ask Artelia who Leto was, the woman to whom Prisca had negatively compared her many months before. Artelia told her that Leto was the mother of the Greek Artemis and offered to take her into the art gallery where they stored votive offerings not on display in the temple. The art gallery included a special room where paintings and sculptures of Leto and her babies Artemis and Apollo were arranged.

Mary told Artelia that Paul admired the temple's work and their focus on celibacy. Artelia was annoyed that Paul was using his tent-making business as an opportunity to proselytize to Artemis' pilgrims. "He's trying to convert people away from the Goddess at the same time he's making money off Her," she fumed.

"He's not having any success," Mary pointed out. "Especially not with women."

"Why should women want to join his guild? They have freedom and power in Artemis Ephesia."

Mary knew that if she was ever to try to explain the worship that had developed around her son, this was her opportunity. But they were interrupted before she could speak. A silversmith wanted to talk with Artelia about a new shrine design he planned to start making right away, in time for the Thargelion, Artemis' birthday celebration in two months. When finally Artelia and Demetrius the silversmith completed their business, they had reached the Leto room. Artelia began showing Mary images of the Titan goddess Leto being seduced by the god Zeus, disguised as a swan. The opportunity for explaining had passed.

She thought: "My son, help me to honor the immense expectations that are building up around me."

20

"Divine bliss expands the heart, spiteful flesh restricts it."

Five months later

D own in Clothmakers Street, Mary haggled with the shopkeeper for cloth for a new chiton for Salome. He spoke the local Ephesian language, not Greek. Although she wasn't proficient, Mary had picked up enough of the language over the years for shopping.

Once she had the cloth she wanted at the price she wanted to pay, she looked up at the sky. It was around fourth hour, time for her to meet Salome and Theodora at the Three Graces fountain at the harbor agora. She started pushing herself through the people in the crowded, narrow street.

Near the harbor she heard a woman orating to a crowd. Most public speakers were men. She slowed down to hear what the woman was saying then stopped abruptly when she heard her speak the name "Jesus."

A man in the crowd noticed Mary and said excitedly, "That's Jesus' mother, right there!"

The people all turned to look at Mary while the speaker pointed at her accusingly and said with a sneer, "Liar! Our Lord was not born of woman— he had no earthly flesh! He is a powerful Spirit who appears as a man only when he chooses! This woman is lying if she says she is his mother! Are you claiming to be his mother?"

Mary looked around for a way to leave, but the hostile people crowded around her. "I-I...Jesus was my son," she said nervously. "I gave birth to him. He was a man."

A man standing near said, "I saw the blood spurt from his flesh and flow down his back when he was lashed at the prefect's palace in Jerusalem. I saw him jerk from the pain. Jesus was definitely a man."

Mary looked at him. He was a big man, with a confident manner and expensive clothes. The crowd looked from him to the orator, with her shrill voice and dusty, rumpled chiton.

"Jesus was a great magician who could make people think anything he wanted them to think," the woman said, but she could tell that this man had more credibility with the crowd than she did. She gave up. "My friends were right," she said in angry frustration. "The masses aren't capable of knowing the truth." She stepped off the plinth and pushed through the crowd away from Mary.

Someone else claimed the plinth and began exhorting the people to go back to the old ways of worship, to return to the arms of the great mother Cybele and her brave son Attis. The crowd was less interested in this message and people moved away.

The man who'd spoken came over to Mary, who felt about to collapse now that the press of the crowd no longer held her up. He put his arm around her, a strong support. "Where do you need to go?" he asked gently.

"Thank you." She leaned on him. "I'm meeting my family at the Three Graces."

"I'll walk with you." She clung to his arm as they walked through the streets to the harbor agora.

Salome and Theodora weren't there when they reached the fountain. Mary sat down and the man joined her.

"So you're his mother."

"Yes."

"I heard he was crucified; is that right?"

"Yes."

"Sad business, that. I don't remember why I was at the palace that day. I was usually at the temple. Maybe I had a message to deliver or pick up. I don't remember," he mused.

"What did you do at the Temple?"

"I'm a stonecutter. The Judeans made me a priest so that I could work on their temple. They paid well, so I let myself be mutilated and everything. But now I'm back home in Ephesus."

She actually found herself getting a little angry, and part of her was surprised at her own response. They let this pagan into the Temple—let him be a priest!—but she, who'd been faithful her whole life, could never enter past the Nicanor Gate.

She realized that she had truly been in Ephesus too long. She thought like a Greek now. The old Mary would never have questioned the treatment of women in the Temple.

"If you're Jesus' mother, then you must be a Judean too."

She nodded. "Yes, I am."

"Have you ever been to the mikvah here? I built it."

She smiled at him in delight. "I'm the mikvah attendant! It's a beautiful mikvah!"

He grinned, glad to hear appreciation of his work. "Thank you."

"I've always wondered why you made it so big."

He shrugged. "I built it the same way I built the others. In Judea, when I wasn't working at the temple I built mikvot for pilgrims. It holds eighty seah of water, just like the others."

"That's twice as big as a mikvah has to be. But it's nice having so much room in there." She found herself ashamed of her earlier anger—if this gentile had not been given access to the Temple, the Israelite community in Ephesus wouldn't have their beloved mikvah today.

"How did you decide to go to Jerusalem to work on the Temple?"

"I'm a member of the guild of Dionysiac Architects. We built the original temple of Solomon. When Herod sent out the call for builders for the replacement temple, we responded."

"They've been building the Temple my entire life, I think."

"We've been working on it for over sixty years. But I've heard it's almost done now. I think when it's done I'll go back to Jerusalem for a visit. I'd like to see the finished temple."

Mary realized that she too would like to see the finished Temple. She began to think: maybe it's time to return home to Judea.

They talked further, and Mary learned that the man's name was Lysandros. Salome and Theodora arrived, effusive in their gratitude to him for rescuing their mother from the spirit-woman. Mary invited him to visit her at the proseuche. After he left, Theodora bought Mary and Salome a meal from a street vendor in the Judean market and then they returned home.

Mary often found people waiting for her in the proseuche, but the visitor waiting today was a surprise: Damonikos the playwright sat on a cushion by the hearth. And he was crying.

"Oh, Holy Mother, thank God you're here!" he said. Mary glanced at Salome, who was staring at Damonikos with wide eyes.

"Salome, go outside for a while," she said. Disappointed, her daughter left.

Mary sat down on a cushion beside Damonikos. He flung himself at her, dropping his face into her lap as he wrapped his arms around her waist.

"Oh, Holy Mother, please help me!"

"Shhh." She patted his head, comforting him as best as she could. "Of course I'll help you, my son. Just tell me what the problem is."

"Paul expelled me from the church," he said between sobs. "And he told the other Nazorenes to shun me."

"He expelled you?" She had never heard of Paul doing such a thing.

"Yes." His teary voice was muffled in her lap. "And I'm scared that now Jesus will reject me and that I won't be allowed to enter heaven."

"My dear, Jesus will never reject you. But why were you expelled from Paul's church?"

"Porneia," he whispered.

"What?"

"Porneia." His voice was heavy with shame. "Sexual impropriety."

Mary felt overwhelmed by this. The Patriarchs said any sexual activity not intended for procreation was sexual impropriety; this was all she knew about it. But she couldn't believe Paul was expelling all people who had sex without trying to make a baby.

She had no special understanding of the admittance rules for heaven anymore. She did not know what Paul had been teaching about it. She did not understand what this had to do with Jesus.

She never knew how to respond to the utter devotion of strangers to her son.

"Do you love the Lord your God with all your heart and all your soul and all your might?" she asked finally.

"I do," he said with great sincerity.

"Do you love everyone else as much as you love yourself?"

"I think so. I want to. I try to."

"Then Jesus will not reject you. The only thing that ever mattered to him was that people love one another."

"But how can I show that I love him, Holy Mother?"

She thought for a moment. "Well, you need to pray, of course."

"I do," Damonikos said fervently. "I am. I will."

"And you need to undergo purification. But first you must atone for your sins." She wished they were in Jerusalem. Then she could tell him to go find a perfect animal to sacrifice in the Temple as an atonement offering. He could spend time scrutinizing the sacrificial victim, contemplating its perfection, and reflecting on the need for perfection within his own soul.

But there wasn't a sacrifice available for him here…

"When you pray, tell Jesus that you wish to atone for your sins," she said slowly. "Be clear about what you're atoning for. Say that you wish God to forgive you."

"Will he forgive me?"

"He will."

"What if I sin again?"

"You should try not to sin. But if you sin again and ask for forgiveness again, you will again be forgiven." She remembered something from Quartillia's scrolls, about forgiving seven times seventy times. "He will always forgive you."

And then she wondered: If all the Law is gone and the only thing that matters is living a good life, loving each other, and believing in Jesus, what does porneia mean, for someone who believes?

How could anyone be expelled from Paul's church?

"Did Paul speak to you about it before you were expelled?"

She could feel Damonikos' shoulders shrink with his shame. "He did, Mother. And I repented. But then I sinned again, and this time I was expelled."

"You will always be welcome at the Friends of Jesus church." She would need to let John know about this, but she was confident he would agree with her decision. "Go home and pray, and when your atonement is complete come back here to purify yourself at the mikvah."

"Yes, Holy Mother."

"And if you'd like, you can help me sometimes." She surprised herself; she hadn't known she would say these words before she spoke them.

"Help you?"

"Yes. Sometimes I visit people who are sick, lonely, hungry, or in prison. Apollos used to go with me, but he's in Achaea now. If you like, you can go with me."

Damonikos kissed her cheek. "I would be honored to assist you in your good works, Holy Mother."

A few days later, Paul came up to the proseuche to see Mary. He had heard about Mary's experience with the spirit-woman in the street.

"I'm so sorry that happened, Mother. The spirit-filled people cause me all sorts of trouble.

"They think they have special spiritual knowledge that the rest of us are too dim-witted to understand. There are some in my church in Corinth. I think I told you that once."

"The people you said were too prideful to accept your authority?" Mary remembered this, because she had wondered briefly if that was why she didn't accept Paul's authority—her pride.

"Yes. They believe that there is darkness and there is light; that darkness is evil, flesh, and ignorance, and light is goodness, spirituality, and knowledge."

"That sounds all right."

"I agree, but they take it too far. They believe that Jesus was the light and that therefore he was spirit only. They believe he was never flesh, because they think everything pertaining to the world and to flesh is evil. Israelites and Egyptians believe in the resurrection of the body after death. The Greeks believe that the soul escapes from the body after death. But those people think that this life of the flesh and body is an illusion and that their spirits are already resurrected with Christ Jesus, are already enthroned with him in heaven."

After a few silent moments Mary spoke. "Paul, you teach many things that I don't understand. I accept this, because you have to follow your own visions, your own messages from God about who or what my son was. But this I can promise you: He was flesh and blood, a child born of woman, a kind and loving man, a man with dreams, tears, and laughter. He died in torment, his flesh torn and bloody. That is my truth. I pray you won't let it be forgotten."

He came over to her and hugged her. "I'll never let that be forgotten, Mother. Never."

His next comment was hesitant. "I also came up here today to rebuke you, Mother."

"Rebuke me?" Not the temple stuff again, she hoped.

"I promised James that I wouldn't allow people in the church who couldn't abstain from porneia. I understand you told Damonikos that he would always be welcome in the Friends of Jesus church."

"You banned him from your church, Paul. He needs somewhere to belong."

"He is guilty of porneia, Mother."

"And he's repented."

"He's repented before. Yet he continues his behavior."

"And that's why you expelled him? And told the congregation to shun him?"

"There was nothing else I could do. He won't stop sinning. He sets a bad example for the rest of the church."

"Why don't you have him arrested then?"

"He's not breaking the law of Ephesus or Rome. They consider this type of porneia to be perfectly normal. He's breaking the Law of Moses."

"Breaking the Law of Moses? Circumcision is the Law of Moses, our covenant with God. Yet you've completely eliminated that requirement. And you yourself told me that the only Law now is Jesus."

"Did you know Damonikos is a member of the Dionysus guild and has one of the god's ivy leaves tattooed on his body?"

Mary actually knew something about the Dionysus guild. "All of the theater people are members of that guild," she said. "The tattoo is how they show their membership."

"Well, many of the theater people do a lot of other things with their bodies more sinful even than tattooing, Mother. You would never understand."

"I understand my son said to forgive the sinner seven times seventy times and you gave up on Damonikos after two. I once heard Jesus tell someone: 'Never be glad except when you look at your brother or sister with love; it is a crime to sadden your brother's or sister's spirit.' Yet you told Damonikos' brothers and sisters to shun him."

Paul was just as frustrated with her. "Mother, if you understood what Damonikos did—what he continues to do—you'd know why he has to be expelled. His sin is one of the abominations that defile the land and the sanctuary of God."

"We are not in the land and your church is not the Temple. Impurity from porneia is not contagious, and even if this was the Day of Atonement, there is no altar to God here in Greece where Damonikos can make a sacrificial offering. He is welcome in the Friends of Jesus church."

Paul left soon after, still in dispute with Mary about Damonikos.

The following day Rebekkah and her slave Naomi came up to the mikvah. Rebekkah had never remarried after Enoch divorced her, so Mary didn't see her very often. She was glad to see her today.

"My dear, how are you doing?" she asked. Rebekkah's mother, Judith, had died last winter, and her children Rebekkah, Martha, and David still grieved.

"Much better, Mary, thank you."

"Would you like to go into the proseuche to pray first?"

"Yes." Then Rebekkah smiled, remembering her mother. "Let's have the tevilah tefilah."

Mary hugged her, and they went into the proseuche for the first part of the immersion ceremony. When they emerged for the tevilah, they saw a donkey cart coming up the road. They stood by the mikvah and waited for the arrival of the new people, so that the two immersion rituals might be combined.

But the people in the donkey cart weren't Israelites. A slave was driving the cart. Inside were two women. One was holding a baby and crying.

They stopped near the mikvah, and Mary recognized Julia, the sobbing woman from Paul's church.

"I've brought you the child, Holy Mother," she said. Julia was stony-faced today. It was the woman with her, the one holding the baby, who was crying.

"What's happening here?" asked Rebekkah.

"The woman with the baby is a slave," Mary said. She hated to say the next words, hated to hurt Rebekkah. "She belongs to this other woman, whose name is Julia. Julia's husband fathered the baby. Julia has decided to give the baby away."

Rebekkah jerked back. She had lived this experience. But in her case, the father of the baby chose to divorce his wife and marry the slave.

"Why are they here?"

"The Holy Mother said that she would take the baby," the slave's mistress said. She turned to the crying woman. "Give your whelp to the Holy Mother," she said coldly.

Rebekkah gently pushed Mary aside. "Is your slave for sale?" she asked Julia.

"What? You want to buy this lazy slut?"

"Is she for sale?"

The woman looked at Rebekkah for a moment. "Why would you want her? You'll never be able to trust your husband around her, you know."

"I don't have a husband anymore. And I need a new slave to attend to my clothes."

Julia sniffed. "We might be able to come to an arrangement. If you can pay me enough to replace her. She's a wonder with hair. That increases her value, of course."

"How much?"

The two women haggled and finally reached an agreement. Rebekkah told the woman that she'd have the money sent to her that very day.

"Before fifth hour," Julia said. "I'll be in the baths this afternoon. And I'll need the money for tomorrow morning's slave market."

"Of course," Rebekkah said.

The slave and her baby climbed out of the cart and came over to stand by Mary and Rebekkah. Her former mistress stared at her a moment, her eyes welling with tears, then told the donkey cart driver to take her home.

Mary told the slave to take her baby into the proseuche to warm up. Rebekkah's slave, Naomi, took the woman gently by the arm and led her into the building.

Mary looked at her friend, seeing the luminous eyes of God. "Why?" she asked.

"It's wrong to take a baby away from its mother." Rebekkah sighed. "You may not know this, but I could have taken Aspasia's son away from her."

"Oh?"

"Yes. That was Enoch's first suggestion, when Aspasia became pregnant with Seth. We would free Aspasia so that her child would be freeborn and then raise her child as our own. I couldn't do it. I loved Aspasia. I couldn't take her baby away from her."

Mary took Rebekkah into her arms and hugged her tight. "Oh, my dear, my dear, my dear. I think you are the kindest woman I have ever met."

"No, I have a fierce temper," Rebekkah said, laughing.

"Do you really need another person working for you?"

Rebekkah shrugged. "Most of my parents' slaves are old and unable to do much anymore. I'll find a place for her."

They turned back toward the mikvah and stopped at the changing tent.

"Did she really call you 'Holy Mother?'" Rebekkah inquired.

Mary laughed. "Don't worry about it." Rebekkah entered the changing tent to remove her clothes. They walked down the steps into the mikvah bath for her purification and tevilah.

She thought: "My son, I honor the pure heart. May I equally honor the polluted heart that yearns for purity."

21

"I can hold the pain of all the world."

Late spring, twenty-one years after the crucifixion of Jesus

When Damonikos arrived with the donkey cart, Mary told him that they were going to Caesar's villa that morning to see one of the emperor's relatives. The slave Libo, whom she'd met a couple of years ago when Paul was in prison, had come by this morning and asked her if she could lay her "healing hands" on his mistress, Tiberia, an elderly cousin of Emperor Claudius.

"She has a terrible fever," Libo said. "And she smells even worse than usual."

"Why don't you bring in a doctor for her?"

"She won't listen to any doctor. But she was interested when I talked about you."

Mary told Libo that she wasn't a healer nor was she a miracle worker, but she would certainly try to help the old woman.

Damonikos was happy to be going to Caesar's house. He and Mary had developed a good working relationship over the last year: he would escort her where she needed to go and help her carry heavy objects. That sometimes meant corpses, but usually it just meant jars of unguents or crates of food. Mary would do all the actual touching of dirty and sick people. He always took the latest play he was working on with him because Mary didn't care for only poor people—waiting for her meant that he often spent hours writing in an atrium or kitchen while household slaves brought him cups of tea or wine or bites of food. Caesar's villa would be a particularly pleasant place to work, and perhaps it might serve as a source of ideas. His new play took place in a palace.

When they arrived at the villa, Libo was waiting at the door of the vestibulum.

"Thank you, Holy Mother. I'm so grateful to you for coming. I know you'll be able to help my poor mistress."

"This is Damonikos, Libo. Please have someone find a nice room where he can wait for me while I visit her."

Mary could smell the woman even before the door of the bedroom was opened.

The old woman lay on a thick feather mattress in the middle of a large bed. A beautiful embroidered bedcover lay over her body, along with a multitude of flies—this despite the efforts of two slaves who waved large fans over the bed.

Mary got as close to the woman as she could stand and then she spoke. "Lady Tiberia, I can't do anything for you until you take a bath." The woman's face was caked and flaking with layers of makeup, her hair was matted and greasy, and Mary could hardly bear to imagine the filth that must lie under the covers. But hidden in the folds of skin and makeup, Mary could see the Eyes.

"You Judeans bathe too much." The woman's voice was old and cracked.

"Most Romans bathe frequently too, I'm told."

"Foolish habit."

"I can't help you until you've bathed," Mary said again. She turned to leave, saying to Libo, "I'm sorry. There's nothing I can do."

"Wait," the woman said. "I'll bathe."

Libo's face lit up with his smile. "I'll get the bathing room ready." He rushed out before his mistress could change her mind.

"I'll wait in the atrium while she's bathing," Mary told the woman's attendant. "Have her thoroughly cleaned, including her face, hair, and teeth, and have all her bedding changed before she gets back in bed." She left to find Damonikos.

In the atrium, the playwright was talking with a Roman. "Mother, I've had a nice surprise this morning. This is Lucius Gratius Cinna, an old friend of mine and a relative of the woman you're helping. He's been elected asiarch for Smyrna again, and he's staying here at the villa while the Confederacy of Asiarchs is having their annual meeting."

Mary walked over to meet the man. "I think we've met before. The same day I first met Damonikos—I think you and another gentleman were Alexander's guests at Damonikos' play."

"Were you one of the party with Alexander the Judean?" Lucius asked.

Mary nodded, and Damonikos said, "I was just telling Lucius about my new play. He's suggested that I could premier it in Smyrna."

"I know it would do very well there," Lucius said with a fond look at Damonikos.

"Why aren't you with Tiberia?" Damonikos asked.

"I've sent her to take a bath."

Lucius gave a hearty laugh. "Good for you! I've tried to get her to bathe for years, and I know her slaves gave up on it long ago. I am very impressed that you succeeded. What did you say to her to make her change her mind?"

Mary shrugged. "I just told her I couldn't help her until she bathed."

"The mistress thinks the Holy Mother is a Judean sorceress." Libo entered the room with a pitcher of wine and three glasses. "She'll do whatever the Holy Mother says she must do."

"Libo, did you tell her I was a sorceress?"

"No, Holy Mother, I just told her you were a holy Judean woman. She made her own interpretation of my words."

"Why does he call you Holy Mother?" Lucius asked.

"Have you heard yet about Jesus Christ?" Damonikos asked.

"Do you mean the founder of the Christians?" Lucius asked, distaste in his voice.

"Some of our enemies call us that," Damonikos said. "But let me tell you about him." He and Libo spent the next hour telling Lucius Gratius Cinna about the kingdom of God and the resurrection of the savior Jesus Christ. Meanwhile Mary asked a girl she saw in the hall to show her around the villa.

She was admiring the herb garden when Aculeo, the other slave she'd met when Paul was in prison, came to get her.

"The mistress is all clean, Holy Mother." They walked back to the old woman's bedroom. "But the water in the bath is a nasty mess!"

"I'm sure it is. You must empty the bath out before anyone else uses it. Did you change the bedding?"

"We did. And already there are fewer flies in the room."

They entered the room where her now-clean patient was sitting up in an equally clean bed.

Mary sniffed. She did not smell the odor that had accompanied Adonis and Judith in their last days. But there was another strange smell.

The old woman's female attendant stood by the bed. "What's your name?" Mary asked.

"Lydia."

"Lydia, did you find any open wounds or sore areas on her?" Mary examined Tiberia's face, arms, and hands. Her face was raw and blistered from the removal of perhaps years of accumulated cosmetics. Mary gently rubbed on the skin of the woman's arm and old skin peeled away.

"You hadn't bathed in a long time, had you, my dear?" she asked the old woman with a compassionate smile.

"No, and I don't plan to do it again in this lifetime," Tiberia said. She was still fevered and miserable.

Mary shook her head. "I'm afraid you're going to have another bath next week and one the week after that, and also one every week for the rest of your life."

The old woman stared at her in dismay.

"It won't be so bad," Mary promised her, trying to coax a smile from the woman.

"There are some sores on her back and the backs of her legs," the attendant said, "and there's a large sore on one of her thighs."

"Well, let's look at that then," Mary said. Lydia pulled down the covers and pulled up the old woman's robe so that Mary could see the large, oozing abscess on the woman's thigh.

"I think this is what has been making you sick," Mary said. She turned to Lydia. "We'll need to lance this. Let's go into the kitchen and see what we can find to use."

In the kitchen she found a thin metal spike, which she had the kitchen maid clean thoroughly, and she also found a bronze ladle in the cold room.

"I'll need wine, vinegar, or pomegranate rind," she said. "Also, I saw some mint in the garden—someone should gather some of that and crush it for me and also bring me some boiled water that has cooled."

Back in Tiberia's bedroom, Mary swabbed the swollen boil and surrounding skin with vinegar. Just touching the skin made the unfortunate woman cry, and Mary knew that lancing the abscess would be very painful for her.

Mary moved to the front of the bed and stroked the old woman's hair, now released from its filthy wig. The thin white hairs tangled together in a ratted mess, and she wondered if she should have Tiberia's head shaved. Perhaps on her next visit. "I'm going to teach you some words that you're to repeat every time you're in pain or scared or worried about anything." For the next ten minutes she taught Tiberia the Shema, repeating it with her until the woman had it exactly right.

"Keep repeating that now, over and over until I tell you that you can stop." The woman continued to repeat the Hebrew words in her old, quavering voice, and Mary spoke the words along with her while she guided Lydia's strong hands to quickly lance the abscess and press the poison out.

When she thought they had released as much poison as possible from the poor woman's body, she wiped up her skin and applied a cold bronze ladle on the area to freeze the surface of the skin in order to prevent the heat from escaping outwards.

"Keep doing that for a while." Mary handed the ladle to Lydia. "It needs to be cold, so as soon as the bronze begins to warm up have the kitchen bring you another cold one."

She walked back to the head of the bed, where the woman still muttered the words of the Shema. "You can stop now," Mary said. "I won't hurt you anymore."

"I hardly felt it at all," Tiberia said. "Those magical words of yours are very strong."

"Yes, they are. Now, some instructions. First, you need to bathe at least once a week. Will you do that?"

"Yes, I'll do that."

"And I don't want you to make up your face for at least a month. Your skin needs to heal from the poisons in your cosmetics."

"I understand. Do you want to examine my urine?"

"No, that's all right. I'm not a doctor."

"Do you have a magical amulet to give me?"

"No. Just the words. They're enough."

The woman nodded and then closed her tired eyes to sleep.

Mary turned back to Lydia. "After the skin has cooled, cover it with a mint paste and then wrap a cloth around it."

"All right," Lydia said.

"Can she walk?" Mary asked.

"She can, but she doesn't."

"Tell her I said she has to get up from her bed and walk around her garden or her house at least three times every day, reciting the words I taught her. Those sores on her legs and back are because she spends all of her time in bed. Someone should support her up if necessary, but make sure she walks."

"I'll tell her."

"Do you know how to continue to treat her wound? How often to change the dressing and so on?"

"I do. She just never let us touch it before."

"All right," Mary said. "I'm glad to be leaving her in good hands." She smiled at the slave and left the room.

Part of her felt guilty about treating the Shema as though it was a magical incantation, but then she thought: if this most important prayer to God resulted in a woman being healed of her pain, then surely God would not mind its use.

Damonikos was still in earnest conversation with Lucius when she came back to the atrium, but he excused himself when he saw her.

"Did your magic touch do the trick, Holy Mother?"

"I think the bath should get most of the credit."

"Do you mind if Lucius goes back with us up Mount Kouressos? He wants to hear more about Jesus. After I let you off at the proseuche, we'll go down to the baths to talk more."

Mary listened as Damonikos and Lucius discussed Jesus and the Parousia throughout the journey from the top of Mount Pion down into the city and back up to the top of Mount Kouressos and home. By the end of the trip, Lucius was calling her Holy Mother and treating her as reverently as Damonikos did.

When they arrived at the proseuche, she saw Paul and his assistant Titus sitting on a bench in the sun, along with two people new to Mary. She was glad to see Titus; Paul had been anxiously awaiting his return to Ephesus.

Paul had gone to Corinth just before Yom Kippur to visit his troubled church, and he had been devastated by the problems he found there. A woman deacon from that church had come to Ephesus on business, and Paul had sent a letter along with her, telling the saints in Ephesus of his deep disappointment with what he found in Corinth. When he returned to Ephesus he wrote a blistering letter to the church in Corinth and sent it off with Titus. Once he calmed down he worried that his letter to the Corinthian church might have been too strong and angry. Anxious to find out how they responded, he had spent a fruitless month trying to catch up with Titus, chasing all around Macedonia and Troas to get the news. Things had been pretty quiet in Ephesus while he was gone.

Lucius helped Mary out of the cart, and she hurried over to Paul and the others. "I'm glad you returned safe, Titus. How are things in Corinth?"

"Titus smoothed things over for me," Paul said. "Unfortunately the Judaizers have gotten to them, and so now some church members are saying everyone needs to be circumcised and worry about what they eat. But at least they're not angry with me for scolding them."

"That is good news." Mary smiled at the strangers and hoped their names would be easy to remember. Paul brought so many people up to see her, delegations from churches all over Greece and Asia, and she was always challenged to remember their names.

"Mother, these are our brothers Gaius and Aristarchus," Paul began, and then she saw from his scowl that he'd just noticed Damonikos walking hesitantly toward them behind Lucius.

"Paul, this is Asiarch Lucius Gratius Cinna, a friend of Damonikos," Mary said quickly. "He's here for the Confederacy of Asiarchs meeting. And you'll be glad to know that Damonikos has just converted him to the worship of Jesus."

Paul's expression changed with the news of such an important convert. "I am indeed glad to hear that. And I'm glad to see you again, Damonikos."

Mary, smiling, greeted Gaius and Aristarchus. She waited patiently while they did their obeisance at her feet and then she left the men and entered the proseuche.

She heard crying from the bedroom. She hurried in to see what it was about.

"Dearest, what's wrong?" She rushed over to where Salome lay sobbing on the bed.

"It's Euphemia. She's gone."

"What do you mean, gone?"

"They sold her," Salome said. "Helene and Aristobulus. They sold Euphemia."

Mary took her child in her arms and rocked her, unable to think of anything she could do to take away her pain.

Paul and his friends entered the proseuche after Damonikos and Lucius had left. "Mother, this has been a wonderful day!" Paul said happily. "My dear friend Titus has returned safely from Corinth with good news from the church there. Gaius and Aristarchus have come down from Thessalonika and Macedonia to give me news about those churches. The collection for Jerusalem received a huge gift from Ephesus today, the largest gift we've ever received. And now Damonikos, one of our lost sheep, has returned to the fold, bringing an influential Roman citizen with him. This has indeed been a good day."

Mary came into the room. "Not everyone is so happy. Salome's friend Euphemia has been sold."

Paul's face fell. "I know. And I'm sorry that Salome's so hurt by that. But Euphemia's new master will treat her kindly, I'm sure."

Mary stared at him. "What do you know about this, Paul?" Behind her she could hear Salome coming out of the bedroom.

"It's the collection for the saints in Jerusalem," Paul said. "Helene and Artistobulus understand that the collection is important and that we haven't collected much money from the church in Ephesus yet. They sold one of their slaves to donate the money for me to take back with me to Jerusalem, to James."

Mary felt herself filling with a rage such as she hadn't felt in decades.

"You sold Salome's friend so that you could give money to James in Jerusalem to feed the people who are just standing around waiting for Jesus to return? Those people who sold everything they had, just so they could wait? You sold Euphemia for them?"

"Mother, I didn't sell anyone," Paul protested. "I don't own any slaves. It was Helene's and Aristobulus' decision—and I think it was very generous of them."

"Generous?! To sell a girl like a, like a burnt offering on the street, and donate the money to those layabouts in Jerusalem? You're always talking about sacrifices, Paul, but what right do you have to make Euphemia a sacrifice? I tell you, it's a sacrifice I won't accept. You will find out who bought that girl and you will buy her back, even if it takes all the money from all your church collections for the saints in Jerusalem, and you will give her papers of freedom, and you will do it today."

"And how will the girl live then, Mother?"

"She will live with me."

"With you? Mother, respectfully, you're not young. What will happen to her when you die? Who will care for her then? At least now she has a master who has an investment in her—he will provide for her, because she's worth money to him. At least this way she has someone to care for her."

"Care for her? How do you know? Do you know who bought her? Do you know what her new tasks will be? You're always talking about porneia, Paul. Well, Euphemia is an eleven-year-old girl. What kind of life do you think is planned for her, eh? Who exactly is it who's caring for her now?"

And then she thought: If this wasn't Salome's little friend, who would save her then? Who would care enough? And then through the red haze of her mind came an odd stray thought: What about the slave Sophos, whom I haven't seen in years—who's caring for him now? And then, incredibly, she suddenly thought about all the other slaves she'd known, people whose lives and comfort depended entirely on the people who owned them—even rich slaves like Arsinoe, who had to change the very god she worshipped when she was sold to a new temple. Mary had always been uncomfortable with slavery, but now for the first time she saw it as an abomination. She felt something shift inside her head.

Suddenly Mary's mind and sight filled with a new awareness, and she felt her body as though lifted from the ground. In front of her she saw all of the slaves in Ephesus—at least half the population of the city, she thought—and then that awareness expanded, and she saw all the slaves in all the world; she felt the waves of pain, misery, and despair that flowed around and out of every individual one of them. And then she saw all the other people who weren't slaves but who still had no say in their lives—wives who were beaten by their husbands, like Marcellina, and men who worked in the mines, like Andronicus and his son, and people who were victims of their family traditions, like Myia and her stone baby. She felt the desperation of the old and sick who couldn't care for themselves anymore, like Adonis and Tiberia; the physical pain of those trapped in diseased bodies, like her dear husband Joseph; and then she felt the deep sadness of those whose riches could never fill their hollow hearts, the empty, lonely ones like Judith and Eugeneia. And then that awareness broadened and the burden of the Great Fire and the Great Earthquake fell upon her heart. She felt every hurt that befell the victims of those disasters, including the searing agony felt by Salome's parents as they burned to death and the heavy crushing weight of the synagogue as it collapsed on John's mother's chest.

Her breath caught as the immeasurable grief rushed through her of all those people who, like her, had experienced the death of a beloved child. Then her breath stopped completely as she took on her son's pain as he hung bleeding on the cross, followed in the next pulse with the pain of the many thousands of other crucified ones; and then she felt the excruciation from all of the world's brutality, all the wars, all the hacking, rending, and severing of flesh. Even that awareness expanded, and she found herself opening up to all the pain of all the people who lived now, which then broadened to include the suffering of all those who'd come before, and then finally she knew the anguish of all of the people who would come even after her own death.

She just stood there with all of the pain of all the world through time throbbing through her, all the tortured, all the damned, all the sad, lonely, sorry souls, and she tried to breathe.

The immensity of sorrow was beyond fathoming, yet here she was feeling the physical and emotional agony of hundreds—thousands—millions of people. She realized that she must be having one of her visions again, after all these many years, because she knew that in real life, no one person could possibly bear the weight of this much horror and still live.

She fell to her knees, and a great wrenching screaming sob to God tore from her throat before she collapsed insensate to the ground.

When she finally opened her eyes, she saw only a cluster of worried faces—Salome, Paul, Titus, Gaius, and Aristarchus—leaning over her. The vast awareness of the world's suffering had faded, but she still remembered the immense weight of all that she had felt.

"Paul?"

"Yes, Mother?" Tears were streaming down his face.

"If you don't save Euphemia, I will never allow you in my presence again."

"I'll save her, Mother."

"If anyone from your congregation objects, they can take it up with me."

"Yes, Mother."

"Tell James that I said that he should tell his saints to return to their livelihoods. It could be another twenty years before Jesus returns."

"Actually, I said that very thing to my congregation in Thessalonika. But I don't have the authority to say it to James."

"Well, I do."

"Yes, Holy Mother."

Three days later Caesar's slave Libo brought a small jade jar to her. Mary had never seen jade before. The slave told her it was from the other side of the world and very costly.

"My mistress is feeling much better. She's very grateful."

Mary decided to keep holy oil in the beautiful jar, for anointing during sacred rituals. She remembered a lovely alabaster jar she saw used for that purpose long ago and smiled her first smile in three days.

But she never laughed again.

Paul purchased Euphemia from her new master and freed her. It took all of the money he'd collected in Ephesus for the saints and a large part of the money from the Corinth collection as well. Though glad to see Salome and Mary, Euphemia remained subdued in her manner. Paul confessed to Mary that she had been right to worry about the possibility of porneia.

The day after Euphemia moved into the proseuche, the priest Hieronymos stopped by. Salome asked Mary if she and Euphemia could go with her to the temple.

Mary hadn't taken Salome with her to the temple since she was a baby. She thought visiting the temple of an idol might be confusing for a young Israelite girl. But she worried about Euphemia and her understandable silence since her unspeakable experience, and Mary thought the beauty of the temple might give her pleasure.

"All right. You girls can go with me." Salome was thrilled. Even Euphemia smiled.

During warm weather Hieronymos brought only a small donkey cart up the hill, which didn't easily hold four people. The girls were glad to take turns walking alongside during the trip to the temple. When the road curved around the base of Mount Pion and the temple of Artemis first appeared, he stopped the cart for a moment so that the girls could enjoy their first sight of the enormous marble building lifted high on its platform, its gilded roof reflecting the light of the sun.

"Oh, Mother, how beautiful it is!" Salome smiled with delight.

Mary looked at Euphemia, glad to see that her face was also lit up and smiling. "Yes, it is," she said. She nodded to Hieronymos, and he flicked the reins to make the donkey walk again.

Artelia was standing near the steps of the temple. She graciously welcomed the girls and immediately sent for a couple of young mellieras to show them around. These novices weren't much older than Salome and Euphemia. It gladdened Mary to see the four girls run up the steps to the temple, full of joy and laughter, enjoying together the peace, beauty, and freedom of the glorious spring day.

But as Mary saw Euphemia enter the temple, she had a sudden thought.

"Artelia, I didn't think—I'm sorry, but I didn't think about the pollution of your temple. I think Euphemia isn't a virgin anymore."

Artelia looked at her. "That young girl is married?"

"No. She was a slave who was mistreated." She told Artelia about Euphemia, Paul, and the collection for the saints.

When she was finished, Artelia nodded. "It's good that you saved her. We'll have a renewal ceremony for her. Let her pass the virginity test. That will help her, I think."

"You can renew virginity?"

"Virginity of the body is meaningless, really. But if a body has been polluted, it can create pollution in the mind. It's the mind's purity that matters. That child's purity has been tainted not by what happened to her body but by her heart's awareness of her betrayal by people who were supposed to care for her."

"Yes." Mary embraced her friend. "Thank you, Artelia."

"But I can see there's something different about you," Artelia said as they began to walk in the garden. "Has something else happened?"

So Mary told her about her vision, about feeling and seeing and holding all the pain of all the world through all of time. Artelia fell silent after hearing this, and Mary felt compelled to tell her about her other visions, the ones from long ago.

"I used to have visions when I was a young girl. Visions about God. And about my son Jesus."

"Oh?" Artelia stopped walking and looked at her friend.

"Yes. I told Jesus about them. They affected him profoundly."

Artelia just waited.

"I think it was my visions that made him take the path he took with his life." Then Mary said the words that had been weighting down her soul for all these years. "I think that my son would not have been crucified if I had not told him of my visions."

After a moment Artelia spoke. "Don't you think he probably had his own visions? His own visions about God? From God? His own reasons for taking his path?"

Mary listened to these words, felt the truth of them in her heart, and then she released the deep breath she had been holding for over twenty years. "Yes. Yes. Of course he did." She took her friend's arm and they began to walk again.

"I think it's time I tell you the last mystery of the eggs of Artemis," Artelia said.

"You mean there's another one?" Mary already knew the mysteries of the star eggs, the bee eggs, and how the many breasts of Artemis the Mother Earth represented the many paths available to reach the same source of sustenance, the one Eye of God.

"The eggs are also the birth of the aeons out of the pleroma of the Goddess," Artelia said. "Within the pleroma—the light heart of the Mother—all things spiritual or material exist and are manifested as the aeons—wisdom, truth, intelligence, logos, goodness, power, light, love, and so on. The aeons are the divine, incorporeal, and eternal realities of all that ever has been or ever shall be.

"The next time this vision comes upon you, you'll probably find yourself also feeling the sorrow of animals and then of the plants and then of the rocks and finally of the stars themselves. And when you do, you should know that most of the time you will be unable to fix the pain of people or things. You can only hold it and be witness to it, with compassion in your heart."

Mary sighed with the burden of it all.

"But sometimes you will be able to change it. You'll make a little shift inside you, and the sorrow will be healed."

"It will?"

"Yes. And then," Artelia said with an enormous smile, "then you will finally be ready, ready to feel all the joy of the world and of the stars, all the great, profound, wondrous, glorious joy that ever has been and ever shall be."

Mary was still smiling two hours later when the four girls found them again.

"Mother, Euphemia has something she wants to ask you," Salome said with excitement. Mary smiled inquiringly at Euphemia.

"Holy Mother, can I stay here?" Euphemia asked hesitantly. "Be a mellieras, like Demetria and Sophia? I like it here."

Mary and Artelia looked at each other, and then Mary nodded. Artelia laid a gentle hand on Euphemia's shoulder. "Of course you can join us, my dear. Demetria, Sophia, take Euphemia to meet with Mistress of the Novices. You can go with them to see where Euphemia will live, Salome, but then you'll need to return here to your mother."

"I'll still be able to see Euphemia sometimes, won't I? When Mother comes to visit you may I visit with Euphemia?"

"Of course," Artelia said, and the girls ran off.

"Thank you," Mary said.

Artelia shrugged. "I'm glad Artemis got to keep one of your rescued ones, for a change."

"Euphemia's a free person now, and she wants to be here. I think it will be easier for her to start a new life here, to forget the awful things in her past."

"Did she really call you 'Holy Mother'?"

They walked over to a fountain and sat. "I think it's time I told you the whole story about my son Jesus," Mary told her friend.

She thought: "My son, I can hold the pain. I'm ready now for the joy."

22

"I am the most me when I lose myself in God."

When John brought the scraggly man into the proseuche, Mary didn't recognize him. When finally she realized who he was, she was filled with happiness.

"Judas!" she exploded as the reality struck her. She threw herself into his arms.

"Thomas, Mother, Thomas," her son said, laughing as he hugged her. "Or Didymus, if you prefer. Call me Twin in any language. But no one calls me Judas anymore."

"Son, son, son," she repeated, over and over. She hadn't seen him in twenty years.

After many tears and embraces, she finally asked, "Why are you here?" They had filled in the missing years for each other. She had told him of her life and introduced him to Salome. He had been impressed by his mother's fluency in Greek and had cried over her scarred hands, once so strong and soothing. He had told her of his life, his children now grown with babies of their own; his wife dead now for six years; how he had set up the church in Galilee and how his sons were now the elders there. He had spent many years preaching in Syria and was planning next to go to India to preach.

"Before I go anywhere else, I wanted to come see you, Mother, and bring you back home to Judea."

"Go back home? Is it safe now?"

"No, Mother, it isn't safe. But we don't think it's ever going to be safe. And your children and grandchildren miss you and want you to return."

"Oh, Thomas, I miss them too. I will be very happy to go home with you." The words rushed out of her mouth without a moment's thought.

They decided to leave in a month. Mary would need time to say good-bye to her friends.

Thomas spent most of his days over the next month with Mary, but he also spent time visiting with John, whom he remembered with great fondness. One afternoon at the proseuche, John asked him if he would be willing to preach at the next Friends of Jesus meeting.

Thomas brought something out of his pack to show them. He carefully set it on a table and unwrapped it. "It's my scroll of the words of Jesus," he said. "I use it when I preach."

"Is that a copy of Quartillia's scroll?" Mary asked.

"No," said Thomas. "This is the one I wrote."

Mary stared. Jesus and James had been the scholars of the family. Thomas hadn't even gone to Hebrew school.

"I learned to read and write for this."

"Thomas, how wonderful!" his mother said. "I'm so proud of you."

Her son beamed. "Would you like me to read it to you?" Mary, John, and Salome all insisted that he do so.

As he read, Mary saw John frequently nod his head or smile, as though he remembered Jesus saying the words. He waited until Thomas was done with his reading before he asked any questions.

Mary wanted to be polite too, but she kept finding herself interrupting her son.

When she heard the saying "He who has ears, let him hear," she smiled, but when Thomas continued to read "A man of light has a light within that lights up the whole world; if he does not shine, he is darkness," she spoke up.

"I remember him saying something similar. He said that when a sighted man and a blind man are in darkness, they are both the same. But when the light comes, then the one who can see will see the light and the one who is blind will remain in darkness." She frowned to herself. Wasn't that what Paul said the spirit-people talked about—the light and the darkness? She would have to ask Thomas his opinion about them.

She spoke up again when she heard that Jesus said that when he left, James was to be their leader because it was for his sake that heaven and earth came into being.

"He was joking when he said that, surely. He was always making jokes about James thinking he was the center of creation, God's anointed."

"We all thought it was a joke at the time—I remember we all laughed," Thomas said. "When he said it, James was still convinced Jesus was mad and was trying to stop him from teaching because he thought he was an embarrassment to the family. It wasn't until Jesus appeared to him after his death that James really believed."

"I still think he said that as a joke. I don't think you should include that part."

"Maybe, but in fact James has been a wonderful leader. Everyone looks up to him. He's the only person who can ever talk any sense into Peter. Even that lunatic Paul looks up to James."

"You don't like Paul?" Mary asked.

"I'm sorry, Mother. I shouldn't have said that. John said that Paul is your friend. And James likes him too."

Mary was struck by how different Thomas' teachings about Jesus were from Paul's. Paul preached that people must believe in Jesus' death, resurrection, and special relationship with God in order to receive atonement, salvation, and eternal life. He hardly ever mentioned Jesus' teachings.

Thomas spoke only about Jesus' teachings, and most of those sayings were mysterious and difficult to understand, often echoing things Mary had heard at the temple of Artemis. Listening to Thomas recount the mysterious sayings of his brother, Mary felt again the pull toward learning more, the urge that drove her to listen to Artelia at the idol's temple. One saying seemed like something Artelia would say: "Jesus said to them, 'When you make the two into one, and when you make the inside like the outside and the outside like the inside, and the above like the below, and when you make male and female into the same, so that the male shall not be male nor the female female; and when you make eyes in the place of an eye, a hand in place of a hand, a foot in place of a foot, and an image in place of an image, then you will be walking in God's empire.'" Many more of the sayings were equally mysterious.

She wondered whether James preached about Jesus the way Thomas did or if he preached the way Paul did or if his church had yet another set of beliefs. She found herself looking forward to spending time in Jerusalem with James.

"I've always been so glad that James made up with Jesus at the end," Mary told her son. "I'm glad you and he were both able to be there with him for the last evening he had with his disciples. I've heard that the guards who came to arrest him were confused when they came upon the three of you together, all looking so much alike."

"Judas kissed Jesus so they'd know which one to take," Thomas spat. "I would have gladly gone in his place. As would James."

"I know, son."

After a few silent moments Thomas continued reading his scroll. When he read that Jesus' disciples would see him when they were able to strip without shame and trample on their clothes, she interrupted again.

"Are you sure he said that? That doesn't sound at all like him. He was very modest."

Thomas shrugged. "I heard him say it. It's like his sayings about hating your family—you need to let go of all of the old attitudes and beliefs that are holding you back. Modesty is just another one."

"But even Adam and Eve were ashamed."

"Maybe we have to get past them too."

She smiled when he read: "Love your brother like your own soul, protect him like the pupil of your eye."

"He learned that from me!" she said. "I used to tell all you children that."

"I remember, Mother. But when Jesus talked about loving your brother or loving your neighbor or loving your friend, he meant everyone."

"I know." She remembered Jesus' commentary on the Shema, when he was asked what the most important commandment was: "Love the Lord your God with all your heart and with all your soul and with all your might, and love your neighbor as yourself, which is the same thing."

She sighed. "He really did love everyone." She remembered something that had always bothered her from Quartillia's scroll. "Do you think he ever said 'he who is not for me is against me'?"

"No," Thomas said. "I know some people remember it that way. But what I remember him saying is: 'he who is not against me is for me.'"

They discussed how some of Jesus' words were being misremembered after all these years. Thomas said that was one of the reasons he had written everything down. He urged John to do the same thing.

"I don't remember his words much," John said sadly. "I didn't even speak Aramaic when I first met him. And I was too young to really understand what he was talking about anyway."

"What do you remember?" Thomas asked.

"The miracles," John said. "I remember the signs that showed he was the Messiah."

"Then that's what you should write down," Thomas said.

At the end of the week Thomas took Mary and Salome down to Alexander's house for synagogue. When John announced at the meeting that Mary would be going back to Judea, everyone was very sad. Mary was a Mother of the Synagogue now and would be deeply missed. Deborah said that they'd have a special new moon ceremony before she left.

Alexander was not around for Sabbath and missed the synagogue meeting entirely. He was in negotiation at the Prytaneion to argue the gerousia's petition to maintain the rights of the Judeans to observe the Sabbath and the Laws of their fathers, something he did every ten years or so. Thinking about Alexander working on the Sabbath to protect the Sabbath, Mary remembered what John had told her long ago: his father emulated the Maccabees, who violated the Torah to protect the Torah.

Thomas attended the Disciples of John the Baptist meeting on First Day and honored Enoch and the others by sharing his own memories of their master. Afterward he accompanied Mary and Salome down to the harbor agora, so that Mary could show him more of the city. Later on the whole family, except Alexander, would join them at the Friends of Jesus church meeting at the house of Calandra and Narcissus. Today Thomas would be preaching. Even Enoch, Seth, Deborah, and Deborah's husband, Daniel, planned to come to the meeting, in respect for Mary and her visiting son.

At the harbor agora, Mary and her family walked quickly past the many shops and booths selling shrines, figurines, and other sacred items in honor of Artemis Ephesia. She wanted to show Thomas her two favorite objects: the soap stones, still being sold at an exorbitant price, and the pearls and seashells that she had been assured long ago were acceptable for an Israelite to enjoy.

Salome showed him the cinnabar shop where John's family's products were sold. They also dragged Thomas over to Abraham the Samaritan's shop of herbal and medicinal wares, but Mary's old friend wasn't there today to meet her son.

Thomas himself was drawn to a shop that sold elaborate water clocks. He was so fascinated by one that rang a gong at different hours that at first he didn't hear when his name was shouted.

"Thomas! Thomas, is that you?"

Mary tugged at the sleeve of her son's tunic. "Thomas, do you know that man?"

He turned around. "Mark!" he yelled in delight. "What are you doing here?" He walked over to embrace his friend then introduced him to Mary and Salome. "Mother, this is Mark, the cousin of Barnabas. Did you ever meet Barnabas, back in Jerusalem?"

Mary said she didn't think she ever had, but that she was glad to meet Mark.

Thrilled to meet Mary, Mark said: "Holy Mother, I have heard so much about you from Paul, and I feel especially blessed to be seeing you here with Thomas."

"Paul?" Thomas said. "Are you with Paul?"

"Luke and I are here to meet with him and then we're going on to Macedonia to preach," Mark said. "What about you? I heard you were going to India."

"I am, but first I want to take my mother back home to Judea."

Mark smiled. "James and the apostles will be so happy to have you back home," he said to Mary.

"I'm looking forward to seeing them too."

Mark turned back to his friend. "Thomas, why don't you come along with me to find Paul? I was supposed to meet with him and some of his people, but I seem to have missed them."

"I'd like to, but I'm here with my mother."

"Go ahead, Thomas," Mary said. "I'm feeling kind of tired anyway, and I'd like to just sit and rest at the Three Graces fountain for a while. You take Salome with you and then come find me later when you're ready to leave for the Friends of Jesus church. Bring Mark with you to the meeting."

They escorted Mary to her favorite fountain, located just past the masses of souvenir shops selling shrines and images of Artemis Ephesia. Thomas hesitated to leave his mother alone amidst all these gentiles and idols, but he accepted that she'd lived here for twenty years and had her own way of doing things now.

He bent down and kissed her, and Salome did the same. "We won't be long," Thomas said.

Mary waved them on. "Take as much time as you need. Greet Paul for me."

But in fact, Mary saw Paul first. She was sitting on her bench, enjoying the warmth of the afternoon sun on her back, listening to the sounds of the agora, the barkers, the heralds, the philosophers, the people haggling and laughing, when suddenly the voice of one orator stood out from all the others in her ears. Perhaps it was hearing the name "Jesus," which always grabbed her attention. She looked around to find the voice. Paul stood above the crowd on a plinth, exhorting people to turn to the blood of their savior Jesus Christ and turn against the wicked worship of the idol Artemis Ephesia.

He made this declaration right next to the shops and kiosks that sold Artemis souvenirs. The Thargelion, the birthday festival of Artemis and Apollo, would begin next week, and there were many pilgrims in the city. The souvenir shops were doing a brisk business, or at least they had been before Paul began his preaching.

He was not here alone. His new visitors, Gaius and Aristarchus, had accompanied him. They were working the crowd, encouraging everyone to join the mass of people forming up around Paul, listening to him tell about salvation through Jesus Christ.

Then Mary began to see other people she recognized in the crowd— Timothy, Junia, Helene, Andronicus, Titus, Tychicus, Trophimus, and others from Paul's church. They all seemed to be encouraging the crowd to listen to Paul and were also exhorting people to turn away from the worship of idols.

The public space of the Three Graces fountain soon emptied as everyone around her moved toward the souvenir shops to see what was happening.

"Artemis is a false god!" she heard someone yell. She thought she recognized the voice of Julia, the woman who'd sold her slave to Rebekkah.

It occurred to Mary that this must be why Mark was planning to meet with Paul here at the agora today. This confrontation with the crowd at the souvenir stands had been planned in advance.

Then another voice rang out, the voice of an angry man. "Great is Artemis Ephesia!" he yelled. "Our Savior, our Ruler, our Holy Mother, our

Heavenly Goddess! Artemis is the protector of Ephesus, and Ephesus is her sacred city! Great is Artemis Ephesia!"

Mary craned her neck and saw a man standing on a plinth across from Paul's. She thought she recognized him as a silversmith from the temple of Artemis.

Soon other voices were chanting, picking up the popular song from the Artemisia festival, "Great is Artemis Ephesia! Great is Artemis Ephesia!" Mary remembered the time she had sat right here in this same place as revelers from the Artemisia procession of the previous night continued dancing into the morning, singing their chant through the agora, their voices cracked and their legs tired from their many hours spent celebrating their devotion to their goddess.

"The Lord God of Judea is the only God!" Mary heard one of Paul's people yell. Then the two insistent crowds merged, Paul's crowd of Jesus worshippers colliding with the mass of people who now looked to be everyone else in Ephesus.

"Great is Artemis Ephesia!" yelled the larger crowd, while the smaller took up the chant "The Lord God of Judea is the only God!"

As the crowd of Artemis supporters swelled it began to flood the road, picking up Paul's followers like flotsam, and soon the river of people was a deluge pouring down the street toward the theater, hundreds, thousands of people, chanting as one voice: "Great is Artemis Ephesia!" Occasionally a voice of Nazorene dissent would sound, only to be quickly drowned out.

Paul, still up on his plinth, was not swept away with the others, but as the crowd passed him Mary saw him trying to get down to join them. Then she saw Damonikos and Lucius Gratius Cinna grab his arms and hold him back, out of the crush of bodies headed down the street.

"Mother! Mother! Are you all right?" she heard an anxious voice yell before she found herself surrounded by her family, Thomas, John, Salome, and Theodora, all embracing her in relief.

Mary looked around. "Where are the children?" she asked apprehensively.

"They're at the villa," Theodora said. "I didn't bring them today. Thank God."

"Thank God," they all said in unison.

"Did you see it, Mother? That riot Paul started?"

"I did. This was a good spot to see everything."

"We were down the street," Thomas said. "We were talking with John and Theodora when the chanting began. Mark joined the crowd, but we were worried about you."

"I heard people saying terrible things about Judeans," Theodora said. "About how we needed to be punished for our blasphemy against Artemis Ephesia."

"Why would people care about that?" Thomas said. "They have so many gods here—what does it matter if someone speaks against one of them?"

"It's eusebeia," John said. "The devotion to Artemis is the same thing as devotion to Ephesus. When you say anything against Artemis, it's as if you're speaking treason against the city."

Thomas sighed. "So now Paul has people thinking the Hebrews are traitors to Ephesus."

John's face was worried. "Everything my father has worked for, all of these years. What will this do to him?"

They decided to cancel today's Friends of Jesus meeting. Today did not seem like a safe day for Hebrews to congregate. Instead they walked back up Mount Pion to John's family house. Even up the hill they could still hear the chant from the theater: "Great is Artemis Ephesia! Great is Artemis Ephesia!"

Mary thought: "My son, how do we honor our God without dishonoring the divine in another's heart?"

23

"God and Man, Life and Death, Watcher and Watched, all present in the Now"

Three hours after they had arrived at the villa and sent a slave to spread the message that the Friends of Jesus meeting had been cancelled, Epenetus ran into the house, puffing and crying. "Master Alexander is hurt! Master Alexander is hurt!" he shouted. Everyone in the house rushed toward the vestibulum to see what had happened.

Behind him through the door came Enoch and his son Seth, carrying Alexander between them, his arms over their shoulders. Daniel, Deborah's husband, walked close behind, assisting them with their burden as needed. Deborah was walking behind them, crying, and much to Mary's surprise Rebekkah was next to her, her arms around her, supporting her. John rushed over to assist his brother and nephew with their father.

Theodora took charge. "Thales, Heron—go to Master Alexander's room and help them get him into bed. John, be sure to come back and tell us the

news. Epenetus, go into the kitchen and calm down. Everyone else, let's go
pray in the atrium."

Enoch interrupted. "Mother, would you come with us? You can help
until the doctor gets here."

The men gently lowered Alexander onto his bed and tried to make him
comfortable. His face was gray, cold and damp to the touch. Mary gently
placed her fingertips on the pulse at his neck. She was troubled to find that
the blood rushed rapidly but weakly through his body.

"What happened?" she asked.

"He tried to address that mob in the theater," Enoch said angrily. "He
tried to calm them down, tried to tell them that the Judeans are not the enemy
of Artemis, tried to remind them that we are her friends in Ephesus. But the
crowd kept yelling at him and squeezing in closer, and suddenly he clutched at
his chest and fell to the ground."

"Is the doctor coming?" Mary asked.

"Epenetus sent Pelagios over to Jacob's family hospital. Someone should
be here soon."

Mary nodded. "Alexander, can you hear me?" she asked, brushing his
wispy hair off his forehead. She didn't think she'd ever seen him without any
covering on his head before.

"Mary...Mary..." he said weakly.

She moved closer to hear him and he whispered a name in her ear.

"I understand." Mary turned to the men. "Tell my son Thomas to step
in here, please." Thomas was the only person in the house who wasn't too
distraught to be sent on this journey, and it wasn't as though the place would
be hard to find.

Thomas came in, and Mary pulled him aside. "Thomas, I need you to go
to the temple of Artemis," she said.

"What—"

"It's important. You can get a horse from Alexander's stable. You remember that main road we walked down earlier, the one with the tombs? Get on
that road and ride east, out of the city. Around the base of the hill. Soon
you'll see the temple. Ride up to any guard or priest and tell him that I sent
you with an urgent message for the high priestess."

"Tell the guards at the temple of Artemis that my mother is sending a message to the high priestess?" Thomas had heard rumors that his mother consorted
with idol worshippers, but this seemed far worse than he could have imagined.

"Yes," she said. "Tell them it's Mary. If they don't recognize the name, say it's the guardian of the sacred spring. If they still won't listen, tell them to let you speak with Hieronymos or with Okeanos. They'll listen to you. When you see High Priestess Artelia, tell her I said that Alexander is dying."

"You want me to tell the high priestess of Artemis that the archisyna-gogos is dying?" he whispered.

Behind them Alexander moaned and vomited. The slaves rushed to clean it up.

"Yes," Mary said. "And he wants to see Artelia. Now go. Hurry!"

When Jacob the doctor arrived, he spoke a few soft words with Alexander and then placed his ear on his chest to listen to his heart. After a few moments he raised his head, smiled gently at Alexander, and then he went over to speak quietly with Enoch and John. Mary could tell by their faces that he was telling them their father would not survive. She wished she could do something to alleviate their pain but knew she could not.

There was a loud pounding at the door. Artelia and her attendants strode into the house.

"I am here to show respect to Archisynagogos Alexander, the friend of Artemis Ephesia," Artelia announced loudly from the vestibulum.

Mary looked at Alexander and saw a slight smile twitch his lips. She walked to the door and said, "Show High Priestess Artelia to the archisyna-gogos' room." Epenetus looked at her askance, but hurried to the vestibulum to do as she said.

Before Artelia could enter the bedroom, Enoch rushed over to Mary. "Mother—" he said in confused concern.

She patted his arm. "It's all right, Enoch." She smiled at him. "Trust me."

Artelia entered the room alone. She was dressed in the grandest of her finery, and Mary could tell she'd rushed to put it on—some of the sashes were crooked and her hair under the embroidered silk head cloth looked as if it would fall down her back at any moment. The high priestess walked to the bed, dropped to her knees, and took Alexander's hand in hers.

"Oh my dear, my dear," she whispered, her voice breaking.

The men in the room stopped their praying to stare at Artelia then stared even harder when they saw Alexander lift his weak hand to caress her face, his expression tender.

Mary went over to Enoch and John, gently encouraging them to leave. John nodded and gestured to the doctor, the slaves, and the other relatives to exit with them. Artelia was left alone with Alexander.

When Artelia finally left Alexander's bedroom, her face was wet with tears. "He wants to see his children and grandchildren," she said.

As the family entered Alexander's room, Mary noticed that Rebekkah was with them, her hand clutched tightly in Enoch's. The rest of the friends and household were still praying in the atrium, so Mary walked Artelia out to the peristyle to sit.

"I'm going to have an inscription made, from Artemis Ephesia," Artelia said. "On it, She will honor Alexander the Judean as one of Ephesus' greatest citizens and a valued friend of Artemis."

"That's good of you," Mary said. "And the Israelites will be especially glad of your support now."

Artelia nodded. "Yes. Your son told me what happened down at the agora. I'm sorry I couldn't have met him under more joyous circumstances."

The two friends sat together quietly. After a while Artelia took Mary's hand in hers, holding it tightly as the tears poured silently down her face.

Eventually Enoch and John came to find them. Their clothes were torn over the heart, and Mary knew that Alexander had died.

"I'm Enoch, and this is John," the older brother said. Mary realized that although Artelia had been to this house at least once before, after the Great Fire, she had never met either of Alexander's sons.

"I am honored to meet the sons of Archisynagogos Alexander," Artelia said.

"We want to thank you for your years of friendship with our father," Enoch said.

"Has he passed now?"

"Yes, Lady Artelia," John said. "He's gone now."

Artelia nodded and her tears stopped. "I was just telling Mary how I would like to put up an inscription at the Temple, showing our esteem for your father. Will you accept this?"

"We would be deeply honored by such a thing," Enoch said.

"I would also like to do something else for him," Artelia said. "I own a large house, a hall, really, down by the harbor. I would like to donate it to the Judean community for use as a synagogue, in Alexander's memory."

Enoch and John looked at each other, then at Artelia. "It would belong to us?" Enoch asked hesitantly. The mikvah and proseuche were on leased land, not owned by the Judeans. A large house by the harbor would be among the most luxurious and desirable locations in the city.

"It would belong to you," Artelia said. "It would not be subject to lease negotiation or rent or the caprice of some future high priestess. It would be yours." She thought for a moment then said, "I know your father was troubled by the schism between the Judeans. But I say if the others don't want to come to your beautiful new synagogue, that's their own concern."

"That shouldn't be an issue," Enoch said. "I'll be able to get a minyan to agree to accept your offer. And the schism would have ended soon anyway with my remarriage to Rebekkah."

Mary was glad to learn that Rebekkah would once again be part of the family.

"So now we just have to decide how to punish the wrongdoers, the ones who started the riot," Artelia said. "Do we know who should be arrested, besides this Paul?"

"We can give you their names," John said. "Even Mother saw them."

Artelia looked at the horrified expression on Mary's face. "No," she said. "Keep Mary out of this."

"They're responsible for my father's death," Enoch said. "They should be executed."

Mary gasped, and Artelia patted her hand. "We can discuss the proper punishment later, after your father's been buried. But first the miscreants need to be arrested."

"Epenetus will know who was involved," Enoch said grimly. "He'll be lucky if I don't beat him to death."

"Then let's go talk to Epenetus," Artelia said. She stood and gave an arm to each of Alexander's sons, and they escorted her out of the room. Mary trailed sadly behind.

During the following days, Mary went several times to the proconsul's palace prison to see Paul and the other prisoners, Timothy, Gaius, Aristarchus, Epaphras, Mark, and several others Mary had never met before. Though he'd been beaten, Paul was in good spirits, a result of being surrounded by so many faithful friends. Epaphras had just come to Ephesus to deliver a letter to Paul from one of his churches and got caught up in the riot, and Paul and Timothy spent much of the time answering the letter Epaphras had brought from Colossae.

Thomas escorted his mother into the prison each time and visited with the Nazorenes. He even showed a few of them his scroll of Jesus' words. But he never had much to say to Paul.

Mary worried about what would happen to Paul and the other imprisoned Nazorenes. She had learned that the reason Alexander had been near
the theater in the first place was because he and Rebekkah had decided to
accompany Enoch, Deborah, Seth, and Daniel to the Friends of Jesus church
meeting, to show their love for Mary and respect for her son who had come to
escort her back home to Jerusalem. It would have been a nice surprise, Mary
thought, to see Alexander at a Friends of Jesus meeting—and she knew it
would have meant a great deal to John.

When the crowd started rushing toward the theater, people had recognized the Israelites walking down the street and dragged them along inside to
answer for the Judean blasphemy. Enoch would not waver in his insistence on
execution for Paul. He blamed Paul for starting the riot, for killing his father
and almost causing Rebekkah and his sister to be killed by the crush or by
the angry mob.

For his part, Paul was genuinely sorrowful over the death of Alexander.
Every time he saw Mary he asked her to tell John and Enoch of his deep
remorse. Mary had passed his message on to John, but Enoch was not open
to hearing it.

After Alexander's burial, his sons and other male relatives and close
friends sat in mourning together, so Mary didn't see either John or Enoch
until after a week had passed.

In the meantime, Thomas borrowed an oxcart and took Mary to the temple so that she could ask Artelia for clemency for the prisoners. Salome went
along to visit Euphemia.

Thomas waited for his mother and Salome outside the temenos, because
although he had come to appreciate what a good friend Artelia had been
to the Hebrews in general and to his mother in particular, he still felt very
uncomfortable being near the idol's temple. He was anxious to get his mother
back home to Judea, where this sort of nonsense would end.

Inside the temenos Salome ran off to the novice's quarters to find her
friend. Mary asked the first guard she saw if he knew where she could find
the high priestess. The guard, recognizing Mary, told her that High Priestess
Artelia could be found in the treasury this morning.

Mary walked over the treasury building where she found Artelia
in an inner room, arguing with an administrator about the temple
income. Mary waited patiently until their business was completed, looking through the locked bars at the towering piles of brass and wooden

chests, all of which, she knew, contained gold, jewels, and other precious objects—most of which belonged to the governments, private individuals, and other temples who paid an annual fee to keep their money locked safely away here.

Finally Artelia won her argument with the official and joined Mary. The two friends left the building and walked into the sunshine.

"How are things going with the new synagogue?" Artelia asked.

"Deborah says the remodeling has started already. Enoch and Rebekkah plan to be married there and then they'll travel with us to Judea to make sacrifice at the Temple, in gratitude for their remarriage." Then she told Artelia about a surprise she'd received that morning: Apollos and Chloe, unaware of the recent tragedy, had sent a letter from Corinth saying that they would be returning to Ephesus to be married. Mary hoped that they too could be married in the new synagogue. But that would be the couple's decision. She didn't even know if Chloe was an Israelite.

"Are you really going to leave?" Artelia asked in a wistful voice.

"I am," Mary said. "But I'll see you often before I go. I won't leave until my son Apollos gets here, so that I can tell him good-bye."

"It will be hard on me, you know. Hard losing you and Alexander both at the same time."

"I know. I'm sorry."

"I know you are. So tell me about the synagogue."

"Well, you were right—it is a big building. It's big enough for a decent-sized assembly hall, a prayer hall, and a school. The community is very grateful. They're working on the assembly hall first, for the wedding. Then they'll build the prayer hall and finally the school. Deborah says that not much remodeling is necessary for the school, but that they'll need to do quite a bit of work for the proseuche." And best of all, the Friends of Jesus church was moving their worship to the new synagogue. Mary was so glad. That's where the church belonged.

Artelia nodded. "I'd like to see it. Do you think you can get me an invitation to the wedding?"

"I know they'd both be thrilled if you would come," Mary said, although part of her started thinking about which members of the new congregation would be most likely to fuss if they had to eat in the presence of a gentile. She considered what she'd need to do to contain their indignation.

"I'll leave before the meal," Artelia said, reading Mary's mind.

Mary smiled. "Say, I thought you once told me you didn't own anything," she said.

"I don't."

"So where did the synagogue building come from?"

Artelia shrugged. "Artemis has many properties she doesn't use, so many that not all of them are even written down in the records and are managed at the discretion of the high priestess. And the Goddess is grateful to Alexander for his devotion to the city. She is happy to give the building to his family."

They walked along in silence for a while before Mary got up the courage to ask her question.

"Artelia, will you please release Paul and the others?"

"It's that important to you?"

"It is."

"I'll need to get Enoch's agreement," Artelia said. "He's after blood."

"I know."

"Well, as a matter of fact, there is something Paul can do for me." Artelia grinned to see Mary's look of astonishment. "That surprised you, eh?"

"Indeed. What do you need Paul to do?"

Artelia took Mary to a set of buildings they'd never entered together before, the barracks for the people who sought sanctuary with Artemis.

"Get Onesimus the slave for me," Artelia told the guard at the door. Guards were needed at the barracks because most of the people who sought sanctuary were criminals and there were many valuables in storage and on display in the temenos.

The guard returned shortly with a man dressed in a simple tunic, wearing a slave collar around his neck.

"Mary, this is Onesimus," Artelia said. "He belongs to a man named Philemon, who lives in Colossae. Onesimus ran away, but after a while he discovered that life is quite difficult for a runaway slave. He decided to seek sanctuary with us, to ask us if we would intercede with his master for him."

"And what does this have to do with Paul?"

Artelia gave a sly smile. "Onesimus, this is Mary. She is the mother of your lord Jesus Christ."

Onesimus' eyes went wide, and he fell to the ground at Mary's feet. "Holy Mother, have mercy on me," he cried.

Mary looked at Artelia. "One of Paul's converts?" She nudged Onesimus to stand up.

"His master, Philemon, is."

"So you want Paul to intercede with Philemon on Onesimus' behalf?"

"I think Paul would have more influence on the man than the Temple of Artemis would. I think that if the request for mercy for Onesimus came from him, it would have more likelihood of success. See, we don't have that much influence outside of our part of Asia. A few times we've asked slave owners in distant lands to show mercy on their remorseful returning slaves, but instead they've been tortured or even executed. And that's not good for our reputation as a place of sanctuary."

"And you're saying that if Paul intercedes with Philemon, you'll release him and his companions from prison?"

"I'm saying that if he intercedes with Philemon I will talk with Enoch about releasing them."

Mary nodded. "Thank you, Artelia."

"One more thing, Mary."

"Yes?"

"Tell Paul that if he is released from prison, he must leave Ephesus by the following day and never return. If I ever hear that he's come back to this city, I will execute him myself."

Artelia sent a slave to go find Salome, and soon Mary, Salome, and Onesimus had left the temenos and joined Thomas in the oxcart.

In the proconsul's prison, Paul was delighted to meet Onesimus and grateful to Artelia for asking him to intercede with Philemon. Mark and Timothy immediately pulled the slave aside to preach to him about Jesus.

"And don't forget, Paul—if you're released, you must leave Ephesus immediately and never return," Mary said. It hurt her to see her friends in their manacles, heavy chains, and iron collars.

"I'll leave Ephesus immediately after I come see you to say good-bye," Paul said, giving Mary an affectionate smile.

In the end, Artelia's intercession with Enoch wasn't necessary. The kind-hearted Rebekkah told her husband that she refused to begin her married life with a man who had blood on his hands.

A few weeks after Alexander's death, Paul and his companions arrived at the proseuche. Down the road to the city wall, Mary could see a contingent of temple guards waiting to escort Paul out of town.

"We're leaving for Macedonia," Paul told her, "and I came to tell you good-bye and to thank you for everything."

"I'll miss you, Paul." This was not altogether untrue.

"Perhaps we'll meet again in Jerusalem," he said.

"You're going to Jerusalem?" She was ashamed to hear the lack of enthusiasm in her voice and rallied a smile.

"Yes," he said. "I'm taking the collection to James, remember?"

"Ah yes. The collection."

"But there won't be anything in it from Ephesus," he said.

"No." She knew Paul disapproved of the fact she had allowed the girl purchased by the collection to become a novice priestess of Artemis. But she also knew Euphemia could have no affection for the Nazorenes.

She asked, "Will Prisca and Aquila continue your work here?"

"Prisca and Aquila have left for Rome. They started a church there long ago and they're returning to it."

"Really?"

"I plan to join them there," he said. "After I deliver the collection."

"I hope you're not going by yourself. Carrying all that money, I mean."

"Oh no." He waved toward the others. "I have plenty of companions going with me. Timothy, Mark, Luke, Gaius, Aristarchus, Tychicus, Trophimus, and perhaps one or two others will go with me at least as far as Macedonia. Epaphras and Onesimus have left for Colossae, by the way. Onesimus is like a son to me now. 'Onesimus' means 'useful,' and he was indeed very useful to me while I was in chains, carrying messages back and forth to the saints. They asked me to express their affection for you."

"That was kind of them. So will anyone be left to continue your church here?" Perhaps the Friends of Jesus church guild could go back to normal now. She wanted everything to go smoothly with their move into the new synagogue.

"Apollos and Chloe will stay in Ephesus to guide the church here. And most of the Ephesians are staying. It's a strong church. Not like Corinth. They'll do well."

They stood smiling at each other for a few moments, Paul unwilling to actually leave her. She made a sudden decision. "I have something for you, Paul."

She went into the proseuche and returned carrying Jesus' tunic. She handed it to him, saying, "I have the memory of him, you have the hope of him. I would like to give you a bit of what I have. It's no true loss to me, for I will continue to remember him wearing it."

A deep voice whispered to her: You are indeed a kind mother.

In her mind she whispered back: It didn't smell much like you anymore anyway.

Paul stood there for a long time, staring in wonder at the precious relic held in his shaking, outstretched hands. Finally he spoke. "I know Jesus said it is more blessed to give than to receive, but I will never give this away. After the gift of salvation, it is the most treasured thing I have ever received. I will hold it close to me every day of my life, and I will pray God I have it next to me at the moment of my death."

"You're welcome." Mary gave Paul and each of his companions a kiss and a loving embrace. She watched them as they walked down the hill, Jesus' tunic now folded tightly next to Paul's heart. The temple guards followed them through the break in the city wall.

Thomas took Mary to the villa to tell Enoch and John that Paul had left Ephesus.

"It's good that he's gone," Enoch said. "He had better never come back, for if he does I'll make sure it's the last thing he ever regrets."

Enoch and Rebekkah were going to Jerusalem along with Mary, Thomas, Salome, and a few others from the synagogue. They would take the Temple tax with them, the first time it had been delivered in several years. Mary was nervous that Enoch and Paul might be in Jerusalem at the same time and hoped they would manage to avoid one another.

John wanted to go along too, but somebody needed to stay back to take care of the cinnabar business. He told Mary that as soon as Enoch returned to Ephesus, he and Theodora would come with the children to Jerusalem, possibly as soon as next year. Mary knew that of all the people she would miss in Ephesus, John and Apollos, her two sons in Asia, would hold the saddest place in her heart.

The other sad place, of course, would be that part of her heart that belonged to Artelia. Mary kept her promise to visit her friend often before she left.

"Why do you have to leave now?" Artelia asked during one of these visits. "Why can't you wait until the fall? Or even better—wait until next spring."

"No," Mary said. "We expect Apollos and Chloe to return to Ephesus any day now, and that's all I'm still waiting for. I like the idea of leaving Ephesus at the same time the storks leave, in summer, after their children have grown. All kind mothers should know the proper time to say good-bye."

They walked together as Artelia inspected the statues and set-up for that night's Thargelion procession. She had decided years ago to do the inspections in two stages so that the final inspection before the torches were lit would not be rushed. This morning was the inspection of the lineup of the shrines and statues. Mary and Artelia were alone, as most of the procession participants were still sleeping off last night's celebration.

"So…you're the mother of a god?"

Mary took a deep breath then let it out. "Yes." It was much more complicated than that, of course.

"I know what I'll do," Artelia said, in her cheeriest voice. "I'll commission a statue of you, to add to the procession of the gods. We'll dress it up every year in pretty clothes—blue, of course—and I'll ask the musicians to write a new song in your honor."

"Why can't I wear gold? I never get to be shiny."

"You and Artemis don't want to both show up at the procession wearing the same outfit," Artelia chided.

Mary smiled and then she said, "You know, I never saw one of these processions close up."

"It's just a bunch of people squabbling for dominance, stepping on each other, fighting because this one's too loud and that one's too drunk." Artelia shrugged then sighed. "I'll never be able to see it as you have, from up on the hill. Watching the wondrous serpent of lights floating along to the music, lighting up the darkness, moving all together as one joyful being—that must truly be magical."

She frowned as she saw that somebody had moved Isis in front of Dionysus. Probably that troublemaker priest. She'd known twenty priests of Dionysus in as many years, and all of them had caused mischief. She called for a couple of guards to move Emperor Claudius in between and then continued with the inspection.

"My friend, the mother of a god," Artelia mused. "I always knew there was something that drew me to you. We'll have to put up a shrine to you in the temenos. How about in the northwest corner—there's still some space there."

"Isn't the Priapus shrine in that corner?"

"Yes, but there's still room. It's not the most dignified neighborhood, but it gets a lot of traffic."

"No, thank you. But I am hungry. When we're done here, you can sacrifice a fish to me."

The two friends continued their inspection walk, smiling at their silliness. As they walked, Mary considered the nature of memory. She was an old woman and wouldn't gain many new memories. She knew too that many of the memories she had accumulated during the course of her long life had faded and were no longer accessible to her.

She decided that her memories were ultimately irrelevant, both the good ones and the bad ones; they were bits of dust that would blow away at the moment of her death. So too, she thought, would the memories of all of the people of her generation—the generation of those who had known Jesus in his lifetime.

But if the life and death of her son could symbolize hope or love or joy for the people who would come after, if it would bring people closer to God, then everything, she decided, was worth it. She had realized something as she handed the precious tunic to Paul.

Jesus had never appeared to her since his death because he had never left her side. Whenever she had looked at someone and seen God in their eyes, she had been seeing them through the eyes of Jesus.

She thought: "My son, I understand."

She wondered briefly how people would remember her, and then Artelia pointed to a couple of red birds dancing in a tree nearby, and Mary smiled.

Author's Note

The Great Temple of Artemis in Ephesus was renowned in its time as the greatest of the Seven Wonders of the World. It was destroyed by Goths a few hundred years after the Crucifixion and not rebuilt after the Emperor Justinian had its huge marble columns carried off to be used in the building of the Hagia Sofia in the 6th century CE. When the archeologist John Wood went searching for its remains in 1869, all traces had utterly disappeared, and even the local residents had no memory of it.

The tradition that Mary spent the remainder of her life in Ephesus with John the Beloved Disciple has existed since the early days of Christianity. It may have been true. In the first centuries CE, churches were only named after saints in locations where the saints had lived. The first-ever Church of Mary was built in Ephesus and was the site of the Third Ecumenical Council of the early Christian Church, the Council in 431 at which Mary was given the title Mother of God (Theotokos). It is near the ruins of this church that the only Jewish artifacts have as yet been found in Ephesus.

The House of Mary on Mount Kouressos (today called Nightingale Mountain) is a Christian and Muslim shrine, venerated as the house where Saint John brought Mary to live after the death of her son Jesus. Thousands of pilgrims travel to Ephesus every year to visit the House of Mary and drink water from her sacred spring.

Made in the USA
Charleston, SC
17 March 2013